THE CLARKSBURG TALES

THE CLARKSBURG TALES

R.C. DAVIS

Dedication

This collection of short stories is dedicated to Judy T., Monica C., Wilma T., and Bernita B., four strong women who were there for me, to offer their support and comfort as I trekked the quagmire that were my teen years. May you rest in peace. To all my crazy, kookie schoolmates, without your influence, I may never have been able to write this book. To the only Iowa town that I could ever truly call home, and all the weird, wonderful, and terribly flawed people who lived there. To Cathy H. who, in the summer of 1973, shone like a beacon to light my path to adulthood (R.I.P.). And finally, to my wife, Anne Marie; you are my rock.

Table Of Contents

#1

Karma, Like Pie

I was never, ever, allowed to hit my little sister. No matter what she did to me, I just had to "Buck up and take it," as my pa said one night at the supper table. Not even a minute later, Shandi helped herself to my piece of apple pie. We grew up that way together. As the years went by, she got set in the idea that she was allowed my unhappiness; just like that pie. We were born two years apart, and even though smaller than me, when she got mad, oh man, did she get mad. Then she'd go on the attack like some kind of a wild animal. I had no choice but to run away. If we were alone and I had to get the hell out of Dodge, well… that was fine. But when there were other kids around, I really needed to stand up to her, no matter what was going to come after. So, it was about a month after we moved to Iowa, in 1968, this problem finally came to a head. I was twelve years old, and Shandi was ten.

We had made friends with some kids who lived on a farm close by and we had gone over to play on a Saturday morning. A game of tag got started, and we were soon running around among the big trees in their huge front yard, just hollering, laughing, and having a good time. Shandi was upset because we didn't want to play the game that she wanted to. So, she decided to sit and pout in a tire swing that hung from this big ol' willow.

I made the mistake of nagging her about it. Without a word, she jumped off the swing, picked up this long, willow switch and wacked me as hard as she could across the back of my neck.

The blood started flowing and the neighbor girl screamed. Her brothers just stood there with their mouths hanging open, their eyes as big as pie plates. I started howling like a dog because it hurt like

1

the dickens. Then I had to go and touch it. When I pulled my hand away it was slick with blood. That was it for the neighbor kids, they took off, running, yelling for their ma.

My sister just stood there, her eyes big and mean. I remember seeing a rabid dog once; Shandi was that critter, come back to haunt me. The switch came up for a second go, but I wasn't going to wait for it. Giving her a good, hard shove before she could swing it, she flew back and hit the trunk of that willow tree and fell down. She didn't get up. The neighbor kids ma, who had come out to stand behind me, said, "Well, boy, looks like you done knocked out your sister."

I just stood there staring down at her, hoping I hadn't killed her. Looking at that woman, and her kids flocking behind her, I got the feeling right then that we were never going to be invited back. Oh, well, there were other neighbors.

Shandi soon came around, and looking up at me, she began to call me every name in the book, starting with, "Ca-ca face." and "Doo-doo head." After a long string of others that she made up on the spot, she finally finished with, "You little shit! I hate you!"

Now, I have to admit that's the one that took the wind out of my sails because, well… I knew exactly where it came from. That picture of my pa standing over me, slapping his folded-up belt against the palm of his hand came into my mind like a raging flood, and I kind of cringed.

When Shandi had run out of things to call me, she jumped up and took off in a clumsy run for home. That woman said, "I suppose you should be going, too." I didn't even look at her, I just followed Shandi, keeping my distance. I watched her cross the big, grassy field behind our place and go in our backdoor. I got to thinking about what was coming next. Since it was the weekend, I knew my pa would be in the kitchen drinking coffee and reading the paper. My ma would be flitting about the kitchen like a bird that didn't have a place to land; cooking, baking, trying to keep pa happy. Then there was grandpa, sitting in his Lazy Boy, smoking his pipe, and watching Saturday morning cartoons. My older sister, Karina, would be up in her attic bedroom, dancing around in her PJ's, listening to *Sgt. Pepper's Lonely Hearts Club Band*, or maybe that Joni Mitchell woman singing about being raised on robbery.

I slipped through the wire fence into the backyard but stopped right there. I was wondering if Shandi was now making me out to be bad enough that my pa would finally put me out of my misery. He was always promising to do so, anyway.

Standing there, watching the house, I was trying to put together in my mind all that I was going to say. What you have to understand is, I worked pretty hard at not lying. I didn't want people to have to go around saying I was a liar. When kids got caught in lies, no one trusted them. I didn't want to be that kid.

But here I was, trying to come up with a story to tell my folks that wasn't true. Because, well—the truth didn't seem to matter anymore. There was a chance that a good lie could save me. I knew deep down that unless Shandi actually killed me someday, I was going to have to be alive and made to suffer.

I was soon going through different situations in my head that might make the ruckus, that I knew was coming, a little easier on me. Because I had always tried so hard to be honest, I wasn't good at lying. I really wasn't sure what would work and what wouldn't in the lying business. I imagined my little sister, inside my ma's kitchen, waving her arms around and pointing to where she thought I might be standing at the moment. She'd be adding just enough to make sure that I was the monster she wanted them to see. That's when, what that neighbor woman had said, hit me, "Well, boy, looks like you done knocked out your sister." That gave me an idea.

The door flew open about that time and my pa stepped out onto the back steps, already pulling off his wide leather belt with its big trucker buckle. He was followed by my ma, who just stopped and stood there with a hand over her mouth. That was pretty normal for her.

I needed to get this thing started. So, I took a couple steps, staggered a bit and then fell down. I figured there was probably enough blood on the back of my white tee shirt to stop my pa in his tracks, and of course—to drive my mother to panic. It had worked with the neighbor kids, so… why not with them?

As I lay there on my belly, with my eyes shut, I decided moaning might help move things along. I heard their footsteps running toward me through the grass. Then my pa started to say something, but all he got out was, "What the…" Then my ma screamed, just like those women do in the movies.

"Oh my god! Oh my god! Carl! What happened?"

I kept up the moaning as she bent down and rolled me over. Opening my eyes just a crack, I saw my pa standing behind her. He was scratching his head, not sure what to do. Since beating me had been his goal, and because I was already at deaths door, it kind of left him in a bind.

"We need to call an ambulance!" my ma squawked just as the screen door slammed. That meant the others were on their way. So, I was going to get to put on quite a performance for everybody.

"No! No ambulance!" my pa yelled. "It costs too much. We'll just toss him in the back of the station wagon and haul his ass over to Doc Brandhal's. I ain't spending hundreds of dollars just to go a couple miles for this little shit."

"What happened? Oh, my god! There's blood!" I heard Karina say. So, I moaned one time for her sake.

Shandi whined, "Aren't you gonna hit him, pa? He pushed me down, and ummm… I was knocked up."

Karina laughed really hard and said, "Knocked out, its, knocked out. Jeez, what a doof." I heard Shandi blew her a raspberry.

Then there was my grandpa with his two cents worth and a cloud of pipe smoke, "I'll be damned! That little rascal's lost all that blood and he's still breathing! What a tough little son of a…"

"Papa!" my ma said, trying to make him stop before he said the 'B word'

"Pa! Aren't you gonna smack him? He hurt me; you know!"

"No one's gonna hit no one. There's been enough hitting," my ma said, taking charge for the first time in my life (and probably hers). I almost grinned and gave myself away.

"Get him to the station wagon, now," my pa said.

But my ma wasn't strong enough to pick me up, and even with Karina's help, they still couldn't get me off the ground. My grandpa just walked away, mumbling something about his bad back. When my pa saw that I was too heavy for them, he grabbed me by an ankle and started to drag me across the backyard.

"No! Don't do that! We don't know what's wrong with him. You could make it worse," my ma said—now actually telling my pa what to do.

"Geez, pa, quit being so mean," I heard Karina holler.

She could get away with that. Because, well… she wasn't afraid of anyone. I had only seen him raise a hand to her one time. I remember how he had grabbed her by the arm and then smacked that belt across her back. It kind of surprised us when she slapped him so hard across the face that he lost his balance and almost fell down. Karina ran away afterwards. I mean, really ran away. She was gone for nearly two whole days, hiding out at a friend's house in Clarksburg. When she came back, everybody acted like nothing had ever happened.

Pa never touched her again after that. I figured he was probably worried she might put some rat poison in his oatmeal one morning, or something like that. I started to feel about her the same way I did about my superheroes. So, I was always trying to give her things, or do stuff for her. Sometimes it kind of bugged her, but she never really tried to stop me, either.

Anyway, not wanting to be dragged all the way to the car, I pretended to come around, hollering, "What's going on? Where am I? Oh, my neck, my neck, it really hurts."

"Oh, my goodness! Carl!" my ma sang out.

I jerked my ankle from my pa's grip and sat up. My ma ran over, and helping me to my feet, she walked me slowly to the car. Karina, in her bathrobe and matching slippers, followed along behind us, singing, '*Three Blind Mice*' to a rock and roll beat. I had a tough time not cracking up. My pa just stood by the car, staring at us. I figured he was thinking it was either time for the beatings to start, or we were too far past that time for it to be worth his trouble. He would just have to wait until the next time that Shandi came tattling.

"Get him to the car. But put him in the back on his belly. I don't want blood all over my seats." Pulling his keys from his pocket, he got into the driver's seat of our beat up, '64 Ford wagon and started the motor.

"So, tell me the truth, Carl, what happened?" my ma whispered.

"So, tell me the truth, Carl, what happened?" Karina said, pretending to be an echo.

"Shandi hit me with a stick just because I told her to get off the swing and come play. I think she's going crazy, ma. I think you need to have her put in the nuthouse before she murders somebody."

"Just calm down, were going to see the doctor," she said as the rear window of the station wagon started to jerk and squeal its way open.

My ma popped the tailgate with Karina's help, and I crawled in, keeping in mind I had to act like my brain wasn't working properly. Shandi and my grandpa had been standing on the steps up underneath the carport. They were not saying anything, but now my grandpa had this big grin on his face like he was happy that there was some kind of excitement going on around our house. Peeking back over my shoulder as I crawled in, I saw Karina go past them, saying, "You're nothing but a bunch of meanies."

"This sucks!" Shandi yelled, stomping her foot.

"Well… maybe next time, Lizzie Borden," Grandpa said, patting her on the head, before following my older sister inside.

My ma was working pretty hard at trying to get the tailgate up by herself. I wanted to help, but I figured that would give me away. She finally got it to latch and breathing like she had just run a race;

she practically fell into the front seat. My pa couldn't get the window to go back up, and when its little motor started to smoke, he quit trying and drove away with it down.

I was pretty sure he was going to blame me for that because I knew he kept track of those things. So, I figured he'd probably get back at me, later. He'd probably sneak up on me when I least expected it, and of course, when no one else was around. I sometimes wondered if he knew that I knew that was how he worked. I had come up with a few tricks of my own to make sure that I stayed one step ahead of him.

One time he told me to come out behind the little toolshed to help him fix something. When I asked him what, he couldn't tell me. But I'd seen him hide a whipping stick just inside the shed door, a close twin to the one Shandi had used on me at the neighbors. So, I told him, "Just give me a minute, and I'll be right out."

The thing is, I meant I'd see him from the safety of the woods across that big field out behind our house. I climbed a big oak tree and just sat there watching him pace back and forth, waiting for me, tapping that switch on the wall of the shed and checking his big, silver wristwatch. He finally got tired of it and left. I 'spect he went off to the tavern to drown his sorrows, like my ma was always saying.

Those moments were always good for a laugh. I'd get to tell Karina and all my friends about it and get a few chuckles. My one friend, Eric Graff, said that my pa must be a real dummy. I had to agree and was sure to add that I 'spected he wasn't my real pa.

So, anyway, we drove the two miles to Clarksburg. When we got to the doctor's office on Main Street, my pa just stayed in the car. He told my ma to get me inside and be quick about it. When she couldn't get the tailgate open, he yelled, "Just crawl out, you little faker!"

"Now honey, he ain't faking. You see all that blood, don't you?"

"Ahhh… it's okay ma, I'll just crawl out. I'm better now," I said, slipping out the window, all the while wondering to myself how my pa could ever have been anybody's honey.

As we walked up the three-stepped curb that ran for almost the entire block, there were people walking by. Most of them were going to the Royal Blue grocery next door. One little girl started to cry, and a woman almost fainted when they saw my bloody shirt.

"Oh, my word!" the women crowed and got into a big hurry to get away from us. Some guy went by with a bunch of little kids and started gagging when he saw me. The kids started howling and bunching up around his knees. Then they started gagging too, and one actually did puke on the guy's shoes.

My pa just yelled out the window, "Get that little twerp inside, will you, Ruthie? Can't have people getting sick and puking their guts out all over the sidewalk, you know!"

Ma hurried me through the door of the tiny office, and when the nurse saw me, she rushed us into a room set aside for checking people out. She made me get up on doc's table and lie down on my belly. Then she left without saying anything. Doc Brandhal came in almost right away and checking me out, said, "Well, what do we have here? You get attacked by a bear, this time, Carl?"

I didn't say anything because I wasn't supposed to. I peeked back and saw him eyeing my ma even though he was talking to me. She didn't say anything, just stood there with her hands over her mouth. Doc cut off my tee shirt with some weird looking scissors and then went to cleaning the cut, saying,

"This looks like about twenty stitches, Ruthie, can you afford it?" For some reason, I got the feeling he didn't really mean in money.

Doc didn't wait for an answer and pulling open a drawer, he hauled out some thread and needle, saying, "I'm going to give you a little shot of Novocain, Carl. That way you won't feel a thing when I start sewing."

He was right, I didn't, and he made a pretty good guess about those stitches, too. Even though there were only nineteen, he had to use some extra thread to tie them off. So, that would count for about twenty, I guess. When he finished, he called in the nurse. She went to cleaning up his mess as Doc took my ma's arm and led her out into the hallway. They started talking about me, acting like I couldn't hear 'em out there. His voice was pretty serious, so I figured he was getting tired of always having to patch me up for something. Then he came to the part where he said he wanted to talk to my pa. I got to thinking that I might want to stick around for that.

But my ma took me back out to the car. I didn't have a shirt anymore, but it was summer. Boys were allowed to go around without shirts on, so that was okay. It didn't work that way for girls, but I think you know why.

I wanted other kids to see my stitches. Since I had taken to lying, and making stuff up, I could just tell them that I had been attacked by a wildcat. Getting in the car, my ma turned to my pa and said, "Doc Brandhal wants to talk to you."

"Well, is he gonna come out?"

"Uh... no. He's says for you to come in and meet him in his office at the back."

"Ah, dammit!" he said.

Then making a big deal of getting out of the car, he stopped for a few seconds to make his 'mean face' at me through the window. Then stomping up the curb, he went inside, slamming the door.

He was gone a long time. My ma just sat there, fanning herself with an Iowa Today magazine. I spent my time trying to figure out how far the window crank would turn before it actually moved the glass. The sun was pretty much baking us through the car roof, and I was going to try to talk ma into going over to the soda fountain at Nordon's Drug Store. But my pa came out about then. I could see he was a whole different person, now. That made me think Doc Brandhal was a damn fine doctor. He not only stitched me up real nice, but he may have also fixed my pa.

Instead of slamming Doc's door, he closed it real nice like. Then he walked slowly to the car, instead of running like he was coming to choke me. He didn't make it all the way, though. Instead, he just sat down on the second step of the curb, looking pretty sad. He started rubbing at his face and head like he had a headache and then he just sat there for a minute, staring down at his work boots.

"You all right, dear?" my ma called out.

He didn't say anything. He just stood up and got in the car. He started the motor, backed out into the street and then driving down across the river bridge, we went up the hill toward highway 13. Half way up, he turned to my ma, growling like an old bear.

"Twenty-five damn bucks, Ruthie! It cost me, twenty-five damn bucks!"

"Well... you know, honey, I think you just might find that, and a little more, in Shandi's piggy bank back at the house. In fact... there's probably enough there to get Carl an ice cream cone, as well. I mean... considering his suffering, and all."

I imagined my pa's head exploding about then. He just stared real hard at my ma, grumbling something I didn't quite catch. She just whispered a few words back and he suddenly gritted his teeth, his eyes nearly popping out of his head. But the next thing you know, we were pulling into the Dairy Dreem parking lot.

I got to go in by myself while my parents had words in the car. I tried not to grin too big when I came out the door with that double dip of Rocky Road. Handing my pa back his change, he looked over at my ma and then just mumbled, "Keep it."

By the time we had pulled in under the carport, I had finished my cone. But I was sure not to wipe the chocolate from around my mouth. In fact, I had actually rubbed the ice-cream against my chin, for good measure. I wanted everybody inside to know how much I appreciated my pa getting me ice cream.

Going inside, I stopped in the middle of the living room floor just long enough for Shandi to see me. She was on the couch watching TV and cheering on Moe of *The Three Stooges*. She finally looked over at me and not even a second went by before her mouth fell open. Grandpa looked up from his *Mechanix Illustrated* and started laughing so loud it made the windows rattle.

Going to my bedroom to put on a clean tee shirt, I could hear the music pouring down the stairway. Karina was up there playing her Dylan album and singing, '*The Times They Are a Changin'* at the top of her lungs. I hoped that was true and started humming along.

I pulled the shirt on over my head, doing my best to keep it from snagging my stitches. It was when my head popped out of the collar, that I saw my pa through the window. He was coming up from the tool shed with a hammer in his hand.

Since I'd taken the screen off that window (just in case I needed to make an escape), I was able to poke my head out. My ma was standing on the backsteps, holding the door open for him, kind of grinning. Pulling back inside before he saw me, I heard him stomp in through the kitchen. Then after about a minute, I heard Shandi say just one thing in a scared little voice, "Pa?"

Going over to my door, I saw grandpa shuffle into the hallway. Looking past him, I could just make out my pa standing over Shandi with that hammer in his hand. He was just staring down at her, asking where her piggy bank was. I have to admit, it had been a long time since I'd seen a look like that on my little sister's face.

When I turned back to grandpa, he was already heading into Shandi's bedroom. His stinky ol' coffee cup was in his hand and his huge leather slippers scuffed on the rough, wooden floor. He moved back to stand in the corner where he could see that piggy bank. It was sitting there on her dresser with a big smile on its piggy face. When grandpa saw me watching him through the open door, he took a sip of his coffee, and then cackling like an ol' hen, he said, "Get on in here, you little rascal, you're not gonna want to miss this for the world!"

#2

Rat House

Fiana rode in the back seat of her da's car. Her younger sister, Shannon, was in the middle, and her brother Cos, on the far side. He was gazing out the open window, his longish, brown hair fluttering around and getting in his eyes.

It was 1969 now and Fiana had been fifteen for almost three months. Cos, the middle child, was three years younger, and Shannon, the baby of the family, was only six. Shannon was her da's little princess and got whatever she wanted. She was now hiding her face behind blonde hair, sniveling. Everybody in the car knew she was about ready to burst out bawling. Fiana was on the verge of exploding because she was trying to tune out the argument going on between her parents in the front seat.

They soon passed the sign that said: 'You Are Now Leaving Clarksburg, A Fine Little Iowa Town. Come Back Soon!' Fiana hoped they wouldn't be going too far. She didn't want to have to start at a whole new school and have to make all new friends. She'd just gotten in good with the ones she had made last April; when they first came to Clarksburg.

A Creedence Clearwater Revival song came on the radio. It was number two on the 'Hot 100 List' and she wanted so badly to reach over the seat and crank up the volume; anything to drown out the yelling. They were getting ready to move again. Only two months in their apartment and her da was trying to figure out a way to save money. She figured just so he'd have more to spend on beer. Work and beer. That's all he seemed to care about. Driving that stupid milk truck and hanging out at the Blue Front Tavern, telling all his lies. That was what he seemed to live for.

Fiana let her long curly brown hair flap out of the window as she bopped along to Bad Moon Rising. She wasn't supposed to let her hair do that. If it got caught on something, it could get ripped out by the roots, or so her da said. But if there was a bad moon rising, what would it matter? If there were worst things to come, getting bitched out about her flapping hair shouldn't be the issue.

"Why do we have to move? We have a perfectly good apartment in town?" her ma said.

"It's like I told you a thousand times, I need to be closer to work. If I have to tell you again, I'm going to smack you. So… shut it."

"You're not gonna smack no one, unless you're thinking you're not gonna get smacked back."

"I'll stop this car right now and show you who's gonna get smacked. We're gonna move, and that's all there is to it."

Their da slammed on the brakes and Shannon screamed. Fiana yelled, "Da!" hoping to remind him about her threat of knocking him over the head if she ever saw him hit her ma again.

She looked at her brother whose mouth was hanging open, his eyes as big as golf balls. His hands were on his crotch and she wondered if he had peed on his da's car seat. He had a weak bladder, and it didn't take much to set him to squirting.

Her ma turned in her seat and put her back to the door like she was waiting for her husband's fist to make its mark. Fiana searched the floor for a stray beer bottle. More often than not, there would be one rolling around down there. Instead of stopping the car, her da whipped the steering wheel to the left and rolled down a gravel driveway leading to someone's crappy looking blue house. Fiana saw her da's face in the rear-view mirror and he was smirking like he thought it was funny that he had fooled them.

The old, grey Pontiac wagon barreled through a scraggly hedge; the opening only half as wide as the car. Branches screeched against the sides, sounding like her da had run over a whole troupe of fairy folk. He laughed about it, but she knew anyone else would have caught holy hell if they had scratched his car. His car—his rules. Yeah, well… his bad temper—her beer bottle.

The car came around the back of the house and skidded in the gravel as it came to a stop. They all stared through a thin cloud of dust into a carport attached at the back. It ended in a small horse stall at the far end, like whomever had lived there years back wanted to keep their favorite steed close at hand.

A rat, the size of a small cat, burst out of the unmowed grass in the backyard and streaked across the driveway to squeeze in through a broken basement window. Fiana looked at Cos, his mouth still open, his eyes still bulging. She mouthed the words, "No way." But that was all because she knew her da was watching.

"Uh-uh, no way," her ma said. "We are not living in this shithole."

"Hell, we aren't! I work right across the highway… can't get no closer."

Creedence sang something about how the end was coming soon, and Fiana got to thinking if that were true, maybe now would be a good time to risk that bottle. She would do it just like she saw in the cowboy movies. She was too late, though, because her da climbed out and was no longer within reach. He stopped to stand behind the car door, just staring at the house.

"We can fix this… a little paint, a hammer and some nails…"

"Please, dear, there's got to be something better. What about one of those houses up on the hill?"

"Nope," was all he said.

9

If he would just step away from the car, Fiana could jump over the seat, grab that steering wheel and back the hell out of there. They could take off and leave him there with his precious house. She knew how to drive, but her folks didn't know that she did. An older friend, Rosemary Ryan, owned an old blue Ford and had taught her afterschool. They often rode around Clarksburg for the fun of it and sometimes Rosemary would let Fiana drive on the gravel roads outside of town.

Her ma sighed looked back at the three of them with the saddest face Fiana had ever seen. She suddenly felt bad for her ma, and catching her own face in the mirror, she realized it didn't look different than that of her siblings. She, honestly, just wanted the nightmare to end and had thought it had with the last move to the apartment.

There had been bliss for maybe two months, and now, this. Her da had been so busy hooking up with family, making connections, and looking for work, he had ignored them during that time. She got a taste of freedom from what she called his tyranny.

Her da grinned a mean grin at them, and reaching in, he turned off the car and pulled the key. Oh well, she thought, maybe next time. He walked to the back steps and pulled open the screen door. Taking a shiny, silver key from his shirt pocket, he held it up for them to see before he unlocked the house. Standing, gazing into whatever room was off the back door, he soon turned his face to them with a goofy look, and pointing inside, he hollered, "Welcome to your new home!" and disappeared through the doorway.

Fiana was first to get out, and as she did, she imitated her favorite comedian, George Carlin, by saying, "Well… let's go check out our new shit hole!"

She walked to the door but stopped short and looked back at her family who were still sitting in the car. She stared at each one in succession until they climbed out and came to her. Shannon was holding her ma's hand with her left and picking her nose with her right. Fiana cringed.

Nobody wanted to be first to give into her da and go inside. It was like whoever was first to set foot across that threshold was the loser. So, they did it together, all four of them pushing through at one time.

The first thing Fiana noticed in the kitchen was the smell. It was a lot like a rabbit hutch they used to own. There was a scurrying sound inside a cupboard under the sink and she mumbled, "You just stay in there—whatever you are." Grabbing Shannon's arm, she was careful to avoid the finger that had been mining boogers. She pulled her and her mom into the living room to get away from whatever was occupying the cupboards. Looking back, she saw that Cos had grabbed a nearly denuded broom from a corner and went to work battling the beast beneath the sink. There came a loud squeak and then a splash from the cellar below. The dilapidated broom followed the creature down the large hole that had been gnawed in the cupboard floor. Slamming the door, Cos sighed in relief and said, "That's one down."

Fiana gave him a thumbs up, but her mom and sister just stared like they couldn't believe what had just happened. Their da's heavy boots pounded down some stairs and he yelled out in his gruff voice, "What the hell's going on down there?" Fiana saw her chance and sang out, "Oh, nothing, really. Cos was just checking out our new swimming pool."

They backed into the kitchen when her da appeared. "What the hell are you talking about, lass?" he said, squinting.

"Darling, the cellar's full of water… I really don't think that's healthy," her ma said, pointing toward the cupboard under the sink. Her da moved into the room and reached for the grimy knob to look inside. Everybody else took a step back.

The door came open and a soggy, swamp-like smell rolled out. The sun's rays coming through the curtain-less window entered the large hole and glinted off some ripples rolling across the surface of the dark water below.

"You see, darling? That can't be good for us."

"Well, the door leading down to the cellar is nailed shut. So… it won't be a problem. No one's going down there, anyway."

Cos shook his head in dismay and wandered into the living room. Fiana passed him at a faster pace and going into what looked like a short hallway leading from the living room, she stopped to stare into a small bathroom. She hoped she wasn't the one to be picked to clean it. To the left of that was the doorway to a bedroom and beyond that, the hall ended at a door under the stairs. Long nails had been pounded in around the edges and bent over. Fiana suspected that it must be the one that hid the stairs that led down into the basement. She was going to make up a sign, later, to tack there, saying: 'Pool— Swim At Your Own Risk'

Chuckling to herself, Fiana turned left to enter another bedroom and considering its size, she knew that's where her parents' bed would go. Stepping inside she noticed a single step at the bottom of an open doorway in the wall on her right. Going there, she looked in. A narrow 'L' shaped stairway led to the second floor. Bounding up the stairs, she entered an attic bedroom at the top. The rabbit hutch smell was just as strong up there.

"This is my room," she yelled. Her da said nothing, so her ma shouted, "Okay, darling!" and added, "Did you hear Fiana, Rowan? She's taking the room up the stairs." Her da's response, a grumbling, "Go ahead and take it, see if I care," was hardly discernable as it floated up through the floor. Fiana smirked.

"Shannon gets the bedroom back in the corner off the carport. Cos… you can take the couch."

Fiana's smile faded. Her da was making her little brother take the couch again. She recalled the: 'Man Enough' speech he gave to them once at the dinner table. She knew, even though he told the whole family, his little lecture had actually been for Cos.

The three of them shared a tiny bedroom back at the apartment. Cos was made to throw down a small mattress in the walk-in closet. No one complained; not even Cos. He had told her that he liked it in there, especially when the sun shone through its tiny, stained-glass window at the end of the day.

"Okay, let's get on out of here and get back to the apartment. We got to pack up. Rents due tomorrow and I want to be out of there before ol' Dela even knows we're gone. Fiana! Get your fat arse down here, we're off."

Fiana moved down the stairs slowly, one step at a time, stomping each tread as she did. She knew her arse was just average sized, so, he was calling it fat because that would hurt her feelings. She listened to her family stampede through the kitchen and out into the carport. Her da would be waiting to lock up, shiny key in hand. Slowing down even more, she grinned at the thought of him pacing. He wouldn't say anything, he'd just make a face. But if he did decide to grab her—or slap her, she would make use of that empty wine bottle with the candle sticking out of it that sat on the greasy old stove next to the door.

Her da ignored her when she came out. He was standing out by the edge of the unmowed lawn, staring across the backyard. As soon she slammed the car door, he stomped back to the house and locked up. Fiana wondered why he had even bothered. There wasn't anything in there that anybody would want to steal. She figured her da just wanted to use his shiny new key and be the boss of who went in and out of his precious pile of crap.

They drove to the apartment where her da backed into the short driveway and parked. "We are going to load the car after dark. Go up and start packing your shite. I'm going up to the tavern. Your moms in charge. So, you better listen to what she has to say. If you don't, you can expect to feel my belt burning your arse, so… to it!"

Fiana got out and waited for her da to go up the outside stairs and unlock the door. Leaning against the car with her arms crossed, she stared down the street toward the river bridge, trying hard to appear indifferent. Cos got out and leaned beside her, crossing his arms as well. When their da was far enough away that he couldn't hear them, Cos whispered, "Fiana, this is a bad idea. You know that, right? That place was spooky, and now… we got to sleep there?"

"Yeah, I know. We should all runaway, well… not Shannon, just you and me, maybe ma."

"Where would we go? You know da would just come after us?"

"Grandda's coming in a couple days. Aunt Louise is going to pick him up at the train station and he'll stay overnight. Then he'll come to that stupid rat house to stay with us afterwards. So… we could always runaway to Aunt Louise's?"

"You two get upstairs and get started," their da said and took off across the lawn toward the town square.

"Darling… we have no milk; can you stop and get some at the Royal Blue?" their ma hollered from where she stood at the top of the stairs, Shannon beside her, sucking her thumb.

"Uh… yeah, sure. Going to get me some of my own milk, first," he muttered.

"I didn't know the tavern had milk," Cos said.

"It doesn't, silly."

"But…"

"Forget it, let's get upstairs."

Grabbing the front of Cos's tee shirt, she towed him for a few feet before she let go and ran. "Can't catch me, little boy," she said.

"Hell, I can't," he shouted and took off after her. "And I ain't no little boy!"

"Oh, that's right, you're now the great, Rat Slayer of Clarksburg!" she sang out and bounded up the stairs with Cos trying to catch up.

They packed what clothes they had, their grandmas' silver from Ireland, and Mae McDhai's favorite flower vase which she never used. There were the mattresses, along with her ma and Da's bedstead, all the sheets and blankets, some cups, plates, a stack of LP's (mostly Fiana's), the little phonograph, and a few toys. Most everything small got wrapped in those blankets and sheets. When everything was set to go, and the bed torn apart, they all sat on the couch that had come with the apartment and watched the Dick Van Dyke show.

The tiny, orange Motorola would be the last thing to go. It was the one pleasure their da had allowed, an ancient television the size of a toaster oven, one that he had found at a garage sale. When the whimsical music played at the end of the show and the credits rolled, not one of them was awake to read them.

Their da showed up well after dark when he knew the landlady would be in bed. Waking everyone, he hustled them back and forth several times between the house and car, carrying whatever they could carry. He hadn't gotten too drunk, and of course, there was no milk. Fiana figured he had spent that money buying rounds for his mates.

There was a lot of hushing and threats being made to keep everybody quiet. They were all too sleepy to argue. Bed parts stuck out the back window of the station wagon and every space had been filled with either personal belongings or their bodies. Fiana's da snuck the front door key into Dela's mailbox, and after checking the ropes that bound the mattresses to the roof of the car, he coasted it down the driveway and to the corner before starting the engine. Fiana couldn't sort what the hush-hush was all about, but she was sure her ma knew. She would wait and ask later.

Upon arriving at rat house, everyone stayed in the car until her da got the lights on. Fiana didn't feel that the single bare bulb in the carport was enough to see if a rat was coming for her. So, she didn't spend too much time out there once they got all the mattresses inside. Everything else was to stay in the car until the next day.

"Where am I going to sleep if Shannon gets my mattress?" Cos asked in a sleepy whine.

"Well, I'll just show you," his da said and opening the door to the enclosed front porch, he dragged an old army cot into the living room, stained, and smelling of cat piss.

"That's where I got to sleep?"

"It's going to have to do until we get a sofa, or you can just sleep on the floor. Your choice."

"You'll be okay," his ma said.

"Yeah, and if you don't like it, tough titty! I am going to bed now. Everybody sleeps in their clothes tonight, you can unpack your jammies tomorrow," Rowan said, disappearing into his bedroom. Her ma put Shannon to bed and checking in on Cos, Fiana heard him ask, "Can we leave a light on? This place is scary."

"Okay, I'll leave the light on above the sink in the kitchen, how's that?"

Fiana watched from where she sat on the floor in a corner of the dark living room. Her ma stopped about three feet short of the lower cupboards and stared at the doors for a few seconds before stretching out nearly as far as she could and to pull the string that turned on the light. Wishing them good night she hurried into her bedroom.

"Fiana, you want to stay down here with me?" Cos asked.

"Naw, I'm going upstairs in a minute."

"Well... hold on, will you?" Getting off the cot, Cos tiptoed into the kitchen. Fiana could already hear her da's snores, so there would be no trouble from him. Getting up, she walked in to see what Cos was up to. He had taken a length of cord that had been used to tie the mattresses to the top of the car and was in the process of tying it around the knobs of the lower cupboard doors.

"That should hold it for tonight," he said.

"Yep, that'll do it. Okay, I am going to bed. Try to get some sleep, huh, little brother?"

Cos got back onto his cot and pulled his head inside his shirt so he wouldn't have to see what might come for him in the night. Rolling over, he faced the wall.

Fiana snuck through her parent's room but her ma was awake and whispered, "Good night, Fiana, try to get some sleep, huh?"

"Uh… yeah. Fat chance. Goodnight, ma."

She moved as quietly as she could up the stairs, but they still creaked like crazy. She left the light on and flopped down on her mattress. After a few minutes she got back up and opened the window on her end of the long room—the only one with the screen. Laying down on her back, she watched a fly buzz around and bounce off the lightbulb. Someone had written on the ceiling over in the corner with red ink marker. Straining her eyes, she read: 'Carl Dawes was here!' She had met some of the Dawes at school. Fiana liked them and wondered if this had been their house at one time. They had probably moved out and taken a place in Clarksburg when the rats took over.

The crickets and katydids chirped and buzzed just outside. There was an owl hooting from somewhere far away. Frogs were croaking from the slough on the northside of the yard, and something that she thought might be a whip-poor-will, piped from the trees on the other side of the railroad tracks.

What a dump. She wasn't sure how long she could stay here. Maybe Aunt Louise would let her stay at her place and room with her cousin, Cami. Twenty minutes went by with her trying to figure a way to get out of this mess. At twenty-one minutes she was asleep.

It was about midnight when she startled awake. The house was alive with noise. Rustling came from under the floor boards and in the walls. Tiny feet scampered here and there. Squeaking and squealing could be heard coming from all corners with the occasional screech to raise the hair on her arms. It was rodent central, and not even the dim bulbs left burning had any effect in deterring the late-night activity. She could hear her da still snoring away, along with her ma. Then a noise on the stairs.

Something was coming up. She lay frozen, waiting, imagining some giant rat was making its way up to have her for a late-night snack. She thought about that ballet, the Nutcracker, and the rat king. Clara didn't seem to be afraid of the giant rodent and even threw her shoe at it. Fiana found one of her sneakers and picking it up, she held it high—waiting.

Then, a shadow at the top the stairs—Cos, dragging a tattered blanket. "Dammit, Cos," she rasped out. "You scared the shit out of me."

"Yeah, well, you ought to be down there."

"Did you see one?"

"No, but you can hear em."

"Ain't no different up here."

"Can I sleep with you, Fiana? I promise I won't pee the bed."

"Okay, but no talking. I'm feking tired and these damn rats don't give a hoot."

Cos crawled onto the mattress with Fiana and they lay on their sides, back-to-back. He pulled the cover up over them to hide their heads and they lay listening to the noise for a few minutes before Cos said, "Hey, Fiana."

"I said, no talking."

"Just one thing."

"What?"

14

"You know why they don't give a hoot?

"No, why?"

"Cause they're rats, not owls!"

There came a muffled laugh from Fiana's side of the bed, validation enough for him to laugh as well. It relieved some of the anxiety they had been feeling, and they soon fell into an exhausted sleep. Sometime in the night Fiana rolled over, and without knowing, wrapped an arm around her little brother and they stayed that way until the dawn greyed the morning sky.

She woke with the sun peeking in the window. It was Saturday. She could hardly wait to see her grandda. He was her ma's da, and he had come all the way from Ireland to check up on them. Fiana knew he didn't like her da, much. The thing she loved the most was that she and her grandda got along just famously.

Cos had disappeared, probably back down to his cot before their da woke up. When Fiana came down, her ma and da were trying to put the bed frame together, but her ma couldn't get the side rail to stay attached at her corner. Fiana was hoping they could go to the Davis Café for breakfast, but she could see her da was already steaming. No breakfast today.

Her da couldn't let go of his end to come around and help her ma or the whole thing would fall apart. Fiana went to help, but she was too late, and the heavy siderail fell to the floor with a crash. She watched her da's face turn bright red. He let his end fall and stumbled across the whole mess as her ma backed up, pushing Fiana into the corner. She wasn't sure if her ma was trying to protect her or had forgotten she was even back there.

Her da grabbed the front of her ma's dress and drew back a fist. Everything went into slow motion for Fiana. She saw Shannon standing in her doorway, her ragged teddy bear in hand. Cos's face soon appeared around the door jamb; his eyes wide with terror. Fiana noticed then that her ma's suitcase was open on the floor beside her feet and laying in the folds of a heavy sweater was her ma's China vase. Next to it was the family portrait behind glass and nicely framed in heavy, dark wood.

It was either the vase or the picture. Not wanting to destroy something as precious as her ma's vase, she grabbed the portrait. When her da's fist was half way to her ma's face, Fiana jumped straight up into the air and at the top of her arc, she reached out as far as she could and smashed it over his head.

Time returned to its normal pace and she watched as her da covered his face and fell to his knees cursing. Her ma screamed and said, "Fiana, what have you done!" It was a good time to escape. If she waited too long, she may not get out.

Picking her way across the pile of bed parts, she ignored Shannon, who was now bawling like a banshee. Fiana passed Cos who had returned to his cot and was now hugging himself. Heading for the back door she heard him say, "Fiana, are you leaving?"

"Got a go, Cos. Be a good boy for your ma, huh?"

Cos's face twisted up, the tears came, and a strangled, "Bye," escaped his lips.

Fiana got the door open and took off across the backyard. Climbing the wire fence, she ran barefoot across the big field of long grass. Coming to a second fence, she climbed over and found herself at the railroad track embankment with the woods beyond. After climbing up the loose shale, she stood looking north toward Clarksburg. She knew the tracks ran just behind her aunt's place and all she had to do was follow them and eventually she would get there.

The cinders that the Chicago Northwestern used along the rail line, hurt her feet as she made her way. She tried to walk on the rails at first to avoid them, and when that didn't work, she just walked on the wooden ties. Sometimes she stepped in tiny tar puddles on the wood, but that was nothing compared to the sharp cinders.

It was close to two miles to aunt Louise. Her ma's words kept rolling through her head, "Fiana! What have you done!" Well, ma, she thought, I've got plenty of time to think about that.

Fiana didn't feel the way she thought she would. She was scared, and even though she felt her da deserved what he got—she didn't feel right about it. She had hurt him, and she didn't know how seriously. When he fell to the floor, which was something totally unexpected, a kind of pain swelled in her chest. Maybe she loved him a wee bit, after all? Memories flooded her mind of the days when he was younger and nicer. But now, she had put him on the floor. Maybe he wasn't as tough as he wanted them to think. It was all for show. The only way she could make herself feel better was to keep telling herself that she had protected her ma.

At the city limits sign, she broke down and cried. It had been a long time since she had done that. The tears lasted until she got to the Ryan's house just beyond the lumberyard. She was glad the chairs lining the deep front porch were free of people, she didn't want Rosemary running out to see her red, puffy eyes. Fiana suspected they were all in the kitchen having a big breakfast, just like a real family.

Her Aunt's house soon came into sight after she crossed the railroad bridge. This sparked a need for her to compose herself. When she thought she was ready to face her aunt, she slid down the embankment and came through the back gate in the white picket fence.

She stopped to sit on a bench outside the back door and studied her feet. The bottoms were spotted black with tar, and there were a few cuts. A little rubbing alcohol and that stuff would come right off. She had learned that trick when Cos had run across a freshly tarred spot in the street outside their apartment.

The door suddenly swung open and her aunt came rushing out in her house coat. "Fiana! What are you doing here? And why are your feet all cut up and covered with tar?" Fiana rose and started to explain, but then her grandda's large frame soon filled the doorway and he grinned. Fiana gasped and said, "Grandda! Why are you here already? I thought you weren't coming til tomorrow?"

"Naw, you got it wrong, darling… twas yesterday."

She didn't care. Running to him, she threw her arms around his middle and broke into sobs. He held her, sometimes patting her back and telling her, "Going to be alright, lass." Aunt Louise took to patting her too, and after Fiana calmed down, they walked her into the kitchen and sat her in a chair at the table. When she could speak, she explained to them what had happened while Aunt Louise fixed breakfast. Fiana told them all about how her da had been acting. Aunt Louise grumbled a few things, but Fiana could make no sense of any of it. Her grandda told her, "Now, don't you worry, Fiana, we'll fix this somehow. You just eat your eggs and toast. Maybe Louise can fry us up some bacon. Then we'll get your feet cleaned up. I'm sure you can borrow your cousin Cami's flip-flops while she's away at camp. Okay with you, Louise?"

"That little imp's got half a dozen, she won't miss a pair," said Aunt Louise, who then cackled and winked. Fiana felt a deep sense of relief. She was with grownups who acted like grownups. She could just be herself—at least for a little while. But not even that would lessen the fear she had for her brother, sister, and ma. Well, not so much her little sister. Her da would never lay a hand on Shannon.

"Where's uncle Delbert, aunt Louise?"

"Oh, off to the farm. Left early this morning. You know we're going to give up this place and move out there full time once he gets things up and running, right? Probably this fall. I'll be so glad to sell this old place," Aunt Louise said and shook her head slowly back and forth. "Not much on city living, you know. I'll be glad to get away from that darned ol' train coming by in the wee hours of the morning when I'm trying to get my beauty sleep. And think about it, Fiana, we're only a couple of miles up the highway from your place. What do you think about that?"

Fiana looked at her grandda who was smiling, a question in his eyes. "Well, that's just fine with me," she said, "As long as I can find you if I need you."

"Lovely," her aunt said as Fiana's grandda winked and clicked his tongue at her.

It was late morning when the phone rang. Fiana, now with clean feet, lay napping on the sofa trying to catchup on her sleep. She heard Aunt Louise answer, and right off she knew it was her da. Then her grandda got on the phone and his stern words rolled into the living room where Fiana lay.

"Tis right, Rowan, the girl's here. Poor lass is worn out. No, I won't send her home. Fiana's going to be with us a couple days, and since I came to visit youse, I'll drive her home when I come. I'm sure Louise will let me take her truck. She's still got the car if she needs to be off somewheres."

He stopped talking and Fiana heard the handset fall back into its cradle. "Be damned… he hung up on me."

"Well," Aunt Louise said, "Tis fine. He's got the same trousers to be glad in. Want another cup of tea, da?"

A few minutes later Aunt Louise came into the living room and when she saw Fiana was awake, she said, "Your da just called. It sounded like he was using the phone at the gas station just down from your new place. We let him know you're going to be with us a couple days. How's that sound?"

"Sounds great. Um… Aunt Louise, can I go upstairs and play some records on Cami's record player?"

"Certainly, darling, but take good care of them, Cami doesn't want them scratched. But I know you got your own, so… I'm sure you'll be careful. Go on."

Fiana went up the narrow stairs to her cousin Cami's room. Passing Craig's and Mal's rooms, she found Cami's bedroom nearly pristine compared to the lads. Digging through Cami's stack of LP's she came across a Youngbloods album. Putting it on the turntable, she sat on the floor listening to her favorite song, *Get Together*. Soon, warm, salty tears were running down her cheeks and not because she was sad, but because she had such a great feeling of relief. She vowed to herself that she wasn't going to be so quick to hit and would try harder to find some way to get around it. She wouldn't give it up as a last resort, though. But she knew she never wanted to feel the way she now felt, ever again.

It was Monday noon when her grandda drove Aunt Louise's pickup into the driveway at rat house. Fiana's da's milk truck was parked over in the grass by the fence, leaving the driveway clear for her grandda. She figured her da must be inside having lunch. Hopefully, they'd boughten some food by now. She climbed out of the truck and was met by Cos, who slammed into her with one serious hug.

"Oh man, did I miss you," he said grinning from ear to ear. Then going around, he grabbed his grandda who picked him up and gave him a serious bear hug, his feet dangling.

When they were finished, Cos led the big man toward the back steps, calling for his ma. The screen door swung open to reveal Rowan with Shannon standing behind him, peeking past his legs. She had a brand-new teddy bear in her arms. Shannon didn't like her mother's father much, and he, in turn, ignored her, figuring she might come around some day. She was definitely her da's little princess.

Fiana studied her da's face and noticed the small bruise and cut at his hairline in front. It wasn't as bad as she had imagined and felt a small degree of respite. He acted like Fiana was invisible. She felt that was a good thing.

"Hello, Rowan, long time, no see," her grandfather said, his big hand still resting on Cos's shoulder.

"Angus, see you made it."

"Aye, still fit, you know."

Fiana's ma pushed past her Rowan and nearly fell coming down the steps. She grabbed Fiana in a tight hug, and sang out, "I am so glad you're alright, I was so afraid." Kissing Fiana on the forehead, she dragged her daughter with her as she went to her da, refusing to let go.

"Hey da, glad to see you," Mae said and keeping a grip on Fiana's right hand, she slung her daughter around behind him in order to complete her embrace. Fiana, not knowing what to do, decided to hug her grandda again, only this time from behind, all the while hoping he didn't break wind. She heard the screen door slam and looking past her grandda, she saw that Shannon and her da had abandon them. Now, only Cos remained, just standing and grinning.

Upon completion of their affectionate moment, they all walked into the house together. Fiana's da and sister were sitting just inside at the kitchen table. Shannon was finishing off a bowl of ice cream and their da, a cup of coffee.

"Coffee, da?" Fiana's ma asked Angus.

"Tea, if you got it, darling," he said and continued on into the living room where he stopped and looked around.

"You know, Rowan... I was only going to be here for a week, but it looks to me like you might need some help with this old place. So, I'm going to stay a wee bit longer. Maybe... maybe even a year. Should have this place shipshape by then. Looking back over his shoulder, he shot Fiana a grin as she watched from the doorway. Turning back to face the army cot across the room, he mumbled loud enough for everyone to hear, "Man, what a shithole."

#3

Uncle Liajah And The Amazing Zillia

I've lived by the river all my life. I'm twelve now, so that's a long time, right? My family calls me Wick, but only because it was actually Rick. It's just, I couldn't pronounce it right until I was about seven. So, it stuck. My full name is Rick J. Ryan and I'm the youngest of ten kids. Six sisters and three brothers, every one of them named after a spice except for me. That's because on the day I was born, my pa said there was enough spiciness in our house as it was, and he wanted his turn to name a kid.

So, there was Parsley, Rosemary, and Thyme, along with Marjoram (Marji), Nutmeg, and Cassia. My brothers were Basil, Dill, and Clove. Cassia and Clove, still lived at home with me, but not for long. They were going graduate to soon and fly the coop just like the rest. I'm gonna miss them, especially Cassia, since she was always watching out for me. My ma's so busy with stuff, she hardly has the time. My pa's always working and is away an awful lot because he's what my ma calls a 'railroad man'.

He rides the caboose and takes care of things for the engineer. I think he's a good pa because he makes sure we got food on the table, and when he's home, we go fishing together and stuff like that. Some kids are jealous of me because I went with my pa on the caboose once and saw what he did for our money. No one was supposed to know I was back there and had to hide in a cupboard when some other railroad men came in and had coffee with my pa. We went from Clarksburg all the way to the Mississippi and back on the Chicago Northwestern without anyone catching me. It was pretty exciting. My pa says someday we'll do it again. I can hardly wait. I'm thinking when I grow up, I'm gonna be a railroad man just like my pa. Until then, I'll just have to settle for going to school, climbing trees, and fishing.

Well, then there's our boat. It's an old, flat bottom, row boat. Some of my pals call it a Jon boat, but I couldn't even begin to tell you why. I don't see no name on it anywhere. I'm old enough to handle it now and can row like crazy, but... I want a canoe. They're a lot easier to float around on and you can carry one if you get too far downstream and want to come back. If it's a small one, anyway.

Our house sits right next to the tracks. They run by our place, clear out at the end of our front yard. Most people have a street at the front of their house; we got the railroad tracks. There's a walkway that runs from our front porch out to the tracks where my pa meets the train for its run to Dubuque. The engineer blows the whistle three times to tell pa they are leaving the depot. Then he heads on out with his duffle and just jumps onboard the caboose when it's passing. It's going pretty slow when it does, and when my pa gets inside, he gets on the radio and reports in. Then the engineer speeds up, knowing pa's safe onboard.

He could always walk over to the depot and get on there, but he wants to use that last few minutes to say his goodbyes and get all lovey-dovey with ma instead of having to wait around.

The railroad bridge is about a hundred or so feet farther over to the east. That's where a trail no wider than my butt, runs down to the riverbank and then all the way to this town called Waubeek. Weird name, huh? I think it's American Indian, or something. Anyway, I walked it one day. When I got there, I had myself a grape Nehi at the general store and didn't get back home until way after dark.

Yeah, I got in trouble, but only because I didn't tell ma where I was going. So, she made me wash the supper dishes and shuck sweet corn. I hated that stuff, and she knew it. I'd rather mow the grass or rake leaves. Maybe feed the chickens, slop our two hogs, milk our one cow, and then there was always the garden chores. But dishes? No way!

Now, if I were to go down the river in a canoe, it would be light enough for me to carry back on that trail if I needed to, or maybe, I could leave it in the river, hook a rope to it, and pull it back while I was walking on the shore. Anyway, that was the plan. I've gotta get the canoe first.

I have a paper route, and I carry twice as many papers as the other kids. I have a big white, canvas bag that hangs off my shoulder and it's always full to bulging. On Sundays, I have to make two trips from the DX station on Main Street where the huge, wooden, paper box sits. That thing was painted a pukey shade of green and about the size of a pickup truck!

Now, I have to tell you about this girl. She delivers papers too. Her name was Zillia. Yeah, I know, never heard a name like that before, huh? And she doesn't even have a story for her name like I do. It's just, Zillia. Her last name is Struck. You know, kinda like, hit, or punch? Some guy at school called her Godzillia once and she blacked his eye so dark, it took two months for it to clear up. No one messes with Zillia because even though she don't have a story for her first name, her last name might be a clue as to how you should treat her. So, you better be paying attention when you ask her what it is. You'll only get one chance.

Don't get me wrong, she's not huge, and she sure don't look like that big dinosaur in the movie. She's just a regular sized girl with short, curly red hair and freckles. Her eyes are green, and she wears mostly boy clothes. That's because her folks can't afford her fancy duds. She told me someday she's going to go to Lottie's store up at the square and get herself a complete girl's outfit. So, just like my canoe dream, Zillia, has a girl's outfit dream.

I met her at the paper box on her first day and then she started coming over to my house. We spend a lot of time climbing trees in my backyard and playing in the woods, just stuff like that. Sometimes we would draw pictures, put airplane models together, or she'll help me with my yard chores. She told me once she likes being at my place more than hers. I supposed that was because she has only brothers and they were always beating up on her and stealing her stuff.

Her brothers stole all her underwear from her dresser one day and wore them over the tops of their jeans. Then they went outside and ran around Clarksburg. She had to chase them all over town to get them back. Now everybody knows what Zillia's underwear looks like. She was pretty upset about it. She said they had no right to do that because it was her underwear. If she wanted people to see it, then she'd be the one to show them. I felt bad for her, so I took a couple dollars from my canoe money and bought us ice cream cones up at the Dairy Dreem. It made her happy again, but I think she still plans on getting Zack, Jake, and Pete, back for that prank when they least expect it.

On the first day of summer, she popped over and was standing on our big front porch, looking in through the screen door when I was coming down the stairs from brushing my teeth. Ma was in the kitchen and couldn't hear her knocking. Cassia was at Poppy Johnsons listening to her stereo because Poppy got *The Best of the Bee Gee's* album from last year in 1969. Clove was up playing baseball at the school. He could hardly wait for today and was gone before I even got outta bed. I 'spect if he got there too early, he would have just sat up there on the bleachers for hours tossing his ball up in the air and catching it with his mitt, waiting for the rest of the players to show up. He wants to play for the Cubs, someday.

So, before Zillia showed up, I was wondering what I was going to do with my day. I figured maybe find a new tree to climb, or something. A train was going by and I almost missed Zillia standing there, yelling in the door. When the caboose finally flashed by, she smiled like she was 'xasperated and said in a normal voice, "Hey, Wick," and I just felt happy that I wasn't gonna have to climb that tree alone.

"Zillia! What's up?"

"Why else, silly. I came to play… or something. Got six hours til paper route time. So, I was figuring we could do something fun and then go up together. What do you say?"

"Sounds fine to me. Ma's busy with bread making, so she won't need me. Mrs. Blahnik's coming over to give her a hand, and you know, they're just gonna get to yakking and I'll just be in the way. I'm thinking they'll want to talk about stuff they don't want me to know about. Hey, want to go climb a tree? There's one down by the trail that looks like it might be fun?"

"Yeah, I already wanted to go down by the river, but I don't want to climb no tree today." Pointing at her knee, I saw a big scrape with a band-aide that was too small for it. She was wearing a red tee shirt four sizes too big for her and some bib overalls with the legs cut off. I noticed one of the legs was cut a little longer than the other, but I figured I'd better not laugh or say anything. I didn't want no black eye.

"So, I was stealing apples from ol' lady Edgerly's tree and she caught me. I fell off the branch and had to run like crazy, getting blood all over everything. My ma had a fit!"

Zillia was talking all excited like and waving her arms around. I had to smile because it was so funny the way she was telling me, and then she smiled really big because that's what I think she wanted me to do. Sometimes, Zillia's kind of a clown.

"Okay, so let's go," I said, and we went out the front door, with me yelling at my ma, "Going outside with Zillia, ma!"

"Okay, boy. Ya'll going down to the river?" she yelled from the kitchen.

"I don't know… maybe."

"Well, ya'll be careful. Hear me?"

"Yeah, ma," was all I said. She was always saying that. I 'spose she wanted to stick a reminder in there just in case I forgot that I could drown, get stuck by something sharp, fall off something high, or maybe even get eaten by wolves, or… naw, there ain't no wolves here in Clarksburg. But that would be fun if there were, right?

"Got to tie my shoes," Zillia said and sat down in one of our half a dozen porch chairs to tie her sneakers. So, I'm watching her, and then I get this feeling somebody's watching us. I look up and see my Uncle Liajah standing out at the end of the sidewalk that runs up to the porch.

Now Uncle Liajah, he don't talk. Never could. But he could hear really well. He's my ma's brother. He didn't have a job. Rode the railroad and carried this big Bowie knife in a sheath at his belt. There was a big brown hat on his head, and he wore a black vest over a dirty striped shirt. Uncle Liajah looked just like a cowboy, but he wasn't no such a thing. He was a hobo. I could see his old boots were more broken down than the last time he stopped by, and I figured ma or pa were going to have to buy him a new pair. Uncle Lijah walked everywhere he went. That is, if he wasn't riding the train. Boots didn't last him very long.

His hand come up in a kinda wave and I said, "Uncle Liajah! Come on up." Zillia looked at him and then hollered, "Hey, Uncle Liajah." My ma was running through the living room, saying, "Liajah? Liajah's, here?" The door whipped open and she started yelling, "Hey, brother! What ya'll doing? Thought I wouldn't see ya'll til next month."

Uncle Liajah just stood there grinning like that cat in the Alice In Wonderland story. Now, for a man who didn't have a home, he sure had the whitest teeth I'd ever seen. My ma flung herself at him and squeezed him so tight, he turned super red and couldn't breathe. Zillia and I just stood there, smiling like crazy idiots.

My ma then hustled him up on the porch, saying, "Now ya'll just go out back and sit at the table under the shade tree and I'll get ya'll some coffee and piece of my cornpone; just fresh last night."

Uncle Liajah patted me on the head and then clicked his tongue at Zillia as he went by. I had to wrinkle up my nose because he smelled worse than our ol' milk cow. I looked at Zillia and she just looked back, her eyes saying, 'What?' I didn't dare say a thing. If I did, it would be too much like I was making fun of Uncle Liajah. Zillia wouldn't stand for that. I knew darn certain ma would have Uncle Liajah's clothes washed before he took off, and I was also sure there was a bath in the making.

If pa came home while Uncle Liajah was there visiting, he'd have him uptown at Lottie's trying on boots, but only after they got the old guy cleaned up. Now, maybe Uncle Liajah wasn't that old, maybe forties. He sure looked like he was, though. Ma says life on the road is hard.

Zillia and I followed them in, and ma took him right out to the old picnic bench under what she always called the 'shade tree' Fact of the matter is, there are a ton of trees out there, it's just, only one of them had a table under it. I 'spect it was ma's favorite tree, being it was a really old, red maple.

Then she came back in and went to pouring a big mug of hot coffee and slicing off the biggest hunk of cornbread I'd ever seen her put on a plate. "Son, gather up some of that middling meat from the pan over there and dump it on this here plate with the pone, will ya? Your pa won't mind if I give part of his share to Liajah."

Now, my ma's from Arkansas, pretty close to the Texas border. So, she says things like 'pone' and 'middling meat' I said middling meat instead of bacon once at school and I think the whole class was going to laugh me right out of the lunchroom. Well, all except for Zillia, who was fixing to blacken some eyes. That was until I told her it was okay. They was just poking fun, so Zillia didn't need to be poking eyes.

I went and dumped a handful of bacon on the plate next to the corn bread and then licked my hand clean. Ma grabbed the plate and the coffee mug and headed out the back screen door. Uncle Liajah was sitting at the table with his back to us. His hat was off, and he turned his head and grinned at us. Now, what's got me stumped is, if uncle Liajah couldn't hear nothing, how'd he know to look back? Yeah, if you figure it out, you let me know, huh?

Ma set the plate down on the table and he dug right in. Ma planted herself on the bench across from him and started in asking a ton of questions. They had a system because Uncle Liajah only knew a tiny bit of hand sign. But ma and Uncle Liajah had been together all their lives. They knew how to talk to each other.

"Wick, why don't ya'll be off now, I'm gonna chat with Liajah and see what he's been up to. Ya'll go on now, have some kid fun."

Uncle Liajah was sucking down the coffee and I figured ma had stuck a couple spoonful's of sugar in there. He waved us off and nodded toward the woods behind the house. He knew that's where we were going before anybody said anything. But I figured he knew I loved the woods as much as he and pa loved the railroad.

"See you later, Liajah."

"Yeah, see you later," Zillia said, and we took off down the little grassy hill to the river trail.

"Ya'll heard me, and be careful."

"Ah, ma, don't worry."

"Ya'll heard me."

I didn't say nothing and then I ran right into Zillia who had stopped where the path, met the river trail. "You see that Wick? Somebody's up on the railroad bridge. See em?"

She was pointing and I looked that way to see some old beat-up brown shoes on someone's feet hanging down out of the boxed-in place. Now, I should tell you, the old railroad bridge had some boxed-in places. Ones that you had to squeeze into. They were a good place to hide, but you always had to check to make sure there were no hobos in there, first. That's where they liked to spend the night. Sometimes they'd be there a whole week and ma would send us over with food scraps, or left overs. We'd lower a bucket on a rope down onto the big concrete pier and they'd help themselves. They just had to let us know they were there by hollering out when they walked by our house. They all knew they weren't supposed come up on the porch. So, they'd just go on by and holler out something like, 'Morning, folks!' or something like that. It might be the end of the day before we'd get some food over there, but I've a feeling they figured they could very well not be getting a single thing, so didn't count on it. Most of them were regulars, but I never seen those brown shoes before. Looking at them made me feel afraid and I didn't know why.

"Just another hobo, I'm guessing," I said.

"Yeah, I'm guessing that, too. Alright, let's git."

We ran down the trail, heading for a place where there was this big circle cleared out amongst the trees. There was a place for a fire, and some logs laying around for us to sit on. We had tied some short boards to the end of a couple of ropes hanging down from some tree limbs to use as swings. Then we'd swing out, whooping and hollering. Zillia said one day she was going to dive into the river from one of them, just like Dover Schmidt had done. Zillia would be the first girl to ever do that from our swings. That didn't surprise me none. She was dead set on it, though. I'm pretty sure nobody was going to try to stop her.

So, we were swinging and Zillia was going way out. Sometimes she went so high, the rope picked up some slack and when it straightened out, it would make a loud thump and jolt her so hard that she'd almost fall off. She'd laugh like crazy every time because she wasn't afraid. I knew it was hard on her, though, because she only did it a couple times and then quit, complaining about how much it hurt her butt.

"So, when you going to dive in? You got a time all planned out?"

"Nope, sure don't. You see, I've got a problem. I don't have a bathing suit and if I jump in with my clothes on and go home wet, my ma will have a fit, and my pa would probably beat the crap out of me. So, I'd have to jump naked. What do you think? What should I do? You see, I'm not gonna give up. It has to be done. I made a bet with Dover, and a whole bunch of other kids that I'd do it. But I only need one kid as my witness, you know? To see me dive off, that is. I want you to be that kid. Everybody knows your honest and wouldn't lie, even if we are best friends and you'd probably lie for me for no reason other than that we are. You know darn well they'd expect you to, for just that reason. I mean, lie and all. But most of our class knows you don't lie. So, I'm safe with you being the one."

At first, I thought she might have been joking. Then I could see she wasn't. I needed to talk her out of it. "But… you'll be naked, or… in your underwear. So, you know I'd see you, and if I remember correctly, you didn't want anyone to see your underwear."

"Well, it won't be in my underwear. You see, Wicky boy, underwear is clothes too. So, it'll get just as wet. Someone has to see me do it, just not the whole town. You're all I need."

I didn't know what to say. Zillia had a problem and I could help her if we did it her way. But I'm not sure. The thing is, if I said no, she'd get mad. I didn't want that, so I said, "Well, maybe. Hey! We could come down here at night and you could do it and I could just sit over there with my back to you and…"

"What's wrong, you afraid to see a girl naked? Didn't you ever go skinny dipping with your brothers and sisters?"

Well, yeah, but we were younger, and besides, we're kin."

"What? Aren't I kin enough? We're pretty close, right? Your kinda hurting my feelings, Wick."

"Uh… no… I mean, I'm sorry, it's just… yeah, I'm a little nervous about it."

"Oh, come on, Wick, it's just one time. Maybe, we could go skinny dipping together and I could do it then. We'd be even-steven because we'd both be in our birthday suits. So, you just think about it and let me know. I'm thinking maybe next week sometime… now that we're out of school and all. Okay?"

"Okay," I said. "I'll do that."

"Don't let me down, Wick… okay? Everybody lets me down. I can hardly bear it sometimes."

I just smiled and we went back to swinging. I was feeling a little nervous now. Zillia and I were good friends, maybe the best that anyone can be. I figured there was a heaping pile of trust between us. Maybe I was nervous because I was a chicken. I don't know. But I decided I was going to talk with Cassia about it. She always had good advice. I didn't dare talk to my friends, or Clove because I knew he'd say something like: "What? Are you crazy? A girl wants to let you see her naked and you don't want to? What? Are you chicken or something?" And besides, Cassia would keep it a secret—Clove would tell everyone. The same for my friends. I was in a pickle now because I wanted to help Zillia out, but I didn't want to cause her no trouble.

So, we were swinging away, and we weren't talking because I was thinking. That's when I looked up toward the railroad bridge and saw some guy squeeze out of the boxed-in place. I could tell, even though he was far away, that he was tall with a big, black beard. His pants were too short, 'high-waters' my ma called them. They really showed them big brown shoes.

"You see that?" Zillia said.

"Yeah, I see him. Another hobo, but one I don't know. Maybe Uncle Liajah knows him."

"Maybe they're here together, you know what I mean?"

"Yeah, maybe. I'll ask him, or maybe I'll tell ma and she'll ask him for me. The thing is, she'll want to feed that guy. But you know, he kinda gives me the creeps. The way he moves and all."

"Well, we don't need to go over there while he's hanging around. If we want to go up to the town square, or when I go home, we can go the river road past my place. The bridge is a short cut anyway. Not supposed to go short cuts. So, I think we're safe."

"Uh-huh," is all I said as I watched the guy sit down at the far end of the bridge and light up a smoke. I got the feeling he knew we were watching him.

"Let's go, I've had enough swinging for one day."

"He's scaring you, isn't he? Okay… kind of scaring me, too. So… let's go."

We swung back to the river bank and dropped off. Then we were just standing there looking at each other, so Zillia jumped up on a log and walked along its top, holding her arms out for balance. "So, did you think about it? You gonna be my witness?"

"Zillia, I need more time."

"Okay, so… maybe you can tell me tomorrow."

"That'll work."

You see, I figured that would give me enough time to talk to Cassia tonight after Zillia went home.

"Okay, good. Hey, let's go down to the fairgrounds and see if the horses are running. Maybe they got the sulkies out. The fair's coming up and they have to get ready for the harness races. What do you say?"

"Sure, let's go," I said, still thinking about my new problem and that stranger up on the bridge.

We ran down to the fairgrounds, racing each other. Of course, Zillia beat me there and then had to wait. But she had sneakers on, and I had boots. Ever try to run in boots? We spent the day in the grandstand watching the horses and their owners doing time trials.

It was about dark when we headed back. I knew Zillia would be with us for supper and then she'd stay til way after dark. I heard somebody say once that she liked to stay out as late as possible because by that time her pa would be passed out from drinking too much and she could sneak up to bed without him or her brothers knowing. She slept in the attic. I figured her ma might get mad about her missing her supper, but when I asked Zillia about that, she just said, no. Her ma wouldn't care one way or the other. When I asked why not, Zillia said her ma figured if she didn't show up and missed the food, too bad, more for everybody else. I 'spect Zillia was pretty happy that my ma liked to feed everyone in the world. So, Zillia would always have a little food in her.

When we got back, I didn't see Uncle Liajah anywhere. "Where's Uncle Liajah, ma? Did he leave?"

"Ah, no. He's out in the shed where he always sleeps. Can't get him to sleep in the house. So, he had enough of my cooking, and he needed to go lay down. I got his clothes drying, so he's got nothing but your pa's old nightshirt to wear. He don't want no one seeing him running around in nightwear. So… take Zillia and go wash up. Ding Bat's ma brought us a roasted chicken. So, we're having chicken and dumplings tonight. Ya'll go on now and wash your faces. Where ya'll been, by the way, boy?"

"Fairgrounds!" I said and then we ran upstairs to the bathroom. Zillia had to pee and she wasn't waiting around for me to leave, so I had to run out and shut the door before she got her pants down. I had to wait for her to get done (so, I covered my ears). She called me in after she flushed, and we shared the sink. I just figured because all she had was brothers that she was alright with me being in there. Then I realized that maybe that's why she didn't mind if I was there when she took her dive.

Pa wouldn't be home for another day, so it was just me, Cassia, Clove, and Zillia eating at the table. Clove picked on me a lot, but Cassia and Zillia were on my side and got him right back. Zillia had a pretty slick tongue and I couldn't figure out why she did and I didn't. We were the same age, but she was way ahead of me in that area. Of course, ma always said I was too serious, and Clove said that I could play a good straight man in a movie; whatever that was. Cassia just cuddled me and said, "Don't listen to Clove, he's just a big meany."

Clove was almost six years older than me, so there was no way I could fight him. One time I kicked him in the butt and ran out of the room. Then he went and put a garter snake in my bed that night and scared the crap out of me. So, I either had to get back at him, or just let him have his way. I think I know what Zillia had to put up with all the time. The thing is, she pounded her brothers every chance she got. I think they were just real careful with her so as not to get black eyes.

We were sitting on the porch til late, talking, and eating popcorn. Clove finally left us and went up to his room to read some mystery story. Cassia went right after him to sit by her phonograph, listen to Simon & Garfunkel, and write in her diary. Then she'd spend nearly a whole hour brushing out her long blond hair before bedtime. Ma was seeing to Uncle Liajah, making sure he had dry clothes in case he wanted to skedaddle.

"Wick, I think I'm going home. Getting kind of sleepy. So, unless your ma's gonna put me up, I think I'm heading out."

"We'd put you up if you want to stay? You can have my bed and I can sleep on the floor."

"Naw, I don't want to put you out of your bed."

"Well… okay, um..."

"We could share it, heck, I don't mind."

"Oh, okay. But you got no PJs here."

"You know, Wick, I think I'm going home. Got something I want to do. Going to stick Jason's hand in warm water after he falls asleep and make him pee the bed. Makes ma mad as hell. She'll whip him for sure, and he deserves it for picking on me because I'm getting boobs now. I couldn't help but look when she said that, but I didn't notice anything different about her. She jumped up then and ran off the porch. I followed her to the railroad tracks and she stopped, hugged me, and then was gone in the gloom. Gone in the gloom, now that's funny! Gloom is the new word I learned watching *Night Gallery* on TV. That Rod Serling, what a weirdo.

"See you tomorrow, Wick," I heard her holler out of the dark. I stood there watching until she showed up underneath the first streetlight. She lived in a little house about half way to the Main Street bridge. I didn't go there. Her brothers were too rough and every one of them would want to wrestle me to see what I was made of.

Where I was standing, I could see down to the end of the railroad bridge and every once in a while, there'd be this little orange glow that got brighter for just a second. Someone was down there smoking and watching me.

I turned around and ran back in the house. After I went inside, I hooked the screen door, so no one could come in behind me. Ma was coming in the back door doing some last-minute checks on her brother and I hollered, "Going to bed, ma."

"Zillia staying?"

"Naw, she went home."

"Poor girl," I heard ma mumble. "She coulda stayed. Ya'll coulda shared your room. She can stay over anytime, she wants. Be sure to tell her, huh, boy?"

"Okay, ma, I'll tell her."

"Poor girl," she mumbled again as she walked by, going into our laundry room. I was thinking I should tell ma about the hobo on the bridge, but I figured I'd wait and see if he was still there tomorrow. Maybe have a talk with Uncle Liajah about him.

I got into my PJs and climbed into bed after brushing my teeth. I lay there with the light on wondering why ma thought Zillia was a poor girl.

Cassia came in to say goodnight. Her white sleeping gown was pretty thin, and she didn't wear no bra. I rolled over and faced the window so she wouldn't think I was looking. She might get embarrassed and I'd feel bad about that.

"Cassia, why don't you wear PJs like me? You hardly got anything on."

"Oh, Wick, your such a sweet boy. PJ's are too warm. I'm just so glad to get that bra off. You don't know what it's like. I should do what all the girls are doing now and go braless."

"Ma'd raise the roof, you know that, and all the boys would be staring all day long."

"Yeah, I know. But that's okay, everybody knows I've got boobs."

"Yeah, but… you really got boobs, and I mean, really, really got 'em!"

Cassia giggled and patted my back and then rubbed it real slow like ma used to do. If she did that for too long, I'd be a sleep in the blink of an owl's eye. The thing is, I still had my question to ask.

"Just trying to be a good boy, huh?"

"What do you mean?"

"Looking out the window instead of at me."

"Well, ma says…"

"Ma says a lot of things, Wick. You don't have to listen to all of them. Just the important ones."

"Speaking of important ones… Cassia, I've got a question."

"Ask away, little brother. You know you can talk to me."

"Zillia wants to dive off the swings into the river."

"What's so hard about that? How is that a question?"

"No, you don't understand. No girl has ever done that in the history of the swings, and she made a bet with Dover Schmidt that she could. He don't believe her."

"Wick, what's the question? She could just do it and show him that girls can do anything boys can do."

"Well, the question is—she don't have a swimsuit. So, she wants to do it naked."

"Little brother, please, the question. You're putting me to sleep."

"She… she… wants me to be her witness. Someone she can trust."

"So, your question is, should you? And the answer is, yes… as long as she doesn't mind. She asked you, right?"

"Yeah, she said it had to be me. But that's just it, I don't want to hurt her feelings and…"

"Wick, if she asked you to be there, then… be there."

"But she was wondering if I could be there with no clothes on, too. You know, like… even-steven?"

Cassia got up, messed up my hair, and went to the door. Before she walked out, she said real serious like, "Wick, look at me." So, I rolled over part way and looked at her over my shoulder. She was in the shadow, so I could hardly see her.

"You know as well as I do, it's got to happen someday. Quit being so serious all the time and have some fun. You gotta grow up sometime, you're almost thirteen now. Honestly, my sweet little Wick, this is all a part of it. Don't expect ma to talk to you about it… or pa. You have any questions; you can ask me. Okay, that's all. Good night."

"Good night, sis," I said, and she left. I heard her bedroom door shut and then I heard the phonograph start up with a song Cassia really liked called '*Unchained Melody*'. She told me it was the best song in the whole, wide world. I realized I didn't know if Cassia had a boyfriend or not. It might be a secret. I'd have to ask.

I lay there in the dark and a breeze was blowing. I could feel it's coolness on my face. Uncle Liajah was in the shed. A candle was burning, and I could see him through the window, sitting on a crate. He was dressed in his clean clothes and was drinking from a bottle. When he wasn't tipping it back, he looked like he was thinking about things. I had so many questions about him, but I wasn't allowed to ask. He was kind of a mystery. I just didn't think that kind of a life was so great. Being alone all the time and never having a place of his own.

Pretty soon he took out his big knife and started throwing it, then he'd get up, go get it, come back, and throw it again. After a while he just started dropping it on the floor so the point would stick in the wood. Then he took to sharpening it with a stone. I could hear it grinding. Every once in a while, he'd take a drink and then make an, "Ahhh," noise like it must have been the best tasting thing in the world. I fell asleep not long after and dreamed I was a hobo with a big black beard that was a problem because it wouldn't stop growing and got so long, I was tripping over it.

After breakfast the next morning, I went out and stood on the back porch. It was big and deep, just like the front, it's roof hanging way out. Sometimes ma liked to do laundry out there, or can vegetables and fruit, or… all those things ma's do. Uncle Liajah was at the bench eating a stack of pancakes. They were the ones that were left over from our breakfast. Steam was coming up off his coffee. He started to take a drink then stopped like he got a feeling and looked back over his shoulder at me and grinned. Waving me over, he patted the seat beside him. I had what I think they call a 'realization'. Uncle Liajah didn't have to hear people; he could feel them. I decided I was going to practice that to I see if I could learn to feel people behind me or when they were hiding and spying. Then maybe I could teach Zillia how to do it and make me worth her salt. Sometimes I was afraid of the day Zillia wouldn't be there, but I don't want to talk about that right now.

"Wick, Liajah wants ya. Go on over there, now, and sit a spell."

"But ma, he don't talk, and I don't know what to say."

"Just go on over there and sit for minute. He'd really like it. Now, go, boy!"

I went over and Uncle Liajah twisted around and reached out his hand for a shake. I did that and then he patted the seat next to him again. I sat down and he offered me his coffee, so I said, "Uh… no, thanks."

He grinned and made a noise like he was laughing. Then he shrugged and drank it himself. I sat there just looking at the river through the trees. He smelled a whole lot better than the day before, so, I could stand to be next to him. I just needed to think of something to say.

"So, how are you, Uncle Liajah," I asked.

He just nodded his head really fast and then patted me on the back. So, that's how it went. Me coming up with questions and him making motions and faces, to answer those questions. Cassia had gone to the Dairy Dreem with that really annoying Stacy Anderson and I don't think I need to say where Clove was. So, there was no one to answer the door when Zillia showed up. She came around the house doing some kind of dance, and singing, '*Willy and the Hand Jive*' It's the singing that brought my face around and seeing me sitting there, she ran over to the table and sat across from me and Liajah.

"Hello, Mrs. Ryan," she called out to my ma.

"Morning, darling. Have your breakfast, yet?"

"No, I left early."

"Well, I'm gonna get ya'll some pancakes. Just sit there with the boys and I'll bring em."

Zillia sat down and made a face at me like she couldn't believe my ma was so nice. Then she said, "Hey, Uncle Liajah, how are you?" and laid her hand on top if his big, rough mitt. He grinned, nodded his head, and patted the back of her hand with his other one. I have to admit for as long as I've known Uncle Liajah, I had never touched him til today.

Ma brought Zillia her pancakes with maple syrup, and butter, plus a glass of milk. It didn't take Zillia long to finish them up. Ma went to washing clothes on the back porch, and I was glad it had that big ol' roof so the sun wouldn't bake her to toast. She sure liked to work hard, and I think every day that came, she'd try to outdo herself from the day before.

"Let's go down the trail, Wick. I was thinking we should build a fort, or maybe a tree house or something. Come on, let's go."

She jumped up and shouted, "Thanks for breakfast, Mrs. Ryan. It was real good!"

"You're welcome, darling, come on back for noon dinner, now. Don't be late."

"I won't," she said. "Come on, Wick, let's go. See you, Uncle Liajah."

He grinned and nodded toward her. I put my hand on his shoulder for the first time ever and said, "See you, Uncle Liajah. Nice talking."

He turned his face to me and instead of grinning and nodding like he normally does, his face just stayed blank. I didn't know what to think or say. Zillia and I just stood there, not talking. Then I saw a tear come out of his eye. Just one. Then he smiled and wiped it away. Zillia and I took off in a run for the trail. I don't know why Liajah did that. Maybe I hurt him when I patted him because he had a sore muscle, or something. Zillia waited til we got down on the trail before she said, "I think Uncle Liajah is feeling sad. I feel bad for him. He should settle down somewhere or just live in your house and quit riding that railroad."

"Ma says that's his life. The one he chose. But I don't know why he'd be crying."

"He's sad, that's all. Grownups get sad. My pa cries sometimes, but that means it's time for me to get out of there because he's going to open up a can of whoop ass."

"Well, I don't know if I'm ever gonna get sad. Doesn't seem like such a good idea."

"It's only natural, Wick. I get sad sometimes, and so will you. So, come on, lets git. Not gonna stand around all day talking about being sad. It'll just make us sad." That's when I realized I had lied because when I thought about Zillia going away some day when she was growed that I was feeling just the thing she was talking about. I wanted to tell her that I'd lied by accident but she just turned and took off running, "You can't catch me, Wicky boy!"

I watched her for a few seconds before I went after her because I just realized another thing, Zillia was wearing a dress! Zillia never wore dresses. It only went part way down to her knees and was kind of burgundy with tiny, yellow flowers all over. It had short puffy sleeves with lace at the collar but was pretty ratty looking like I've heard Cassia say. I don't think her running in it was such a good idea, either, because it kept flipping up showing her unmentionables.

I chased after her and caught her before we got to the clearing. "You're wearing a dress! Since when do you wear dresses?"

"I don't know, since today, I'm guessing. I just wanted to wear something different. I'd forgot all about it, then I found it in the back of my closet and thought, why not? It might be nice to be a little different once in a while. It's old, gots some holes, and maybe a little too short now, but what the heck, right?"

"Well, you best not climb any trees or somebody's gonna see London... or France, and I don't care about either of those places."

"You gonna go around telling people all about my flowery underwear?"

"Well, no. Of course not. But I think your brothers might have already done that, right?"

"So… okay. Let's go build a tree house, then. Or at least… find a tree to build one in."

Just as we started walking, I heard the bushes moving behind us and we both turned around at the same time to see that tall hobo with the big black beard. He was just standing there, staring at us with these big, dark eyes under that big black hat. He didn't say anything, he just stood there in his sickly-looking skin with red splotches all over it. Zillia came up beside me and we just stared back. I figured she would have said something by now, but when I looked at her, I saw she was scared. I'd never seen Zillia scared, but that didn't mean she was any less brave.

She yelled, "What are you doing here?"

"Yeah, what are you doing here? Why aren't you up at the bridge. We could bring you some food up there."

"I don't want no food," he said in a raspy voice. "I want money. You got any money?"

I looked at Zillia and she looked back at me. Her eyes were big, and I wondered if mine were too.

"Well, do you?"

"No, we don't have no money, we're just kids," I said.

"Well, kids or not, you could still have some money. Kids always got money for candy and such. And why you speaking for this girl? Why don't you let her talk for herself. You got money, girl?"

"No, I don't have no money. You see any pockets? Where would I put it?"

"Don't get smart with me, missy," he said and then grinned at us, showing some really brown teeth. Then, just like a magic trick, there was an ol' rusty, butcher knife in his hand. I figured if he cut anybody with that ol' thing they were going to get that tetanus ma was always going on about.

"Now, boy, you give me all the money you got, and I won't stick you with this."

I started to shake, and I was trying hard not to pee my pants. Zillia was just standing there, but it wasn't like she was staring for the sake of staring. It was more like she was studying him. Like she was looking for something.

"I'm gonna count to three, boy, and if that money isn't out in your hand, I'm gonna give you your very first shave. Hearing me, mister?"

"But I haven't got no money, I'm telling you."

He started walking toward us, holding out that rusty knife. For some reason, Zillia stepped in front of me. "You better leave him alone; he told you he ain't got no money and I don't neither. So… so you can just go away."

"I'm not going anywhere, missy. Maybe you got something else for me," he said.

I couldn't figure out what he meant by that. Did he want our clothes, or, maybe our shoes?

"Why don't you just pull up that pretty little dress and show me what you got. You're a pretty little thing. I'll bet your pappy just loves to bounce you on his knee now, don't he?"

Zillia reached back and took my hand. I felt her shivering. I thought to run away about then and I was going to pull her with me. I looked behind me to make sure I had a clear shot down the path, and then I heard Zillia kind of squeak. Kind of like something surprised her. When I looked back, Uncle Liajah was standing about ten, maybe fifteen feet back of Blackbeard. He had on his big brown hat, but it was pulled down low so you could just barely see his eyes. He didn't make no noise, he just appeared like out of thin air. Zillia and I just stared, and that made ol' Blackbeard turn around.

Now, it was Blackbeard's turn to look scared. It was like, at first, he thought he was the most serious hobo in the world. Then he saw my uncle and realized he was nowhere near that. Blackbeard turned all the way around to face Uncle Liajah, and said, "What the hell do you want?"

Uncle Liajah grinned at the man, only this time it was a scary grin. A crazy man's grin. Then he took out his Bowie knife. It slid out of his sleeve in one smooth motion and made like a little hissing noise when it did; kind of like it were a poisonous snake. The sun kind of danced over it, making it seem almost like a magic thing. Blackbeard's knife was nowhere as serious as Uncle Liajah's.

Uncle Liajah motioned with his head for us to get out of there. Zillia didn't waste a second pulling me off the path into the trees. Blackbeard tried to grab my arm, but I was gone too quick.

We came out behind Uncle Liajah and ran for the house. I looked back once as we were flying down the trail and I saw my uncle still standing there, just like we left him. He was shorter than the other man, but if you ever seen a little terrier pup take on a bigger dog, than you'd understand what was going on. Blackbeard looked at me like he was afraid, and the face he was making was like he realized he'd made a big mistake. I saw him gulp and I'm pretty sure uncle Liajah seen it, too.

Zillia and I ran like crazy and came out of the woods right where it met our yard. That's when I heard some shouting. I stopped and looked at Zillia and she looked back.

"You heard that, right?" I said.

"Darn right I heard that, whatcha think? I'm deaf?"

We ran up to the house. Ma was sitting on the back porch. She was just sitting there, not even looking at us. She was crying. Not like a little baby or anything, just tears coming down her face and her looking off toward the woods. Zillia and I stopped at the bottom of the steps and just stared at her. I was feeling embarrassed and I could tell Zillia was too. But she didn't stay put, she let go of my hand and walked right up there and threw her arms around my ma. So, because she did that, I went and did the same; only from ma's other side.

"Liajah's gone, just up and walked away down into the woods. Didn't say goodbye or nothing. So, I suppose he ain't coming back."

"He came to save us, ma. There was a bad man down in the woods coming after Zillia and me. Uncle Liajah saved us."

About then we heard a scream. I have to say I never head a man scream before. Can't say I ever want to hear it again. My hair stood up and the goose flesh covered my arms. I saw Zillia face turn white, just like she lost all her blood to her legs. Before I could say a word, ma jumped up and just kind of whispered, "Liajah," like it was a secret or something. Then she grabbed our hands and towed us off the porch to run in that direction. Zillia and I were trying our best to keep up. I didn't know ma could run so fast.

We busted through the horseweeds and came out on the path, still moving like a striped tailed tomcat. We got to the clearing and stopped. There was no one there, just a bunch of blood on the old, dead leaves. Not big puddles, mind you, just some drops here and there with a little trail of it leading off down toward the fairgrounds.

"I think Liajah's been hurt! Oh, my word, what we gonna do?" Ma said and then just sat right down on the ground kind of hard like and started crying like that baby I was telling you about earlier. She put her hands over her face and started making so much noise it scared me. Then Zillia started in and sat down next to her, her head leaning on ma's shoulder. So, of course, I started in too, but I was doing it kind of quiet like, the way I thought a boy was supposed to. Ma started saying, "Liajah's dead. Liajah's dead." Then she started turning her head from side to side and Zillia let out kind of a yowl and started crying harder. I just walked over, and even though the tears were rolling out of my eyes and the snot was running like a river from my nose, I put my hand on my ma's shoulder and told her, "Oh, no, ma, uncle Liajah ain't dead. He's too quick. Uncle Liajah ain't dead, I can just feel it." That's when I thought that I didn't need to practice too hard to kind of feel for folks. If I just concentrated hard enough, I could feel them even if they was a long way off. So, I 'spect, I'd been doing it for some time and just not seeing it.

Well, patting ma seemed to help a little and when we were all cried out, ma got up and took Zillia's hand and then mine. We walked back up to the house and on the way, ma said, "Wish your pa would git home. I'm missing him something terrible. I know it's only been two days, but I got the loneliness."

I didn't do nothing, just looked at Zillia and wiped off my face. All that crying had made her eyes really bright and then I suddenly felt a little different about her. Couldn't put my finger on it, but it put a funny feeling in my tummy. It was like some kind of a light was shining on her as we walked there, and I wondered what it would feel like to kiss her. That was kind of weird. I don't have a clue why that was, but I figured I could reckon it later.

We went into the kitchen and ma set us down at the table and gave us lemonade. Then she stood looking out the window toward the bridge, drinking a cup of coffee. "Wish I could see Liajah out there. Just wish I could." Zillia and I just looked at each other and shrugged.

My sister came in the front door, stopped, and stared at us. Ma turned around and set her cup down. Cassia made her, 'Oh no,' face and stretching out her arms, ma walked right inside them. Then they were hugging. Ma went to crying again and Cassia walked her out onto the front porch where they sat in the chairs. I heard ma say, "Cassia, I think Liajah's dead, there was blood."

Cassia asked her to tell her what happened. So, she did. Zillia and I just sat there, drinking out of our glasses. I decided I was going to help myself to the chocolate chip cookies that were cooling on a plate in the middle of the table. I gave Zillia two. She never said nothing, and we just ate cookies and drank lemonade.

Pa was supposed to be home about seven o'clock and we were sitting on the front porch waiting. Cassia knew the whole story by then and we were sure to add our part about Blackbeard, even the part where he asked Zillia to pull up her dress. Both ma and Cassia made a strange noise and slapped a hand over their mouths with their eyes getting real big. They looked at each other and then we all looked at Zillia, who made a face like it was no big deal and said, "Well, my brothers are always pulling up my dress if I wear one. So, most the time, I don't. Fooled em, huh?" she said and giggled. Thinking about her brothers doing that, made me mad. I don't know why.

Soon, the train whistled, coming around the bend just east of the bridge, and we heard the brakes just screaming to get stopped in time. We all jumped up and ran out to the tracks and waited. The engine went by and the engineer waved. When he stopped clear down by the lumber yard and the depot, my pa jumped off.

He was smiling pretty big when he did, and just dumped his bag and grabbed ma in this big hug and started kissing her. We all kind of piled up around him—even Zillia. After we got through with that, he took ma's hand and walked her toward the house. "Grab my bag, hey Wick," he said. So, I did.

"Honey, I have some bad news," ma said.

"What's that?"

"I think Liajah's been killed."

Pa stopped and faced her. Putting his hands on her arms, he said, "Now, why you thinking that, Priscilla?"

"We're thinking maybe another hobo killed him in the woods below the house. There was blood."

"Now, don't you fret none. Liajah ain't dead. No one can kill..." That's all he got out because there came a loud whistle, like someone was calling up their hunting dog. We all turned and looked. It was Uncle Liajah. He was leaning out the door of one of the box cars, waving that crazy wave of his. The train made that loud noise that trains make when the brakes come off, and it started to move. It was gone before we knew it, everybody waving like it was going to be the last time we'd ever be able to wave at Uncle Liajah.

Ma just kind of fell into pa's arm's. Cassia just stood there, smiling, and patting ma on the shoulder. Zillia looked at me, and then she fell into my arms. I didn't know what she was doing, so I almost didn't catch her. But then we were hugging, and I hardly ever hugged Zillia. It was only ever that quick thing when she was leaving. But I have to tell you, it wasn't so bad. This time it lasted longer. She had her chin on my shoulder and her face was warm against mine. I decided right then and there I was going to do it more often.

We didn't watch any TV that night because pa was telling us all about riding the caboose and other stories. He told us about being in Dubuque and how it was too big a town for him. Then they got to talking about uncle Liajah and if ma thought uncle Liajah might need new boots because if he did, pa was going to buy him some and have them ready when he came back around.

They talked, and we listened, sitting around the kitchen table, drinking lemonade, and eating popcorn. Well, not pa—he had a beer. Clove came home, got all excited and took to shaking pa's hand and patting him on the back and such. Then those two went out on the front porch and sat in the dark just talking about Clove and his life. Zillia went home and Cassia went off to bed. I fell asleep lying on the big, round, rag-rug in our living room and barely made it upstairs.

I woke up the next morning and it was sunny and the birds were going on about it being so. There were locust (actually cicadas, Cassia told us, but we liked using locusts, instead) cranking out their noise already and I could hear the chickens out in the yard, clucking away about nothing. Cassia came in all dolled up, looking like she might be heading up to meet a boy at the Dairy Dreem.

"Ma and pa are going uptown to do some shopping at Lottie's and The Royal Blue. You want to come? I'm going with them. So, if you stay, you're going to be home alone."

"Where's Clove?"

"Oh, don't be silly. You know where Clove is."

"I'm staying. Going to lay here for a while and think a spell."

"Well, don't break your brain," she said. Then she kissed me on my head and left the room. She yelled up from the bottom of the stairs, "Oh yeah, ma says feed the chickens and sweep the porches before you go running off to the woods."

"Yeah, yeah," was all I yelled back.

I laid there a long time before I got up and got dressed. Then I ate cold bacon and a pancake folded in two and soaked in syrup. I topped it all off with a glass of milk. Afterwards I went out to do my chores. It got to be afternoon and still no Zillia. I started to worry about her the whole time I was working. By the time I got done, my family was back home. They got all kinds of food, boots for Liajah, and a bunch of other clothes. They even got stuff for me, but since it was clothes, I didn't bother to look at it. I was pretty sure it would find its way up to my room.

I was up there, digging through junk looking for my yoyo, opening drawers and such, and fretting about Zillia. I couldn't get her off my mind because I was afraid something bad had happened, like, maybe Blackbeard kidnapped her and was right at that very moment, pulling up her dress to see what she had for him. Then Cassia had to go and sneak up behind me, yelling out, "What you doing?" I about peed my pants.

I spun around to yell at her and there she was, posing for me in an orange two-piece bathing suit with white polka-dots. Cassia was a woman now, no doubt.

"Do you like it?"

"What you asking me for? I'm not going to wear it. Besides, I'm worrying about Zillia right now—she never came."

"Oh, don't worry about Zillia, we met her on the way uptown and she went with us. She's back home now. Said she'd be over later. She was going on about taking that dive today. You know, the one you were so worried about? Anyway, so be nice, Wick, and just tell me, does this look good on me? It's my first real two piece, you know? Pa bought it for me. Said I'm too old for skinny dipping, now."

She turned around once for me and I wanted to tell her the bottoms were too small, but because pa had bought it for her and because she wanted to hear me say it, I told her it looked good. When she danced out of my room to go back to hers, I almost yelled for her to pull out that wedgie. I was too late though because she slammed her door shut. Then she put on The Guess Who and started singing 'American Woman' at the top of her lungs. I went out onto the big landing where you could pick a door to go into anyone of the bedrooms up there and that's when I saw a shopping bag on the big rug out in the center. I peeked inside and there were two pairs of swimming trunks in there. I had a question, so I went and knocked on Cassia's door.

"Don't come in, unless you want a show!"

"I don't want no show, I want to know about these here swimming trunks."

"One's yours, the other's Clove's. Take yours and toss his on his bed, will you?"

"Okay... uh... thanks?"

'No Sugar Tonight' came on and Cassia started singing that real loud, too. I didn't see any sense trying to talk to her. So, I walked away. One of the swimming trunks was smaller and blue, so I figured the other one must be Clove's. I was glad because his was yellow with a white stripe up each side. Not my favorite. It was right then I remembered what Cassia said about Zillia wanting to do the dive today and that got me worrying again.

I was in my room trying on those trunks when I heard Zillia downstairs talking to my folks. I was buck naked with my door open. Zillia was halfway up the stairs before my new trunks were even halfway up my legs. It was a close call. If I hadn't heard her, she would have caught me without a stitch of clothes.

"Hey, Wick! Whatcha doing?" she said and gave me a weird little smile.

"Getting dressed, what's it look like?"

"Did I almost catch you naked?"

She had that dress on again, but no socks, just those old, torn sneakers. "Yeah, almost. So… looks like we're not going tree climbing today cause you got that stupid dress on again."

"Yeah, well… it's diving day. So, no trees. But… you ready to be my witness?"

"No."

"Oh, come on, Wick. It's got to be today. So… let's go. Get your pants and shirt on and grab your boots."

"Ain't wearing boots today, I'm going barefoot."

"Fine! But let's go."

She grabbed my arm after I finished pulling on my tee-shirt and down the stairs we went. Running through the kitchen, I saw pa at the table drinking coffee from his favorite mug and ma was going around doing stuff with a brand-new apron on.

"Where ya'll off to," ma asked.

"Down to the river."

"Well, ya-all be back by noon dinner, and ya'll better come running when ya-all hear the bell. Get them chickens fed, Wick?"

"Yeah," I said about the same time Zillia pulled me out the back door. I looked at pa and he was winking at me. He wasn't going to git in the way of kids fun. He always said that's the best time in anybody's life. I hoped he was right.

It took a whole five minutes to get to the swings, and all the time we were running, I was wondering how I was going to tell Zillia I didn't want to be witness to her dive. She was going to take off all her clothes and then I'd be stuck. I figured she'd ask, 'Ready?' and I'd just say, 'No, sorry.' But she didn't say anything like that.

We got there, we stopped, and she turned around and looked at me. She made big eyes and then did that thing where you raise your eyebrows a whole bunch of times. Then she grinned, bent forward and grabbed the hem of her skirt at the front and started pulling it up. I had just enough time to get my eyes shut.

"Wick, what you doing?"

"I ain't going to look, Zillia. Just go do it, and then you can lie to Dover that I saw you. Being here is good enough, right?"

"No. Wick… just open your eyes."

I turned and faced the other way before I did.

"What you doing, now?"

"I opened them. They're open."

"Yeah, but you got to be looking at me, silly. Come on, Wick, don't be ridiculous."

I imagined I'd would turn around and there would be Zillia in all her glory. I tried to prepare myself for what I was going to see. Then Zillia yelled in my ear, "Do me a favor, okay?" and it scared me.

She sounded mad, so I slowly turned around and there she was, standing there in a swimsuit just like Cassia's, except it was green. I felt so relieved I almost fell down.

"What… where'd you get that? You said you didn't have no swimsuit. All this time I was worrying, giving myself a gut ache, and you had this all the time?"

"Nope, just got it today. So, I didn't have it when I told you. So, I wasn't lying or nothing. Your ma and pa bought it for me. Cassia helped me try it on. It's the only one that came even close to fitting."

I looked her up and down and I could see what she meant. It was kind of baggy, so she wasn't haven't that wedgie problem Cassia had. I figured she'd grow into it, though. All I cared was that it covered all the important parts, and when Zillia said, "Come on, let's get this done," and ran to the swing—I was right behind her.

4

A Mischief Of Rats

Cos never thought in his thirteen years of life that he would be abandoned. It had never happened before and the thought of it had never crossed his mind. He had to assume that is what had happened as he sat in the quiet living room of the dilapidated house that he called home. It had been his da's idea to live there, which was grand for him as he was hardly ever home. It took a while to get used to it, and there had been resistance, but once they settled in, he hadn't given it much more thought.

Happiness had finally come to him when his family moved to Iowa. The west had been hot and dry, a solid contrast to the lush greenness, the woods, the river, and the tree lined streets of nearby Clarksburg. A word he never used but had heard on the Disney shows was: Enchanted. That was him.

He soon got caught up in this new world of four seasons, fishing in the Summer, sledding and skating in the Winter, and just wandering during the Spring and Fall months. He could walk everywhere he wanted to go. The railroad tracks that lay across the field behind the house took him straight into Clarksburg. Song birds sang, the frogs croaked from nearby ponds, and there were fireflies (actual fireflies!) that made an appearance at the end of May. He and his sisters would catch them in jars and then sit in their pony's stall, in the dark, to see who had the brightest one. There was wildlife everywhere and Cos liked that. Well… all except for the rats.

They had occupied the place long before he and his family had come. It became a struggle to keep them at bay. They had holes everywhere, and if no hole was convenient, they would make one. Cos's ma had to take precautions to protect what food they had so the rats couldn't help themselves. His da, on the other hand, never took the time to try to stop them. Rowan left it up to Mae and Cos to deal with the problem. He never experienced the full brunt of the situation, so was indifferent. Fiana and Shannon always called on Cos to rescue them from the little beasts. Fiana had the attic bedroom, Shannon, the one in the back corner opposite his folks.

After a month or so of putting up with the infestation, Fiana started spending a lot more time away from home at aunt Louise's house in town, or at her best friend, Poppy Johnson's house. They were like sisters. Shannon was hardly ever home. She was either with their da someplace fun, at school, or at their aunt's as well, spending time with her cousin Cami.

Cos wanted to look after his ma since no one else seemed to want to and because she was always alone at the house. Nobody ever came to visit and she had a great fear of going outside. For her there was terror inside the house as well as out. Aunt Louise said Mae had always been her sensitive sibling.

Nighttime was party time for the rats. When darkness settled on the land, they would begin their raucous affair, and the house would fill with their noise. Squeaking, squealing, fighting, gnawing, running from hole to hole across the floor in the dark, and worst of all, the bigger ones stopping and glaring at him as if he was the intruder. Cos would wrap himself up in a heavy blanket where he slept on the couch, being sure to cover his head in case they should conduct a taste test of his face. He had mentioned it to his classmate, Eddy Beltzer. Eddy told him not to worry about it. They were more afraid of him than he was of them. It would take a great deal to convince Cos that Eddy wasn't just blowing him off.

Cos feared those bigger ones more than the others and there were two or three of them. But one was enough. He remembered his uncle Delbert telling his da a story about river rats and how they could grow as big as cats. Uncle Delbert wasn't kidding. The bigger ones were also the bravest. They were vicious when he faced off with them. Instead of running away, they came at him, squeaking and hissing. They tried to jump on him, snapping their teeth. It was usually Cos who had to back off.

Now, he sat alone. Completely. Just him and the rats. The change had all come about in one days' time. Darkening his day like a cloud blocking the sun.

Nearly a week had passed since that morning he had climbed onboard the school bus with his sisters to head off to school. There had been no clue at breakfast that anything was amiss. His da was already off for his milk run, picking up enough at the local farms to fill the truck's tank, and then off to the dairy.

There had been eggs and bacon and toast for breakfast. Cereal for his little sister who didn't like 'cackleberries' Lunches were made and carried in brown paper bags along with school books and homework. The day had been a typical day at Clarksburg junior high. What Cos didn't know, was that uncle Delbert had paid his ma a visit during the day, bringing her the bad news about a telephone call he had received at his farm from Rowan. The world was about to tilt on its axis for the McDhai family.

Cos started to suspect something was wrong when he got on the school bus for the return trip home and his sister's never showed up at the waiting place.

"You're going to have to wait for my sisters," he hollered at Mrs. Lorens, the bus driver. She shut the doors anyway.

"If they ain't here, they ain't going," she said and pulled away from the long, yellow curb at the front of the school.

Cos didn't like Mrs. Lorens. His friend Lester said she was a bitch. Maybe he was right. When he was dropped in front of the house, he stepped out of the bus and immediately got a bad feeling; something was really wrong.

He found his ma standing at the door of the attached pump house looking out toward the highway, crying and ringing her hands. It had been tough to watch. Then when she screamed at him to go next door to the gas station and have the owner, Jerry, call an ambulance. That had pushed him over the edge. He yelled, "Why don't you straighten up and act like a parent should!" Then he too burst into tears. Screaming at her, he ran into the bathroom, slammed the door and began to the beat on the sink with the stick they used to prop up the window.

It had been a gift to her from him so she wouldn't have to use her good kitchen knives. He had cut it to the right length, sanded it smooth so she wouldn't get splinters, and proudly presented it to her.

It didn't matter anymore, so he destroyed it on the rim of enameled, cast-iron sink. Smashing it to splinters. His revenge for her stealing his childhood. He felt bad at first and then realized that she would never need it again. Eric Graf's ma told him she wasn't coming back for a long time.

Now, his sisters lived in another woman's house with his father, and his ma, was in the nuthouse. The deputy that showed up with the ambulance that hauled her off, sent him to stay with Eric, who lived up on the hill in a row of newer homes. That lasted almost a week. Then Eric's ma told him he could no longer stay with them. There were older girls in the house and they couldn't take the risk that Cos may not act in a gentlemanly fashion. She couldn't have her daughters getting pregnant. Cos hadn't a clue what she was talking about. How did that involve him? She sent him packing; back to rat house.

Sitting on his couch, his overnight bag on the floor in front of him, he watched as several sets of baleful eyes watched from the hole in the baseboard between the greasy stove and the noisy refrigerator. Cos didn't know what to do. He was not used to asking for help. Eric's ma had been mean to him for no reason, and about something he didn't know anything about. His da had ingrained in him that he needed to do everything for himself. The world was a hard place and that was the only way he was going to survive.

"You have to look out for yourself, no one else will."

Cos wasn't much on swearing at his age, but after that line had been used on him for the thousandth time, he turned away, making sure he was out of hearing distance before whispering, "Bullshit."

No one makes it alone, however, here he was, alone with the fear that 'he wasn't going to make it' looming like a bad storm on the horizon.

The sun was setting. He needed to eat. Going into the kitchen, the eyes at the hole pulled back into the dark and quickly returned to the safety of the water filled basement, the little hairy bodies making splashes that were barely discernable. Cos stood in front of the open refrigerator drinking from the milk bottle and after draining it, he chowed down on raw hot dogs, slices of American cheese, and Wonderbread. He could have made a sandwich, but that would have taken more time and besides, it was all going to the same place, anyway. He needed to set up his defenses for the night.

The refrigerator was the safe place for the food. The rats couldn't chew their way into it, so taking all the food in the cupboard that the little beasts hadn't already ruined, he put it in the refrigerator and made sure the door latched tight. If things got too bad and he found himself losing the battle, he could always retreat outdoors. Cos was an expert camper. It was one thing he knew how to do. He could set up the mildewy tent in the woods just across the tracks, gather firewood, and set up a proper campsite. He had been a Boy Scout out west. Camping there meant heat, rattlesnakes, Gila monsters, and scorpions. Certain defenses needed to be set up to deal with them, as well. It's just, they were outside the house. The rats on the other hand...

Cos wondered if the rodents would be braver because it was just him, alone. Did they know it was one against one thousand? He didn't think he was going to get any sleep this night. So, first, he needed a weapon. His baseball bat was too heavy; he needed something lighter.

After making sure there were no rats hiding in his parents' bedroom closet, he rummaged through the things piled on the floor and coming across his father's so-called shillelagh, he smiled to himself as he read, 'Blackthorn' engraved in its side. Perfect. Taking it to the couch, he laid it there. Then going back into the kitchen, he grabbed his ma's stack of plastic dinner plates and a roll of masking tape from the drawer. Taking them back into the living room, he set one against each of the big holes in the baseboard and taped those that he couldn't push furniture up against. He had only covered the holes in that room, there were at least twenty-five others scattered about the house.

He could use books, but the thought of the rats chewing them to pieces, troubled him. He loved books and other than his da's mechanics manuals, he didn't want to spare any of them. The public library was his sanctuary and damaged books only brought a feeling of unease.

The library had the Encyclopedia Brittanica and Cos spent a great deal of his time reading them. He learned that a group of rats was called a 'mischief' and that they had some kind of kingdom. Male rats were called 'Bucks' and females were 'Does' just like with deer, except mama rats were called 'Dams' and their kids were 'Kittens' or 'Pups' just not the kind Cos wanted to cuddle. He also discovered that it was the Black Rat, or, river rat, who dominated the kingdom at Rat House. They were bigger and meaner than the brown rats.

It all made him think about a ballet he saw once on TV. The Nutcracker. The girl, Clara had to deal with the rat king who was as big as a man. Cos just kept telling himself that it was just a man in a rat costume, but that didn't lessen his fear. Clara had only used a shoe to vanquish her foe, and there had been wooden soldiers who also came to her defense. There would be no wooden soldiers coming to help Cos, and he doubted that shoes would do any good. He knew how to swing a baseball bat, though, and the lighter Blackthorn would allow for a quicker recovery on the backswing.

The door to the kitchen opened right into the living room so he could watch from the couch. The upstairs, bedrooms, and bathroom, all opened into the far end of the hallway. Technically, he only had to keep watch on those two doorways. The door to the basement had been nailed shut, something somebody did before the McDhai's arrived on the scene. The previous renter must have done that after they discovered the basement had flooded and the rats had turned it into their indoor swimming pool. The little beasts hadn't chewed through that door yet, but they had all night if they'd a mind too.

Cos turned on the single table lamp to give him some light since the one at the ceiling didn't work. The bulbs in the kitchen light had burned out and there was no money to buy new. Beer at the pub was more important. His ma had been using a kerosene lamp borrowed from a neighbor. She had hidden the matches so Cos wouldn't find them and accidently burn down the house. At the moment, Cos didn't think that it would be an accident.

The light in the bathroom still worked and he turned that on to cast a little light into the hallway should the rats try an offensive from that direction. Cos left the back and front doors unlatched in case he needed to make an escape. Taking all the camping equipment from the enclosed front porch, he piled it out back in the carport, so it would be ready on the run. He didn't think the rats would bother it; or at least, he hoped.

Grabbing the last can of root beer from the fridge, he turned on the TV before retreating to the couch. Wrapping up in his thick wool blanket, he lay the Blackthorn next to him, popped the top on the root beer, and sat with one eye on the Dick Van Dyke show, and the other, vacillating between the hallway and the kitchen door.

After a while he forgot to check the doors and the TV took all of his attention. The sun disappeared from view and the room grew dark. The evening movie was *Willard*. A recently released movie about… rats. Cos shivered and changed the channel. He needed comedy. But the Willard announcement reminded him what he was supposed to be doing and occasionally he'd lift his eyes to check out those doorways.

It was during a commercial while watching, *Leave It To Beaver*, that he glanced up to see the three pairs of eyes that normally watched from the hole in the kitchen, now gazed balefully from the middle of the floor. Uncle Delbert was right, they were nearly as big as cats, which made him wish he had a few of those. But Cos doubted even cats could overpower these critters. He watched their noses twitching like they were trying to catch his scent. Goosebumps rose on his arms and the hair at the nape of his neck now stood at attention.

He felt the need to act, there needed to be a show of force. They needed to know who they were messing with. His hand crawled to the stick and once he had it, he flung off the blanket with a shout and leapt from the couch. They started to scramble, their claws not getting a foothold on the old linoleum. Cos dashed toward them, raising his shillelagh with both hands, preparing for that first swing. They were too big to go into their hole all at the same time, so one went in, one ran behind the fridge, and the third tried to dash past him into the living room. As if golfing, he caught the little beast squarely and sent it against the cupboard with a loud bang.

Cos thought it was down for the count, but the rat acted as if it hadn't felt a thing and getting up, it scurried out the door and into the hallway.

His actions, even though fruitless, had empowered him. As long as they didn't swarm him, he could probably hold them off. Moving back to the couch he climbed on and sat. The rat party was just starting. They were now in the walls, in the ceiling, and there was the consistent splashing in the basement.

He turned up the TV and tried to get lost in the show. The Beav was his usual hilarious self and Wally was doing everything he could to keep his little brother out of trouble. But Cos couldn't get into it. *The Twilight Zone* followed and he had to change the channel again. He was scared enough; he didn't need Rod Serling creeping him out any more than he already was.

Eleven o clock rolled around and Cos felt his eyes grow heavy. The rat noise hadn't lessened any and every once in a while, he thought he saw a rat poke it's head around the side of the stove and glare at him, its eyes showing red from the glow of the table lamp.

Cos remembered the flashlight. It was in the drawer in the table that the lamp sat on next to the front door. Getting up, he grabbed it and took it back to the couch, adding it to his arsenal. Then thinking twice about it, he gathered all the shoes by the front door and piled them down at the end of the couch where his feet would be when he was sleeping. He thought about coffee to keep himself awake, but he hated that stuff. It was going to be hard to keep his eyes open.

Ten minutes later, he fell asleep, the late-night news droning on with the weather for the next day. He had been dreaming about a cute girl from his class; Denise Donnelly. She wanted to hold his hand, so he let her. She was nice to him, even though no girl had ever held his hand before or wanted to. He liked it, it was soft and warm. She even squeezed his hand once while laughing over some stupid joke that he had made. The she turned to him, her lovely blue eyes got really serious, and she said, "They're coming."

Cos snorted awake and tried to clear his eyes. There had been a noise, something loud enough to wake him. When the fog cleared, he felt the fear creep in. There were now five of them sitting at the threshold of the kitchen door. The one in front of the other four was bigger and it's snout appeared scarred like it had once had a bad accident but had survived.

Cos's eyes traveled to the hallway entrance. There were more over there, seven or so of the smaller ones. A few of them were already in the room, running back and forth behind furniture. It was like they weren't sure which one of them should lead the charge. Then, several things happened all at once. The MGM lion roared on the TV, Cos screamed because it surprised him, and the rats in the hallway scattered back toward the bedrooms.

He jumped to his feet to stand on the couch, making sure none of the rats had snuck up on him. The couch was high up, but the rats could jump, and catching the fabric with their claws, they could climb. Letting go with his version of a war cry, he jumped from the couch toward the kitchen. All but Scarface fled. Instead, it came for him.

Cos back peddled, jumped up on the couch and just as he landed, he saw Scarface was in midair, its teeth bared, its eyes seemingly red with hate. It was headed for his leg, and Cos imagined it was looking to take a big hunk out of his calf; blue jeans and all.

As if by instinct he swung the Blackthorn, holding tight onto the tip. The ball of the big end came around and contacted the little monster when it was a foot or so from fresh meat. It squealed loudly at the impact and changing direction, the beast smacked into the wall and fell motionless onto the armchair.

Tears had leaked from Cos's eyes to dry on his cheeks, but more out of rage, than fear. His attention remained on that grayish black pile of fur lying across the room. Cos suspected he had killed it. He had never killed an animal before. It might have been trying to hurt him, but it was still an animal and he wasn't feeling too good about what he had done.

Cos sat down and tried to calm himself. The rats were gathering again. They weren't going to wait until he fell asleep. He groaned and shouted, "Git out of here!" They didn't scatter this time. He had killed their leader and they knew it. Now they wanted their own revenge, he could just feel it. Getting to his feet, he held the stick like a baseball bat and said, "Come on, you little maggots!"

They inched across the floor, the ones in the rear running back and forth like they weren't sure about this. They were coming on two fronts this time; from the kitchen and the hallway. It was all so surreal. This was something that only happened in movies like… *Willard*. He wondered if he was only imagining it. But, nope, it was really happening. They were going to do the thing he feared most—swarm him. Cos had read where when wolves attacked as a pack, that they had a strategy. It seemed to him that rats did to.

Electricity snapped under the lamp table and the room went dark. Cos screamed in a way he had never screamed before. By the bluish light of the television, he could see one of them lying dead underneath it, the smell of burnt fur and rat flesh floating to his nose. It had chewed through the cord.

Now there was only the light from the TV and the hall. He felt a thump on the couch and saw one of them must have climbed up the back where he couldn't see it. He swung and missed. The creature jumped back onto the floor and formed up with the others. Then they came, all at once.

He began swinging, hitting some, but missing others. After about the tenth time that he contacted one with the heavy end of the stick, they scattered and moved away across the room to regroup. Finding the flashlight, he shone it at them. They moved out of sight behind things, some going back down the hall. "Git out of my house!" he shouted and jumped onto the floor, his stick at the ready.

Cos didn't see the eager set of eyes peering in the uncurtained window to his right. Something was perched upon the upside-down milk crate that he used to climb in when he got locked out. They had been watching his every move and closer inspection would have revealed a murderous light within.

Running toward the kitchen, Cos sent the rats that had gathered there scurrying for cover. Then he waited, the flashlight in one hand, the stick in the other. He felt the panic creeping in. The thought that he might have to actually flee his home was becoming more of a reality. Yet there was also an anger blossoming inside him, a rage much like the one that enveloped him the day the ambulance came for his ma.

Something was scratching at the backdoor!

Cos cut loose with another war cry and flinging open the warped wooden panel, he raised his stick for the first blow. But it wasn't a rat, at all, but… a rat terrier.

Samantha (Sam for short), Eric's dog. She and Cos had become good friends over the year and she would often wander down to Rat House to play and hang out when she'd had enough of Eric and his weird family.

She looked up at the stick hovering above her head and then back at Cos's face, her eyes saying, "What the…?"

Cos said, "Sam, what are you doing…?" and lowered the stick. Sam jumped into his arms, just as she always had when he went to Eric's. He hugged her as she gave his face a good licking.

She wasn't in his arms for long, though. One of the rats made an appearance in the kitchen doorway. It was almost as big as Sam. She gave a long, drawn-out squeal of delight and leaping from Cos's arms, she had that rat's neck in her jaws, before it could even think about turning and running.

Cos kept the flashlight on her and amazement flooded in at how quickly she dispatched that creature. She shook it with such ferocity that Cos was surprised that the rat's skin hadn't split open to spray the walls with rat guts. She dropped the little fiend, and stood panting, looking at Cos with eyes that said, "Okay, who's next!"

Another one appeared squeezing in under the pumphouse door. Why someone would want a noisy pump in a small room attached to their house was beyond Cos. Sam dispatched that rat in the same amount of time as the first. Then Cos and Sam worked their way through the house, confronting and annihilating every one of the beasts that was dumb enough to show itself.

Cos with his stick and Sam with her centuries old rat killing skills went to battle together. Rat bodies were left where they lay and by two o clock in the morning the house had quieted with the exception of the sound of Cos and Sam panting together.

He gave Sam some water in a small bowl and after she had her fill and he had drunk a glassful, himself, he curled up on the couch and wrapped himself in his blanket. The rat battle had exhausted him and having never stayed awake until such a wee hour, Cos soon fell into slumber, the test pattern on the TV giving off a low hum. Sam, after doing a once-around of the rooms on the first floor, jumped onto the couch and curled up at Cos's belly. She slept with one eye open as Cos's purring snores filled the room. It was the first time in a long time he had slept with his head uncovered.

It was about six o clock that morning when someone rapped on the backdoor. Sam woofed and ran through the living room into the kitchen. When whoever it was, knocked again, she let go with a raucous string of warning barks.

Cos jumped up and stopped to look around. Rat bodies were scattered around the living room and in the kitchen. There wasn't time to clean them up, so he unlocked the door and opened it to a smiling Rick Faris.

Rick worked with his father at the dairy. Cos liked Rick. He was nice guy and would give Cos chewing gum and offer to take him fishing. He took Cos once to meet his family who lived in a cabin in the woods. They were all just as nice as Rick.

"Hey Cos, your dad home?"

"Uh, no."

Sam sniffed Ricks pant leg and then moved over to the water bowl for another drink. Battle always made her thirsty.

"Well, your dad hasn't been showing up for work. So… is your mom home?"

"Uh… no, she's in the nuthouse."

"The nuthouse?"

"Yeah, that's what Eric's mom called it, anyway."

"Where are your sisters?"

"Don't know."

"Can I come in?"

"Yeah, sure."

Cos stepped aside and Rick moved up into the kitchen. Stopping, the blond man with his Elvis haircut, looked around at all the dead rats. His eyes got big and he rubbed at his forehead and then looking back at Cos, he said, "What the hell happened here?"

Walking into the living room, Cos heard him say, "Ah… geez," as he scanned the floor. Sam walked in and sat down. Then looking up at Rick, she made a face that Cos interpreted as saying, 'Well, how'd I do?'

Rick turned and looked at Cos and coming back into the kitchen, he said, "How long you been here alone, Cos?"

"Oh, it's been a couple days, I imagine. Was up at Eric's for a while but his ma kicked me out because she thought I might try something with her daughters. I don't know what… but I didn't argue."

"Okay, well. I want you to pack some clothes, you're coming home with me until we get this figured out."

Cos thought that was a grand idea. So, after pushing some clean clothes into his old gym bag, he slipped on his shoes and met Rick in the kitchen where he sat in a chair, Sam now on his lap and getting a good scratching behind her ears.

"Okay, kiddo, let's make like a shepherd and get the flock out of here." Standing up, Sam jumped off and Rick walked to the back door. Cos turned and looked at all the dead rats lying about and felt glad he wasn't going to have to clean that mess up.

Going outside, Sam was the last one out. Rick shut the back door and they headed for Rick's maroon '67 Ford Mustang. He had bought it new, five years prior, but it was still a good-looking car, and it was fast. Cos's ma said she thought that Rick might be a lady's man. Cos hoped someday he'd too be a lady's man, if that meant being like Rick.

He got into the front seat and Rick soon climbed in. Sam sat in the dirt of the driveway, scratching and watching them. Cos shut his door and Rick said, "What about your dog?"

"Sam? Oh, she's not my dog. She just came down to help me fight the rats. As much as I'd like to have her… she's Eric's dog."

"Okay, then," Rick said and started the car. As soon as the motor caught, Sam did a stretching bow in the manner that dogs often do, barked once as if to say 'Good bye,' and then sped away up the hill toward home. Cos watched her race away like she was late for breakfast, and when the tears came, he turned his face toward the window so Rick wouldn't see him cry.

#5

For The Love Of An Epiphany

The world was unfolding as usual, but it didn't do it the same way for everybody. It wasn't the planet looking at itself doing the thing it had done for its entire existence, but the humans that rode the spinning ball in a vast, gas filled universe. This much Zane McShane knew. He couldn't stop it, he just had to hold on. Somebody told him once that life was like a rollercoaster ride. He felt it was more like that teacup thing. Just spinning and spinning with the occasional slow turn and troubling jolt of the cup. It was designed to protect the rider from the more violent forces of nature. Those things looking to rip him limb from limb. Zane was still debating whether gravity was a friend or not.

At fourteen, he was smarter than most of his peers. The problem was, he didn't feel the need to prove it. So, he didn't try. Some of his teachers thought he was lazy and possibly had a case of mental retardation. They even considered transferring him into the Special Education classes because that's what you did in 1970. However, a couple of the educators understood his humility and believed Zane had great potential. So, they went to bat for him, and the school decided to keep him right where he was at, seemingly waiting for their next opportunity to bring him low.

That left those who supported him in a constant state of vigilance, and they would remain that way until he got into high school. Then, they would pass the baton off to those like themselves in the upper grades, who would see him through to his graduation. Zane never showed his gratitude, but only because their efforts were cloaked in compassion and a humility all their own. So, he didn't know who to thank. He just thought, 'That's life.'

The planet just kept spinning.

When he first came to this small, sleepy town, just two years before and was introduced to his classmates, they had a blast with his name. That's the trouble with first names that rhyme with last names. Thanks, ma!

They spent months coming up with variations. Then one of the boys started calling him Hunchy because he was round shouldered. After a while, they forgot about his real name and the fun ended. Hunchy couldn't decide if that was a good thing, or not. He became just, plain, ol' Hunchy, and fell snugly into his slot. The one they had created for him.

If anyone showed an interest in being friends, he gave them special consideration. Time would be spent doing things together that boys do in their free time. Yet more often than not, the relationship turned into a pissing contest and a quest for dominance. It would fall apart and then Hunchy would be on his own again. It wasn't that he couldn't hold his own in a fight, it's just, he didn't see the sense in it.

He spent a good deal of time alone, exploring the woods, the seemingly endless river bank, and the vast expanses of flower and grass covered prairie. He knew about Naturalists, and that's what he wanted to be. Unlike other kids who adored Superman and Captain America, it was John Muir, Audubon, and Henry David Thoreau who were Hunchy's heroes.

On really nice days, he could be found lying in a boat on his back, floating in the placid waters above the village dam. The hours would just fly by as he studied the infinite blue sky with its fluffy white clouds. It was something he found much more interesting than predictable relationships and the curse of approval seeking behavior with all its consequences. He began to think 'best friends' was a myth.

It was in the autumn of his third year living in Clarksburg, that Hunchy experienced what could be considered his first epiphany. He didn't know that's what it was called, he just knew how it felt. The excited feeling lifted his spirits and he smiled to himself. Sadly, he didn't know that epiphanies were something that fell into the category of the 'few and far between'. It was a good thing that he didn't, otherwise it would have just been one more thing to be unhappy about. Ignorance is bliss.

The subject of his revelation (attending an after-school event to test his 'best friend' theory) didn't matter as much as the feeling it may bring. Hunchy decided, for that reason, he would have to act on it. Homecoming was just a couple of days away. He would go and see what 'the big to do' was all about. Then he would decide for himself if the others had just blown it all out of proportion, or that it was actually something beneficial to him.

So, he planned. Step number one: find some money. It cost money. For two dollars you could get a ticket at the principal's office. Then you were given access to the football game on Friday and the dance on Saturday night. The ticket was shown at the gate when arriving at the game and then taken from you the following night at the gymnasium door where the 'sock hop' was held. You could also pay two dollars for either at the gate or door, without the ticket. But then it was four dollars total. More money than he had ever had in his pocket at any one time.

The dance was supposed to be for the high school kids. But there weren't enough of those to make any money at it. So, if Jr. high kids showed up and paid their money, no one said a word.

He almost gave up the idea because it created such a problem. But… he didn't. The moment was all too special, and he would feel the fool if he quit. Hunchy was going to sacrifice himself to the system—just this once. The future beyond that was out of his hands.

Step number two: match socks without holes. Hunchy worried about finding a pair of socks in his drawer that didn't have holes. If he was going to be hopping in his socks, he wanted them perfect. He would also have to wear his best jeans—and without asking permission. His 'Sunday Go To Meeting' jeans were for formal occasions only. That's what his ma said. But Hunchy didn't attend formal occasions. So, the jeans just remained folded in his drawer and had been for the last four years. Luckily for him, his ma always bought big. That way he could grow into them over the space of a lifetime. Hunchy suspected he had grown into them by now. Saturday night would tell. He decided he wasn't going to the football game; it was too rowdy. Going to the dance itself would be enough to meet his objective.

Finally, step number three: Find a way to the school. There would be no school bus to pick him up and he didn't know anyone who had a car. His bicycle had a flat tire and a patch kit at Hale's Hardware was a buck, five. He would walk. That way he could save the money for the event. It was just… he had never gone there at night, so he didn't know what to expect. He had walked the fields, the woods, and even the railroad tracks after sundown, but never the north end of Clarksburg where the school was. He found the unknown, in this case, inviting.

He declined many requests to participate in the parade. Creating the float or getting things to put on it, didn't appeal to him. His most spoken word on Friday was, "No." Every time somebody asked him if he was going to the game, he loudly stated, "No." If they had asked him about the dance, it would have been a whole different story. But only one person asked that question. Mandy Vale. The fact that she stared at him a lot during the school day wasn't a mystery. He had caught her time and time again. Then she'd smile and he'd look away, pretending something else had caught his attention.

When she asked the question, he just stared at her face and that line of freckles bridging her nose. Then, at her eyes; big and brown. At first, he was surprised that someone had actually asked the right question. He smiled by accident and when he realized he had, he just said, "Yeah."

"See you there," was all she said and walked away, grinning from ear to ear.

Hunchy knew she didn't have many friends. It was because she had a problem with her right hip. That leg just didn't work properly, and it was like she always had to pull herself to the left on purpose when she stepped just so she could walk in a straight line. Then there was her hair, long, brown, and super curly. He heard the other girls talking about Mandy. They were scared to be seen with her. The boys just made fun. She always kept her head up though. Hunchy figured she cried about it when no one was around—just like he did on the big rock down at the river bank.

He worried that she might try to be friends with him. Then it would end up like those other brief associations. But she was a girl. He never had a friend that was a girl. So, maybe it would be different. He just didn't want to waste all that energy on something that was doomed to fail.

Later, he found himself hoping there would be another epiphany. Only this time, about Mandy. A revelation that would assure him that it was worth it to be friends with her. But until that happened, he had to stay focused on the first one.

Saturday morning found Hunchy on the move. Pop bottle patrol. He had found a quarter under the cushion on the sofa. Now he only needed one dollar and seventy-five cents. The Royal Blue Grocery on Main Street would give him a nickel for each bottle found. The Jack & Jill grocer farther up the street would send him away. They didn't want to be troubled with bottles. So, he did the math and estimated he would need thirty-five of them. That was a lot. It would take him all day.

Hunchy located a cardboard box and dropped the bottles inside each time he found one. Twenty-four of them soon filled the carton and it was almost too heavy for him to carry. Stopping at the store, they would only accept them if they could keep the box. He would have to get another. Walking out with a dollar forty-five in his pocket, he began his search, not only for pop bottles, but also a box to put them in. The containers he found were either too big or too small. He took it as an omen that his quest was already failing.

He soon found himself on the south end of town, just on the edge of the woods. That's where the lumber yard was. Those guys were always drinking bottled pop, doubling down on the really hot days. Hunchy suspected cutting and hauling boards around was hard work. Maybe there would be bottles left sitting on the fence rails or stuck in a corner because some people were just too lazy to walk the bottle to the rack.

The yard was closed because it was Saturday. The sky was cloudy and growing dark. It looked like rain. Not good. That would slow him down. He walked around the buildings, searching. First the sawhouse, then the office building with its modern metal siding, and finally, the lumber storage building. Being it was the oldest building there; it was huge and slatted to let the air pass through. Making sure no one was watching from the Ryan's back porch; he slipped in through some loose slats on the side.

It was dark in there, but his eyes soon adjusted to the dim light and he could start his search while enjoying the smell of newly cut pine boards. After a considerable amount of time without results, Hunchy started to wonder if maybe he was out of luck and that the dream of the sock-hop was dying. He stood in the sawdust of the center isle built for the trucks to pass through, saying to himself, "Don't give up. Don't be a quitter." His words sounded weird in the quiet where only sparrows chirped and pigeons cooed.

He had the rest of the town to comb, so he had to get moving. Time was getting short, the dance started at seven. The big clock above the closet-like office where the attendant sat, said it was ten after four. There were pop bottles in there, but the door was locked. The feeling that came was like he was sinking. It felt very similar to that moment after jumping into the deep end of the pool and letting himself just descend slowly to the bottom. Hunchy didn't get angry too often, but it was coming now.

Hunchy hurried toward the walkout door. It was set right in the middle of the big overhead panel that slid open to let the trucks come in. Grabbing the knob, he pulled hard. It didn't budge. He just kept yanking and yanking, turning the knob left and right as he did. He felt the tears coming, and along with them, that familiar feeling of frustration. With a ma like his, there was no way around it. It was one of the first emotions he ever had to deal with in his young life.

Tugging on the door caused the big overhead to sway in and out. Several boards, longer than he was tall, had been left leaning against it down at the end. They clattered to the floor. It gave him a fright. He stood in silence, waiting to see if anyone was going to come running. When no one did, he thought to pick up the boards and put them back (leave it like you found it his ma was always saying).

It was when he walked over to do just that, he saw them sitting there. Three wooden trays of pop bottles stacked in a corner behind where the boards had been standing. Old, dusty, dirty pop bottles in filthy wooden crates. They had been there a long time. Nobody would miss them he was sure of it. He wouldn't be able to carry all three. But he didn't need that many. One crate would do. That's all he would take. Now, all he had to do was figure out how to open that door.

He studied it closely for about a minute and almost kicked himself, saying, "Ah, geez." There was a night latch that he had ignored for some reason. It required a key from the outside, but you only had to turn a knob on the inside and you were free.

Hunchy took just the top tray of bottles and found his way out. Hurrying up the drive to the roadway, he could only hope no one was watching. Life in a small town told him that the odds were in his favor. He would have to stop at the boat ramp and wash the bottles before taking them to the store. There was still time for that.

Just as he stepped onto the asphalt of the river road and began his trek north, it started to rain. He had a mile to go before he reached the bridge and then another two blocks to the store. It started coming down in buckets and he walked the middle of the street, holding the crate out in front with both hands. By the time he got to the halfway point where the boat ramp was, he didn't need the river anymore. The rain had taken care of it for him. But he was soaked through to his underwear, his long hair dripping like crazy. The picture in his head of himself, didn't look good. But it was okay, it wouldn't kill him. The people at the store would wonder what he was up to, though, coming in there all soaking wet.

Grandma Schneider opened the door for him, and he walked in dripping on the dark greasy boards of the floor. She pointed to a corner and said, "Put them there," and then called back, "Paul, get up here." Paul came from the back wiping his hands on his apron. "What you kids won't do for a pop bottle. Ma, give him his money," he said and returned to the meat counter where he had been cutting pork chops. Grandma Schneider rang open the cash register and 'NO SALE' popped up on a tab at the top. She took out a dollar and two dimes. Handing them to Hunchy, she said, "Now go home and get into some dry clothes before you catch your death."

"Thanks," was all he said. When he got outside, he laughed at what she had told him. The rain wasn't going to kill him. Being wet didn't kill you. He was practically skipping now and stomping puddles as he did. It was the day the rain became his friend. Just like the river, the woods, and that big rock down on the riverbank.

At home, Hunchy found his ma napping on the sofa. After slipping out of his wet clothes, he hung them on the wet clothes rack and climbed into the shower stall that sat in the corner of their galley kitchen. He stood in the fusillade of droplets and soaped up good. When he rinsed off, he tipped his face up to the shower head, his eyes closed, pretending he was standing in a warm rain. Smiling to himself, he wondered why people thought getting caught in the rain could kill you but didn't think twice about taking a shower.

Using his ma's blow dryer, Hunchy dried his hair. He found fresh underwear in the basket by the kitchen table, and after picking his best pair, he pulled them on before going in to match socks. He would have to wear two 'righties' because it was the 'lefties' that were the ones with the holes. Sneaking his good jeans from the bottom drawer of his dresser, he wondered if there might be something wrong with his left foot, or maybe it was his boot that was making those holes. He would worry about that later.

Pulling on his jeans he found them tight and hard to button, but he got the job done. Catching sight of his butt in the mirror that hung on the back of his door, he had to laugh. They were the tightest pants he had ever worn, and his backside had never looked like that before. He hoped the other kids wouldn't make fun of him.

There was only one clean tee-shirt and it wasn't good enough for the dance. It had holes in the armpits. It would be hard to walk around without lifting his arms. He wished he had checked sooner. Maybe he didn't truly believe he was going, so hadn't bothered. There was doubt.

His eyes fell on his favorite brown sweater folded on his chair. It was a little fuzzy, but it just might work. Pulling it on over the tee-shirt, he checked it in the mirror and almost shouted with joy. He thought he looked like one of those kids in his ma's J.C. Penney catalog.

Finding his little peace sign on its chain lying atop his dresser, he slung it around his neck and left it hanging outside the sweater for all to see. After putting on his boots, he stuffed his money in his pocket and slipped out the front door before his ma could wake up and try to delay him with never ending questions.

It had stopped raining. The clouds remained, though. Everything was wet and the smell of rain was fresh in his nose. The street lights were just coming on and the pavement shimmered. It was pleasant, and Hunchy felt happy.

After walking nearly a mile, it was totally dark by the time he arrived. Kids were running in and out of the door, chasing each other. High school kids were standing around in couples just outside and he could hear the music floating out on the night air. There was no line of kids waiting to get in the door. So, throwing it open, he walked right in. No one recognized him at first. He thought that made it fun. He proudly handed over the money and the older girl behind the table with the big sock hop banner, thanked him, and stamped the back of his hand with the face of a wildcat. The school mascot. She had no idea how hard he had worked just to get that two dollars, or the additional sixty-five cents left over so he could buy a piece of homemade pie or a soda.

Hunchy walked up the hall to the gymnasium door and looked in. The Bee Gees were singing *I Started A Joke* and high school kids were slow dancing. Hunchy grinned to himself. He had made it. The quest was over. The incredible epiphany sensation had been honored.

Scanning the gymnasium floor from end to end, his eyes caught Mandy's about the same time hers, caught his. She was at the pie and punch table, drinking out of a paper cup. She set it down and turned away from Alison Pearl, the girl she had been talking to. It was like she had something more important to do. She was coming straight for him and was grinning bigtime. Alison followed and grabbed her arm. Hunchy heard, "Mandy, answer my question." Mandy turned back and did as Alison had demanded. But she kept looking over her shoulder at him and it made Hunchy nervous. He backed up across the hall, and a little bit to the left, so she couldn't see him anymore. It might be best for everybody if she thought he had gone.

Hunchy just stood listening to the music from the big stereo sitting on the stage and watched the other kids goofing off. He figured he could probably go home now. He had done what he came to do. Well, maybe a piece of pie first. Dessert didn't come around too often, and he could smell all the different kinds on the table from where he stood.

Then, two things happened. A group of kids came down the hall on his left from the music room with musical instruments in their hands, and a deputy sheriff, who had been hired to keep everybody in-line, came up the hall from the cafeteria. The deputy came around the corner about the same time Hunchy turned to talk to the kid with the trumpet.

"Can I try it? Please? Just once, I've never played one before."

The kid acted unsure, but then handed it over. Hunchy took it and held it like he had seen them do during the pep rallies and blew a single note. It was perfect. He grinned and handed the horn back to the kid, but before the kid could take it, it was yanked out of Hunchy's hand by the deputy.

He then shoved it at the kid and said, "Take it and get out of here." The kid did, and then the deputy grabbed a handful of Hunchy's sweater at the shoulder and pushed him toward the door, saying, "You can just get the hell out of here, we don't need no troublemakers." Hunchy was literally stunned. He had never in his life even talked to a deputy, let alone been near one. There had never, ever, been one inside the school before. The cop pushed him outside and he was left to stand staring in through the window as the deputy shut the door. He then pointed at Hunchy through the glass like he was saying, "Yes, you! Troublemaker!"

Hunchy looked past him and saw Mandy standing in the doorway to the gymnasium, a hand at her mouth, her eyes open wide in disbelief. Other kids stood around talking and pointing, like they couldn't believe it.

Hunchy walked away to a bench that sat along the walk just outside. The second he planted his butt on the seat, it started to rain. A slight sprinkle at first, and then, buckets. Everybody else ran inside. The last kid in, held the door for him and yelled, "Coming?" Hunchy shook his head, no. The kid let it close, saying, "Suit yourself."

Hunchy just sat, looking up into the sky, the big droplets beating on his face. It didn't bother him. The rain was his friend.

He was soaked in less than a minute. His best jeans dripping at the cuff, his hair plastered to his head. Looking at the door, he saw the deputy still stood guard. Hunchy turned away and just stared across the bike racks to the lawn beyond.

He heard the door open and figured the deputy was coming out to make him leave the school grounds. Hunchy figured the cop was just going to have to carry him, because he wasn't going to budge an inch.

Somebody sat down next to him and he let his eyes stray in that direction. Small feet in sandals with red lacquered toe nails. Allowing his eyes to move up slender legs clad in blue denim, they passed over a bright white blouse now soaked through enough to show the lacey accents of a brassiere, and then he looked straight into the eyes of Mandy.

She said, "I'm sorry, Zane." Hunchy looked away, putting his eyes on the concrete at his feet. The rain pounded the back of his head, the drops splashing up from the pool around his boots. He was at a loss for words.

Mandy was getting just as wet as he, but she wasn't leaving. Maybe… she too had a friend in the rain. Maybe she, like he, didn't believe it would cause them to catch their death. She then slid up against him. He felt the warmth of her, but no girl had ever touched him before. He really didn't know what to expect. But—it was all good. Good like the epiphany was. Then she took his hand and that surprised him even more. He tried hard not to show it. So, he just let her hold it, and they sat there in the rain for the longest time—together.

#6

Sheep Shed

The two boys took their time crossing the narrow, well patched highway just outside of Clarksburg. With the taller one in the lead, they stumbled down into the weed filled ditch and then struggled up the other side. Their forward motion was soon cut short by a barbed wire fence. They stood together, running dirty fingers over rusty wire, checking out the vast field beyond.

A small herd of cows stood silhouetted on a hill to the south, their lowing barely audible on the breeze. They were of no interest to the boys, though, because their adventure lay in the other direction. After a brief debate regarding navigation (which included pointing fingers for effect) they tossed each other a grin and started over.

It wasn't an easy climb, especially for the smaller, lesser experienced boy. For him, the crossing was more like a tightrope walk. The wires quivered and shook. His body swung in and out as barbs scratched his legs and ripped at his knee length cut-offs. After a brief struggle, he gave up and just let himself tumble into the ankle high grass on the other side. The taller boy laughed, slapping at his thighs. He even went as far as to ball his fists and pump his arms while spinning around one time in his mirth.

"Geez, Charley, you ever climb a fence before? Oh man! That was hilarious."

Charley (also known as 'Little Charley' to his closer friends), brushed himself off, his once excited grin, now a scowl of discontent.

"Wasn't funny, Lester! Oh man! That hurt like heck."

"Geez, what a whiner. Most kids round these parts are pretty tough by the time they're thirteen. Sure can tell you're a city feller."

"Yeah, rub it in, will you. Hey, you know… I'm still trying to figure out why I even hang around with you, Lester Valey."

Shoving his hands in his pockets, Charley threw Lester a look of defiance. Then casting his eyes down, he flattened a gopher mound by kicking it until it was just a brown patch in the weeds.

"Well, you know, I think it's because I'm the coolest seventh grader you know. I will make a man out of you… city boy!"

Whipping his greasy, dark hair out of his eyes, Lester directed his snaggled toothed grin to the nearby hills and said, "Let's go, slow poke, I want to find those sheep before lunch."

Charley ignored the taller boy. Pulling a hand from a pocket, he licked a fingertip and rubbed it over a scratch on his knee. Lester, seeing that his pal didn't give a damn about sticking to the plan, shook his head in annoyance. Deciding that he'd waited long enough, he took off without another word.

Driven by impulse to follow, Charley moved forward without looking where he was going and tripped over a large tuft of grass. Catching himself just in time to defeat gravity, he checked to see if Lester had noticed.

His pal was still moving away, not looking back. Charley put extra effort into catching up. They were soon loping along together, discovering the perils of farm fields. Wet, emerald green cow pies presented themselves unexpectedly causing the need to swerve. Rushing through shallow, muddy wallows, their shoes were soon soaked through and their legs spattered with muck. Then there were the low, unseen, cut banks carved by a narrow creek that meandered through the field with more 'S' curves than a full-grown bull snake. Since they had chosen to run rather than walk, they either had to come to a skidding halt, or launch themselves out into space with reckless abandon.

When it was the latter, they would let go with a "Yippee!" or a "Yahoo!" before touching down on the other side, always bringing their feet together at the last second to create a satisfying thump. Then looking at each other and laughing at having survived, they'd take off again with the long-legged Lester still setting the pace; much to Charley's dismay.

Sheep droppings soon made an appearance, bringing another challenge to the duo's quest. Loosely constructed pyramids of dark green marbles lay scattered about in the now well shorn grass. Charley, catching the taller boy's attention, nodded toward a pile of poop and raised his eyebrows in question.

Lester grinned and said, "Yep, sheep crap! Good sign we're getting close. I 'spect just over that rise, there."

Still focused on the taller boy's face, Charley ran smack-dab into a patch of waist high thistles. Lester let go with a wicked laugh and just for the heck of it, he kicked a pile of sheep manure in passing. He didn't wait for Charley.

"Ooow! Dang it!" Charley hollered. "Ain't funny Lester! How would you like it?"

He bent to examine his thighs and shins to see what damage the thorns had done. Rubbing at them, he gave a heavy sigh and looked up to see that Lester wasn't paying him any mind—or even stopping for that matter. Charley whined out, "Will you stop?"

Lester came to a halt with a growling sigh. Turning around, he put his hands on his hips, rolled his eyes, and shook his head, saying, "Ah geez Charley, take all day, will you."

He started back toward his partner but came to a halt half way there. Why he had chosen to ask Charley to come along, escaped him. Then he remembered. There had been a sudden epidemic of tidiness among his usual gang. When he asked if they wanted to go do something fun, like chasing sheep, bedrooms suddenly needed cleaning, lawns needed to be mowed, and two friends even said they had to wash the car. He only hung out with Charley on a 'need to' basis, and the little bookworm had been the only one free this particular Saturday.

"So… remind me again why we're chasing sheep?" Charley said.

"Are you going to start complaining about that again? Heck, I told you already. Just because it's fun. My grandpa has sheep and I chase them all the time. Why do you think dogs like doing it? Ah dang… you'll see what I mean. Just keep your mouth shut til we get there, okay?"

"Hope you're right, hate to think we came all this way for nothing."

Lester shot him a look of irritation which soon changed to a smirk. Charley's usually well combed hair was now a bird's nest and his face was red and sweaty. Then there was that drop of snot hanging off the end of his nose.

Charley pulled out a shirt tail and wiped away the drop, exposing his pale, chubby belly. Lester rolled his eyes again, and looking up at the sky said, "Ah, geez."

Turning away, he took off at a jog, leaving Charley to his own devices. He'd had about enough of the wimpy behavior.

Charley trailed after him but was fast running out of breath. His side hurt and he ran bent forward at the waist. Wiping the back of a hand across his forehead, he looked back to the east. The sun was well up in the sky now, and the day was heating up fast.

"Gosh, already feels like a hundred out here," he mumbled as he plucked his shirt from his sweaty armpits.

A short time later he arrived where Lester had paused at the top of that rise. They both stood together now, just gazing down the long, grassy slope into the shady hollow.

"Took you long enough," Lester said without looking at the shorter boy.

"Didn't see any sense in running. Not like the sheep were going to pack up the field and go on vacation, you know."

"I told you, I wanted to do this before lunch and it's almost that, now. I've got other things I want to show you. Stuff that a city feller like you needs to see."

"I ain't no city boy! I been living in town for only a year. Besides, you don't live that far out of Clarksburg, yourself, mister hypocrite."

"Yeah, but my house is outside the line, so… I ain't no town kid. Besides, you probably forgot everything you learned when you was in the country. I just need to remind you of things. That way you don't get to be too much of a sissy."

"You know what, Lester? I think you're one of the meanest kids I know."

"Yeah, so? What's wrong with being mean? What's being nice ever get you, huh? You ever hear that saying, 'Nice guys finish last'? Well, it's a tough ol' world like my pa's always saying. You're going to learn that someday."

At that moment, a flock of sheep appeared, moving out past a long, white shed down at the bottom. The animals stuck close together as they chomped away at the overly grazed grass. Cutting his lecture short, Lester grinned and said, "Damn! There they are."

"Yep, those are sheep, alright," Charley said, happy for the chance to get back at Lester.

"Ahhh, blow it out your butt. I bet you actually thought they were goats, or something."

Lester gave Charley a menacing look even though he felt a tiny bit of admiration for him. The little guy was starting to show some spunk, and that was something he could appreciate.

Charley didn't give Lester's look much attention because a scary thought had wormed its way into his head. His elation at getting 'one up' on Lester dissolved away with worry.

"You know Lester, they look kind of big. Are you sure they won't bite?"

"Ah heck no! It's 'count of all that wool that they look so huge."

"But… will they bite? I mean, they have teeth, right?"

"Well, they might bite you because you're such a pain in the rump! We're kind of lucky today, though. I don't see a ram hanging around, anywhere."

"A ram?"

"Yeah, you know, a boy sheep?"

"You mean with the horns and all?"

"Yeah, a ram—with horns and all. So, you have to be careful, or they'll stick one right up your wahzoo! Naw, just kidding. They cut the horns off when they're young, but… they can still bite— YOU!" Lester said and chomped his teeth at Charley. Then making a fist, he startled the smaller boy by lightly punching him in the upper arm and giving him an angry sounding, "Baaah!"

Charley meant to punch him back, but Lester startled him with a loud, "Yahoo!" and took off down the slope at a dead run. Charley's fist found only air. Letting out a loud sigh, he too broke into a run, his shorter legs pumping, his knees rising high.

The sheep hesitated for the longest time as if they couldn't accept what was happening. Then upon receiving all of the clues necessary to indicate that they just might be in danger, they also ran, making tracks for the woods on the far side of the hollow.

When the boys reached the bottom of that long slope, they stumbled and fell because of the sudden change in gradient. Their momentum caused them to slide on their stomachs, ploughing through gopher mounds and fresh pyramids of manure.

When they came to a stop, they looked at each other with surprise and broke out laughing.

"Let's get 'em!" Lester sang out, and springing to his feet, he sped away, dirt and dung falling from his shirt and shorts.

"I'm coming," Charley crowed, and getting clumsily to his feet, he took off after the taller boy, and for once, he didn't give a thought to the filthy state of his clothing.

He stayed a short distance behind Lester on purpose, just watching to see how it was done. Lester closed the gap between him and his prey in no time. When he got close, the flock seemed to explode. The sheep scattered in all directions. Some even ran back toward Charley. He chose one that looked like it might be a first-year runt while Lester went after a plucky, old ewe.

After a minute or so, Lester hollered, "Hey, Charley, don't chase the same one for too long, it might have a heart attack. Switch off once in a while, huh?"

Then to demonstrate, he chose a different target and yipping like a coyote, chased the beast toward a small ravine that cut up through the trees. Charley stopped running and looked around for the least threatening member of the flock. Spying a large lamb, he did his own version of an urban coyote, and rushing toward it, the lamb sprinted away, bleating in terror for its ma.

This continued for nearly fifteen minutes, and the boys, even though panting like sheepdogs, were not ready to quit. Their wicked laughter mixed with the frightened exclamations of the sheep, and neither boy noticed the bank of storm clouds rolling in. It wasn't until they blocked out the sun, that Charley stopped and turned his face to the sky.

"Lester! Lester!" he called, but the taller boy didn't hear him. It wasn't until a bolt of lightning flashed, followed by a serious crack of thunder that Lester stopped to give the forth coming storm some attention.

The wind came all at once, and it was almost like it had jumped out of a hiding place. The leaves on the trees shivered, bringing their own noise into the unfolding chaos.

"Looks like a heck of a thunderstorm is coming, Lester! Suppose we should go?"

"I don't think there's time to get back to my place," Lester stuttered out as a snaking bolt of electricity struck a tree on the hill to the west. They both felt it through their feet, and it caused them to shirk away and gasp. A large branch crashed to the ground as sparks flew, and a small flame erupted where the lightning had found its mark.

"Oh crap! What are we going to do?" Charley cried out as Lester did a fast walk in his direction.

"Let's get inside that shed over yonder before we get struck by lightning—or worse."

"What could be worse?" Charley whimpered, as Lester passed him on his way to the sheep shed.

The taller boy didn't answer the question but stopped to look back at the flock of sheep, a look of disappointment on his face. Charley followed his gaze, and they watched all the animals bunch together and hightail it for the tree filled ravine. Then looking at Charley's fear contorted face, Lester said, "Come on, let's git."

"I want to go home. This ain't no place to be right now, Lester. We could get killed."

"Ahhh shut up and get inside," Lester said, sprinting away toward the sheep shed.

The lightning flashed again, and the thunder resonated loud enough to deafen them both. This set Charley's feet into some serious motion, his sneakers trying to find traction as he scrambled, the wind bullying him along. Halfway there, they could hear the heavy rain as it marched across the timber, pummeling everything in its path. Soon the dense wall of water was on them as they fled for a presumed safety.

The outbuilding had two large overhead doors on the side that faced them, one at each end with a row of small windows, about shoulder high, in-between. The door down on the right was closed. The one in front of them, stood wide open; an invitation to enter.

They almost made it. But within that few seconds just before they burst through the door, they found themselves soaked to the skin as the deluge engulfed the shed. The noise it made pounding on the metal roof left them to think Mother Nature hoped to frighten them back outside so she could finish them off.

The lightning flashed and danced among the roiling clouds. The thunder never seemed to stop as the ground vibrated beneath their feet; again, and again. It grew darker as the boys stood in the opening, shivering in their wet clothes. The wind made the building creak and groan, seeming to squirm in the grip of the gale.

Soon, another bolt of lightning struck, this time at the top of the hill where the cows had once stood. Its noise, like cannon fire, brought the boys out of their anxiety induced trance and Charley said, "What are we going to do, Lester? What are we going to do?"

"Ah, just calm down, will you? We're going to have to wait it out."

"What about tornados? Are we going to have a tornado? I heard…"

"I said, calm the heck down before I smack you. We ain't going to have no tornado. If we were—we'd hear it by now. They sound just like a damn freight train is coming, and I don't hear nothing like that."

"You ever been in a tornado, Lester? How would you know if you haven't been in one?"

"Ah, shut up, you! I've been in millions of them. This is just a stinking ol' thunderstorm. Geez Charley, you're such a chicken."

Charley said no more and stood rubbing his hands together as he stared out the door. He now felt truly offended. No boy wanted to be known as a chicken, and he was no exception.

Lester sniffed the air and turning to look past Charley toward the dark end of the room, he said, "Speaking of stinking, do you smell that? Smells just like an ol' raccoon, or something that got hit out on the highway, except—a hundred times worse."

Charley was thinking that maybe he should just ignore Lester from now on. But the thought was fleeting because it occurred to him that maybe now was not the best time. So, pushing his feelings aside, he said, "Yeah, I smell it. Makes me want to puke. What do you suppose is down there?"

"What you asking me for? Who knows, could be your sister," Lester said and snickered.

Charley decided that was the last straw.

"Hey! I don't make fun of your sister, for ummm… being fat." Then squinting his eyes at the taller boy, he balled his fists.

"Charley, dang you! Don't you go making fun of my little sister. I'll kick your butt right here and now, mister."

"Well… you started it," Charley said, and squaring off, he made himself ready for the taller boy's attack.

Lester looked down at his companion and then back out the door like Charley wasn't worth the trouble. Besides, if his pa got wind that he had been beating up on Charley, he'd get a beating of his own, and there would be blood. So, they just stood in silence, the wind whipping their hair and clothes.

The rain cascaded off the edge of the roof in torrents, making a loud splatting noise as it hit the ground. Then, just like someone had thrown a switch, it stopped. After ten minutes or so, the sky brightened in a narrow band beyond the trees, and the wind fell to just a breeze with the occasional gust. But the lightning still flashed, and the thunder rolled like the bass drum of their school's marching band.

"I think we can make a run for it now, before the next one comes," Lester said.

"The next one? There's going to be another one?"

"Could be… you never know. But I don't want to stand here all day waiting for it. Let's get the hell out of here."

Lester didn't wait for Charley to make up his mind and dashed out to disappear around the corner.

Charley said with a stuttering shout, "Hey! There's still lightning."

But his pal didn't hear him, and about a minute later Charley heard Lester bellow from a distance, "Come on, Charley, you nitwit. Git your butt out of there."

Moving to the back wall, Charley peaked through a knothole in the siding. He saw Lester skidding around as he made his way up the slope, sometimes falling, only to get back up and fall again. The lightning still lit the sky and Lester seemed to be running straight toward it.

Charley pulled his eyes away from the hole in the wall and said aloud to himself, "He left me. He dang well left me. That skunk. I hope he gets the crap shocked out of him, but…but doesn't get killed. That'll teach him."

He heard a noise down at the dark end and peering into the gloom, he watched a large field mouse squirm out through the crack at the bottom of the closed door. He shivered at the thought that there might be something bigger than just a mouse lurking in the blackness.

He turned his eyes to the open door and saw it was growing even lighter outside, but the rain had returned and was now just a steady pitter-patter on the roof. The lightning still flashed every few minutes or so, and the thunder hung out in the distance.

Charley's imagination got the better of him and he wondered if maybe the storm was waiting for him to come out like a bully he used to know. The creep would hide just out of sight around the corner until Charley started home, and when he got to the bully's hiding spot, the guy would pounce on him.

A realization hit him, and he scoffed at his own stupidity, saying, "Oh geez! How stupid am I? There's not going to be another one." Then, as if his partner-in-crime were still in the room, he added, "Lester Vailey, you are such a liar."

Turning his face back to peer into the dark, he muttered, "I'll show that so and so. I'm going down there and see what's making that stink. Then I'm going to tell everybody that I did, and that Lester ran away. So, we'll see who's chicken."

Charley started slowly toward the other end, always ready to bolt if necessary. The old concrete floor was littered with moldy straw and dried sheep droppings that crunched underfoot. There were several old wooden pallets scattered about and he nearly tripped over one.

The lightning flashed again, making flickering images of the windows on the back wall. Every time it did, he could make out a little more of what was waiting for him down in the murk.

He leaned forward as he walked, believing that made it easier to see. With one hand stretched out in front, he covered his mouth and nose with the other. Then he gagged as a wave of foul-smelling air washed over him, the stench of whatever it was, driven by a gust of wind through the gap at the bottom of the closed door.

"It's got to be somewhere around here," he whispered.

Inching past the last window, he could now make out what looked like a large pile of dirty cotton. It lay on the floor just a few feet from the end wall.

Lightning suddenly strobed across a skull, and a single, dark eye socket glared. He stopped with a gasp and pulled back.

The bile rose in his throat, so he knew the puke wasn't far behind. His breathing sped up, and goose flesh covered his arms and legs.

"I ain't afraid. I ain't afraid," he repeated over and over again between gulps, as he forced himself to move ever closer.

That's when he heard a low buzzing sound coming from somewhere. Looking around, he noticed what looked like a couple of wasps bouncing off a pane of glass at the window. That confused him because the sound in his ears was that of an entire squadron of flying things.

Trying to hold his breath as much as possible, without getting dizzy, he took his hand from his face. A weak flash of lightening came, this time without the thunder. But it was just enough for him to put the puzzle together. The pile of cotton was a dead sheep.

Taking a single step forward, his foot kicked something, and bending low, Charley saw it was a board that had broken loose from one of the pallets. Picking it up, he tossed it at the carcass, wishing seconds later that he hadn't. A large cloud of big, bloated flies lifted off and swarmed over him. He made a loud, "Guh!" as he spun and twisted, swatting at the air.

Flies crawled on him everywhere, in his ears, on his eyes, and some even got under his shirt. An "Ahhh!" came from his mouth as a large hairy one landed on his lip and tried to crawl inside. Slapping at his own face, he spit and sputtered as the bug took off for safer parts. He grabbed the front of his shirt and shook it, trying to help the ones inside find their way out. Then slapping at his arms and legs, the mob of vile vermin left him alone and went back to snack on something that wasn't trying to get away.

The sun, just visible above a scud of clouds, soon cast a dim light on the shed. Its illumination filtered in through the dirty glass, showing more of the festering mass that now lay before him.

Charley stood up straight and smoothed down his shirt. Then pushing his hair back out of his face, he mumbled, "I've had enough of this." But just as he started to turn away, he saw it move.

The horde of flies rose to hover above their disgusting buffet, confirming that it wasn't Charley's imagination.

"That's just not possible," he whispered, his attention on the rotten corpse. He watched closely, wanting to be sure he wasn't just seeing things. Then, it did it again, only lifting a bit higher this time like it was trying to sit up.

With his eyes feeling as if they'd grown as big as saucers, Charley felt a cold numbness take over his body and he froze. With his mouth hanging open, he watched in horror as the things neck swelled, shrank, and swelled again. Every time it did, the skull lifted off the floor and then made a sickening clack upon its return.

He was finally able to slide his left foot backwards a couple of inches—the first step in getting the heck out of there. But he realized he couldn't make himself leave. As scared as he was, he still found himself fascinated by what was happening. A dead thing was coming back to life right before his very eyes. Scenes from a movie he had watched a week before called, *The Night of the Living Dead*, ran through his mind, and there was now no doubt—the dead sheep was a zombie.

Charley stared in awe as the skull started to sway back and forth, the neck swelling and shrinking. He could now see the bottom side of the skull where strips of rotten flesh hung down, and swinging right along with them, something that looked like an eyeball at the end of a short string. Then, with the loudest clack ever, the skull hit the floor. The neck started to expand again, and this time, it didn't stop.

It ballooned up to the size of a watermelon. Charley thought now would be a good time to run. But the boy's life was cursed with delayed reaction. Within that stagnate couple of seconds, the ripping of rotten skin filled his ears and the neck exploded, spewing putrid flesh all over him.

His bloodcurdling scream rang to the rafters. It spilled out of every crack in the shed's walls and open door. Terrified sparrows, pigeons, and swallows, who made the shed their home, all tried to leave at once, bumping into each other as they flocked and fluttered out that opening. Charley's lengthy shriek had been so loud, it even perked the ears of the sheep in the ravine across the hollow.

Wiping at his face like a mad man, Charley flung putrid chunks of sheep flesh onto the floor and the walls. A few even made it to the rafters, where they stuck for a few seconds before falling back to land on his head.

From the carcass came a loud gurgling hiss, and then a high-pitched kind of growl. Having cleared the stinking mess from his eyes, Charley stood stock still, staring with a look of terror, mixed with fascination.

A smaller head was emerging from the dead sheep's neck. Its eyes popped opened and glared angrily at Charley. They were demon's eyes, turning from green to red, and back again as the head whipped from side to side. Its fang filled mouth snapped at him between burbling growls. Its dagger like teeth gleamed as bits of decaying mutton sprayed out.

Another scream, louder than the first, tore from Charley's throat. This was followed by retching, and then he did barf. His breakfast cereal shot forth, creating a kaleidoscope of color over the filthy straw. His cut-off jeans darkened at the crotch, his bladder deciding it too wanted in on the action.

Gathering what was left of his wits, Charley spun and rocketed toward the open door. He nearly made it, but miscalculating his turn, he bounced off the door jamb and spun like a top out into the light.

The flock of sheep, now moving out from the ravine, were witness to the boy gyrating from the doorway of the building to fall flat on his face in the wet grass. Every wooly head came to attention at the sound of the boy's crazed blubbering. Getting to his feet, the kid moved around the shed in a lurching run, bleating in terror for his ma.

Ten pairs of unsympathetic eyes watched him slip and slide his way up the hill in the wet, manure covered pasture. After the boy's silhouette disappeared over the top, they turned their attention back to grazing and whatever else could be considered the business of farm animals.

***

The hollow grew quiet as the last of the clouds followed the frightened boy, northeast, toward the highway. The sun now cast its warmth on the placid scene as the flock continued with their forage. A short time later, motion was detected near the shed and a few fluffy noggins rose to cast a curious eye in that direction. They were soon privy to a spaniel sized opossum waddling from the open door, its once white fur now matted with the putrid slime of one of their dead. It stopped just long enough to look around. Then giving itself a couple good shakes, it made its way into the cool shadow of the nearby woods.

#7

The Little Red Motorcycle

The paint was faded, and the chrome was speckled with rust. The rubber had grown brittle, and the engine was clad in a filthy coat of oil. A small, round badge floated in a sea of metallic red on a bulbous fuel tank. DUCATI was written in faded green and white letters across eagle's wings, the once bright feathers dulled by age. Cos had no idea what Ducati meant, but he figured it was probably something Italian because of the way it rolled off his tongue. That didn't matter, though, because it was one of the most beautiful things he'd seen in a long time. That's the way love works when you're a fourteen-year-old boy.

His ma had surprised him by suddenly jumping up from the sofa, kind of like she had stumbled upon a thought that she had lost earlier. Taking his hand, she towed him out the back door and down the rickety stairs to the loading dock of Ralph's TV & Stereo. He followed her as she moved to the gravel lane that came up from the alley. Passing the sign that read, 'Deliveries Only! No Parking!' they stopped next to a patch of horseweed and she pointed it out to him. He wondered why he had not seen it there before. It must have just arrived; Ralph was always bringing junk back to his shop. Probably in trade for a secondhand television.

"Would you like to have that? I saw it there when I was out hanging laundry."

Cos didn't answer right away. He thought she was joking. Was she going to steal it? They had no money for this kind of thing. She had even said so many times before. Now staring at him for what seemed like forever, he finally decided she wasn't kidding. He gave her a simple, "Sure, ma."

"Then I'll buy it for you, okay?"

Now that was a question. Cos didn't like questions. Mostly because he never seemed to give the right answer. The rules changed constantly with her ever since his da had run off. It drove him somewhat mad. The look on his ma's face said she wasn't going to settle for a 'Sure, ma.' So, forcing a smile, but also trying to hide his crooked teeth, he looked down at the gravel and said, "Yes, ma... thanks." He had whispered it just loud enough for her to hear.

He didn't want his ma to know that he was having mixed feelings. There was excitement, yes. But he was also afraid. Afraid it was going to be just another broken promise. This was how she tried to bring him joy. It usually happened when she realized that she had been neglecting him (as their social worker had said), then she would try to give him things.

A moment would come in the middle of her telephone gossiping sessions or some commercial for laundry detergent while she lay on the couch watching her soap operas. She would suddenly look at him like she realized she had forgotten something.

That always made him squirm. It meant change. She was going to mess up his day. Probably get in the way of his plans to go down to the river or to the village park to meet the guys. Always something to steal his freedom. It normally took a couple days for things to get back to normal. But lately, he noticed that somethings weren't going back to the way they use to be. He wondered if that's what growing-up was really about.

Cos figured a motorcycle was serious business. She wasn't giving him a plastic model to put together, a goldfish, a hamster, a puppy, or a kitten—nope, a real motorcycle. This just might be worth his time. He was going to hide his excitement and fight the feeling to shout and throw his arms around her. He knew if he held back, she might actually follow through with her plan. If she figured out that she had made him happy long before making good on her promise, she might believe she had accomplished her goal. Then she'd forget the whole thing and spend the next month coming up with excuses as to why. So, he had to stay cool. He needed to resist.

Ignoring her, he drifted away to a place in his mind where he was already riding the little, red motorcycle. In his daydream, he saw himself buzzing across a green meadow, the wind blowing through his long, brown hair. The whine of the engine was in his ears, and the sun's light danced across polished chrome. In that picture, he saw himself smiling—and his teeth—were perfect.

Minutes went by without any words between them. She grew impatient. Then she just turned and walked away toward the back of Ralph's TV shop, tugging down the hem of a dress two sizes too small. Upon reaching the steps, she shook her head and muttered, "Kids, don't appreciate nothing, these days."

That snapped him out of his daydream, and he thought to say something to let her know he did appreciate it. But that was her last-ditch effort to make him confess that her plan had made him happy.

No! Stick to your guns!

So, he stood and watched her walk up and mount the loading dock. Then wading through a sea of derelict TV's that were scattered about the deck, she went inside.

He squinted, trying to force his eyes to see her as she moved around inside the shop. He could just make out the little pink flowers on that tight, blue dress. He followed her shape as she made her way into the showroom at the front. The sunlight, reflecting off the white paint of the furniture store across the street, cast her into shadow. Only the top half of her body was visible above the waist high wall that separated the sales floor from the repair area. The sound of her voice floated out to him, but the words, when they arrived, were never formed enough for him to know what she was saying.

Someone popped up to stand in front of her, their silhouette showing well coiffured hair, and a bushy mustache. It was Ralph, himself.

She now yakked away, nodding her head and talking with her hands. Then Ralph did the same, looking like one of those bobble-headed dolls. Cos thought he saw a smile come across Ralph's face, his white teeth gleaming in the light. But Cos wasn't certain, maybe that's only what he wanted to see.

His ma stuck her hand out toward the TV man, something flapping in her fingers. The money. It had to be the money. But Ralph shook his head from side to side and the smile disappeared. No. He was saying, no. So, she shook it at him like that would help.

Then her hands went to her hips and her voice got loud. She looked out the door at Cos and pointed. The conversation stopped and her head tilted in a way that he knew all too well; she was begging. He almost walked away because that was something he didn't want to see. It was not something he wanted her to do for him, not for something that he didn't need.

Then it happened. Just as the sun peeked above the top of the TV shop to bathe him in its light, Ralph's head stopped shaking no, and switched to yes. The money hand came up again, and this time, it was taken. Now, the two silhouettes moved toward the back door and Cos cast his eyes to the gravel, pretending not to notice. They were coming, and there would be questions.

The June sun now shone hot on his head, so he moved to stand in the shadow of a nearby telephone pole. Turning his back to them, he kicked at a small stick that had worked its way out onto the drive.

"Cos! What's happening!"

That was okay, not really a question. That's how you said hi in 1971. Ralph's voice was deep and loud. Cos waited to feel the concussive wave as if a cannon had been fired; but it never came. He knew that was his imagination. It was just, something as deafening as Ralph's voice should have ruffled your hair. Like that documentary about the government dropping that atom bomb on that island. Everything for miles around just fell over.

He turned to look at the village's only TV man. Cos thought about the, "What's happening?" greeting and debated with himself on how he should answer. Should he be a smart ass, or just answer politely. Feeling it might be a good idea to be nice, he decided it was worth a couple words.

"Not much."

"So, you are now the proud owner of a motorcycle, huh?"

Closing one eye, Cos focused on his ma. She was now standing behind Ralph and to the right, her face beaming as if she was about to shout, 'BINGO!'

Ralph was smiling widely, too, kind of like they were doing him the biggest favor in the world.

"I don't know, am I, ma?" slipped out of his mouth.

"You sure are. Fifty bucks now, and fifty more next month when my check shows up."

Ralph had to get in his two cents worth and said, "And even though it's not all paid for, yet… I'm gonna let you take it today."

He turned and grinned at Cos's ma, nodding his head. Then turning back, he looked at Cos, his head still moving like some kind of a weird puppet. Cos just stood and looked back and forth between the two. It made him even more uncomfortable, but he was able to mumble a, "Thanks," and went back to pushing the stick around with his toe.

A little green inchworm was crawling across the gravel, moving like it was trying to get to the other side of the drive before getting smashed. Bending down, Cos picked it up and gently put it on a nearby weed. It stood up on its back six legs, the front two thirds of its body waving about like it was trying to sort out the sudden change of scenery. Cos felt he knew just what the worm was feeling. He too had been put in places that left him confused. That's when those familiar words rolled into his head, "You'll be a whole lot better off where you're at, little guy." He wished he could remember who said that.

Suddenly Ralph's voice was in his ears again, "It's a 1958 Ducati TS98. It was my very first cycle. Boy, I sure loved that bike."

Loved that bike? So, not anymore? He had used it for all it's worth and then just dumped it and walked away. That's something rich people do. Just use it, abuse it, and throw it away. Then you could just go out and buy another one. Cos decided he didn't like rich people very much. He faked a smile at Ralph because his ma would have wanted him to, and he wondered if the TV man could tell it was phony.

"That bikes a classic, now. So, take good care of it," he said, and Cos could hear the dismay in the TV man's voice.

Ah! So maybe there was still a little love left for the old machine. Cos felt maybe he had been too quick to judge the guy. There was a good chance that Ralph had spent a lot of time with that bike and had grown quite attached to it. Pretty much in the same way Cos had become attached to some of his own playthings as a boy. He was going to have to give it some more thought. Just—not right now.

"Well, I guess… that's that, huh, Mae?" Ralph said to his ma and they turned together to walk back up the drive toward the shop. His ma couldn't stop thanking Ralph as he stuffed the crumpled bills into his properly creased, dress slacks. Have to look good if you're going to sell TV's. Cos looked down at his Levi's. He would never give up his blue denim for slick polyester. They weren't worth the thread that held them together, and they surely wouldn't last a day on his backside.

Figuring it was okay to do so, he walked over and pulled the Ducati from the weeds. Wheeling it over to his back yard on flat tires, he heard Ralph holler, "You have fun with that, now."

Great, another person telling him how to take care of his stuff. Then his ma hollered out, "Thanks again, Ralph, you're an angel." It almost sounded like she was hoping for a date, even though she was twice Ralph's age. Cos just figured that maybe she was starting to get lonely now that his da had run off. She sure talked about it a lot. Sometimes just rambling on and on about men that she knew in Clarksburg. Men, he knew, who wouldn't give her the time of day.

He stood with his new treasure leaning against his leg, just like a faithful dog that had found its master. He watched his ma work her way up the dilapidated stairs that led to their rear balcony, her hand constantly searching for the railing.

"You're ever so welcome, Mae," Ralph called back. Cos decided he wanted to get in the last word.

"Thanks, ma," he shouted. But she just raised a hand as if to dismiss him, and squeezing in through the half-open screen door, she disappeared inside.

Rolling the little bike out of sight to the other side of their unpainted garden shed, he propped it up on its own kickstand so it wouldn't have to lean on anything. Now it could look a little more dignified, not hiding in a patch of weeds like it was ashamed.

He sat down in the grass a few feet away, and pulling up his knees, he wrapped his arms around his legs and studied it.

Cos was suddenly overcome with emotion and unexpected tears spotted his boots. He lowered his face so no one would see, and he began to rock back and forth, trying to keep from making any noise. The feeling went away after a few minutes, and wiping his eyes with a sleeve, he looked about to see if anyone was watching. He didn't know why he cried. Maybe because this kind of thing just didn't happen to him, or because they were poor, and forking over fifty bucks for anything other than food or rent could bring trouble.

Memories filled his head of the landlord, or grocer, standing on the front stoop waving a piece of paper around and demanding money. His ma would be stammering and stuttering, promising she'd pay as soon as her check came. Cos decided he was going to make it up to her. He was going to make her proud. He would fix up the motorcycle and turn it into a dream machine. A classic, Ralph had said. Well, it would be again. He would show them.

Images of the finished cycle pushed those bad memories out of his mind. Within the realm of his imagination, the bike had a fresh coat of candy apple red paint, shiny chrome, and five coats of wax. With its engine purring, he would roll up in front of Eddie's house and make him jealous. Eddie was the only friend Cos had who owned anything like a motorcycle. It was a Cushman scooter, nothing like his Ducati. But it still had two wheels and a motor. That was enough. Cos felt like he might be getting too big for his britches as his ma always said.

Eddie's dad was the local motorcycle mechanic and if Cos started to give Eddie the impression his bike was 'one up' on the Cushman, all Eddie had to do was talk his dad into letting him have the old guy's Triumph Scrambler, or that BSA Bantam. Eddie would then blow him out of the water and make him look like a fool. Cos felt he needed to be cool about his new prize around Eddie, otherwise he might be riding alone in the future. He imagined Eddie's face when he told him that he now had a cycle. Eddie would want to ride it and would stop being so stubborn about letting Cos ride anyone of the motorcycles in the Beltzer's stable.

The screen door at the back of the TV shop suddenly slammed, and loud voices pushed away the daydreams. Cos poked his head around the corner and saw Ralph and his repairman, Frank. They were sitting on the back steps smoking cigarettes. Cos pulled back so they wouldn't see him. He was going to listen-in on their stupid gossip. Sliding his butt over, he moved his back tight up against the rough boards of the shed and cocked an ear.

"So, you sold em that hunk of junk for a hundred bucks?"

"Wasn't junk, you prick!"

"Sure it was."

"Hey, that was my first bike, and it ran really good the last time I started it."

"You better hope it still does, or you're gonna have that crazy woman back over here with a butcher knife in her hand."

"Aw geez, Frank, go back to work. Got to get that set done for Schneider, today."

He heard the door slam again and peeking back, he saw Ralph was alone, the smoke from his cigarette slowly drifting upwards. The guy seemed to be in a trance, just staring down the drive. He seemed to be worried about something, and Cos imagined that he was making a plan just in case Mae actually did come after him with a knife. Cos imagined his ma chasing Ralph through the streets of Clarksburg, Ralph screaming like a little girl. They were jumping over stuff and running in and out of the stores. A giggle slipped out of Cos's lips and he slapped a hand over his mouth before peeking around the corner to see if Ralph had heard.

Seeing that he hadn't, he pulled back. Then came an ugly, intruding thought. Maybe they were all thinking he wouldn't be able to do anything with the Ducati. Just maybe… they were thinking that when he tried to start it and couldn't get it to run, he would just give up. That's what his da would have thought. But he knew his da wasn't a very nice guy, that's why he had to disappear in the middle of the night while they were sleeping. Uncle Delbert had to be the one to stop by the house and tell his ma that his da had met another woman on his milk route and wasn't coming back. His ma had started crying really loud and then started wailing when Cos had walked in the door after coming home from school. He had wondered where Aunt Louise was at the time. She was her sister after all. Cos later learned that his aunt was so broken up by it that she couldn't face Mae. Then his ma went to the nuthouse. They were still living in Rat House, back then, and Cos was soon to go and live on uncle Delbert's farm.

His da was never coming back. He didn't know how to feel about that. There would be no more beatings and that was good, but also—no more money. No food, no rent, or the fuel oil that kept the huge furnace that sat at the back wall of the dining room of their home, now, growling in the cold of winter. He'd worried more than he ever had before.

When his ma came back and they moved into the apartment, she knew that he was fretting and told him to stop. It wasn't a kid's place to worry about such things. There would be something called government assistance, and they could get food stamps. So, she told him to be thankful to the good ol' US of A, and some guy named FDR who was the president who had started the assistance program way back before Cos was even born.

"We're getting by, lad," she said, "No thanks to yer da."

So, Cos sat leaning against the shed making plans. The next time his ma and Ralph saw this bike, they wouldn't be able to recognize it. Getting to his feet, he moved the Ducati inside the little shed. He felt it would be best if it stayed out of sight. He didn't want anyone to know what he had done to it until he was ready to roll it out. When that day came, he was going to let it just stand outside in the sun for a little bit, the new paint gleaming, the chrome sparkling.

What if someone tried to steal it?

One time, someone stole Eddie's Cushman and left it on the railroad tracks. Luckily, it was found before the Chicago Northwestern, running a load of coal down to Cedar Rapids, ran it over. Wick Ryan, a kid who lived over by the lumber yard, had found it. He and his girlfriend, Zillia Struck, had dragged it off the tracks and then ran up and told Eddie. They now get free rides anytime Eddie's out riding around Wick's house.

It dawned on Cos that he would have to find a padlock. He needed to make sure it was one that was too big to get cut off. He'd have to find some money and go buy it from Hale's Hardware. Ol' man Hale knew everything there was to know about hardware, and he could help Cos pick the best one.

The next problem for him to solve was that he didn't have many tools of his own, just a couple of screwdrivers, a hammer, and an adjustable wrench that was practically worthless. So, he would have to go down to the lawnmower shop on the corner and convince Ernie B, the gimpy, old mechanic who owned the place, to loan him some good tools. He knew Ernie would do it. Cos swept his shop on Saturdays and shoveled the snow in the winter. No one else would do it for the old guy and Cos did a good job; Ernie even said so.

There was no electricity to the garden shed, which meant, no light. And to make it worse, it didn't have any windows. He would have to work in the sunlight that streamed through the open door. On rainy days he would have to either work by the light of the noisy Coleman lantern that they had from way back in their camping days or go over and hangout at Nordon's Drug store and fret.

They had a soda fountain, and he would have to spend the few bucks Ol' Ernie gave him after sweeping up, and only after Cos promised he wasn't going to buy marihuana. Cos really didn't know what that was, but figured it probably wasn't as good as a milkshake.

The next morning was the fourth of June, school was out so Cos had plenty of time on his hands. He set about putting his plan in motion and just as he expected, Ernie loaned him some of his older tools, reminding Cos to show up the next day to sweep and straighten things up. Cos promised and putting all the tools in an old metal bucket, he carried them back to the shed. He had found a small padlock in the junk drawer in their kitchen, but it wasn't big enough. Someone could just hit it with a hammer and that would be the end of it. But it would have to do for now, least until he could afford to buy a bigger one.

Sitting on the concrete floor of the little out building, he studied the bike perched over in the corner. He had spent a great deal of time with Eddie working on old junk bikes and helping Eddie's da, Arnold, in his shop. Cos knew just about everything that he needed to know when it came to small motorcycles. They were pretty simple machines. The bigger ones were a whole different story. They were complicated. He certainly wasn't ready to overhaul an engine or rewire an entire bike. So, he felt he might need to go up some day and watch it done. Arnold might let him help if he was in a good mood, or, half drunk. Then him and Eddie could jump in and help with any of the hard parts. Those were the days that he and Eddie relished, the hard part: having to hang around outside the open overhead door, waiting to be called. Arnold said that he thought that Cos might have a photographic memory because he was pretty slick when it came to tearing stuff apart and putting it back together. It made Cos feel pretty good, least on that day. He just wished the old guy didn't drink so much.

Cos felt a need to be precise about taking the Ducati apart. He felt a need for order. So, he fought the urge to just start unscrewing nuts and bolts and then carelessly tossing things every which direction. The first thing he did was take off the seat and then the gas tank. This was followed by pulling the engine, which he placed in a corner on some cardboard. He would save it for last. He would have to adjust the carburetor too, but that wasn't a problem, it was one of the first things he had ever learned to do.

There was considerable scraping and sanding. Stealing a can of degreaser from his ma, he used so much of it, he had to go outside a couple of times just to clear his head. Then there was the oiling of the old cables, the chain, axles, and any other thing that swung or rotated. Eddie found him two old tires in Arnold's junk heap of old motorcycle parts. He told Cos they had come off a bike of the same size as the Ducati and had been tossed out to be replaced by new ones.

Then Eddie showed up one day with some new inner tubes that he had swiped from his da's shop. He confessed that he was mad at his da and if Cos didn't want them, he'd understand. Cos was happy to take them, but then worried for days that Eddie's dad would show up and take them back. He ended up giving Eddie a stack of his old Cycletoons comic books for his trouble and then demanded that Eddie promise to never tell his da where the tubes had disappeared to.

By Friday night, Cos had the Ducati completely dismantled, cleaned up, and ready for paint. When Saturday morning came around, he fulfilled his promise to Ernie B and cleaned up the shop, going as far as to even organize the greasy shop manuals in the rack on a wall in the tiny front office. Then he spent the rest of the day collecting pop bottles. He showed up at the hardware store an hour before closing, and sadly found that cans of spray paint were too expensive. He only had enough for two cans of candy apple red. He could only hope that would be enough.

Then he remembered the paint booth out behind Slade's body shop. They used it for small parts on cars and sometimes they left half full cans of spray paint behind sitting on the metal table just inside the doorless opening. It was stealing of course, but they wouldn't miss it. Slade's was closed on Saturday, but those guys were scary, and Cos knew they hung out inside the Blue Front tavern on the corner. The booth, even though at the back, could still be seen from the tavern windows. If they caught him, they might hang him by his feet from the engine lift just like they did his classmate, Jimmy Soor.

All he really needed was red and black because everything else was chrome or rubber. Those things didn't need paint, just wax and maybe a good buffing. He already had the red. So, slipping in through the horseweeds, between Slade's and Whitcomb's insurance office just after sundown, he went around the back and peeked into the booth.

There were rows of used spray cans in there. Moving inside, he sorted through them until he found several labeled Gloss Black. Tucking his shirt into his pants at the front, he pulled out his collar and dropped them inside, one at a time. Gleeful with his find, he forgot to be careful and ran out on the street side, instead of the way he had come. He could not have timed it worse. The tavern door opened and out came Slade himself followed by the Silber brothers. They were the meanest men in Clarksburg, and Cos avoided them at all costs. His heart started to thump in his chest and looking around he realized he had no choice but to duck back inside.

He was so afraid he found it hard to breathe, and he couldn't swallow because his throat was so dry. Hoping they wouldn't come his way; he got ready to run for it. He heard two cars start up and head east on Main Street. When he couldn't hear the engines anymore, he ran back to the alley and followed it all the way home. Dumping the cans out onto the floor of the shed, he sat inside, gulping for air, and vowing he would never do that again.

The motorcycles seat was really going to be a problem. The seams were splitting, and the foam was coming out. Cos decided he would have to tell his ma what he had been up to so he could get her to sew the leather where it had separated. They didn't have a machine, but she went to work and did it

71

all by hand. With carpet thread and needles, she had it done in three days' time. She even went as far as to put some shoe blacking on it. When she brought it back to him, he was shocked because it looked like new. He was so overjoyed that he kissed and hugged her. She didn't know how to react to that, so she just smiled her crooked tooth smile and said, "Just trying to do my part, lad," and then walked away, beaming.

When he finally got around to the engine, he realized the challenge that lay before him. It would require a lot of time, more than he had anticipated. Luckily for him everything rotated like it was supposed to. The crankshaft was not yet bound by rust and the piston's compression was still good. So, the rings were still intact. He cleaned it up with a crappy wire brush and some stainless-steel pan scrubbers he found in the trashcans behind the Davis Café.

Ernie gave him a new can of motor oil to fill the crankcase with, as well as a sparkplug in trade for an old garden tractor transmission that Eddie had given Cos as a peace offering. They'd had a fist fight over Eddie making fun of Cos's love interest, Denise Donnely. Eddie had won. The guilt must have been too much for him and Eddie had come begging clemency. The transmission was really a piece of junk, but for some reason, Ernie practically slobbered over it.

With the Ducati's engine gleaming, Cos had to carefully put it back into the frame. This required great care to keep it from scratching the paint and after several tries, he finally got it to seat in its cradle. It was an awkward job and exhausted him so much, he had to quit for the day and go fishing.

The next morning, he was up early securing the motor in place with new bolts and nuts that he'd bought at Hale's. They were mere pennies apiece, so Cos got two of everything. He even used new lock washers with the flat ones to show any professional mechanic, who might inspect his bike, that he was serious about his work.

The motor's side casing caught the rays of the suns light shooting in through the cracks in the siding. The metal flake paint sparkled, and the leather seat gave off a soft glow. Cos started to feel a strange excitement. The big day was coming, and he could hardly wait.

As he stood in the door assessing his progress with the Ducati, he felt the sun on his back. He got a profound thought that the sun was like a person, always pushing its way in. "Poking its nose in," as his ma would say. But it always made him happy. Almost like it was a friend that wanted to cheer him up.

He would often find it peeking through the curtain into his room or sneaking around the corner of the apartment as he sat in the dirt, harassing the local ant population. He recalled one cold, cloudy day when he had been walking along the river. The sun had suddenly broken through the clouds and sneaking up behind him, it felt like it had given him a warm hug.

Now turning to meet it, he tilted his head back and closed his eyes. The warmth played over his face and he vowed to himself that he would dearly love the sun for the rest of his days.

By the end of July, the Ducati was ready to go. His ma had followed through on her promise and had paid the final fifty-dollar payment to Ralph. The motorcycle was truly his now, no question. He had worked just about every day from sunrise to sunset. From the first of June through the twenty fifth of July, Cos only allowed himself time away for sleep, the 'pop bottle day' and the Fourth of July (to run with his friends and go fishing).

His buddy Harry had found where the city workers had hidden the fireworks and had filched some of them. Harry then gathered the gang together to spend a portion of the early evening setting them off in their hidden spot behind Slade's. When the sheriff's deputy showed up, they scattered, leaving the officer not knowing who to chase, so he chose Harry. It was a bad choice; Harry was the fastest of all Cos's friends. Having to remain out of sight until dark, they ended up watching the main fireworks show from a large hayfield just to the north of the county fairgrounds.

On the morning of the twenty sixth, Cos was up early trying to convince his new found love to start. He had scrounged up thirty-five cents for a gallon of gas and was soon dashing up Fourth Street to the Standard Station on the town square. They almost didn't let him have it. He didn't have the proper gas can, just a gallon milk jug he had found under the kitchen sink.

Old Earl quit fighting him when Bill Johnson, the owner, told Cos that he and Earl needed to go out back for a minute and that Cos could just leave the coins next to the cash register and go pump it himself. Then he was to leave as soon as he was done. Bill said that would give him and Earl plausible deniability. Cos had no clue what that was, but if ol' Bill could use it, more power to him. Least Cos wouldn't be stealing. Returning home he filled the tank, and hardly spilled a drop. He wasn't sure what everybody was so worried about.

The moment of truth had arrived. It took almost an hour of kicking, tinkering, and adjusting carburetor jets to get the Ducati to pop just once. When she did, he flopped down on the concrete floor, exhausted. Rivers of sweat bathed his face and his shirt was completely soaked through. The large black cloud of exhaust that the machine had kicked out, rolled through the door and then skyward as if it couldn't wait to get out of that shed. Cos rested for all of ten minutes and then tried again. This time it roared to life after just two kicks. The little 100cc engine was loud inside the shed and when the muffler rattled off and clattered to the floor, it became deafening. That was the only bolt he had forgotten to tighten.

Grabbing the chromed steel with his bare hands, he quickly dropped it. Stupid! Mufflers are hot! "Shit!" he hollered, examining his palms. Luckily for him, it had not run long enough to give him second- or third-degree burns. Grabbing a rag, he was able to work the muffler back on the pipe and screw down the clamp.

Rolling the Ducati outside, he stood beside it, revving it up, the engine noise rising and falling. He looked around to see if anyone was watching. About that time, Ralph shot up the delivery drive on a brand-new Rickman Matisse motocrosser—all aluminum and plastic. It had a powerful, air cooled 'two stroke' engine that was painted flat black. The beast had a tuned expansion chamber that could rattle the windows for blocks.

Catching sight of Cos standing there with the little red motorcycle, Ralph gave him a surprised look and then promptly ran into the dock stairs. He fell over, the engine sputtered to a stop, and the large knobby tire on the rear, stopped kicking up a spray of rocks and dirt. Ralph drug himself out from underneath the Rickman, cussing up a storm. Standing it upright and setting the kick stand, he examined all the scratches on the fiberglass fuel tank. The 'F' word issued forth a dozen times like machine gunfire. Ralph stomped his foot several times before he brought himself under control. He then turned and walked toward Cos.

"What the hell! Is that the Ducati?" he asked, scratching his head through his wild mop of hair.

"Uh huh," Cos said sheepishly.

Ralph walked around the little machine still scratching his head. "Well, I'll be damned. Are you sure?" Cos thought it was a stupid question and said nothing. Stopping beside the Ducati, Ralph ran a finger along the tank and then the rear fender. Cos turned off the key, silencing the engine and just stood, squinting up at the TV man. He found himself growing ever fearful that the intruder would somehow find a way to take away his little treasure. Ralph circled the little bike a second time, and Cos moved with him.

Finally, Ralph turned and walked back toward the TV shop, shaking his head, and repeating over and over again, "Unbelievable." When he reached the bottom of the dock steps, he called out, "Frank!" and entering the screen door, he met the repairman just inside. There was a brief discussion and Frank came out onto the dock, clicking a wire stripper in his hand just for effect. Looking hard at Cos and the Ducati, he howled, "I'll be damned! Good job, kid!"

He just stood there smiling a kind of wicked grin. That troubled Cos and he grabbed the handlebars to push the motorcycle back inside the shed. Slamming the door, he sat down with his back to the panel to keep it closed. Nobody was coming in if he could help it.

Grabbing a three-foot long 2x4 from the floor, he held it like a club. Every so often he would peek out through a crack in the wall to see if anyone was outside. Frank had gone back inside and there was no more activity on the dock for the rest of the day. Cos remained in the shed until dark, just thinking and looking at the Ducati. He had not anticipated that he would feel this way. He actually owned something that someone else might want. Now there was fear of loss. He had imagined at first that it would be wonderful to make the other kids jealous, but he was not prepared to deal with what might follow.

Slipping out of the shed, Cos locked the old, rusty padlock and taking the key from its hiding place above the door, he shoved it into his pocket. Tiptoeing into the apartment past his snoring ma, he made his way into his room and threw himself onto his bed. He lay there, staring up at the water-stained ceiling, worrying about everything he possibly could. Shortly after midnight, he fell into a half sleep, remaining somewhat aware in case a thief tried to pry off the hasp and make off with his prize.

Cos slept for maybe three hours and then exploded awake from a bad dream about rats. Looking about wildly, he realized that he was safely in his bed in the apartment and no longer at rat house. The danger was in the past. He lay for a couple more hours, planning his day. When the room started to lighten with the sun at the horizon, he crept to the backdoor. His mother was still in her bed, unfortunately, it sat just a few inches from his exit.

Her snoring suddenly halted and it gave him a start. It was when she started talking in her sleep about why carrots had to be so expensive at the Royal Blue, followed by something about stray cats getting into the refrigerator and eating all of the baloney, that he relaxed. He had to fight the urge to snicker and decided that it was too bad she couldn't be this hilarious when she was awake. Cos didn't blame her though; she had actually been a funny person before her husband had abandoned her. She rarely smiled anymore.

He peered out of the dirty window in the door and could see that the padlock was still intact. Returning to his room, he got dressed, and after pulling on his boots, he quietly departed by the front—less chance of awakening his ma.

Arriving at the shed, he unlocked it and stood leaning in the open door just ogling his bike, finding it hard to believe that what sat before him was all his. The sun was just topping the trees in the east, bathing him, and the little red motorcycle in its rays. There was a feeling of magic in the air.

Cos rolled the Ducati out into the yard. With one last look back at the apartment, he ran, pushing the motorcycle through the ground mist that blanketed the wet grass. Finally breaking out of the alley onto the street, he coasted to the south edge of town and didn't stop until he reached the railroad bridge. He would have to push it across the trestle, but if he ran fast enough, the wheels would glide over the gaps between the ties. Arriving on the other side of the river, exhausted, he stopped to rest just past the Ryan's house.

After dragging the bike sideways over the rails to clear the trestle, he climbed aboard the Ducati and just sat in the tall grass, catching his breath. His destination was the Sandpits, Clarksburg's proclaimed recreational area. It was where they used to dig sand for the concrete so desired by the 'movers and shakers' who visualized a simple village's growth into something more prosperous.

After many years of digging, they called it quits and moved their operation, leaving behind some quarry deep pits. The holes gradually filled with water and became some of the best fishing holes in the county after the conservation department started stocking them with farm grown fish of all kinds. There was a spider web of paths that covered the area, making for some serious trail riding.

Walking the bike to the mud road that ran through the lumberyard, Cos stopped and stared south toward the Fairgrounds where he knew he would find the entrance to The Pits. Climbing aboard, he propelled the Ducati forward with just his feet until he was at least a good ten yards from the city street. Now, safely outside the city limits, he was legal to ride without a license. He opened the valve to the gas tank, set the choke, and flipping out the kick starter, he gave it a quick push with his foot. The Ducati roared to life and Cos whispered a thank you to the motorcycle god. Pulling in the clutch, he clicked her into first gear, and letting the lever out ever so slowly, he buzzed away into a new found freedom.

***

That's the way it went for the next two years, and he did everything he had hoped to do. He even rode around the town a few times in broad daylight, knowing the deputy sheriff rarely made an appearance before seven o'clock at night. One evening, Cos pushed his luck a wee bit too far. Deputy Jonny Herman had cruised into Clarksburg a little early and had caught him. Cos was let off with a stern warning and forced to walk the Ducati home, however, he got the feeling that the deputy knew what it was like to be a boy with his first motorcycle. The officer's concern seemed to be 'all for show' Cos would be able to get his license sometime the next year and then he'd be perfectly legal, or as his ma put it, "To go out and get himself killed."

He and Eddie rode together a great deal, mostly on the country roads. Cos had to learn to negotiate loose gravel and was soon keen to detect the second before his tires were going to break loose and send him into the ditch. A quick acceleration or shift of gears corrected the problem and allowed him to continue in the preferred direction.

Sometimes he and Eddie cruised the gravel to Coogan, the small town north of Clarksburg. The trip was exhausting, though, so they didn't do it too often. They were racers, not road riders, and the allure of the open highway had not yet taken hold.

Most of their time was spent at The Pits. There, they could compete against each other. Something they considered to be preparation for the upcoming days when they would become professionals, riding courses all over the nation, winning trophies, money, and—girls. Eddie had told him that not only did rockstars have groupies, but so did motorcycle racers. Cos hadn't even thought about that part. He wondered if Denise Donnelly would want to become his groupie. He'd have to drive by her house someday when she was outside.

The two boys often traded bikes, but Cos didn't like the scooter as much after having ridden his Ducati. It was the same for Eddie. Once he rode Cos's dream bike, the Cushman wasn't good enough. His father had acquired a German made Sachs, and Eddie traded his da the Cushman for it. The change was like night and day for them. The Sachs was faster and torquier but was what the two boys called a 'weird ride' because it had a swing arm style front fork and took some getting used to. It wasn't as advanced as the Ducati with its telescopic front fork, and there was a lot of bouncing to contend with.

A strange kind of intimacy grew between Cos and his bike. He knew this guy, Buzz, who had been a sailor at one time and always referred to his ship as a 'she' To Buzz, all ships were women. The Ducati had become Cos's girl and he dubbed her 'Wee Linny' after a girl he knew back in Ireland.

He and Eddie sometimes entered local races together as a team, never expecting to win. They just wanted to make a name for themselves and brag about their achievements. Technology was changing with the influx of the high torque, Japanese machines. It seemed almost ridiculous that Cos and Eddie ever enter any competition after the 'new bikes' came on the scene. But they were lovers of motorcycles, not of speed and power. They adored the ingenuity of archaic design. Machinery that had once been the going thing. They loved the classical machines that the pioneers of transportation had brought to them. Something that Kawasaki, Suzuki, and Yamaha, could never change.

In the spring of his seventeenth year, Wilhelmina Theobald, HACAP director and town busy-body, had wrangled a scholarship for Cos at a summer camp that was to take place at a college in Cedar Rapids, Iowa. Wilhelmina convinced him to attend, saying it was something he didn't want to pass up. He decided spending a summer away from Clarksburg just might be a good thing.

Cos needed more credits for high school and the camp would bring him that. He would depart the village in June and return at the end of July to prepare for his junior year in high school. Two days before he was to be off, he decided to attempt an overhaul of Wee Linny's engine. He never got the opportunity to watch Arnold overhauling any motorcycle engines or receive any tutelage from him on the subject, but Cos wanted to take the risk and give it a go. He felt confident that he could do it. Pulling the motor out of the frame, he snuck it into his bedroom, making sure his ma didn't see. He spread newspaper out over the cracked and faded linoleum of the floor and began to remove different components. Laying them out on the paper, Cos used a black marker to print a number beside each one, showing the order in which they had been removed.

By late evening he had the engine completely dismantled and the parts covered half of the bedroom floor. Taking in his work, he chuckled to himself as he was sure that anyone's first impression, as they entered the room, would have been that it was some kind of an art project. Cos was overwhelmed with pride for what he had accomplished. Pride was a dangerous thing, it blinded him to the knowledge that, to go off and leave it as it was, for almost two months, might just be the worst idea, ever.

His Ma never came into his room, though, and he didn't believe that she would ever have any reason to. He had done everything he could over the years to keep her out and she had caught on quickly. Since the night his da had left, his bedroom had become, solely, his domain. So, he presented her with his laundry on wash day, including his sheets, making his own bed and putting away his own clothes from the basket she left outside the curtain that hung in his doorway when she was finished.

While he was away, there was no need for laundry. So, no need for her to ever come inside. Cos told her he would clean and dust upon his return and to remember who's room it was. He never got an acknowledgment, but she had been busy watching *All My Children* and had only glanced his way and smiled before returning to the soap opera and her usual, trance-like state.

When he came home at the end of July, his Ma greeted him at the front door with an awkward hug and a, "Howz it, lad?" She didn't wait for an answer, though. Returning to the sofa she lit a Pal Mal Slim and turned her attention back to, *As The World Turns.* Cos went into his room and threw his bag onto the bed, almost walking out before realizing that the floor was bare. The old, cracked linoleum was newly waxed, and a little rug, with a strange pattern lay next to his bed. He almost screamed like they do in the horror movies. A scream that his theater teacher had once referred to as, 'The 'Wilhelm'

Cos ran into the living room to confront his mother, but when he arrived, he couldn't speak. She glanced up at him for a few seconds as he stuttered and stammered. When she felt he was taking too long, she turned her attention back to the television.

He growled and stomped out the front door and down to the town square. Then he ran back the other direction to stop outside Ernie B's shop. He figured he could, at the least, tell Ernie what a stupid thing his mother had done. But it was Sunday, and the shop was closed. Hurrying back to the apartment, he burst in the door and hollered, "Where's my Ducati, goddammit?"

Without even the courtesy of a look, she said, "You mean that shite that was scattered all over your bedroom floor was the motorcycle?"

"It was the engine. I was fixing it!"

"Well, you can still fix it. It's in a box under the stairs," she said, raising her voice an octave, her eyes darting back and forth between him and the TV. Cos ran to the door that opened into an alcove under the stairs.

Swinging it open, it smacked into the sofa. This gave his ma a jolt and the ash tray that had been precariously balance on the arm, fell onto the floor. She looked up at him, her eyes turning to slits. But before she could say anything, he disappeared into the dark interior of that closet, soon to reappear with a greasy cardboard box. He stopped and they exchanged looks that could have peeled paint. Then, stomping to his room, he dropped the box on the floor, rattling the windows.

He heard her come to the curtain and express a meek, "Sorry." Then he heard her fall onto her own bed and her sobs soon filled the air. It was something she always did to make him feel bad for her and their sad situation. He knew better than to react and remained in his room to show her that he was going to stand his ground.

His own tears soon came. But he would keep them silent because they were not for her. They were real tears, tears of despair, and not intended to hurt anyone. He sat on his bed and stared at the greasy parts in the box. Plaster dust covered every one of them. There were chips of gypsum and bits of paper. He would never be able to sort out that mess. His pride and stupidity along with his mother's neurosis had destroyed his dream. The two of them, together, had killed Wee Linny.

Cos lay down on his bed and rolling onto his side, he pulled up his knees. A framed photograph of his ma sat atop his nightstand, a picture of her in a happier time back in Ireland. A period in his life when his whole world centered on her. A feeling blossomed within him. The need to flee. To get away from Clarksburg. To get away—from her.

Now the guilt came. He tried to push it to the back of his mind, but it wouldn't leave him alone. A thought began to formulate in his head. His ma had conditioned him to feel that way. Mae McDhai was the master of the guilt trip and she used it like a tool. She would often try to convince him that the reason his da had left was because of him. "Your da could have been happier with me, if it wasn't for you," she had said many times in their past. One time he had yelled at her, saying, "Maybe I should just kill myself." She just said, "Maybe," and walked away. It had knocked him for a loop. She never said she was sorry. He even demanded that she apologize. She refused.

It was those kinds of moments that were eroding their relationship. Cos's devotion to her was waning. "I'm not going to live with you forever," he mumbled to the picture. The time for him to fly the coop (as his Aunt Louise was always saying) was coming. His excursion to Cedar Rapids for the summer had been confirmation that he could live his life away from her. The realization of a new goal and hope for some kind of a future forced the guilt out, and he smiled to himself.

Cos's knees started to ache and upon stretching out his legs, a crinkling noise came from his back pocket. It came as a reminder and reaching inside, he pulled out a heavily creased photo, an image of a mousy haired, teenaged girl with olive skin and a large toothy smile. A narrow line of freckles lay across the bridge of her nose and her eyes were a sharp green. At the bottom, written in scraggily cursive with red marker: 'Great Summer!' and 'With Love, Sandy K.' There was also a heart, pierced by an arrow.

He flattened out the picture the best he could and then using his ma's framed photograph as a support, he leaned Sandy's picture against it, blocking his ma's image. Laying back, he studied the girls face for the longest time.

They had met in art class. She had grabbed his hand during the scary part of a movie, but even better, she didn't let go until the credits rolled. Then one day he found himself in a crowded hallway between classes. She was pushing her way through the mass of students and when she saw him, her scowl ran away from her face and she grinned from ear to ear. He smiled and said hello. The tightly packed hallway forced them to go chest to chest. Her small breasts had pushed into him and a bolt of fear shot through his body. He was afraid she might think it was intentional on his part.

"Sorry, sorry..." Cos said, blushing and trying to pull away. But instead of taking offense, she wrapped her arms around him to keep him right where he was at. Then she surprised him by rising up on her toes and kissing him softly on the lips. Sandy smiled shyly afterwards and said, "Thought I'd never get up the nerve to do that."

Cos said nothing, he just stared in shock. "See you at lunch, huh," she said and turned to push her way through the crowd. Looking back one time, she grinned and waved before disappearing into the throng of students.

The sensation of her lips on his, remained with him for the rest of that day and even though the feeling had waned by the following morning, the memory of the moment never would. He had heard about the magic of the first kiss. It had been perplexing; thrilling. Wee Linny had never brought him that level of exhilaration. He wanted more. Even though he knew in his heart that the Ducati was done, and the summer was ending; Cos McDhai was just getting started.

He studied the photo in the dim light of the streetlamp that stood just outside his window. More memories flooded in, like the moment he had to say goodbye. They had been standing at the curb behind the dormitory with Sandy clinging to him. She had been fighting back the tears and even though it was a sad moment, it couldn't have been more uplifting. To think somebody cared enough for him that they would shed tears upon his departure. Cos needed to see her again—no matter the cost.

His eyes grew heavy and sleep came, the kind that took him down deep, where the dreams were. Visions also came, unlike any he'd ever had before, and even though he wouldn't realize that's what they were until he woke, he was left without a doubt. They had shown him the future.

#8

The Rafting Boy's Tale

My name is Conor Sullivan, I am thirteen years old, and I've got a story to tell. I reckon all my friends back in Clarksburg think I've drowned, but that's not true. If anyone should come to my pa's cabin a couple miles down the river, they would see me, still breathing, burping, and farting, just like any normal kid.

It's just... it would be better if certain people thought that I was. These two mean guys at my school to be exact. But now I am feeling kind of bad for the people that cared about me. I mean, my ma found out right away, because my pa made me call her when I showed up on his doorstep—cold and wet— but still very much alive.

After I got warmed up and dried off, he walked me about half a mile to the Rudd's farm to use their phone because he didn't like going into Clarksburg with all its commotion. Old farmer Rudd and his wife were kind of quiet and kept to themselves—kind of like pa did. They weren't likely to mention to anyone that we were there. I 'spect they didn't like commotion, either.

When pa got ma on the line, he made me do all the talking because they've been separated for quite a few years and that meant phone calls were thin ice. My ma chewed me out real good, blubbering all the time she was doing it. Then she started laughing and crying at the same time, telling me how I would always be her boy and that she loved me more than words could say. After that, she said it would be alright with her if I stayed with pa for a while, but before she hung up, I begged her not to tell any of my friends where I was.

It wasn't even a week later that a sheriff's deputy showed up at my pa's place. He had to come by boat because we're closer to the river than the highway. He didn't seem none too happy about that, but it was easier than walking all that way through the timber and getting his nice, clean uniform all muddied up.

He came to tell my pa that ma had been arrested for causing a ruckus over at the Blue Front tavern, and how afterwards, they had to stick her in a place where she could dry out. The deputy told my pa that he would have to take care of me now and make sure I got everything a kid needs, and that, was that.

Pa wasn't too pleased with me about a sheriff's man showing up at his door. The only thing worse than that, would have been the Game Warden. Pa was stuck with me. He told me he wasn't going to make me go back to school, but he was sure to add that I could use his flat bottom boat with the motor if I'd a mind to. I had to give that some thought.

I was helping with the hunting and the trapping, and soon we'd be casting our fishing lines together. Then one day he told me right out of the blue, while we were out working his trap line, "Ain't right you left your buddies to think something bad happened to you. So, I've been a thinking, you should let them know, somehow, that you're still breathing. Write 'em some letters, because I know you can write, or take the boat and go back up there to show them you've risen from the dead. I don't care how you do it, but I want it done. You hear me, Connor? Ain't right for you to leave them fretting, and… well… that's all I have to say about that."

I'd been given a choice, and I almost wrote those letters. There would have been three of them for sure. One of them being real important because I was starting to have dreams about her. The other two would have been to my pals, Benny Blahnik, who we called Ding Bat. He was kind of a weakling but was really smart. He still greased his hair, even in 1972, and kind of looked like this kid called Opie from a TV show I knew.

Then there was Dover—Dover Schmitt. He was this tall, lanky kid, whose shaggy dark hair was always hanging in his eyes. He wanted us to call him 'Thunderhead' because he had a thing for storms and those huge, anvil shaped clouds that went clear up to that one sphere (I can't never remember which one). Anyway, it was a serious macho name, and I reckoned he wanted us to call him that because he so badly wanted to be kin to those big ol' clouds. I think it was just that, secretly, he wanted to be powerful.

If we called him Dover, he'd give us a dutch-rub or a serious snake bite on our arm to remind us. So, we made fun of him as much as we could by calling him Dover the Head, or, Thunder Butt. Anyway, we got lazy and just started calling him Thunder after a while. He settled for that.

We hung around together all the time, mostly down on the Wapsi River. It ran right through the middle of town, but we didn't hang out in there. That stretch of riverbank was high school kid territory, and if we were seen poking around, there would be hell to pay. We learned our lesson the first time we tried. Having to explain to my ma why I had a black eye wasn't easy. So, our secret spot was just outside of Clarksburg, down the river, by the sewer plant.

There was this big ol' levee that surrounded all the buildings, and it was on the south corner that Mother Nature had stuck a sand bar poking out into the river. Now, the Wapsi wasn't that big, not like Huckleberry Finn's Mississippi (yeah, I read that book about half a dozen times). But in the late spring, when the ice and snow was melting, it would flood, and the sandbar would disappear for a while.

We'd have to go and hang out at the railroad bridge just upstream. We would climb down from the catwalk and sit on the concrete piers, just goofing off, eating candy bars and stuff, waiting for the day our sandbar would come back. Sometimes we'd squeeze into these boxed-in places that Wick Ryan had showed Ding Bat. Then we'd wait for the train to come and would holler all kinds of weird stuff (sometimes swear words) as loud as we could while it went right over our heads. It was scary and exciting, all at the same time. When the sandbar finally came back, it was always a different shape from the year before. We didn't mind, though, because that kept things interesting.

The guys and I had been friends since kindergarten, and the thing that really brought us together (and maybe, pushed us apart) was our raft. We started building it back in the sixth grade and didn't get it done until the summer after. I want you to know, though, if it wasn't for Ding, we may never have gotten it finished. He was the brains behind it—but it was my idea. Thunder was the muscle because he sure liked showing off how strong he was when we were putting it together. I figured someday he was going to get one of those hernias my pa was always going on about.

Ding wanted to put a sail on the raft, but we argued because a sail did you no good on a river. He finally won out because we were pals. So, Thunder and I went ahead and made a big wooden 'T' and stuck it on the raft in a way that made it stand straight up. Then Ding stole an old bed sheet from his ma's laundry basket and hung it on the crossbar to make a proper sail. Not that we ever used it or anything. Ding just wanted it to look like the one he saw in the book. The one without all the bees and big yellow flowers flapping in the breeze.

After we put the finishing touches on everything, those guys were too afraid to try it. That left only me—of course.

"You going to be the one, Boy? Or we going to have to draw straws?"

"Ahhh, naw, I ain't afraid, and because you guys are..."

Thunder squinted with his left eye and said, "Okay, Boy, since you think you're so tough, you get to be the test pilot. Come on, let's see you do it."

My nickname was Boy because I called some kid at school, 'Boyo' just one time (it was one of my pa's favorite words). Then everyone started calling me Boyo as a nickname. Which of course, got shortened to Boy, because, well… like I said, people are just plain lazy about that sort of thing.

I grabbed an oar that we stole from somebody's rowboat up above the dam and climbing on board, I pushed out. Thunder had tied the raft to a piece of metal rebar that he'd pounded into the sand, leaving just enough slack in the rope for me to get a good ways out.

The raft worked just fine and never tried to sink or anything. Then we all tried it together, and even though it sunk a bit from all our weight, it still worked just like a raft was supposed to. So, we spent the rest of the summer hanging out on it.

We kept it tied to the sandbar and we'd push out to midstream with the oar. Then, we'd throw our concrete block anchor out up river, otherwise the current would push us right back to the sandbar. We'd dive off it where the channel was deepest, always hollering weird stuff and laughing about it. After a couple hundred times of doing that, we'd lay around in the sun, drinking the root beer Thunder always brought, and trying to get a suntan. Well, all except for Ding. He always burnt real bad and had to walk around all slicked up with lotion.

Other kids must have heard about the raft and came down to watch us out there having a good time (so much for our secret spot!) We whooped it up like it was the best thing in the world and they'd all stand around, staring at us like we were creatures from outer space. That got their juices flowing, making them wish they had a raft. Thunder started charging a quarter for a ride out to the middle and back—one kid at a time. But because we didn't want no one except us hanging out on our raft when we were swimming, we were pretty quick about getting them back to the sandbar. Then one day, the weirdest thing happened, Willowbough Boyd showed up.

Willowbough was this real shy girl. You didn't see her around town much outside of school. If you came across her it was because you were out in the woods or cutting across somebody's pasture. Willowbough wasn't afraid of the rain, either. She'd be out there soaking it up while everybody else was hiding inside. Honestly, I thought that was the coolest thing.

I remember one day I saw her spinning around in the kiddie pool in the little city park during a downpour. The pool was down by the river bridge, and if you stand in my bedroom and look out the window of our attic apartment, you can see the pool between the houses across the alley. It was the first and only time I'd ever seen her wear a summer dress. It looked like one of those flowered numbers that left your shoulders bare and hardly made it down to your knees.

I was changing out of my wet clothes because I'd been caught out in the rain, and there she was, just spinning away, her arms straight out to the side and her face bent up to the sky. I'm not real sure, but I think she might have been laughing.

She was poor like me, and usually dressed in dungarees that were too big for her, and this jean jacket that was way too long. She also wore flannel shirts because I don't think she had a pretty blouse like most of the other girls. Her face was round, and her skin was the color of my ma's coffee with cream. But I don't think Willowbough had a tan, because, well… she looked like that all year long. Her hair was a darker black than mine and was cut into one of those Bobs. Mine, on the other hand, was a flattop.

Thunder didn't like her nose and told me once that it really bugged him. I couldn't figure out why it was such a big deal. It was just a little bit bigger than most folks. But noses are just plain weird anyway. So, there ain't one person who's got any room to talk—not even Thunder.

Some of the other kids said she was kind of ugly, but I couldn't understand why they thought that. I have to confess; I thought the opposite. Her eyes were this really dark brown and when she looked right at you, (if that ever happened) you could see how pretty she was. Someone told me once that her ma was an American Indian from over Tama county way, and that she had married some guy named Boyd who was from Clarksburg. Now, this made perfect sense to me.

For some reason, a few folks in Clarksburg didn't like Indians, or anyone else like them. I could easily have been that way too, but we had some Mexican in us because my pa's ancestors had come from what he called, 'The St. Patrick's Battalion' It was this bunch of Irish guys who fought for Mexico against America. But that was clear back in the 1800's. So, I figured if there were any hard feelings over that, they had all gone away by now.

Willowbough lived in a place down by the railroad track embankment. There was this little row of tiny houses in the trees that looked like they just might fall down at any minute. Ding told me that his pa told him that the town should just go ahead and bulldoze the whole lot of them because that would make Clarksburg a better place. I was thinking—maybe not for the people who lived there. So, I told Ding that maybe Clarksburg would be a better place if they just went ahead and bulldozed his pa. It was just a joke, but Ding didn't talk to me for the rest of that school day.

Anyway, Willowbough sat behind me in Mrs. Bowmen's English class and sometimes I'd sneak a peek back under my arm pit just so I could look at her. She never seemed to be paying much attention to what the teacher was saying and was always drawing stuff like wolves and birds and horses and things like that in her notebook, or on her desk with a pencil. Now, I have to admit, she was pretty good at it, and I reckoned someday she was going to be a great artist.

She could never make it through a whole school day without being made fun of. Shelly Anderson called her Injun Josephine. Doug Moore kept pestering her about why she didn't have an Indian name like, Two Crows, or Girl Who Doesn't Talk-A-Lot. After a while, the mean kids came up with a nickname for her and started calling her, Branch. I supposed because that's what a willow bough was. I didn't call her that, though because, well, she never did anything mean to me and... I really liked her.

People are always saying revenge is supposed to be sweet. So, I figured I'd try it and see. I took to getting the other kids back for being cruel to Willowbough. I mean, she just ignored them and went right on drawing those pictures, not doing a thing about it. I have to admit that drove me a little crazy.

Whenever Shelly started in on Willowbough, I'd start in on her. First, I asked why her last name wasn't Ander-daughter because a girl can't be a son. So, there was no way she could be a real Anderson. Then we started studying Prehistoric Man and I thought it might be fun to start calling Shelly, 'Neanderson' after that one kind of cave dweller that our history teacher, Mr. Mann, told us had gone extinct. I asked Shelly when she was going to go extinct. All the other kids laughed real hard and she got so mad; she bounced her eraser right off the side of my head. But I never heard her make fun of Willowbough ever again.

It was on that very same day that I came back from lunch and found a really cool drawing of a hawk on a piece of notebook paper inside my desk. I didn't ask Willowbough anything about it. I just took it home and hung it in my room.

Then one day, the Scruddup twins, who were these seniors, came into the lunch room while we were eating. They were these big, scary, farmer boys that everyone was afraid of, including some of the teachers. Willowbough was sitting at the lunch table behind mine, facing my back while eating a peanut butter sandwich. They walked right in and leaned against the wall behind her. Of course, they were there to pick on her, and that's the day that things kind of changed for me.

"Hey, fatty... yeah you, fat butt Boyd. How'd you get such a fat butt, anyway?" That was Pete Scruddup's big mouth.

"You know Pete, she's not really fat... she's just big boned." That was his brother, Vern, whose mouth was a whole lot bigger.

I looked back and saw Willowbough was staring at them over her shoulder but wasn't saying anything. She turned back but didn't go right to eating because she was crying. Not like most kids, though, with all the noise, just these quiet kind of tears.

Mrs. Nelson, the lunchroom monitor, and the meanest woman in town, yelled over, "What's going on over there Pete Scruddup? And you… Vern Scruddup, what are you doing in here? This isn't your lunch period. Is there something wrong?"

The whole room went so quiet you could hear a mouse fart. Before they could answer, I blurted out, "Yeah, there's something wrong, it's because they're… they're the 'Screwed-up' brothers."

I of course was trying to be funny but saying that surely signed my death warrant.

"Mr. Sullivan, you mind your own business."

"Yes, Mrs. Nelson," I said, and pushing my tray away, I put my face down on the table and wrapped my arm around it. I then snuck a peek back at Willowbough. She was staring right at me with her eyes looking like two dark pools of water that I was swimming around in. The tears were still there, and she was sniffing a bit, but she was smiling in a closed mouth kind of way, and I swear, I saw her eyes twinkle.

The Scruddups walked out then, with Pete mumbling, "We'll get you later, Raft Boy." And of course, Vern had to add, "And you too, Branch-o-roony."

I had now gone and made enemies of the Scruddup brothers.

Which, up until that time, I'd been invisible. But I had also made a better friend of Willowbough, and I have to say that it just felt worth it.

So, like I said, she showed up at the sandbar and brought her little dog, Pan (which, if I'm not mistaken, had been Peter Pan at one time before she went and got lazy). He was this little Jack Russel and was always with her when she wasn't in school. Sometimes he'd be waiting just outside the door when the bell rang. But you couldn't pet him or nothing, he wouldn't let you get that close.

Laying on the raft on my belly, in just my swimming trunks, I could see her sitting crossed legged up on the corner of the levee. She was just up there watching us, petting her dog who was coughing at us. I just figured that's how he barked.

Thunder hollered out, "Hey guys, its Branch! Look Boy, its Branch. See her?"

"Don't call her that."

"Why not?" Ding asked. "Everybody does. I mean, isn't that what a Willowbough is? Ah hell, Boy… what kind of a name is Willowbough, anyway?"

I wanted to say a pretty one, but instead what came out was, "Why don't you shut your mouths, you pricks." That just kind of slipped out, and to make matters worse, Thunder had to go and tease me.

"Uh oh! Boy's sweet on Branch. Got yourself a girlfriend, huh, Boyo?"

Ding took it one step further by saying, "Yeah, Boy, you got yourself a girlfriend? Kind of an ugly one with a big nose, if you ask me."

"If anyone's ugly… it's you, Ding Bat bohunk."

I gave him a shove with both feet, and he fell overboard. He came up sputtering about the time I grabbed our oar and turned-on Thunder.

"Hey now, Boy! Don't you hit me with that."

"Well, then, shut up, you."

"Geez, don't have a cow. Come on, we're pals, remember? So…"

"So, shut your big trap about Willowbough… and about me having a girlfriend."

"Okay, geez…"

Thunder looked away and started shaking his head, like he couldn't believe how I was acting. Ding was hanging on the side of the raft, looking up at me, his eyes big with worry.

"Who's the prick, now?" he said, and swam back to shore.

Willowbough saw him coming, and getting up, she took off into the trees. She didn't want to talk to Ding, I'm guessing. He put on his shoes that he left on the sandbar and stomped off.

Thunder said, "Prick," and then he dived into the river and swam to shore as well. When he got there, he ran after Ding, leaving me alone to bring the raft in by myself.

Ding got over being mad after a day, and the three of us were back on the raft in no time, trying to forget all about our little disagreement. That's the way it went clear into winter. We'd come down after school and hang out on the weekends. Soon we had to start wearing our coats, and of course, work a little harder at not getting wet.

Willowbough usually came too, following us at a distance or hanging out back in the trees, just watching us fish and stuff. Sometimes I'd see her teaching Pan some new trick or just playing some kind of a game that only girls, who hung around by themselves, played.

When the snow came, she didn't seem to mind that either. But instead of sitting up on the levee, she'd stand. Her jacket would be done all the way up, a big fuzzy stocking cap would be on her head and her long ol' scarf would be blowing in the wind. She had these big, knitted mittens that didn't match and some furry topped, black boots that I think might have been her ma's.

The three of us didn't want to give up the raft until we absolutely had too. We were pushing our luck to be out on the river when the winter winds came. I got a feeling it was more like we just didn't want to let go of summer.

Soon the river froze, and the raft got stuck in it where we docked at the head of the sandbar. We finally gave in to the fact that we would have to wait until spring came and went back to climbing around on the railroad bridge. On the really cold days, we goofed off in town. The high school kids hung out at the Dairy Dreem up by the highway in winter, so we took over the soda fountain at Nordon's Drugstore.

Willowbough still followed us around. The railing for the catwalk at the railroad bridge was two thick cables strung between posts. If we were down on one of the piers, she'd sit on the bottom cable, with the top one running under her armpits. That way, she could sneak a peek at us once in a while as she swung. She always chose the same spot, which was right at the end of the bridge. I reckoned she thought that way she could escape if need be.

One day we were at Nordon's having root beers, and Willowbough was pretending like she was shopping, just walking around the shelves, peeking at us between the shampoo bottles. I was getting kind of tired of it, so I got up and walked over there. She must have lost track of me because I cornered her at the Aftershave. I could tell she was wearing perfume because that wasn't a man smell I was smelling. It was more like flowers.

"Hey, Willowbough, what's happening?"

"Hi, Boy," she kind of squeaked out, and that was all. Then giggling, she pushed past me and left the drugstore, meeting Pan on the sidewalk out front. She kind of skipped away across the street like she was happy. Pan went right after her, bouncing off of her butt, with his front paws, every couple of steps like he was trying to hurry her along.

"She's so weird," Ding said.

Thunder put his two cents worth in there, "Yeah, you said it, Ding."

"Yeah, but… don't you think she's kind of pretty?" slipped out of my mouth as I watched her skip away. Then I looked back at them and they all laughed like they thought it was supposed to be a joke. Even old man Nordon laughed from behind the counter. I walked out right then and went home. I didn't need that kind of crap.

Now the Scruddups' were starting to be a problem at school. Not only was I fighting all the time with my pals because of Willowbough, but I was also trying to avoid Pete and Vern. They knew about the raft because they were always calling me Raft Boy whenever they were giving me a dutch rub, sticking me in a locker, or tripping me in the hallway. But I never saw them around Clarksburg when school was out, not even on Friday when all the farmers came to town for supplies. So, I figured I was safe. I was a little worried about the raft though and was afraid one day they'd come down and wreck it.

It was soon 1973. My ma was drinking way more now and acting like she was crazy. I was afraid one morning I'd wake up and she'd be completely cuckoo for coco puffs. I'd get up early and sneak off before she got out of bed and not come home until way after supper time, always hoping she'd be passed out by then.

The first three months went by with the same ol' routine, me trying to come up with things to do and places I could be—away from home. It was in April, when Ding and I were down hanging out on the soggy sand bar. The snow was seriously melting and the Wapsi was getting ready to commence with its flooding. Big, flat chunks of ice were floating down the river, and I figured because they were so thick out there, if a guy had a mind too, he could skip right on across without wetting a foot.

Thunder showed up pretty soon after we got there and started jumping on the ice shelves that when the level of the river fell, were left sticking out from the bank. He'd break one off and jump back real quick before the chunk slid into the river. Then he'd go to the next one and start jumping on it. So, Ding and I joined in, thinking it might be fun. We knew it was a little dangerous, but that made it more exciting, and of course, I had to learn the hard way about being the guy on the outside.

We started jumping on one that was as big as a trampoline and about a foot thick. We got it to break off. Ding and Thunder jumped back on shore, but I couldn't get around them in time. I ended up riding it like a surfboard down into the water. It didn't go far because the river eddied back up into a pool behind the foot of the sandbar; a place where trash and other stuff got stuck. I ended up just spinning around with all that other junk.

"Cool!" Ding hollered.

"Yeah! You're braver than me, Boy. I wouldn't do that," Thunder said.

"Well, it's not like I did it on purpose, you know?"

Even though that was the truth, I still felt kind of proud, and just grinned at them like a crazy man, standing there with my hands on my hips. My eyes went to the woods behind them, and sure enough, Willowbough was back in there leaning against a tree with Pan by her feet. I raised a hand real high in the air, not expecting her to do anything. But a big purple mitten came up, and I saw her smile. She was so quick about it that I had to wonder if it had been my imagination. When Thunder and Ding looked to see who I was waving at, she ran away as usual with Pan doing his cough-bark as he chased after her.

I know Ding wanted to say something mean about her, but decided instead to say, "So… ice makes a good raft too… huh, guys?"

"Yeah… but a dangerous one," Thunder added, even though he was still watching Willowbough. Then he looked back at me and said, "I don't think I'd ride that out into the Wapsi. What if it broke apart or melted? You'd be screwed. Well, maybe not you… Raft Boy!"

He laughed after he said that, so I knew he was trying to be funny. But he had called me Raft Boy. That made me mad. So, I hollered, "You're a raft boy too, Dover Schmitt! And don't you think you're any different, Opie bohunk!"

"Ah geez, Boy, calm the hell down, I was just teasing," Thunder said.

"Teasing or not, that's what the Scruddups call me. So… unless you want to be brother number three, shut your mouth."

"Alright, sorry! Don't have a litter of pups, huh?"

Ding just stood there with this look on his face like he was sad. I could only think it was because he had actually tried to be nice and Thunder had ruined it. They both got real quiet and started kicking at stuff on the ground. I got off the ice and we walked back into town without talking. Something was changing, I just couldn't tell what.

We walked along, not looking at each other, our eyes on the road. I wanted to say something, but I wasn't sure what it would be. I really couldn't tell what was going on between us. One thing I did know was that lately, when I thought about hanging out with Thunder and Ding, it felt kind of like I didn't want too anymore. But when I thought about a chance to hang out with Willowbough for the first time, I got excited.

Looking back, I expected her to be there, and sure enough, there she was, plodding along about half a block behind. I gave her a wave, but the guys looked too, so she turned and ran away down the mud road that led to her house. It donned on me that it was the guys who were keeping me from Willowbough. Realizing this, made me think I might have to decide between them or her. You want to talk about feeling sad! My brain felt like it was squirming around inside my head trying to figure out a way to be with her, and them.

Two days later, on a Saturday, I was alone down at the sand bar. I had slept in and when I woke up, my ma was leaning against my door jamb with a glass of vodka in her hand. She was saying my name over and over again trying to sound like a croaking frog. Then she'd giggle, take a sip, and start over again. I just covered up my head with a pillow. She quit after a minute or so and went to the john. I got dressed real quick, and grabbing my coat, I got out of there.

I went to the guy's houses first to see if they wanted to hang out, but they made excuses, so I reckoned I wouldn't see them again until school on Monday. The way they acted made me wonder if they felt about me, the same way I was feeling about them.

I hoped to see Willowbough following me around, but then I realized I didn't know how she knew when I was out and about. I passed the mud road that went to her place, but I didn't see her down there, either. So, I decided to go and check on the raft, thinking it might be free of the ice.

The day was kind of dark, and the clouds were hanging real low. There was a thick fog on the river just a little ways down from our spot, and it was like a big ol' cloud got tired of floating and came down to sit a spell.

The raft was still stuck, and I didn't want to waste any energy trying to break it loose. I figured I'd go over and check on that big chunk of ice and maybe float around on it for a while. It was a little smaller now and bounced around inside that turn-back like it was restless and wanted to join the other hunks of ice that were racing by.

I was standing there in the slush, just staring at it, when I heard someone running up the other side of the levee. I was hoping it was Willowbough and that I might get a chance to talk to her without the guys around. But it wasn't. It was Pete and Vern. They saw me, and Vern hollered, "There he is, let's get that little creep."

I had a choice to run or fight, but neither one was good because those guys were bigger and faster. So, I broke the oar loose from the snow where Ding had leaned it up against a tree. I figured I could at least use it as a weapon and maybe scare them off. But I knew in my heart that they would just take it away from me. Then my eyes came back to the ice raft and without a second thought, I jumped right onto the center of it, using the oar for balance. Then pushing against the river bank, I forced the ice raft out of that little pool and into the current.

"Damn it! You little worm, Sullivan," Pete yelled.

"Geez, Pete, you see that? He's getting away on a piece of ice, I never…"

"Ah shut up, Vern, you stupid idiot, I can see he's getting away."

I drifted down toward the cloud and just before I went in, I caught sight of Willowbough running through the trees, kind of chasing after me; Pan, hot on her heels. For the first time in my life, I heard her speak more than just two words. Coming out of the trees, she stopped to stand on the shore, and calling out to me in a way that made me feel pretty sad, I heard, "Come back, Boy! Come back, I want to go with you!"

It was too late, and the fog swallowed me up.

#9

The Cut Of One's Jib

Palance Turner was a kid who loved anything that could float on water. Everybody called him Pal, and he liked that. It made him think that he could be anyone's friend. He had just turned twelve in the spring of 1972. Pal wanted to do something great on his birthday, something that would make people talk. But that didn't happen. Two days later he was still wondering what had gone wrong. He couldn't stop thinking about it. His friend, Tommy, said he should try harder to think about something else because the other kids were afraid Pal was going to hurt himself; and maybe, them too. That was because Pal took a lot of dares and didn't seem concerned about risk. His ma said he was obsessed with glory and that he should just let destiny takes its course; whatever that was supposed to mean.

They didn't have a dictionary at home. So, Pal went to the tiny, red brick building that was the Clarksburg Library. He didn't want his ma to know that he didn't know those big words. Obsessed and destiny, were way out of his league, but he did know glory.

Thumbing through the pages of the massive book sitting atop a big, wooden pedestal, he kept glancing over at the librarian who was sitting close by at her desk. She was watching him, making him feel weird, and that made his task harder.

Pal continued, anyway, and when he finally found the word, 'destiny' and read the definition, he decided that was one he didn't need to worry about. It would just happen. As for 'obsession' well… he understood it as something that could control his life if he wasn't careful. He thought about what Tommy said and it made him feel like he just might be an idiot. Pal wondered if the librarian thought he was. If he was obsessed, it was mostly about the boats staked to the shore above the dam. They just floated, seemingly neglected. If they were his boats, he'd be with them every day.

Just about everyone in town owned one, except for him. He was pretty sure that's what drove his obsession. Row boats, flat bottoms (a lot like a rowboat), and canoes—mostly canoes. Of all the boats, they were his favorite. Harder than hell to paddle up stream, but light enough to carry if you needed to. They were inexpensive, too. You could float around in them and go just about anywhere you wanted. Well, except for the ocean. There were sharks there, some of them bigger than any canoe. Taking that risk would be like agreeing to be something's lunch. Pal knew, at the least, that he wasn't that big an idiot. So, he reminded himself to just not go there. That way he wouldn't have to ever worry about sharks.

Finally, there were the pontoons. They were too big for a kid. They were a dad's boat. It didn't matter, though, Pal didn't like them. You could have the same kind of fun on a raft and any kid could build one of those, himself. He knew one such kid, Benny Blahnik, (his friends called him Dingbat) who had built a raft with his buddies. Pal had to pay a quarter to get a ride on it and that's all it took to get him hooked. Pal knew if he ever got a boat, it would surely cure him of his so-called obsession.

Saturday rolled around and Pal found himself heading down to the river. April was way warmer than it was supposed to be. The sky was clear, and the temperature was going up. The word was, the ice had broken upstream and the Wapsipinicon River was on the rise. He heard there were ice floes and he just wanted to be sure that was the truth. He needed solid evidence to share what he knew with the guys.

Stopping in the middle of the bridge, he looked north toward the roller dam. It didn't register at first, because his mind had a tough time wrapping itself around why there were three pontoon boats, a bunch of canoes, and four rowboats, all nosing into the slimy concrete of the dams curved surface. They'd spin and slam into it sideways and go right back to nosing it again. Some were nearly rolling over in the churning water. They were all caught between the massive boils at the base and the water rushing over the top.

When one of the canoes finally did roll over, and got crushed by a pontoon, Pal snapped out of his initial shock. He figured the ice floes that were moving pretty steadily over the dam had been the culprits. They must have hit the boats that had been frozen in the ice over the winter and tore them loose from their moorings. He needed to tell somebody. He just didn't know who.

The gas station!

The little Standard Station sat on one corner of the square. Most of the fisherman in Clarksburg gathered there to tell their fish stories, and even more so in the winter months. They didn't have much else to do while they waited for the fishing season to come around. Those guys would surely know what to do.

Pal ran. He didn't know what to say when he got there and he was afraid that he would just stutter or freeze up with all those eyes staring at him; but he needed to try. Bursting in through the door, he found seven old guys standing around in striped bibs and assorted winter hats, plus a few wearing grease spotted coveralls of the insulated variety. All of them were drinking coffee out of brown stained cups. They had been telling their tall tales to Earl, one of the guys that worked there.

Now, Earl didn't like kids, and Pal was afraid the old guy would tell him to get the hell out. But Pal also knew Earl's boss, Mr. Johnson, really well. If he was there, then he would tell Earl to shut the hell up and would probably give Pal a grape Nehi or a root beer for his trouble.

"The boats went over the dam!" Pal hollered.

A warmth filled him from head to toe. He had gotten it all out at once and hadn't stuttered a bit. But then Earl said in his mean voice, "What the hell you talking about, boy?" Now Pal did stutter and had trouble repeating it. But Mr. Johnson came out of his office and stood in the doorway brushing donut crumbs off his tidy gray Standard Oil uniform. He wasn't as hard of hearing as the rest.

"You heard him, fellas! Get your butts in gear!"

Earl scowled and stepped out of the way as the seven old guys rushed out the door. Pal was barely able to get out of the way. He watched them jump in their pickups and jeeps and race away down Main Street toward the river. Bill Johnson was picking up the phone when Pal left at a run, chasing after the old guys.

The seven men soon became twenty, as trucks and cars pulled up, all of them parking just about anywhere they wanted. There were people running down to the shore with big coils of ropes. The ones who had the 4x4's, drove down to the edge of the river and up to the dam stopping just short of the big rocks. They drove slowly, trying not to do too much damage to Walter Soors' front lawn. Pal knew Mr. Soor, and he knew it wouldn't matter how slow they went, the old man was going to get madder than hell, and even kids, Pal's age, and younger, would be hearing about it.

The jeep drivers pulled out cables from their bumper winches and inspected the big hooks attached to their ends. They were ready to do some serious pulling.

Big men in heavy coats and dungarees pulled on leather gloves before forming big loops in their ropes. "You going to lasso those pontoons?" Pal hollered. They all looked at him for a second and then each other. Without a word they went back to preparing to toss their ropes. Pal figured that was okay, it was probably a bad time to be asking a stupid question.

A few of the boat rescuers were hearty women who did some fishing of their own. They had pretty much taken charge and Pal felt they were doing a damn fine job of directing the operation. Within ten minutes of Pal's arrival, there where ten men standing along the shore tossing ropes. They started getting in each other's way and those women had to get in there and get them to spread out, some of them going up the rock covered levee at the end of the dam to toss their lasso's from a higher spot. Other men stood behind them, just watching, cheering them on. Pal decided if he was going be hollering and not helping, he should join that group.

When somebody would hook a pontoon, they'd all drop their lassos and form a line on that rope and start pulling. Getting tired of standing with the cheer squad, Pal grabbed the end of the rope to help out. It was tough going and some men got pulled into the water and had to climb out and move to the back of the line. They didn't even bother to dry off first. Eventually pal was in the middle and getting kind of crushed. So, he too dropped out and returned to the end.

They eventually got one free and pulled it to shore. It pushed a small canoe in front of it as it came. Another guy lassoed a second pontoon and taking advice from one of the woman directors, he hooked the rope up to his cable winch and pulled the boat back to shore without a problem. The precedence had been set. Now they just needed to save pontoon number three. Everybody went to throwing ropes like it was some kind of steer roping contest. Some really big kid that Pal only knew as 'The Goon' had been trying for the third one but snagged a row boat by its oarlock instead. He hollered, "Got it." and started pulling it to shore all by himself. Sadly, it rolled on its side, took on water, and sunk.

Luckily for him it was well out of the boils and now closer to shore. Pal knew they'd be able to salvage it come low water in June. Goon had lost his rope; the rowboat had taken it down. No amount of yanking could get it free. One of those fisherwomen whispered something in his ear and the big guy begrudgingly joined another team, mumbling swear words as he went.

A new problem arose when it was seen that the last pontoon was slowly working its way toward the other side of the river. A few men took off and ran back across the bridge with their ropes, heading for the opposite shore. Before they even got half way across the bridge, old man Hale from Hale's Hardware got a rope on it. There came a chorus of shouts and everybody ran to grab the rope. Crazy Vaughn Earhart showed up out of nowhere and moved to stand at the front of the line. He was this big, muscle-bound roofer who was also a student at the University of Iowa. Some of the guys whooped and hollered like he was their hero. Pal figured they must have been other roofers.

They all set their feet and began to pull, while old man Slade backed up his 4x4 toward the bridge so he could pull out his hook and cable. He never got that far. The pontoon began to spin and one of the long metal floats hit the dam. This pushed the boat under water at the front and then the whole thing just seemed to explode. It came apart with pieces flying everywhere. The rope parted at the half way point and snapped back causing Vaughn to let go and duck to avoid flying pieces of boat. Everyone else in that line fell like dominos. The pontoon disappeared into the boils with small chunks of it floating away downriver, the striped awning, that had been its roof, twisted and squirmed through the water like a live animal.

By the end of the day, two pontoons, a canoe, a couple of flat bottoms, and Goon's rowboat had been saved. The people who owned the boats got them to shore and tied them to the trees in a grove along Soors property. Then they went to inspecting them to assess the damage. Everybody else who was just there to help and didn't own any of those boats, fell into line and paraded back up to the sidewalk. They were heading back up to the Standard Station, coiling up their ropes and bragging about the part they had played in saving their fellow fisherman's watercraft.

After pulling the one lone canoe from the water, Pal pushed it up into the trees to make sure it wouldn't float away. Afterwards, he joined the procession, feeling a little excited about the whole affair. He hoped he would see some kid that he knew so he could brag; just like the old guys.

Everybody gathered in the mechanics bay at the little gas station, drinking Mr. Johnson's coffee, sodas, and yakking up a storm. Bill Johnson came out and asked, "Well, how bad's the damage to my pontoon?" he asked some guy that Pal didn't know. "Well, Bill, one of the railings is bent and there's a small dent in one of the floats, but other than that, not much."

"And my canoe? It was tied to the pontoon."

"Its fine. Fact is, it came out first. I seen that young feller over there pull it up out of the water and put it up in the trees," the guy said, pointing a finger at Pal.

"That right, Pal? A dark green canoe with a yellow stripe?"

"Yes, sir, Mr. Johnson, I tied it to a tree."

"Well, you know young feller, if it wasn't for you, we might not have been able to save any of those boats. Howz about it, fellas, a cheer for Pal?"

They all whooped and hollered with some of them actually doing an old-fashioned hurrah. Pal blushed and thought about running out of there, but Bill Johnson hooked his thumbs in his webbed belt, stepped in front of Pal and asked, "You got yourself a boat, yet son? Every kid needs a boat, you know? I'll tell you what, you can keep that ol' canoe. I'm fixing to get one of the new fiberglass jobs. One big enough to hold four men. You go on and just take that one. Don't forget, though, call Martha over at the town hall cause you're going to have to register it in your name. Got that?"

Pal just nodded because he was grinning so big that he couldn't talk. "Now you just go get yourself a Nehi from the fridge. You deserve it." Bill patted Pal on the head and he went to the fridge and pulled out a soda. Popping the cap, he took a good, long swig to wet his throat so he could speak, and nearly shouted, "Thanks, Mr. Johnson." He turned and ran out the front door with his soda in hand. Pal needed to get home to tell his ma that she didn't have to worry about him being obsessed anymore, he'd finally got himself a boat.

#10

The Goon

Kids are mean, and I'm saying every kid—including me. I didn't know why other kids were mean, but I knew why I was. Now, school was the worst place for it. It seemed like when you get a bunch of kids all together in one spot, things are sure to go to hell in a handbasket. My ma has a hand basket, and it ain't all that big. If hell were to break loose in that little thing, it would be bad.

That kind of thing made going to school, scary, and running out those front doors when the bell rang at the end of the day was always reason for celebration. There was nothing the school could do about the meanness that was inside us. It wasn't something rules could make go away. Besides that, all the teachers really cared about was the war in Vietnam, and if it was going to last through 1971. I figured just one more year wasn't such a bad thing. Ma said it would give President Nixon time to get things cleaned up and apologize to all those poor folks for us bombing the crap out of them.

So, because our teachers were always looking in a different direction when the crap was about to hit the fan, they didn't see how afraid we were, oh, let's say, when walking by the high school lockers. To make it worse, they could never accept our excuses why we were always late for class. You probably know as well as I do how hard it was to get out of a locker from the inside.

I had been coming to this school in Clarksburg for a little over two years now. I came from a place that was very different from Iowa. It took all the other kids that long just to get used to me and accept me as one of their own. But that didn't keep them from testing me every once in a while. They just wanted to make sure that I was shaping up to be one of them.

Then there was the whole name thing that was causing my family a lot of trouble. I guess names like Fiana, Shannon, and Cosantoir were not very Iowan names. My sister's names were easy enough, but mine was a wee bit too difficult for them. So, it got shortened to Cos and that helped solve that problem. Our last name, McDhai, wasn't too hard for people who didn't know Irish. But I still got a lot of crap like, "Your gonna die, McDhai!" or "Hey! Tie-dyed McDhai!" That was the last time I'll ever wear that shirt to school. Then there were the comments about how that famous burger restaurant was going to name a sandwich after me. It took a while for me to sort that one, but then I decided it didn't matter.

I soon fell in with a group of boys that were known as troublemakers. They weren't so bad that stuff was getting broken, or anybody was getting killed. Just mostly things that the grown-ups said were, 'bad behavior'. Stuff we thought was fun.

So, there was Eddie Beltzer, who seemed to be the only redheaded boy in the entire school. I figured all those freckles probably got him as much crap as my name did me. We used to ride motorcycles together and got along just fine, that is until Lester showed up. Lester Vailey was this tall, skinny guy who never seemed to stop joking, but was also the meanest kid I knew. Then there was Carl Dawes. He was a small kid (I know what that's like!) who was pretty tough, but kind of shy. A really smart guy who mostly kept to himself. The thing is, if he got mad at you, then you needed to look out because you were in for trouble.

There was this one time when Carl went out of the classroom to use the toilet. The next thing we knew, this big kid ran by the door screaming because Carl was sitting up on his shoulders, pounding him on the top of his head. The whole class started laughing and then we all got in trouble because that wasn't supposed to be funny.

Anyway, I told you all that stuff so you could get to know us. But I really wanted to tell you about this weird kid whose name was Mike Belsky. He was Lester's cousin. I didn't know him, and Lester said it was because Mike didn't like me. So, he would never hang around with the gang when I was with them. At first, I believed Lester's lies, but then realized, how could Mike not like me, if he didn't know me? It didn't matter, though, because I was with Lester, and he was kind of the leader of our gang. So, Mike had no say.

Lester said everybody called Mike, 'Goon'. Well, except for Carl, who thought that was just too mean, so he was going to stick with Mike. I kind of agreed with Carl. I didn't think I could bring myself to call him that, either. But I didn't even know the guy. I never saw Mike in school, but I never gave it much thought. I just figured he was one of the high school kids that hadn't gotten around to getting in a fight with me—yet.

On the day I met him, I was walking down Fourth Street and Lester came along. He was looking for a bicycle to steal because he wanted to hang it from the flag pole at the high school.

"I'm not going to help you steal some fella's bike, Lester. You can go to jail for that."

"Ah geez, Cos, you're always worried about stupid stuff. I'm too young to go to jail. Besides, they'll just take me to my ma, if I get caught. She'll give me a good ass whupping with her paddle, and she don't even hit that hard."

"Well, I'm not helping, even though it might be kind of funny to see. So, I'll come and watch."

"Fine, but I'm gonna go down and get the Goon. He's strong enough to help me get it up that pole. Not like some weaklings I know."

He said this like he was trying to make me feel bad. Like I was no good to him. So, we didn't talk for a while, almost like he was trying to figure out jobs for weaklings like me to do. He stopped in front of this little white house with blue trim. Then he spun around really quick and bumped into me on purpose with his hip. I almost fell down and he started laughing about it as he walked up to the front door. I followed him, but I wasn't too happy about the bumping thing.

"You're a prick, Lester. I hope you know that."

"Yep, sure em. Now shut up and listen. When you meet this guy, just call him Goon, OK? He won't mind. He looks so much like that guy from the Popeye cartoons that you won't believe it. He's a freak of nature."

When we got to the door, Lester knocked with that 'shave and a haircut, two bits' kind of knock. It swung open right away and it was Mike who answered. I knew him right off. Lester hadn't been pulling my leg about what Mike looked like.

At first, I was afraid, then I felt sorry for him. That guy was even taller than Lester. His body was huge like he was already full grown. The problem was, he had a real small head, and his hair was short but had these big curls. Nothing fit. His hands hung to his knees, his legs were too short for his long upper body, and on top of that, he had this giant belly. His face was like a five-year old's and his nose was way too big for it. He looked at me through his thick glasses, and said in a voice that sounded like a giant's, "Whose dis guy, Lestah, I don't know dis guy?"

"Ah, it's okay, Goon. This is Cos, he's my new pal."

"Uhhh… hi?" Mike said, looking down at me.

"What's happening, Mi… ummm… Goon," I said, trying to sound cool.

"Hey, Lestah! Dis guy talk's funny!" He was loud, like he wanted the neighbors to hear. He started bobbing his head up and down like there was music playing and then he grinned at us, showing all his missing teeth. I already felt bad for him, and now, I was feeling worse.

"Well, so do you, you fuckin' idiot!" Lester said, pushing his way inside the house, me following.

"My mom's home, Lestah, we're gonna have to play outside."

"Ah shit, Goon, every time I come over, we gotta play outside."

"Well, my mom says so… yuh know, and she's the boss."

"Well, then let's go. Geez, quit standing around like a freaking jerk off."

Now, I suppose you noticed that Lester liked to cuss a lot. I think he did it just to impress his buddies, as they say here in Clarksburg. I was afraid if I hung around with him too much, I would start cussing a lot, too. Then some day without thinking, I would cut loose in front of my ma and that would be the end of me. I suspected she would probably kill me and bury me in the back yard, especially if anything I said took the lords name in vain. I guess I could be grateful that she just might use one of her precious tomato stakes to mark my grave. So, anyway, not only did I have to be sure to use my American words, but I also had to try to keep from saying the bad ones.

We had to go through Mike's kitchen to go out the back door. It smelled like macaroni and cheese. Mike's ma was standing there, mixing something in a bowl. She looked up and said, "Hey boys! Mike, if you're going to play in the backyard, stay outta the barn, you know your dad doesn't want you in there."

She didn't look anything like Mike.

I mumbled out a, "Hallo, mam."

Lester snickered and rolled his eyes as he followed Mike out the back door. The screen slammed shut, leaving me inside. So, I just stood there, grinning at Mike's ma. She grinned back, showing me that her and her son did have one thing in common. She certainly wasn't making regular trips down to see Doc Theobald, the dentist, that's for sure.

Lester called out, "You gonna hang out with Mike's ma, Cos, or are you going to come with us?" That made Mike laugh and slap his leg. I pushed through the door and onto the concrete pad that was all they had for a back porch. Lester and his cousin were standing out in the grass, looking at me like I was nothing but trouble. "Come on, you bozo!" Lester hollered. Mike laughed even harder. Doing my best to ignore it, I walked over to them and then we just stood there looking at each other like idiots.

"Hey! Let's go in the barn," Lester said.

Mike started to argued, but Lester won out. So, we snuck around to the alley side and went in. We spent the afternoon breaking Mike's dad's empty liquor bottles against these huge poles that held up the haymow. We were talking about what company made the best cars, the fastest motorcycles, and what the best cowboy movies were. Lester wanted to break a bottle over Mike's head, just to see if it was as easy as it was in those movies. So, he spent nearly fifteen minutes trying to talk Mike into it. He got so riled up, he threatened to punch us both just to show Lester and I how easy it was to knock somebody out with just one punch.

That's when we dropped the subject and went to trying to catch pigeons. We climbed up into the rafters and walked the big beams. Lester almost fell once, and I tried to save him, but his cousin stopped me, saying he wanted to see what would happen and whispered, "Don't be a pahty pooper." We soon gave up that idea and just lay around on the moldy, old straw bales, talking about who was the toughest movie actor. Lester wanted to go to Nordon's and steal some cigars to smoke in the barn. I was against that idea and they made fun of me for it. So, not only was I against letting Lester fall off a beam and die for Mike's pleasure, but I also didn't want to get cancer, or burn down a barn.

Lester seemed to have forgotten all about stringing a bicycle up the flag pole at the school and switched to trying to talk Mike into a sleepover. The bigger boy didn't like the idea, but then gave in when Lester promised we'd stick to being at the Vailey house instead of going anyplace people wouldn't know him.

That was the plan for the Friday night coming up. We could invite any of our pals and meet at Lester's place just before suppertime. We knew Eddie would jump at the chance to get out of having to babysit his little brothers. Carl was a 'maybe'. He was the kind of guy who just wanted to hang out at home and read comic books. The little guy just never seemed to be interested in any real adventure. I sometimes felt that it was more because he didn't want to be pushed into anything he didn't like, and of course, he wasn't afraid to tell you so. Or maybe, he just didn't like Lester.

The next few days went by really slow, and I chomped the bit during every one of them. I was pretty much free to do as I wanted because my ma thought it was important that I spend time with my new friends.

The weekend finally came around, and I remember running into the apartment to change out of my school clothes. Grabbing a crappy old sleeping bag, I yelled to my ma that I was off to Lester's for a sleepover and that I'd be back in the morning.

When I got to Lester's, Eddie was already there, but he only lived just up the hill. I was pretty sure that once his ma gave him the go-ahead, he probably shot out the door like a rocket, running all the way to the Vailey's house. Lester told us that Carl didn't want to come. He said sleepovers were for little kids, and that we were only doing it so we could walk the streets at two in the morning. He was right, though. The plan was to be out goofing off when we weren't allowed to be. We simply wanted to know what was going on out there when we were supposed to be in our beds.

Mike got to Lester's just after I did, and he had to walk all the way. It was something he seemed to have a lot of trouble doing. So, he didn't seem to be in much of a hurry. After he got there, we all went into this moldy, stinking, wall tent that Lester's ma had put up for us in the backyard. We sat down in a circle and as soon as we did, Mike pulled out a cigar and lit up.

Lester hollered, "Dammit, Goon! Can't you wait until my folks go to bed! Geez, you're an idiot!"

Mike stopped puffing for a minute, like he was thinking about it, and then pinched out the glowing end of the stogie before dropping it in his shirt pocket. I watched sparks fall on the canvas floor and got a real bad feeling.

Lester hollered again, "Goon! What the… you trying to burn down the stupid tent!"

"Crap! It's on fire! The floors on fire!" Eddie screamed, and jumping up, he tripped over my foot and fell out through the door. He turned over on his back and tried to crawl away with his elbows. His eyes were really big, like he was afraid the fire was going to come after him.

His face got really red when he realized that he was just panicking. That made us laugh. Mike started patting out the fire with his bare hands. Lester had grabbed a metal canteen and was getting ready to dump water on the floor when Mike's shirt pocket burst into flames.

I said, "Mike! Your shirt! Your shirt!"

He let out a weird howl and started slapping at his chest. Then pulling out the now mangled cigar, he spit on the end of it. The slime that didn't stay on the cigar, made a big thick string that ran down to the canvas and put out a few more sparks.

"Damn, Goon, instead of using your hands, I suppose you could have just spit the fire out," Lester said and laughed.

I guess Lester didn't want to let his idea go to waste, so he just splashed the water all over Mike's shirt.

"Lestah, you creep."

"Oh, crap Goon, you big slob, what's your problem?" Lester said, and reaching over, he flicked his cousin's ear.

"Yeah, Goon, what's with you, you big oaf," Eddie said, crawling back inside.

Mike looked at me like he was waiting for me to take my turn. I just shrugged. I wondered if this was the way it was going to go the whole night. The two of them nagging the crap out of the big guy and me feeling sorry for him.

He seemed to have a problem that no grown-ups could solve. But I figured it wasn't any of my business. I just unrolled my sleeping bag by the north wall and pretended like nothing had happened.

We spent suppertime messing around with Lester's pets and going back to the tent on occasion to eat the snacks that Lester's ma had put in there. It bothered me that we wouldn't be getting any supper. I really wanted a hamburger, a pizza, or something. All we were going to get was orange soda, potato chips, donuts, cookies, a box of Coco Puffs, Beer Nuts, beef jerky, and some radishes, because they were Lester's favorite vegetable. Before that moment, I didn't know anybody had a favorite vegetable.

When dark finally came around, we went back inside the smelly tent and waited for Lester's folks to go to bed. We spent the whole time talking about certain girls in our class and tried to impress each other with lies about sex. It was some pretty ridiculous stuff and too stupid to be true. But it was just like fish stories. We had to 'one up' each other, and it was more about who could tell the best one. Eddie tried to talk us into a circle jerk, something he had heard about, once. But none of us seemed to know what that was. So, we changed the subject.

Mike only wanted to talk about one girl in particular: Terri Dormyer. She was his first real crush and probably the only girl that ever gave him the time of day. He went on about how she had said hi to him once and then gave him a stick of gum. But we all had our own loves at the moment, mine being, Denise Donnelly. She was this beautiful, blue-eyed girl in my class who always wore miniskirts. She had light brown hair cut to match Jane Fonda's shag. Her face was always sad though, and someone told me that was because she had found her father hanging by his neck in the garage, deader than a door nail. Supposedly that was the year I came to Clarksburg.

Anyway, Mike kept going on about Terri and what they were going to do when they finally went out on a date. He was going to take her to the Dairy Dreem for burgers. I actually felt kind of good about him having a dream, even though I knew it was all blarney. Eddie and Lester started picking on him about it, and that got him all worked up, making him think it was a lost cause. At one point, Mike got so pissed, he stomped out.

"Where the hell you going, Goon We're not supposed to leave. Get back in here, you big lug."

He just stood outside the door, his hands in his pockets with his head hanging down. I poked my head out and begged him to come back in.

"Come on, lad. They didn't mean nothing by it. They're just putting you on."

"Piss on you, Irish boy, leave me alone."

"Oh, come on, they were just having a wee bit of fun."

But Eddie and Lester didn't help matters by laughing all the time I was trying to convinced him. After about twenty minutes, he finally gave up and crawled back inside. I felt like I had done something good, and also saved our sleepover from being cut short by Lester's folks. I thought that Mike and I might be able to become friends, but he just ignored me. He sat in the corner, facing the wall, picking his nose. Lester and Eddie were now whispering to each other and looking at me every once in a while.

"What you whispering about?"

"Don't worry about it," Lester said. Eddie giggled.

"We'll tell you later, okay? Just before we head out," Eddie said, and then he and Lester looked at each other in a way that made me worry.

When the lights in the house went off and we knew Lester's folks were in their bed, we snuck out the back flap. The zipper was really loud. So, we just left it open, and climbing over the fence, we went into the cornfield. We worked our way between the rows and came out on the street about half a block away. That's when they told Goon, and I, what the plan was. We were going to sneak up to Terri Dormyer's house and peek in the windows. I didn't like the idea, but it had been Eddie's, and Lester was all for it. Lester told me it was supposed to be my initiation into a new club he and Eddie were starting. This didn't make any sense to me, and I started nagging at them about what they meant. They just kept looking at each other in a way that was like, 'If you want to be a part of the gang… then just go along with it.'

When we got to Terri's street, we stood on the sidewalk just outside her huge house. Mike stayed back on the corner because Lester told him to. He was supposed to be the lookout in case Marshal Tylor showed up. The three of us walked over into her yard and Eddie told me to go around back and look in the big window. He was pretty sure that's where her bedroom was. Then I should come back and tell them what I saw.

"I don't want to go by myself. One of you, should come with me."

"What? Are you chicken or something?" Lester said.

"Yeah, chicken! Buk-buk-burraakkk!" Eddie mocked and started strutting around like a rooster. I thought about how easy it would be to punch him in the nose and run away. It was just… the fact that I didn't want to be known as a chicken kind of overrode my need for revenge. Besides, all I had to do was go peek in the window, and then come back and tell them what I saw.

I gave them a dirty look and took off around the house. The window was just over my head. I had to get up on my tiptoes to look. There was a big table with a bunch of chairs around it and I knew right off that it wasn't Terri's bedroom. Someone had made a big mistake. I thought it was funny though because it gave me a chance to go back and tell them what dummies they were. Sneaking back across the lawn, I saw they were now out in the street, looking like they were getting ready to run.

"Well, did you talk to her, Cos? What'd she say?" Lester asked this like he already knew the answer and was talking loud enough to make sure Mike heard him.

Eddie said, "Yeah, Cos, what'd she say? Did she say she thought Goon was sexy and couldn't wait to see him again?" Mike was already walking to us, puffing on his mangled stogie.

I wanted to tell the truth and let them know that someone slipped up, but for some stupid reason, I played along.

"Ummm… yeah! She told me Goon was a great guy, and she wished he'd get his arse back there."

"Great! So… tell him, Cos. Tell him!" Lester and Eddie said this at the same time, nodding their heads and grinning at each other like they knew something I didn't. So, when Mike got to us, like the biggest fool in the history of lying fools, I told him what he wanted to hear.

"Hey, Mike."

"It's Goon, you shithead, call me Goon, I'm, dah Goon!" he said, raising his arms up above his head like he was one of those fake wrestling stars on TV. I didn't like being called a shithead. So, I really poured on the blarney.

"Terri says she can't wait to see you. She's waiting back there with the window open so you can just crawl in."

Mike perked right up, and almost knocked us down when he pushed through us and ran for that window. He did this kind of limping thing across the grass before going around the corner of the house. I stood with the other two, watching him go, waiting. I should have been running. Mike came back around that corner like an angry bear. He was moving pretty fast for a guy who couldn't walk worth a damn and the look on his face said he wasn't coming to thank me.

Now, I know what a haymaker is, but I've never gotten one. And honestly, I didn't see this one coming. There were stars just like in the cartoons, and I was out cold before my brain had a chance to tell me it hurt. Goon may have been slow on his feet, but he was quick with his fists. I remember opening my eyes and looking straight up at the real stars as they shined through the tree tops. Lester and Eddie were standing around me, talking about calling an ambulance. I came up off the pavement pretty fast, but almost fell down again.

"You maggots!"

Eddie whined, "Ah, Cos, it was just a joke, come on now."

"Yeah, Cos, just a joke," Lester said, trying not to laugh.

"You two can just bugger off. Especially you, Lester Vailey, you… you big prick."

I looked around and finding a long, thick branch lying in the grass, I picked it up. I now had a nice little club that I was going to go share with Mike. He was standing in the street about halfway down the block. I started running and so did he—only in the other direction.

Eddie was the first to catch up, with Lester close behind. Snatching the stick out of my hand, he said, "Now, Cos, just calm down, you've got to be the better man,"

"Up your arse, Lester. You put me up to this."

"Just calm down before somebody really gets hurt," Eddie begged.

"Really? Until somebody gets hurt? What the fek… didn't I just get hurt? You eejit! You know, it's your arse I'd ought to be beating, Eddie Beltzer!"

I pushed him hard and he stumbled. Backing away, he stuttered, "Now Cos, you've guh… guh… got to be the better man."

"Ah shite! You eejit! You don't even know what that means."

Lights started blinking on in houses up and down the street. Eddie's place was just two houses down. We saw a light come on in the upstairs bedroom and Eddie said, "Oh, shit." We scattered. I left them and ran down the hill the same way Mike had gone. Cutting over to the train tracks, I found where they crossed the Ryan's front walk and I headed across the railroad bridge.

Sneaking in the back door, I tipped toed to my bed and lay there on my back, rubbing at my jaw and feeling glad that it wasn't my eye or my nose. I fell asleep plotting my revenge.

I woke up late and lay staring at the ceiling, my face throbbing, and thinking about everything that had happened. I didn't feel so mad anymore and kind of figured that I probably deserved it. I stopped thinking about revenge and started thinking of ways I could avoid Lester and Eddie for the rest of my life. It was going to be impossible, there was just no way. I wouldn't see Mike at all, but the other two were with me for about six hours a day until summer.

So, I did my best to ignore them, and they kept their distance. Sometimes they passed me in the hallways or in the lunch room, but they never tried to talk to me. One day, out of meanness, I stomped a foot toward Eddie as he was walking by. He ran away to the end of the hallway and into the high school. All the other kids laughed, and then we saw an upper classmen grab him and stuff him into a locker. So, we laughed even harder, but then we ran away, just in case that guy tried to grab us.

The gossip spread pretty quickly about how I had a fight with Lester's cousin and almost beat him to death with a stick. When the other kids asked if it was true, I just pointed to my bruise and said, "What do you think?"

One night, at the beginning of summer, I was riding a bicycle up the street toward the school. Rolling past Mike's house, I saw a 'For Sale' sign in the front yard. I stopped for a minute and noticed the curtains were gone, and looking in a window, I saw the furniture was too. A sad feeling came over me, but I couldn't figure out why. I felt like something had been stolen from me. Not because I never got my revenge, but because, honestly, I still wanted to tell Mike I was sorry that I had pulled that crap on him.

Now, I would never be able too, and that was unfinished business like my ma was always saying. I figured I would just have to add it to the list of things that never got settled. It wouldn't be easy, but I knew I'd survive. I continued up the street from Mike's place, there was something I wanted to do and didn't want to go home until I got it done. Afterwards, I had plenty of time to think about stuff when I was walking home, and I was feeling a whole lot better about the whole mess.

I woke up about eleven o'clock the next morning. I went into the kitchen for a bowl of cereal and saw ma already laid out on the couch, smoking Pal Mals and watching the first soap opera for the day. I sat at the breakfast table where a copy of the morning edition of the Clarksburg News was scattered over the table. It was quite a mess, but that's how ma always left it. I could see the front page lying there and I pulled it to me. I got a bit of a jolt when I read the headlines.

Only in Clarksburg would that subject be headline news. There was a big, black & white picture showing the Marshal standing with two men, pointing at a bicycle hanging from the flagpole at the high school. They were all grinning like they thought it was the funniest thing they'd ever seen. Underneath, it said that Eddie Beltzer's bicycle had been taken yesterday evening from where he had left it in his front yard. Marshal Tylor had found it hanging from the pole this morning and called some volunteer firemen for a wee bit of help; one of them being the newspaper reporter and the very guy who wrote the article. He was quoted as saying, "Just no way one guy could have done it all by himself.

I just grinned and whispered, "Want to bet?"

#11

An Unfortunate Fandango

I have to say it. It may not be good for me, but I've held it in for too long. I hate that game that boys and girls always play, the one where you have to try and figure out who likes you and who doesn't. For me, I just look at a girl and decide if I like her or not. If I do, then I spend days trying to let her know it and even after all that work, she just might tell me to take a hike. Then, I have to start all over again with someone else. It makes me tired, and sometimes I wish I could just go back to that time when it didn't matter, and we were all just good friends. Like two years ago in the seventh grade when we hung out together, just doing stuff and nobody caring if they had a boyfriend or girlfriend. Back when high school was still too far away for any of us to care.

Don't get me wrong though, we knew back then who was cute and who wasn't, it just didn't matter. If we told somebody in our class that they weren't cute, they'd get sad, madder than hell, or tell us to stick it where the sun don't shine. They might even cry. I don't know if I'd ever cry. It could happen, though. That would be embarrassing. We all usually did that Thumper thing (you know? Bambi's friend?) where if you didn't have anything nice to say, you didn't say nothing at all.

That changed when we got older; I don't know why. Of course, that brought the new rule that if we all agreed someone wasn't 'good looking' then we couldn't like them. So, that left me with a choice to either stick with my friends and agree, or lose all my friends, but still have a choice of whoever I wanted to hang out with; risking nobody liking me at all. Which, when you think about it, is really how you make new friends. I always wondered how I rated but was clueless until Rebecca Holibit got into an argument with Debby Pearl about what made a guy cute and what didn't. She sat in front of me in Mrs. Yahkee's class and turning around, she looked right at me, and then she looked at Doug Moore, who happened to be sitting in the desk next to mine and said, "Now, uhhh… look at Doug, he's cute. But Clint, well, he's…" Now I have to stop there because I have to admit, I was really afraid what was going to come out of her mouth and that it was going to make me feel bad. I kind of held my breath, waiting, trying to figure out what kind of an ugly animal I was going to call her. But she finished it with, "…handsome." Then looking back at Debbie, she said, "There's a big difference, you know?"

Debbie looked at me and then at Doug and then back to me. Then she grinned at Rebecca and said, "Yeah, I see what you mean." They had to stop talking because Mrs. Yahkee was coming in the door. The thing is, everybody else in the class was still looking at me and Doug, who was now blushing. I studied every face as my eyes moved around the room. That was until they landed on Phoebe Lindlee. She was smiling at me, but not like the others. Not like a smart ass, but more like she agreed with Rebecca. Phoebe had this long, straight, brown hair all the way down to her waist and these big brown eyes. Her face was kind of triangular and tanned. She even had a few freckles even though she wasn't a redhead like Shelly Anderson.

The other girls said Phoebe was plain. I didn't know what they meant by that because she and I never talked. We'd be walking toward each other in the hall, and just say hi, but keep on going. Except one time, I looked back because she had on these bell-bottomed jeans with bigger than average bells. I just wanted to get a look at them without her knowing, kind of wondering if they made them for boys, too. The problem with looking back at her, was… she was looking back at me. So, I hollered out to Bailey Barnes who was walking past her and coming my way. That way she'd think I was looking at him, instead.

Now, she was giving me this look from across the room like we were the best of friends. I decided to ignore her and gave Rebecca and Debbie my full attention, just in case they had more to say about me being handsome.

If Rebecca thought I was handsome, then maybe she might want to go out with me. The rumor had it, though, she was dating Craig Campbell, Clarksburg high's football hero. But I had never seen them together. Maybe she would leave him behind for me because of my handsomeness. I mean, I was pretty satisfied with what she said, and really glad no one had argued. So, it was final, I was 100 percent sure that she had spoken the truth. I now knew I was handsome and wasn't going to let anything change that.

So, it was October of 1972 and I had been a freshman at Clarksburg high for nearly three months. That made me an upper classman, but only to the 8th graders because they were the only ones who cared about that. They were now off limits, though. The problem was, I couldn't be friends with the kids above me either because that too was against the rules. Freshman year was 'no-man's land'

You had to spend the whole school year proving yourself to everybody above you by acting cool. The negative side of that was, by the time you became a sophomore, the seniors in your first year were all gone, and the juniors took their place. So, we really needed to start impressing those guys for when that second year came around. That way we'd have friends at the top. Also, I think it was pretty much agreed by all of my classmates that we had to stick together if we were going to survive high school. That brought us a little closer, and I have to admit, I was pretty happy we were all getting along so well as freshman.

One thing that was really great about being in high school was that lunch time was free time. We didn't have to stay on campus and could kill that hour going anywhere we wanted as long as we were back in time for class. I had gone down to Nordon's drug store for a candy bar and was coming up the middle of Fourth Street, just walking and singing *Girl With No Eyes* by that band, It's A Beautiful Day. I was getting frustrated because I couldn't remember all the lyrics when I heard someone holler, "Hey Clit! Clit Torres!"

It was Tony Boneyad. He had been sitting in a car parked alongside the street, smoking cigarettes. I told him a thousand times not to call me that. There were a ton of other students around, sitting in, and on their cars. They were all laughing at me now and whispering, "Clits here. Hey everyone, there's a clit." I thought it was pretty weird that everybody acted like they knew what that was. I doubted they did and figured not one of them had ever seen one. Well, at least not the boys, anyway. Tony flicked his cigarette butt at me through the open window and then got out of the car.

"What do you want? Bonehead. Tony Boner… your Boneness!"

That, for some reason, got more laughs than Tony's remark, and from all the right people, too. So, I felt redeemed. Phoebe, who was sitting on a car hood close to where I was standing, didn't laugh at Tony's joke, but laughed like crazy at mine. I looked right at her and I could tell she was kind of embarrassed because all the kids were laughing about girl parts. She gave me a little wave and I threw up my hand for second without thinking about it.

She leaned over to Denise Donnelly, real quick like, and said something. They both laughed so hard they almost fell off the car. I don't know what that was about, but I figured I'd ask them once I got done dealing with Tony.

Now, that guy was a real joker. He pulled pranks on just about everyone in the school, including some of the teachers. So, basically, everybody had a 'bone' to pick with him and looked for every opportunity to make fun of him. The need for revenge was strong in me. I had actually gotten back at him for everyone that was there, who he had pranked in the past, and I think that put me on their good side. Tony just walked to me, grinning like he didn't care what anybody said or did.

"Thought I told you not to call me that, you prick," I said, pretending I was pissed off. "You don't even know what that is."

"Ah, come on, Clint. We're buddies, right? Buddies should be able to make fun of each other and not go off half-cocked, capeesh?"

I didn't know what a capeesh was, but I still said, "No, not capeesh. I don't care what else you call me, just not that. Got it… bone-a-fied?"

He stood looking at me with one green eye wide open and the other squinting. His forehead was all wrinkled up and his short, bristly blond hair, which he parted on the side, seemed to be standing up like those alley cats when they get to fighting. I prepared myself to take the first punch. Tony was tougher than me and looked it too. He always wore a tight black tee shirt and peg legged Levi's with these stupid motorcycle boots. He tucked his jeans inside so everybody could get a real good look at the shiny black leather and all the buckles.

He brought his fists up and I got ready to duck, but then he laughed and slapped me on the shoulder. "Thought I was going to hit you, didn't you?" I relaxed and shrugged. Then after I had a few seconds to think about it, I clapped him on the back like we were the best of friends. He pretended like he was getting ready to box me, but then stopped and blurted out, "Hey! Dance this Saturday! Prairieville Ballroom! First time legal! Sixteen now, you know? Going? You've got to, Clint. It's going to be a good time! Ain't no fun without you."

He was buttering me up. But I already planned to go and had raked a few extra lawns around town to get some cash to pay the door fee and maybe even have a soda, or two. But I liked hearing him beg. I wanted to hear the great Tony Boneyad sweet talk me into going.

The Prairieville Ballroom was in Prairieville (of course), and it was the place to be on a Saturday night. Most of the bands sucked because old people ran it, and they didn't know what the good music was in the '70's. But this Saturday was the Kenny Can't band and they did rock & roll. Ol' man Kubla would only hire them twice a month because every kid from every county around would show up. It took him, and the rest of the Kubla family at least a week to clean up and make repairs to the building. So, he'd schedule The Czech Party accordion band and the Willy Waltzers in between. But I knew Kenny Can't brought in the big money, and I also knew ol' man Kubla was a greedy bastard. Kenny Can't was going to keep the Prairieville Ballroom alive for as long as rock & roll existed.

Saturday rolled around and all I could think about was going to the ballroom. I had my paper route to get done in the afternoon and the whole time I was tossing them papers, I was thinking about what I was going to wear, how I was going to comb my hair, and if I should wear my tennis shoes or my Sunday dress up wing tips. So, just all that stuff a guy has to deal with when they're going to a dance. Besides, I already had solid evidence that I was handsome. So, I didn't have nothing to worry about. Wick Ryan and his girlfriend Zillia Struck were there getting their papers, too. They were younger than me. I stuck to the rule of not talking to junior high kids, even though Wick was a pretty nice guy. Also, well… I was a little scared of Zillia. She was this little beauty with short, curly, red hair, who could hold her own in a fight. I seen her go at it with an older kid who was picking on Wick. She was on him like a rabid wildcat. To avoid accidently starting something, I just smiled and kept on packing up my papers.

It was collection day, and I was going to rake in about a fifth of the total amount that I got from my customers. That would be about five bucks that I could add to the ten I already had in my pocket. I just knew it was going to be good because the only thing that could ruin the night was that I wouldn't be able to talk some girl into dancing with me, or that there would be a fight.

Fights ruined everything. I won't start one, but I never had a problem finishing them. But then your face got bloody, your clothes got bloody, and maybe you'd lose a tooth or get a black eye that you had to look at in the mirror every day for weeks after. No girl thought a black eye was handsome.

Now, I have to say, the worst thing of all, was that Kubla hired a deputy sheriff to work the dance. If he had to interfere, he would make it worth his trouble by hauling you in and making you spend a night in a jail cell so you could learn your lesson. I didn't need to learn a lesson. I already knew that listening to music, drinking sodas, and dancing with a girl, was a hell of a lot more fun than fighting and going to the hoosegow. If it came down to it, I could only hope that Tony was around because he'd jump right in. Then I could just disappear into the crowd when he made the fight all about him. He wouldn't mind and would even get mad at me if I ruined his chances for that kind of attention.

All he needed for a reason to cut loose, was to know one of his friends was getting pounded. Then he'd turn into that Tasmanian Devil that you see in the Looney Tune cartoons. Honestly, you didn't want to be in his way. Tony had this thing about his friends. If he liked you—he'd do anything for you, and he even told me so. He was in the boxing club over at the community center, and fights at the ballroom were just sparring practice to him.

The dance started at seven o'clock and I was in the john at home, killing time, putting some last-minute touches on my looks. I lived on the edge of town where Highway 13 and Main Street met up on the hill. It turned into a gravel road where it ran up past Pinecone Ridge, the county park. My place was a giant chicken coop that somebody had made into a house. There wasn't a whole lot of room in there, but my dad drove truck, so he was hardly ever around. The oldest of my brothers and sisters had moved out. It was just me, my crazy ma, and my big sister, Florence. If you came to pick me up in your car, you would have to drive by the place, take a right on Hillcrest Street and then another quick right into our driveway. I was standing out front at fifteen minutes to seven when Mike T's '57 Chevy coupe whipped around the corner and roared up to the house.

Now, I have to tell you, Mike T was a sophomore. But he was that one guy in the whole high school who didn't care if you were a freshman or a senior. Mike just wanted to have friends. He had one brown eye and one blue. His hair looked like a helmet made of chocolate and somebody told me once it was that way because he'd played football all his life and the helmet that the football players had to wear shaped it that way permanently.

The '57 Chevy was his personal project. He had fixed it up all by himself. Having a car like that helped him make all those friends I was telling you about. That meant a free ride to Prairieville because he was heading over there, too. His girl, Shelagh Bennett, had her own car (her dad's actually) and wanted to drive it to the dance. So, she wasn't in the Chevy with him. The gossip was, her and Mike got into a lot of arguments about who was going to drive when they went out on dates. Mike was too proud of his car to give in to Shelagh. She was what my grandma called 'strong willed'. Now me, I called it stubborn. But you just have to know Shelagh. She was smart, good looking, and tough. So, you didn't want to get on her bad side, either. Mike had his hands full with that girl. Also, Mike was kind of goofy, but we never said anything to him about it. I imagined once we all got our drivers licenses, Tony would be the first to tell him that we thought he looked and acted just like that hat wearing dog in the cartoons. I didn't want to hurt Mike's feelings. So, it surely wasn't coming from me.

Mike tore into the driveway and slammed on the brakes right in front of me and then had to go and honk his horn even though I was standing right there. It scared me and I jumped about a foot off the ground, and of course, everybody laughed. That's what he wanted, and I felt kind of stupid.

"Hey Clit!" Tony hollered from the backseat. They all laughed again, so I gave every one of them the finger. Billy Blahnik and his girlfriend, Sherry T, who was Mike T's older cousin, were sitting in the front seat. My best friend, a kid we called Pesky, sat in the back with Tony. He was a Fulton (his cousin, Harry, had just got tossed in jail for a year for beating a guy to within an inch of his life). Pesky was just a quiet, smart kid, who smiled a lot.

Billy jumped out and pulled the seat forward so I could get in. Pesky had to slide over next to Tony, who started to look uncomfortable because another boy was sitting so close. Billy got back in about the same time my ma came and stood in the front door (that I'd left open).

"You need to be making all that noise?" she yelled at Mike.

She was wiping down a pot she had just washed and anyone who mouthed off would find out just how well she could throw it. "Don't you be coming up here, honking that damn horn, you hear me?"

Mike just froze and stared at her out of his window. "Oh… uh, okay, Mrs. Torres," was all he said.

She yelled at me next. "Clint, how many times have I told you to shut this damn door?"

"Just go, Mike," I whispered. "Do it slowly—but go."

Everybody else was snickering and I was afraid Tony was going to blurt out something stupid before we were able to get gone. If he did and she could catch the car, she'd hit him with that pot— maybe twice. She might even throw it and dent Mike's car. I can tell you through experience there was a good chance of that happening. The car started rolling slowly backwards to the street about the same time my sister, Flo, came out to stand on the stoop in her green mini skirt. She had blond hair and it was picking up what was left of the sunlight still coming over the hill at Pinecone Ridge.

"Aw, ma, leave him alone. Can't you just let Clint have a little fun? Come on, it's Saturday."

Ma never argued with Flo. She didn't say another word and stomped back into the kitchen. I could see her through the little window at the sink and I knew she was doing that glaring thing she always does.

Flo had a date with some college kid down in Cedar Rapids. He was a Butters. My Jr. high reading teacher's son. Him and Flo had been friends a long time. They were going to the same college next year in August. I figured they weren't going to get much studying done.

Flo was waiting on him to get there and probably just wanted me and my friends to be out of there before he showed up. As soon as we got out on the street, Tony said, "Man, that Flo, she's a looker. How can you live with that? You ever sneak in when she's taking a bath? Man, I'd be horny everyday with her around if I were you."

"Ah, geez, Tony, she's my sister, for cripes sake!"

Everybody was looking at him weird, except for Mike T who had to drive. Tony shrugged but couldn't leave it alone.

"How come your sister's got blonde hair and you got brown? She got a different father?" Nobody laughed. They were still staring like they couldn't believe this guy and were all waiting to see what I was going to do about it.

"Well, Tony," I said, "She's actually your long-lost sister. After your ma gave birth to her, my dad wanted all his kids under one roof. Your ma took fifty bucks for her… and then she went and had you. A sad day in the history of Clarksburg."

Now everybody did laugh. Tony turned red, and Sherry said, "You deserve that one, Tony." "Yeah, maybe," he said, and then laughed before reaching across Pesky to punch me in the leg. He really didn't want it to hurt—but he could have.

Mike T turned up the tape player when we got just outside of town and nobody said much the whole six miles to Prairieville. I didn't get to ride in a car that often, and I just sat there with the window down and the wind blowing through my hair listening to Fleetwood Mac.

When Mike T pulled up in front of the dance hall, some kids in in their folk's station wagon whipped out of a spot across the street, so Mike took it.

"He-he, now I don't have to park out back. Dent city back there; let me tell you!"

Nobody said anything because we were too busy piling out of the car. Going inside, we paid our money to old man Kubla at the door, and then scattered. Billy and Sherry went right to the dance floor because Kenny Can't was doing a slow number called, *Color My World* by Chicago. Tony just disappeared into the crowd, his head pivoting around like a hawk on the hunt. Pesky and I followed Mike T who eventually hooked up with Shelagh. She grabbed Mike in a bear hug, lifted him up off the floor and squeezed. Looking at us at the same time, she said, "Hey, boys."

Shelagh was wearing her typical white sleeveless tee-shirt and tight bellbottom jeans. That girl was really curvy. Dropping Mike, she put her hands on her hips and stuck out her chest. She was really posing for us. A lot of kids didn't like her. I think that was because she had no shame. She had big boobs and she most certainly wanted you to notice. So, sometimes she'd talk about them like they were a new pair of shoes. I secretly lusted after her, but I didn't really know why. She dragged Mike to the floor, and they disappeared into the crowd of dancers.

I looked at Pesky, who grinned and said, "Let's do a walk-around and see who's here."

"Gotcha," I said.

The place had a low ceiling but was as big as the gymnasium at Clarksburg high. Everything was made of pine wood and varnished to be super shiny. It was dark in there with just the wall lights on (except for the bar) and the disco ball at the center of the ceiling that was spinning and throwing dots of light everywhere. Moving counter clockwise, we went along the bar that took up half the wall on the right-hand side and then a bunch of tables in a big open area that must have been an addition they added on later. If you wanted to eat something, that's where you went. I can't say too much for the food, but I don't think people came to the ballroom to eat.

The stage was on the back wall and when we got there, the trumpet player grinned and nodded at us. Probably because he'd seen us before when we were hanging out up front. That guy knew we were serious fans of Kenny Can't. Taking a left at the next corner, we walked past the longest row of wooden booths in the world.

It was crazy on that side. The booths were packed, kids were climbing all over them and squeezing five or six people into a four-person seat. Girls sat or laid on tabletops with boys just staring at their bodies. There was laughing, yelling, giggling, lots of screaming (in happiness—I think), and tons of cigarettes getting smoked. Some of them didn't smell like tobacco either. There were kids hiding bottles of beer and sipping out of them when the deputy wasn't looking.

That guy (I think it was Jonny Herman) stayed closed to where the bar met the wall by the front door. He could see the whole room from there and keep his eye on the drinkers. I could tell he was wanting it all to be over. I don't think he wanted to ruin anyone's night unless a fight broke out. So, if that didn't happen, it would stay fun and we'd all leave happy. Then he'd go home with a pocket full of Kubla's money and no paperwork.

The band ended the one song and went right into *Keep On Chooglin'* by Creedence Clearwater. There was a stampede and three fourths of the booths emptied out onto the dance floor. So, we took one of them. Pesky and I just sat, looking around, the both of us trying to zero in on any single girl who looked like she needed a friend. I figured we both stood a good chance of getting at least one dance.

Now, I need to tell you some more about Pesky. He was tall and skinny. He never seemed to get zits and he had these blue eyes that girls just loved. He attracted them like ants to sugar. There was always one or two girls hanging around with him at school when we weren't in class. Pesky didn't go steady with anybody. He wanted his freedom and the fun that went with it. I'd put my money on him to be the first one to get a dance.

We just sat there craning our necks, trying to make sure everybody knew we were searching. That way, if any cool girl was checking us out, they would know that we were on the prowl. I saw Phoebe standing with her friends, Mary Niemeyer, and Copper, Saleena Birdsongs little sister. Saleena hung out with Cos McDhai, the Irish kid who lived in the old post office. She was Pesky's cousin's girlfriend. I heard it was because of her that Harry had beaten that one guy to a pulp. The Birdsongs were American Indians, and that creep had been making fun of her. I only knew this because Copper was always bragging about Saleena and all her friends.

So, those three girls were over by the stage, carrying on, laughing, and talking with their hands (something Flo was always saying people did). They were having a good time, but they looked like groupies.

They were the plain girls, or at least, that's what everybody said. I wasn't sure what was wrong with that, though. They had everything that makes a girl, a girl. On top of that, they were the smartest kids in my class. I think it's because they weren't cool. I probably should mention that if Tony saw me with anyone of those three, he'd pick on me forever without a moment's peace.

Phoebe suddenly just stopped paying attention to her friends and looked straight at me. She caught me staring. I mean, she zeroed in on me like a hunter who'd spotted a rabbit. She grinned and gave me a little wave. I waved back by just tilting my hand up at the wrist from the top of the table and rocked it back and forth. She motioned for me to come over, but I shook my head and mouthed the word, "No." If any other girls saw me over there, they might think I was with Phoebe, Marie, or Copper. Then I'd never get a dance.

This might be a good time to mention the troublemakers. There were always one or two groups, made up of three or four guys patrolling the floor, trying to find kids that were easy to scare. Then they'd try to get them to fight by picking on them until they'd had enough and would then say something stupid that would get their asses kicked.

One group had already passed us by, but they were Clarksburg upper classmen and once they recognized us, they moved on. They were really looking for kids from other towns, especially our football rival, Coogan high. Prairieville, Waubeek, Buffalo Ridge, and all the kids from over in the little town called Paris, went to our school. That included all the farmers, too. Coogan had their own school and took in all the little towns around it, plus all the farmers up that way. I always skipped the football game when they came down. It was too easy to get jumped and left to bleed beneath the bleachers.

Pesky said, "You should go over and see what Phoebe wants."

"You saw that?"

"Duh! Hey, Clint, you might be blowing it. Go over there!"

"Naw, what if someone cooler comes along? Phoebe might ruin my chance."

"Okay, well, have it your way, but I think you're going to be singing *Mr. Lonely* when this night is over."

"That's what you think. So, do you see anybody?"

"Well, there's a red headed girl standing over by that ceiling column. She's just kind of swaying to the music, with her eyes closed, and no boys around, and... Oh shit! troublemakers coming up behind you. Clint, get ready. They look like Coogan boys and there's four of them."

I didn't bother to turn around, instead, I slid into the corner of the booth and stretched my legs out on the seat with my back to the wall. I pretended like I didn't see them until they stopped beside our table. They had hair down to their shoulders and peach fuzz on their faces. They looked tough, and I knew unless someone helped us, we were out of luck.

A tall kid with a big Maltese Cross hanging around his neck, said, "Hey, Bobby, these guys look like Clarksburg scum."

The shortest of the group, a guy with a chipped front tooth and a round flat face, who I think was the leader, looked at Pesky, then at me, and said, "Yeah, looks like it to me, Timbo. Hey, you guys Clarksburg pussies?"

We didn't say anything and just sat there, waiting to get pulled out of our booth, thrown to the floor, and kicked by four pairs of boots. I could see the deputy was watching and the Coogan boys knew it.

There were four big men sitting in one of the booths over along the front wall. I knew the biggest of the four, Crazy Vaughn Earhart. His name said it all. He was big and muscle bound. Vaughn was a roofer when he wasn't at the university going to class. Vaughn had a permanent tan from all that roofing, wild brown hair, and a Fu Manchu mustache.

He had an eye on the Coogan guys too, and I could tell he was letting the other three know what was going on at our table. They were almost as big as him and every one of them was from Clarksburg. I figured they'd jump in if these Coogan boys grabbed us. I just hoped it would happen before I got too much of the crap kicked out of me.

I don't think the troublemakers knew what was coming, so they didn't know not to kick our asses. Just when I thought they were coming for us, some girl walked up and faced off with the short guy. She put her hands on her hips, stuck her face in his and said something to him. She was mad about something and I could tell they respected her.

The four of them just walked away, and after a few steps the short guy looked back and frowned, but it was at her, not us. Then she put her eyes on me, her hands still on her hips. She had the same round, flat face as that Coogan kid, and her nose was the same. She grinned at me and I saw her teeth were perfect. She had freckles, long, wavy, dark, brown hair and green eyes. This girl, or woman, I should say, had a body like Shelagh. Curvy. Her tight jeans and tee shirt made her look curvier, even though she wore a brown plaid flannel shirt over it. She had big, rough hands, and I suspected she might be a farm girl. I realized that the Coogan troublemakers all wore the exact same shirt. I figured they wanted to be able to recognize each other from across the room or something like that. Coogan colors were purple and white, but they weren't showing them. So, I figured they must have graduated high school already. It was like they were some kind of a Scottish clan. The thought made me want to laugh, but it wasn't a good time for that kind of thing.

"Hey," the girl said. "Can I sit with you guys?"

I looked at Pesky and he shrugged. So, I said, "Sure, free country."

I swung my legs off the seat, and she plopped down. Sitting beside me, I realized she was a lot bigger than me, but she smelled good and I could tell she'd spent a lot of time getting made up for the dance. That's when I saw Phoebe was halfway across the floor, coming toward me. She just stopped, threw up her hands and made the 'Oh well!' face. Turning around, she went back to Marie and Copper.

My new friend pushed herself up against me and I started to heat up. But it wasn't the room temperature that was doing it. She was looking at me real hard and grinning. She flipped her hair back and some of it whipped my face. It smelled like green apple shampoo, one of my favorite smells. I was getting excited now, and that kind of scared me. She kind of scared me. The girl looked at Pesky, and then I looked at Pesky, and he said, "That redhaired girl over there is looking around like she wants company. I think I'll go over there and talk to her."

He started to slide out and without thinking, I said, "Hey, I'll go with you."

"Oh, please, no," the girl said. "Stay with me, I like you."

"Yeah, Clint, stay with her, she likes you. Besides, I don't need you over there ruining my chances of getting a dance."

"Yeah, Clint, stay here—with me," the girl said, and I looked up into her eyes. They were half closed, and she was looking down her nose at me. Then she licked her lips, and I got a chill. Pesky winked at me and walked away. When he got to that redhead, he said something, and she grabbed his hand and yanked him out onto the floor. The song changed to something slow, and the next thing I knew, Pesky had his arms around that girl and they're moving around the floor in some kind of a waltz, her face about an inch from his. One minute later, they were kissing. I was thinking that was just like Pesky. It was that easy for him. He was a lover, not a fighter. I didn't know if I was a lover or a fighter, but I knew I was in trouble if this girl kept looking at me the way she was. The thought, 'She's gonna eat me alive,' rolled through my head.

"Hey, Clint, let's dance, too," the girl said, and she pulled me from the booth. We stopped in an open spot on the floor where everybody could see us and the next thing I knew, she had me in a kind of bearhug as we moved around the floor. She had me crushed to her body and there was no way I could ignore how big her boobs were. She had my face practically buried between them. Then she kind of picked me up and put her face to the side of mine. I had to dance on my tiptoes to stay up there, and then her tongue was in my ear. It shocked me and I almost jerked my head back. But it felt good, so I let it stay. When the song got to the end, she stopped, stepped back, and looking hard at my face, she clamped my head in her hands and kissed me real hard. I heard Pesky do a wolf howl and then—Tony's rebel yell.

He was behind me and I couldn't see him, but I could see Pesky had stopped dancing and he and that redhead were both grinning at me. The band suddenly broke into Sweet's *Ballroom Blitz*. Pesky and the redhead went wild with the whole room right behind them. My dance partner grabbed my hand and towed me back to the booth. She practically shoved me inside and then came in after me. I was right back where I started. I figured she wasn't one for shaking her booty.

She was hot now and kind of panting, but her eyes were glued to me. The Coogan troublemakers passed by again and the short guy laughed. The girl flipped him off, and he returned the same. I watched Crazy Vaughn stick out his foot as they passed. He tripped the tall one, and they all four backed away and kept going. I figured they knew who Crazy Vaughn was, and they didn't want no part of him.

The girl didn't see what happened because her eyes were stuck on me.

I nodded toward the Coogan kids and said, "Who are those guys?"

She looked for a second and said, "Oh, that's my little brother, Bob. He thinks he's tough. Got kicked out of school a couple years ago. Has a job on the Coogan garbage truck, now."

"You're from Coogan?" I asked, pretending like I didn't know.

"Yeah, where you from?"

"Ummm… Clarksburg."

"So, you're not far from where I live."

"So… you don't mind?"

"No, why should I? You thinking about that whole school rivalry thing? That's all crap."

"Your brother sure wanted to beat the shit out of me because of it."

"Yeah, well, it doesn't matter where you're from. If he thinks he can take you, he'll try. Hey, you want a beer. I want a beer. Wait here, I'll be right back!"

Not waiting for me to say anything, she jumped up and walked toward the bar. I watched her go and realized that she wasn't no schoolgirl. That was a full-grown woman. But I couldn't take my eyes off the sway of those hips in those tight jeans. All of a sudden, I didn't care that she might be older.

A movie I had watched once with Flo came to my mind, *The Summer OF '42*. A young boy falls for an older woman and they have an affair. I could be that kid. The thought made me excited and I could hardly wait for her to get back. But the bar was packed, and she had to wait. She kept looking my way and blowing kisses and other stuff like that. I figured she wanted to make sure I didn't sneak away. She would probably run back over to the booth if I got up, even if it were only to go to the john to take a leak.

Tony scared the crap out of me by flopping down in the seat across from me. "Clit!" he shouted. I was glad it was too noisy for anyone but me to hear.

"Boner!"

"That's right! The biggest in town. Hey, we are friends, right?"

"I suppose… sometimes, anyway."

He laughed and said, "Okay, close enough. So… you know who that is, right? She tell you?"

"No, she hasn't said what her name is. Why? Should I care."

"Damn right, you should. That's Deb Schact! She's from Coogan. That bunch of pansy asses walking around looking for trouble, they're from Coogan too. Her brother's the short one, Bob. I call him, Boob. He hates that. I think it's just funnier than shit."

I kind of went into a daze, but Tony just kept talking. I didn't hear a thing as my eyes went to Deb and then to Pesky who had the redhead twirling across the floor, her short dress flying up to show she had matching red panties. I wanted to be Pesky at that moment and be free of this situation that I'd gotten myself into.

Tony said, "Oh look, she's coming with some beer. Mind if I stay and make fun of you guys? Maybe she'll go away and leave the beer…or buy one for me. I'm thinking maybe it would be better for you if I stayed. Lots of other girls here, you know. Tell her to take a hike, Clint. Save your own life."

I ignored him, still trying to decide what I was going to do. Deb came back by way of the front wall, trying to avoid the dancers. She was passing Crazy Vaughn's booth and he stood up to block her way. She stopped so quickly she almost splashed beer on him. It surprised her and she gave him a mean look, but she didn't say anything. He leaned down and said something right into her face. I could see her lips moving and he leaned down further like he was going to say something in her ear.

The next thing I know, she spun right around and walked back to the bar. Putting herself up on a stool she set one beer on the bar top and started drinking the other. She stared at me. Her face was sad. I wanted to get up and go over there, but the next thing I know, Crazy Vaughn was at my table blocking the way.

"Hey, Vaughn," Tony said.

"Shut your ass up," Vaughn said, and sitting down, he pushed Tony to the wall because he was so big."

Tony didn't say anything more. He just looked at me, nodded his head toward Vaughn, and shrugged. Vaughn looked hard into my face, like he was studying me. We hardly ever spoke—just a wave hello, or he'd holler out, "Hey, little buddy," as he drove by in his old pickup. Just like we were pals. I think he just liked kids, and maybe, he missed being one.

"Okay, listen. I'm only going to tell you this once. You don't want that," he said, nodding toward Deb. I didn't look at her, instead, I put my eyes on Phoebe and her friends. I knew Deb was staring our way; I could feel it. When I finally did look at her, she swiveled to face the bar and went on drinking.

"That woman is almost twice your age and believe me, little guy… she's trouble."

I looked at Tony who was nodding his head like crazy, agreeing with everything the big guy was saying. Vaughn looked at him and said, "I told you to shut up."

"But I wasn't saying anything?"

"I don't want to have to tell you again, scrapper."

Vaughn turned back and kind of leaned forward across the table. Then he looked at me out of the tops of his eyes and said, "Take my word for it, you'll thank me later. It's Clint, right? Clint Torres? Yeah, I know your sister, she's cool. I told Miss Schact over there, that your only sixteen. That put a stop to her horny ways, like, right now. So… anyway, think about it, Clint. Do the smart thing," he said and patting my arm, he stood up and headed back to his booth. I watched him walk away and about the same time, I saw the Coogan tough guys stop to talk with Deb. She said something, shook her head, and looked down at the floor. I could have sworn she was crying.

It was when Bob jerked his face around toward me that I knew the storm was coming. She grabbed his arm, but he pulled loose and the four of them came straight for me. Tony was out of the seat in two seconds flat to meet them. Crazy Vaughn and his friends came out of their booth and headed our way. I watched Deb slide off her stool, knocking over her beer. The deputy was standing close by and he said something to her, but she ignored him. He grabbed her arm and she punched him. Tony was going at it with Bob. Vaughn and his pals were mopping up the floor with the other three.

It didn't take long for other fights to break out and the next thing I knew, Pesky had my arm with one hand and the redhead's, with the other. He pulled me out of the booth saying, "Time to go!"

We headed for the door, dodging bodies and fists. I looked back and saw Mike T and Shelagh were right behind us doing the same. I noticed the band had stopped playing and were now taking on a few of their rowdier fans. We got out the door and everybody ran for the Chevy.

I jumped in the back with Pesky and the redhead. Mike T started the car as Shelagh climbed in the passenger side, slamming the door. Mike didn't wait for Sherry and Billy. Whipping out from the curb, he floored it and ran the muscle car through the gears. Coming to the corner, he slid it into the turn and zooming out to the highway, we squealed onto the blacktop and headed west toward Clarksburg.

"What about, Tony?" I said.

"He's on his own. Probably end up in jail, or somebody else will give him a ride. I'm not worried about Tony," Mike T said.

"Yeah," Pesky said. "Tony can take care of himself."

I looked at Shelagh, she was just looking back over her shoulder at me, grinning. "Oh Clint, you're so cute, always worrying about Tony. I could just kiss you."

"Hey!" said Mike T. "Shelagh, I'm still in the car—do you see me?"

"Yeah, but it's the truth. He's so cute when he's worried."

Mike T just shook his head and Shelagh giggled. I looked away to Pesky and then headlights lit us up from behind. I was sure it was the police or a bunch of Coogan toughs chasing us down. "Somebody's following us! Oh crap! Looks like the county mounty!"

"Relax, Clint," Shelagh said. "It's just Billy and Sherry. They got my car."

"I didn't know Billy had a license?"

"He doesn't!" everybody but the redhead shouted at the same time.

The redhead giggled and I looked straight at her. She was cute. Everything about her was cute. In fact, she was too perfect. She looked so much like a little elf that it was crazy. I looked at Pesky's face glowing from the headlights behind us.

He grinned at me and said, "Clint, this is Beebe, Beebe Carlson. She's new to Clarksburg. She just started school this year.

"Yeah, kinda smart too," Mike T said and looked at us in the mirror, grinning. "Good thing you guys hooked up, otherwise…"

"Keep it up, Mikey. Just keep it up," Shelagh said and huffed. Straightening up in her seat, she just stared out of the windshield like she was pissed.

Mike was trying to get back at her. Shelagh looked back and sneered at Beebe. Jealousy. Poor Beebe just smiled to herself and pulled Pesky's arm tighter around her shoulders.

Things were tense enough without Shelagh losing it. "What's up, Beebe," I said, because 'How do you do?' was just too old fashion.

She smiled with perfect teeth and said, "Hey, Clint," and then her and Pesky started kissing.

Halfway back to town, two sheriff's cars raced past us, heading for Prairieville. I was glad we got out of there when we did. I needed some air, so I rolled down the window and let the wind in. I was feeling kind of bad. Mike T had Shelagh, Pesky had Bebe, and behind me, Billy was with Sherry. I hardly ever felt lonely, but the little bit that I had experienced in my short lifetime, was no big deal—

until now. This felt a hundred times worse. I started thinking about my options and seriously felt I was bound for monkhood. Pesky had been right. Figures. The *Mr. Lonely* song by Bobby Vinton started rolling through my head and I had Mike switch on the tape player and turn up the volume to Led Zeppelin's *Black Dog*.

Clarksburg had a curfew. It was straight up midnight on Saturdays and the deputies were serious about it. But our town Marshal, wasn't. Mostly because he knew us and lived in the same town. He'd just tell you to go home even if it was two in the morning. If the deputy told you once and then caught you a second time—you went to jail.

Mike T dropped Beebe off first. She lived in a house I didn't know. It was up on Snob Hill where the popular kids lived. I have to admit, I was confused. Beebe was nicer than most rich kids. I knew that because she had picked Pesky. I figured they just hadn't been there long enough to know how the neighborhoods worked in Clarksburg. Pesky and Bebe got out, said, "See you," and went around the house into the dark backyard, holding hands.

Billy pulled up behind us in Shelagh's car, and got out to come talk to Mike T.

"What's going on, Mike?"

"Just had to drop off the new girl. Hey, can you give Clint a ride home? It's after midnight and I don't want to go back down through town. There might be a deputy."

"All the deputies are over in Prairieville, chicken shit. Hey, let Clint walk home."

"What? No! Your eighteen, so you got nothing to worry about. The rest of us could go to jail for curfew."

Shelagh leaned across the seat and practically laying on Mike's lap, she said, "Hey, Billy, maybe you and Sherry could walk from here? I could just take my car, you know."

I could see her face. She was grinning in a wicked way, but she was stilled pissed about Mike having an interest in Beebe. I figured Billy better give her the right answer. He had no choice, really. Shelagh knew how to put you in a spot. That was her thing.

"Thanks a bunch, Shelagh," Billy said. "Clint, go jump in. I 'll take you home. Then Sherry and I are going down to the Blue Front to play some pool."

"Yeah, well, Mike and I are going up to Pinecone Ridge to watch the submarine races," Shelagh said and giggled before sitting up and sliding tight up against Mike. He grinned at her and kissed her cheek. She softened up and grabbing his head, she turned his face to her in a way I thought might break his neck and kissed him real hard. Then she pulled back and wiped her mouth.

"Oh man, you're making me hot! Sherry and I just might have to go down to the Pits for a little rendezvous before we go to the tavern. Oh, and by the way, Shelagh, there are no submarines in the Wapsi."

"There are tonight!" she said and then she turned to me, "See ya, wouldn't want to be ya! Sorry, Clint... just kidding."

I stared at her. This was too much. Everybody was going somewhere with someone and I was going home. I felt like getting into trouble. So... maybe I'd break curfew anyway. I knew where there was a bicycle that I could run up the flag pole at the school, just like somebody did awhile back. Then I could play cat and mouse with the deputy all night. I knew a lot of good places to hide if he got close. If he caught me, big deal. Maybe Tony went to jail and I'd just be in there with him. We could raise some hell. I know I was just making myself madder. It just wasn't fair that I didn't have a girlfriend, especially since I could have been with Deb. But Vaughn had to go and ruin that for me.

Climbing out of the Chevy, I slammed the door and stomped back to Shelagh's car. I stopped for a minute just outside the driver's window and stared at the ground, kind of balling up my fists. Then, I turned around and stared at Billy. He, Mike T, and Shelagh, were all laughing about something. I think I was on my way to exploding when I heard Sherry say from the front seat of Shelagh's car, "Hey, Clint, everything alright? Come in here and talk to me, maybe we all can do something together?" Sherry's voice kind of calmed me down. It was just that kind of voice. A movie star voice, maybe a Marylyn Monroe kind of voice. I felt the anger start to leave. Maybe I could talk to Sherry about my problem. She was nice, and maybe she could give me some advice or something. I just said, "Hey, Sherry," in a sad kind of way. It wasn't a trick to make her feel sorry for me. I really was sad. The first time in a long time.

I opened the backdoor and kind of fell in backwards. After swinging my legs in, I slammed the door. I started to say something to Sherry, but my nose caught a whiff of cologne. Sweet Honesty, one of my favorites. Flo had a bottle, but only wore it one time. I heard a, "Hi, Clint," and turning my face all the way to the right, I looked right into the eyes of Phoebe Lindlee. My mouth just kind of dropped open and before I could answer, Sherry said, "You know, Phoebe, right?

"Uh… yeah. Hey, Phoebe. What's up?"

"Billy and Sherry are giving me a ride home. We had to get out of there because of the fight. Hey, I saw you there."

"Yeah, I was there. It kind of sucked."

"Oh, I don't know. I was hoping for a dance, but you looked kind of busy… with that older woman."

"Uh, yeah, well… short relationship," I said and laughed. She laughed too, but in a way I'd never heard her laugh before. Kind of quiet, and not like she was laughing at me—but with me.

Billy came and got in, shoved the gear shift in drive and then followed Mike T out to the highway. We followed them 'til we got to Hillcrest, then Billy turned off and stopped just inside my driveway. He parked in a place where the trees could block my ma's view. I didn't get a chance to talk with Sherry, and all that pissed-offness was building back up inside me. Phoebe hadn't said any more to me, but she never took her eyes off me, either. Every time I looked at her, she'd smile like she was just happy to be there. I kind of wished I knew her better. Maybe I should have tried harder.

"Here you go, Clint. Got to run, the Pits are calling! See you later. Oh, and enjoy your date."

"What?"

"Are you righthanded, or left?"

"What do you mean?"

"Your girlfriend? Is she the left or the right?"

"I, uh…"

He laughed and said, "Skip it, just a little joke. Speaking of little jokes…"

"Billy!" Sherry said, "Not nice."

"Sorry," Billy said and bumped into the door panel when Sherry slapped his shoulder.

I got out and slammed the door to make sure Billy knew I was pissed. I just stood there with my back to the car waiting for him to get the hell out of my driveway. To make it worse, I was going to cry, and I don't cry. But I think I had reached my limit along with the 'hopeless case' stage of my life. I would be known as 'Clint the crybaby' for as long as I lived in Clarksburg.

I fought hard to keep the waterworks from starting, wanting everybody to just go away. I heard Sherry say something and Phoebe answered, but she sounded far away. I felt bad about not saying goodbye to her, but then—I really didn't need too.

Billy peeled out backwards and went barreling down the street. I turned around and nearly ran, smack dab, into Phoebe. She was smiling in a way I think was kind of sweet and looking at me like Keli Hale looks at the pieces of cake on dessert day in the lunchroom. The problem, besides being on the verge of bawling, my mouth was hanging open and I couldn't get it to shut. Then I had to go and stutter, "How… how… how come…"

My eyes were wet, but I didn't dare rub them. I just opened them as wide as I could, hoping they would air dry. Phoebe didn't seem to care about any of that, and said, "I thought maybe... since I didn't get my dance, we could at least hang out together for a couple hours. Walk me home?"

It seemed like it took forever for me to answer. Stunned, I think the word is. Here I was about ready to become the biggest loser in town and it seemed to me like Phoebe had saved the day. I wasn't going home alone, after all. I mean, I know I was already home, but Phoebe was with me and that made all the difference in the world. I didn't know her all that well, even if we had been in the same class since about the third grade. But maybe now was a good time to start.

"Well, Clint? You going to say something or…"

"Sorry, sorry… um, yeah… uh… where do you live?"

"Up the hill, after the park road, about a mile. We have to walk the gravel, but it's not so bad."

I didn't have to think any more about it. "Sounds groovy to me! I didn't feel like going to bed, anyway."

"Good, let's go," she said and headed out of the driveway. I chased after her and we walked up the hill. Being that close to her kind of changed things for me. I didn't feel nervous, and she was so friendly in the way that she talked to me. It just seemed so natural for us to be together. Then I noticed she had cut her hair and now had bangs.

"Hey, you got bangs."

"Yeah, I wanted to try something different. Something for the dance. So… Clint, um… who was that woman that you were hanging around with at Prairieville? Was she like… a girlfriend?"

"Oh! Ha! Nope, nobody special."

"Okay, that's good, I guess. Well, I was just asking because, if she was, I didn't want to ruin anything, or have someone coming after me. You know what I mean?"

Before I could answer, the Larson's big Labrador, Toby, let go with a loud bark through the fence. We both jumped and Phoebe made a squeaky little noise before grabbing my hand. The thing is, she didn't let go, even when we were a good distance away from the Larson's house. So, we walked like that all the way to her place. Thanks, Toby!

#12

The Not-So-Great Turkey Heist

So far, 1972 had turned out to be pretty boring. I had only lived in Iowa for a little over four years and only in the town of Clarksburg for two of those. My home now was in the old post office down the street and I had come up to the corner to see if any of my friends were around. The streets were empty, which made me wonder if everybody had up and died. It was a small town, though, so that's to be expected, I guess. My uncle Delbert's all-time favorite thing to say was, "They roll up the streets at six in this town, you know!" He wasn't kidding. It made me want to start some trouble, but that would have to wait until after supper. I didn't want to go back to my place because that would mean PB & J with Kool-Aid. The Davis Café was closed, and I didn't want to go the half a mile to the Dairy Dreem up by the highway to get a burger. Taking the risk, I decided to sneak in the back door of the Blue Front tavern.

If I spent some money, stayed quiet, and didn't bug anyone, I could be in there for as long as I wanted. Arnie, the old guy who owned the place usually treated me pretty good. I could buy the 'Blue Front's Grilled Cheese Special' with money I stole from my ma's purse, and then eat it in the very last booth by the back door. I knew ol' Arnie was worried about the deputy checking in and finding me at the bar. But honestly, I didn't think anybody really gave a damn.

The tavern was on the corner of Fourth Street and Main. The way you got in was on the corner of the building like someone had chopped it off and stuck a door there. I walked right on past it and went down to where the tavern butted up against the bakery. That's where the so-called back door was, even though it was on the side of the building. We just called it the back door because it was at the other end.

Looking around like I was getting ready to cause some trouble, I whipped open the screen door and ran up the short set of wooden stairs. I could either take a right at the landing and go inside the bar or keep on going up to the restroom. Not having to pee, I took that right. Sneaking inside the open door, I jumped into the first booth I came to, and sat still, just so I could get a look around.

I liked it in there. It was cool and dark with a lot of varnished wood. It reminded me a lot of the pubs back in Ireland. Arnie had this huge mirror behind the bar, right in the center of a bunch of shelves that went clear to the ceiling. There must have been every kind of booze in the world back there, along with candy, snacks, cigarettes, tobacco pipes, combs, nail clippers, and a whole lot of cigars and chewing tobacco.

There were four farmers drinking beer at the bar, all watching the weather report. Old Raymond Beasley was sitting in a booth by the front door chewing away on a huge tenderloin. He tipped back a can of Olympia beer and then looked my way, probably checking to see if I was going to be a problem. My friend, Harry, told me once that Beasley was kind of a hermit and lived way down by the railroad tracks in this little, one room shack.

The bar room got quiet after I settled in. The news guy on the TV talked about militants upsetting the first sitting of the Northern Irish Assembly and about an airliner that had crashed in Boston. When I decided no one cared whether I was in there or not, I got up and went to the bar. Standing at the end, I asked Arnie for the Grilled Cheese Special. He looked at me like he usually did, just some stupid kid out to cause trouble. He made a noise that sounded something like, *humph!* and then said, "Two dollars and ninety-five cents there young feller. Did you want a root beer with that?"

"Uh, yeah, I suppose…"

"Well, do you, or don't you?" he said, sounding annoyed.

"Well… that's what comes with it, right?"

He looked at the old man sitting on a bar stool next to me and jerked his head in my direction as if to say, 'Can you believe this guy?' He then turned around and pulling the sandwich from the fridge under the bar, he popped it into the toaster oven. I caught myself in the mirror and noticed that my long brown hair seemed even longer than the last time I looked. I had been trying to grow it out after years of butch haircuts. It was down past my shoulders now and I wished my da had stuck around long enough to see I wasn't doing what he wanted.

The pop of the root beer tab made me jump, and I watched Arnie grab a bag of potato crisps off a rack. He set them on the bar in front of me along with the root beer. I handed him three one-dollar bills and making change, he said, "You go set down, now, and I'll bring that sandwich over to you. Don't want no one seeing you here at the bar for too long."

I did what he told me. A few minutes later, he hobbled over with the sandwich and after setting it down on the shiny plywood top, he leaned on the edge and whispered, "You're that funny talking young feller from down the block, ain't you?"

I didn't answer. I would normally have punched someone who said I talked funny, and I didn't care how old they were. But it was his house, so I had to be nice. "Well, I'm just asking because I'm pretty sure, I know your pa. He used to come in here a lot. He was kind of a funny talker like you. Well, you finish up now and be on your way. I don't want no trouble with the law because of you being in here, Okay?"

I just nodded and started chewing on that sandwich like I hadn't eaten for weeks. He went back behind the bar to wipe down some pint glasses. I felt bad for wanting to smack him. I'm sure he meant no harm. Besides, this wasn't County Monahan. I needed to be more tolerant, as my Aunt Louise put it. I had to understand that some people just don't know how to ask a question proper.

About the time Arnie got done with his dishes, the front door burst open. Red Dog Finney and three other ruffians came in and stood looking around the room. Ol' Beasley finished up real quick and taking his beer, pushed his way through them and went out the door. Arnie went right to pouring four mugs of PBR and then set them in a row on the bar. Without saying a word, those guys downed the beer in less than half a minute and practically slammed the mugs down on the counter top. Arnie filled them up right away.

They stood looking around the room and after making sure that there was no one in there that they could make fun of, they turned back to the bar. Putting their heads together, they talked so no one else could hear them. It didn't stay like that for long. Their talk turned into an argument. Two of them finished up their beers and turned to leave, with one saying, "To hell with you, Finney, we're going down to Eddies."

Now, Eddie's was the rival bar down the street, and people in Clarksburg went to one or the other. It was the bar for local troublemakers. I didn't dare go near it. In fact, whenever I had to go past it, I always ran. I had to be careful in case the Silber brothers happened to be coming out. They were always looking to way-lay somebody who might be passing, and that included kids. They did it just for fun and sometimes it gave me nightmares.

Well, the next thing I knew, Red Dog was standing there beside my table, looking down at me. He was this short, sort of stocky fellow with flaming red hair. He always greased it back in a pompadour like Elvis Presley. Sadly, for him, he had been cursed with a face full of freckles. At his age, it looked kind of stupid. He acted like a rascal most of the time, but he was quick with his wit and always had some good jokes.

Sometimes he showed his nice side, and to be honest, I kind of liked him. He reminded me of some of the lads I knew back in Ireland. He wanted people to think that he might be some kind of an outlaw. But I've caught him doing nice things like helping some old lady with her groceries, sweeping the sidewalk at Darrel's Butcher Shop since Darrel got the arthritis, or trying to hug his kids without anybody noticing. He worked at the only turkey farm in the county as a 'Turkey Wrangler' (that's what he said, anyway) and it seemed he never stopped talking about his job.

"Hey! I know you," he said and then looking back at the other guy, he smiled a dangerous kind of smile.

"What you up to here?" he said, flopping down across from me in my booth.

"Uh, well... I'm eating a sandwich? What's it look like?"

"You leave that little feller alone now, Finney. He's got to finish that sandwich and get the hell out of here."

We both stared at Arnie, the look on his face telling us he meant business. All heads turned and looked in our direction. I felt my face get warm.

"How'd you like to make ten bucks?" Red Dog said, ignoring the others.

"Doing what?"

"What's your name, again?" he said and leaned back in the seat, raising his eyebrows really high, making me uncomfortable.

"Cos," I said proudly

"Cos? Like… Cosby, as in Bill, or maybe, lost cause or…"

He laughed out loud at his own joke. I wondered if I could punch him and get out the back door before he caught me. I decided it wasn't worth it. Besides, he knew where I lived.

"Well, you know, Cos, I work at the turkey farm and…"

"Bollocks! No! You're kidding!" I said and then added, "Is not like you haven't told everyone in the county a million times, already."

My turn to be funny, which only made me feel that now would be the time he would hit me over the head with his beer bottle and toss me out the back door. He just gave me a stupid grin and shook his head like he figured he might be dealing with a moron.

"… and I need a couple of guys to help me corral a few turkeys that I forgot to put away earlier. Buzz, who's standing over there, is going to help me. But I need another guy. Would you help me out? Like I said, I'll give you ten bucks."

He then leaned forward on the table and squinted at me with one eye. I could smell the beer on his breath and his Brut aftershave. I wondered if maybe he was just pulling my leg. I should have asked all the right questions just to be sure he wasn't doing that. But I didn't because I started to imagine all the things ten bucks could get me. I could spend days down at the soda fountain in Nordon's Drug Store. That's where all the girls hung out after school. I imagined myself buying them all phosphate sodas and Green Rivers just so I could get them to like me.

"Okay, sure… what do you want me to do?"

"Just come out with us and help gather up them turkey's. When we get them back into their cages, I'll bring you back to the tavern and pay you. How about that?"

"Alright, when do we go?"

"Right now," he said and grinned. Then he smacked the table top and brought all those eyes back to us.

"Buzz! Come on over here," he said to his friend.

Now this fellow, Buzz, was kind of a quiet man. Peopled whispered among themselves about him being slow witted, but I had to wonder if maybe he might be really smart and just had them all fooled. Coming over to the booth, he looked at me and said, "Hey, you. You're Cos, right?"

Another ruffian who knew my name. I guess I was more famous than I realized. It made me nervous. I looked real hard into his eyes, deciding right then that he wasn't dull after all. He just liked to make people think he was. Probably so he could always be one step ahead of them.

"Let's go!" Red Dog said, jumping up and almost knocking Buzz off his feet.

"Where you taking that boy, Finney?" Arnie called out, sounding like he cared a wee bit about me.

"He's going to help us with some work."

Grabbing my arm, he tried to yank me out of that booth. "Hold up, there," I said and snatching up the rest of my sandwich, I chugged the root beer. Setting the can on a shelf by the back door as we went out, I heard Arnie holler, "Hey! That don't go there."

We walked to a blue Chevy pickup that looked older than the hills, and Red Dog said to me, "Cos, you get in the back. Buzz, you get up front with me."

I climbed in and sat down with my back to the cab. I heard the door hinges squeak from the lack of oil and then the sound of it slamming shut. Red Dog started the truck and backing out of the spot, 'burned them off' as they say, and we raced away through a cloud of rubbery smelling smoke. Heading north on 4th street, we sped up past the high school and out of town on the gravel.

The only light around us came from the headlamps and the farm houses we passed. I bounced around trying to eat the rest of my sandwich, complaining to myself how much I didn't like riding on gravel roads.

We'd only gone a few miles before Red Dog turned east, leaving the dust behind because now we bumped along on an old mud road. It was one of those I figured must have existed back when Iowa wasn't Iowa yet. Not liking mud roads any better than gravel ones, I told myself I could just be glad that we hadn't any rain for weeks. I imagined all three of us trying to get the truck unstuck in a downpour and showing up back at the tavern covered from head to toe with mud.

After about a mile, the headlamps went off and the truck coasted to a stop. It got real quiet, and I stood up to look over the cab. I could hear mumbling from inside with Red Dog's hand going in and out of the window pointing toward some farm buildings in the distance. A coyote yapped from a ridge to the east, metal hog feeders clanged, and I could just make out the sound of a thousand or so turkeys, gobbling away somewhere to the north. Putting it all together, I realized we were on the backside of the turkey farm.

Those two climbed out, shutting their doors real quiet like, and Red Dog whispered, "Come on down here, Cos."

I jumped over the side and landed in the ditch, almost falling on my face. Buzz tried to catch me, but it only made me feel more embarrassed.

"You okay, little buddy?" he asked

"Fine," I answered, slightly annoyed.

"Okay, here's what we're going to do," Red Dog said. "I don't want my boss to know that I forgot, so we're going in the back way. Once inside, just grab a couple of them turkey's by the neck and then just follow me. I'll show you where to put them, and then we'll leave as quietly as we can." He looked back and forth between us a couple of times and then stopped to stare at me.

"Do you understand me, Cos?"

"I understand you! How hard is it? What? You think I'm some kind of eejit?"

Red Dog stared at me and even in the dark, I could see that he looked kind of puzzled. "A what? Where in the hell are you from that you talk like that?" Before I could answer, he laughed and looking at Buzz, said, "Okay, let's go."

I shook my head and told myself that someday I was just going to haul off and smack this guy. I followed them and watched them climb the barbed wire fence. When it came my turn, Red Dog tried to help.

"No, I got it! What you thinking? I'm some kind of a pansy or something?"

"Just trying to help," he said, sounding like he just might be getting fed up with me.

I finally got over the fence and ran to catch up with them. We walked away across this huge pasture and the only light we had, came from the stars. There were a ton of them. I walked with my head bent back, trying to find the big dipper. A bad idea. I kept tripping in holes and stepping in cow pies, making a lot of noise. After a while, Red Dog looked back to see what I was doing and then shushed me. Even in the starlight, I could see he was giving me a dirty look.

We soon came to a big fenced in area and once we got inside, I could just make out a flock of big white turkeys standing over in a corner. They gobbled in a way that sounded like they might be asking each other, "What in the hell is going on?"

Red Dog turned to me and said, "Okay, Cos, listen to me. Just grab em by the neck with one hand and tuck them under each arm. That way, you see, they won't flap you to death. Understand?"

"Got it," I sang out, like I'd been catching turkeys all my life.

"Now, just walk right up to them. They won't fly away, and you can just grab 'em."

He said this with a humorous tone in his voice, sounding like when someone is trying to pull a fast one on you. I thought about quitting right then. I could walk back to Clarksburg. I could see the town's lights in the distance, so I knew which way to go. But a picture of Red Dog handing me that ten-dollar bill kept popping into my head. Then, the face of Denise Donnelly, smiling that great smile at me before taking a chocolate milkshake that I was offering.

I decided to stay. It had been awhile since I'd had any excitement. I had been itching for trouble. So, without saying anything more, I headed over to the flock. The other two did the same, and I found it true what Red Dog had said. Those stupid birds just stood there, bobbing their heads, looking around at each other like they were expecting suggestions. I reached out and just snatched one by the neck. Everything went to hell in a hand basket.

The flock exploded in all directions. The one I grabbed started flapping its wings in my face and clawing at my chest. I tucked it under my arm like I had been told, and it stopped the flapping, but now it was pecking the wrist of the hand that held its neck. I turned to Red Dog and gave him a look that said, 'What the hell?' He had never said a word about pecking. I should have expected it though, most things with a beak on their face will do that. I was going to cuss him out, but I could see he had to deal with some pecking of his own.

Buzz just caught his second bird and whispered loudly, "Do you got it? Do you got it?"

"I got it, for feks sake! What now?" I whispered back as loud as I could without it becoming something more akin to yelling.

"Follow me," Red Dog said, a little too loud for the situation, and instead of heading for the roosting boxes, he ran off in the direction we had come from. Getting to the fence, he ran right up like it was a ladder. I'd never, in my life, seen anybody do that. It was the kind of wire fence that had them four-inch square holes in it and was usually topped with three strands of barbed wire. Well, this one didn't have barbed wire, but from where I was standing, getting over it was going to be a chore. I figured I would do just what Red Dog did.

That was about the time a door opened at the barn and the light from inside shot out across the pen and lit me up. I heard a, "Hey you! What you' doing out there?" I looked that way and saw this man as big as John Wayne, coming out. There was no mistaking the big double-barreled shotgun in his hands. I turned to say something to Buzz, but he was already gone, and those two were hightailing it for the truck.

With no time to think, I took off, still holding onto my turkey. That's when the shotgun went off and I heard the splatter of birdshot hitting one of the metal feeders. That gave me an extra boost, and I took off like a striped cat with its tail on fire. I finally got to the fence and went right up it, just like Red Dog. But when I got to the top, there was another blast, and I felt the sting of it on my backside. It knocked me off the fence. Luckily for me that turkey must have felt a wee bit of attachment for me as its new found friend and sacrificed itself, by cushioning my fall. Getting up, I kept a hold on it and ran, but now with a limp.

Reaching the outer fence, I found a gap in the wire that no one seemed to have noticed before, and I squeezed on through. Red Dog sat in the cab, gunning the engine, his two birds lying dead on the road. Buzz was now trying to put his two turkeys out of their misery by whacking their heads on the rail of the truck bed. Then dropping those in the back, he picked up Red Dog's and tossed them in, too. He came over and took a close look at mine and said, "Well, yours is already dead." I felt sorry for it then. It had given its life for mine and we hadn't known each other for more than a few minutes.

Buzz jumped into the truck bed and I tumbled in after, letting my bird fall in behind me. I heard him pound the side of the truck twice with his fist and the Chevy raced away with no lights.

Once we reached the gravel road, the headlamps came on and the truck picked up speed. "Oh shit!" Buzz hollered "Your bleeding! You've been hit! Christ almighty!"

Getting up on my knees I put a hand to my backside and when I pulled it away, he was right, there was blood, but not as much as I would have expected. Buzz flipped my turkey over and after a quick inspection, we agreed that it, besides getting crushed, had also taken most of the bird shot. A lot of the blood that was on me had come from it.

My backside throbbed like crazy. I couldn't sit anymore, so I stood, looking forward over the top of the cab, feeling lucky it wasn't buckshot. I'm sure the farmer didn't want to kill me, he just wanted to scare me. That way, I would think twice about coming back.

When we got to Clarksburg, Red Dog snuck through town using the side streets. Pulling into the alley behind my place, his headlamps went off. He turned left, coasting part way up the gravel delivery drive that led to the old wooden loading dock behind Ralph's TV's. I jumped out when he stopped and kind of limped around to the driver's door. Red Dog reached out slowly and grabbed my shoulder, pulling me close. I could tell he was trying to be nice, but he also wanted to let me know that this was serious business. If we got caught, there would be hell to pay.

"You go on and take that bird and don't say a word. You hear me, Cos? You can have it instead of that ten bucks, okay?"

So much for my plans to treat the girls down at Nordon's. That was my sole reason for going in the first place. Feeling kind of mad, I said, "But... but I thought you said..."

"Shut up! Not a word, hear me?"

I looked back at Buzz and he made the, 'Oh well!' face and handed me my turkey. It's bloody feathers made it hard to hold on to, so I took it by the neck and stepped away. The truck rolled backward down to the alley with Red Dog looking at me like he meant business. I just stared as Buzz threw me a goodbye salute.

I dumped the dead bird in the garden shed and went up the rickety stairs to the balcony. I found my ma lying in her usual place on the sofa, a bowl of popcorn balanced on her big belly and watching TV.

"J, M, & J, Cos! What the fek happened to you?"

"Ah ma, it's nothing. Just a wee bit of blood."

"A wee bit, me arse! It looks like you've bled out. Come on over here."

She didn't bother to get up and just lay there inspecting my backside.

"Looks like you've ruined a good pair of trousers. What happened?"

"Well… just a wee bit of birdshot."

"So, what's the story lad?" she said, and setting the popcorn bowl on the floor, she probed my backside with a fingertip.

I winced and squirmed because that hurt like hell, but I was able to say, "Grabbed a turkey, and some guy didn't like it much. So, he let me know how he felt about it."

"Told you not to hang around with those hooligan friends of yours. See what comes of it? Well, least you're not bleeding anymore. Go take off your trousers, grab my big tweezers and bring them to me. I'll do my doctoring right here where we have the best light."

I did what she told me and brought the tweezer, now only wearing my underwear. She sat up and taking the little metal pinchers from me, she grabbed my arm and spun me around. Then she yanked down my underwear, leaving me to stand naked.

"Ma!" I shouted and tried to pull them back up.

She slapped my hand away and said, "Can't do this with you wearing them, besides, I've seen your wee arse a million times, lad. What you thinking? Just stand fast, this is going to hurt."

She was right, but there were only about eight pellets in there. She said not to worry because there wasn't enough to get lead poisoning. After she got done, she told me, "Now, you eejit, I hope you've learned your lesson."

I had to put some hydrogen peroxide on my wounds and that stung worse than the pellets when they hit me. Then she had me bring the turkey from the shed and I had to help her clean it. It wasn't her first time, and without another word about it, the bird went straight into the freezer.

It took a couple of weeks for my gunshot to heal. I kind of walked with a limp for a while and sitting meant only on my left cheek. My friends made fun of me and I had to make up a good story about what had happened. I must have done a good job telling my lie because they all seemed convinced by my blarney.

I didn't see Red Dog for a while after the turkey heist. Then one Friday afternoon as I was walking down the street going to Nordon's for some gum, he just popped out of Darrel's Butcher Shop. It scared the crap out of me, and I almost took off running. He got a hand on me and I started to scream, but he said, "Hush!" and I felt him slip something into my hand. Then he let go of my arm and hurried away. I turned around to watch him go. He was looking back at me and nodded once, giving me a big wink. I saw him hold the door at the Jack & Jill store for some old lady and then he disappeared inside.

Opening my hand, I saw a crumpled ten-dollar bill. I grinned so hard it hurt. Red Dog had given me my dream back. Doing a limping run to Nordon's, I swung open the door to see Denise Donnelly and Keli Hale climbing up onto stools at the soda fountain. Ol' man Nordon, in his little white paper hat, was just putting on his apron behind the counter.

"Hey, Cos," Denise said, flashing her silver blue eyes at me as she smoothed down her short, puffy skirt. She must have just got a new haircut because now the Shag she had worn, was now a bob cut. She tried to flip her brown hair back, but it was too short to do that now. My friend Harry told me that when a girl flips their hair back when you show up, it's a sure sign they are interested in you. That made me feel even happier.

"Hey, Cos," Keli said, swiveling back and forth on the stool in her green mini skirt, her knees far enough apart that I could see London and France all at the same time. To be honest, Keli kind of scared me. She looked at me like I look at chocolate cake. She hardly blinked and the grin on her face reminded me of that cat from Alice in Wonderland.

Denise said, "Cos… did anyone ever tell you that you kind of look like Paul McCartney? You know… of the Beatles?"

Keli giggled and looking at her, I saw her hazel eyes kind of twinkle. She stopped her swiveling, and her blonde hair stopped whipping about. She still faced me, her knees still miles apart. That's the problem with miniskirts, girls get used to wearing them and forget to sit proper. I looked away to show Keli I wasn't interested in her flowered underwear and went back to looking at Denise's eyes.

"So… yeah, I get that all the time about that Beatle," I said. "So… hey, can I buy you two some sodas or something?"

I climbed up on the stool next to Denise and she looked back at Keli. They grinned at each other and said, "Sure!" at the exact same time.

Months went by and there was plenty of gossip going around about the great turkey heist, but I did as Red Dog told me and never said a word. Well, except to my ma. Luckily for me, Marshal Tyler never showed up at my door. So, I figured everything was done and there would be no more of it. You can just bet every time Thanksgiving rolled around, I would be reminded of our turkey heist. Then, of course, there was the big payoff of spending time with Denise at the soda fountain. It made me wonder if that guy who said, "Crime doesn't pay!" really knew what the hell he was talking about.

#13

Bad Manners

It was the eighth grade. That special year before the big jump into high school. A guy didn't need to be told that being a freshman was going to be different; you could just feel it. You'd already gone through seven years with classmates that were there from the very beginning. Sure, new kids came, and old friends left, but everybody in your class was familiar, and probably more than you wanted them to be. Small town life meant knowing everybody's business and how everybody had a place, even the poor folks. The rich people seemed to be the ones who set the rules and their kids were no different. It just so happens I was one of those poor folks and there was probably one of me for every ten of the wealthy and popular. I can tell you right now, when the crap went down, it didn't matter who actually started it. If you were around at the time, fingers were going to point your direction and then you were in for the fight of your life to prove it wasn't your fault.

You could count on the rich sticking with the rich. If anyone of them had a heart and their head was in the right place, there was still little chance they were going to speak up and tell the truth. So, the poor would defend the poor, but no one was going to believe anyone of us, simply because of who we were. Poor, for some reason, always meant crooked and no matter how good you were, you were going to have to work like hell to prove it. Sometimes it was better to just go with it, stand your ground, and take what they were going to dish out. I suspected that was because, when you just went ahead and confessed, even though you were innocent, it made them feel smart, or clever, or something. Because of that, they wouldn't be so hard on you. So, it hurt less, but was sure to follow you around for the rest of your life. And after about a hundred times or so, you got a reputation.

My uncle Fred told me once the best thing you could do when you graduated high school, was to just drop out of sight. Go somewhere else and start a new life. Easy, peasy, right? Well, we will see, but for now, I had to try not to get that bad rep. I still had four more years to go and I had been fighting pretty hard to be like that one kid, Ponyboy, from The Outsiders. The problem was, I didn't have any brothers to look out for me and my folks weren't much help. I wasn't a greaser by any means, but it was the early seventies now, so peg legged jeans and pompadours had simply been replaced with bell bottoms and pony tails. The hippies were becoming a thing, and if you weren't careful, Clarksburg folks would just add it to the long list of things that made you who they believed you were—even if you weren't.

"Mickey! Hey Mick!" Jason Brandhal yelled across the ball diamond.

I decided not to go to the lunchroom with the others, instead, I went out to the bleachers to sketch. If I'd known the baseball players were going to show up, I would have gone somewhere else.

"What you doing over there? Hey you… Mick? Are you a mick, Mick? Drawing a picture for your mommy? He looked around at all the other players and they all laughed and nodded at him. That's right, Jason was king.

I just grinned and gave him a short wave. No chance I was going to get any good work done now, but I pretended like I was, and made like I had gone right back to sketching. Jason was doctor Brandhal's son. A kid with short, blond wavy hair, that stuck out all over. He had a mean face and his attitude matched. My ma said I was supposed to be nice to him because she went to see his dad pretty regularly. She was afraid if Jason and I got into it and his dad heard about it, he might accidently stick her hard with a needle or jab that tongue stick into the back of her throat.

Jason was fishing to add more to my list of bad things that he wanted other people to believe, and honestly, I was a little worried. Up until now, he had pretty much left me alone. I mean, short of the name calling. There was the time a bunch of us were camping out in Jimmy Waterman's fort in his backyard, and even though Jimmy had invited me, he was also friends with Jason. Jimmy's ma had brought us out some chips and green onion dip, but when she left, they started snatching handfuls from the bowl and when I grabbed my share, Jason said, "Leech! You fuckin' leech, Bolan!"

Now, I was entitled to the chips too, and I have to admit, it was a mistake for me to be at Jimmy's sleepover. I was the only poor kid hanging out with rich kids, and even though some were being nice to me—the rest weren't. That was kind of where it all started. After that, I'd walk by Jason in the hall and he would make a face or pretend like he was going to hit me in the nuts. And when he did, all the kids around him would laugh, especially if he caught me by surprise and I jumped or tried to run away.

The coach called the players into the dugout and when they had their backs to me, I snuck away. I was hoping that was the end of it for a while and that Jason would be happy with making me look like a clown. It was at the end of math class, that Jason commented, "Hey Micky, what's all those strings hanging from your bell bottoms, you cut those like that, or is it time for a new pair? You can always get some of those girly pants over at Lottie's. Of course, if you get them any tighter, we're going to have to put some lipstick on you and your going to have to start dating Goon. What do you say, Goon? Can Mickey be your girlfriend?"

Goon's actual name was Mike. He was big and slow with tight curly hair and a huge nose. He walked in a kind of bouncing sort of way and always had a comic book sticking out of his back pocket. He sure got picked on a lot. He never started fights, but he sure could finish them. So, he never answered Jason's question, instead he just got up and walked out. Mr. Keller, the math teacher, yelled,

"Mike Belsky, you get back to your seat, mister. We have ten minutes left of this class. You can wait ten minutes." Mike kept going. Mr. Keller chased after him and ran into a desk on the way out. Everybody laughed.

"Just stay in your seats until the bell rings, you hear me," he said and rubbing at his hip, he ran out into the hallway. Nobody said anything. As soon as he was out of sight and yelling at Mike as he chased him down the hall, the whole class cracked up. Jason made a gun with his hand and pretended to shoot me. Pledge Bowman was laughing so hard, her face had turned beet red. Becky Kubla gave Jason the evil eye and said, "Jason Brandhal, you're a doctor's kid, you should be acting like it." Poet Rowett just got up and walked over to the window and stood watching some birds out on the lawn. Natalie Anderson yanked on Copper Birdsongs braid and Copper came up out of her desk and pinched Natalie's nose so hard she screamed. Natalie, like her older sister Shelly, didn't like Indians. But she didn't dare go after Copper because that girl had a bigger sister named Selena, who wouldn't think twice about messing up somebody's face. Natalie talked like she was stuffed-up for almost two days after.

When the bell rang, I had five minutes to get to my locker and then get back to Mrs. Butters Literature class across the hall. Jason hung back talking with his buddies, and when I looked over my shoulder going out the door, I saw they had their heads together and all their eyes were on me. It wasn't over.

I suspected it was going to last most of the day, in fact. I don't get mad easily, but I could feel it coming. On the way down the hall, I thought about my ma and imagined Doc stabbing her by accident with a scalpel. "Sorry, ma," I whispered to myself, "Somebody needs a lesson in manners."

Mrs. Butters was my favorite teacher. She was British—or something like that. Not very tall, short hair, and big glasses. That woman knew her stuff and I liked listening to her lecture. I thought it was sad that today wasn't going to be a good day for that class. Jason sat behind me when I was in there and one row over to my right. He was close enough to grab me if he wanted to. We weren't even in our seats ten minutes, when he whispered, "Hey, Mickey, Copper has some lipstick in her purse, why don't you ask her if you can use it?"

And that's how it went the whole time Mrs. Butters was talking about Moby Dick. When Jason asked me, "Hey Mick, I'd bet you'd like to have a Moby Dick, huh? Maybe Goon has a Moby dick for you?" He snickered, but there were none of his friends around to laugh with him. They were all sitting over in the back corner. Mrs. Butters knew about Jason and had forced him to sit by me over by the windows. I figured she thought I might rub off on him and maybe he'd like books and stuff just as much as me.

Now, I was still boiling from math class, and maybe I should have traded insult for insult just so I could feel like I was getting Jason back. I figured maybe I'd wait until after school and go after him. A good old fist fight was brewing. It wouldn't go much of anywhere, but maybe I'd get a good punch in before all his friends piled on me. I was bound for principal Ehl's office for sure. Not a place I went much, but I'd be willing to end up there if I needed to.

So, he kept poking at me and poking at me, and I'm trying to ignore him. Mrs. Butters looked back at him a couple times when she was writing Herman Melville's name on the bulletin board. So, I knew she was hearing him. I had art class after this, and Jason wasn't in there. I was hoping I would calm down by the end of it and maybe Jason would forget all about me. No such luck.

I had kind of a girlfriend in Tammy Thomas, and we hung out together after school. We've been friends a long time. She had short, dark hair, cut in what they call a Wedge. She wore tight jeans and a short jean jacket every day. It was one of those cowboy jackets. She was heavy chested, as my ma said. Too big for an eighth grader and those tee shirts she always wore. I just never said anything because from the way she talked, she'd trade in those big boobs for a smaller pair if she could. I really liked her. I mean… I really, really liked her. She was always nice to me and was always saying some pretty smart stuff. She always got good grades; where I was just average.

But an artist just needs to know and understand art, not all that other stuff. She told me once, "Micky, you are so cool! I never knew an artist before, and you're pretty darn good." After that I told myself that I was going to be her friend until the end of the world. I had a fantasy we would become a thing and maybe one day we'd get married. I could see myself spending the rest of my life with little Tammy Thomas.

So, of course, that's where Jason went next. Tammy wasn't in my Literature class. She was across the hall in Mrs. Bowman's English class. But that didn't matter. Jason started right in on her boobs and worked his way around to her chubby, little butt. Then it was her weird hair, her stupid jacket, and finally, the way that she talked. I say, 'finally' because that's where I put a stop to it.

You have to understand, I didn't think about it. It wasn't planned. I just boiled over and everything that happened afterwards was all… how do they say, just automatic. Jason was going on about Tammy all the time Mrs. Butters was talking about Ahab, and the good ship Pequod. I think she was ignoring him too. She had stuff to write on the blackboard and seemed to be concentrating real hard.

I opened my desk top and laying right there on the bottom of that little space, right in the center, was a big ol' rubber band. There were little pieces of paper scattered around it that were just the right size for making paper wads. To me, that was like giving an angry man a gun who had just gotten the crap beat out of him and then kicked out of the Clarksburg tavern down on the square.

Like I said, I didn't think about it, I just took the rubber band out and one of those pieces of paper. I folded it up just right and stuck it in my mouth to get it good and wet. Then strapping the band across two fingers, I bent the paper in two and nocked it like you do an arrow on a bow string. Then, I waited.

Mrs. Butters was looking at us, talking about Ishmael and then turned back to write his name on the board so we'd know how it was spelled. About the same time, Jason said, "Hey, Mick, you suppose Tammy would like to hold Goon's copy of Moby Dick? What do you say?"

At that point, he reached out and yanked on my hair. That's when it happened. I just spun around and whispered, "Maybe YOU would," and drawing back on that paper wad, I let fly. It surprised me when it hit him in the eye. He screamed even louder and longer then Pledge Bowman was always doing. I mean, he cut loose with a noise that would raise the hair on your head.

I whipped back in my seat and pretended like I didn't hear a thing. The whole class went quiet as Mrs. Butters spun around and said, "Jason Brandhal! What's your problem!"

He told it like it was.

"Micky Bolan shot me in the eye with a paper wad!"

I had been looking down at the top of my desk and I didn't raise my face. I only looked at Mrs. Butters out of the tops of my eyes. I was waiting for her to tell me to go to the principal's office. Instead, what she said surprised the crap out of me. Dropping the chalk on her desk, she wiped off her hands and then putting them on her hips, she said in a very British way, "Well, you probably deserved it."

Not what I expected.

In fact, I don't think a teacher ever stuck up for me like that, before. That was all she had to say. She turned right around and went back to talking about Moby Dick like nothing ever happened. Jason just sat back there, rubbing his eye and groaning. I looked back just once and his one mean blue eye (the one that still worked) was looking at me and I think I saw murder in it.

"Mrs. Butters, I have to go to the nurse, now!"

She looked back over her shoulder at him, then looked at the big clock on the wall and said, "Yes, go to the nurse Mr. Brandhal, and when you're done there, don't come back. I don't want to see your face in here until tomorrow. Now… go!"

He did, too. I didn't see him again until the next day, but he didn't have a bandage or anything. In fact, except for being a little red, you couldn't see anything wrong. I never had to go to the principal's office, either, but I heard through the gossip (Debby Pearl told me) that she was walking by and heard Mrs. Butters yelling at Mr. Ehl. Debbie said that from the way it sounded, Mr. Ehl was afraid of Mrs. Butters. I never heard any more about it. Doc never cut nothing off my ma that he wasn't supposed too, and people started treating me a whole lot different.

A couple days after I shot Jason, Tammy, and I, were walking through the lunch room on our way back to class. Jason was sitting with a couple of his buddies at a table. I figured that was going to be the moment when he got his revenge, but he wouldn't look at us. The thing is, I couldn't let it go. I'd just finished a paperback version of Moby Dick (an assignment from Mrs. Butters) and I had the book with me. So, I dropped it on the table in front of him and said, "Hey Jason, here, grab my Moby Dick, will ya? You might actually pass literature if you do." He just looked away and everybody started laughing. Tammy took my hand for the first time since we met, and we walked away talking about how nice it was to have a friend, and of course, I thought about Mrs. Butters.

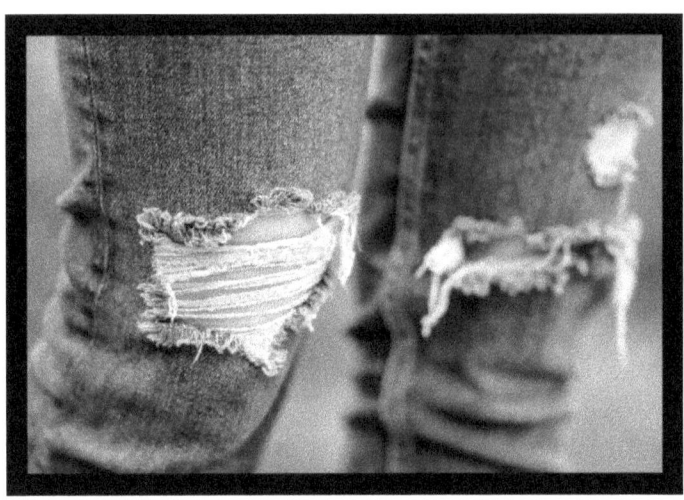

#14

The Weight of Deeds

I was sitting on the front steps of the Clarksburg high school building, feeling free and happy because it was fieldtrip day. I had been taking in the warmth of the morning sun on my face with my eyes closed. After a minute or so, a shadow blocked the light and opening my eyes, I saw the high school principal standing there. He was towering over me, dressed in his pressed grey suit, his hands on his hips. He kind of looked like he had just stepped out of a J.C. Penney catalogue.

He didn't like that my knees were popping out of the holes in my old Levi's. They happened to be my favorite pair and the only one of two that I owned. My ma and I were what people called 'impoverished'. Our money came from the taxes paid by other people because my mother had been abandoned by my da a couple years back. She was physically disabled and couldn't work, which made us look like lazy, no-goods, in principal Trotman's eyes.

He told me I would have to change into something more presentable because torn trousers were not allowed in his high school. "Cos, I'll give you twenty minutes to walk home, change and come back. You might want to actually run, though. I wouldn't want the bus to leave without you. Then you'd have to stay in school all day when all your classmates are out having fun."

It was a good five blocks one way, and the same coming back; of course. I knew by doing it ten times a week that I wouldn't make it in time and would miss the bus, which had already arrived at the curb.

This pretty much confirmed that I was just going to ignore Mr. Trotman. So, that's just what I did, sitting there, picking at the fraying edges of those holes. He walked away after a few minutes to go back inside, but when he got to the door and opened it, all of my classmates came tumbling out. I joined the crowd as they raced by, and together we poured into the open door of the waiting school bus.

Since Mr. Trotman said that jeans with holes were not allowed in high school, I wondered if they were allowed on buses. I mean, the school owned them too, right? But Mrs. Carpenter, the bus driver, just nodded at us and grinned as we scrambled past her into our seats, yelling, laughing, and poking fun at each other. That was until Mr. Trotman climbed in. Everybody got quiet because he just might make up some new rules about having a good time on a fieldtrip. The thing is, we all knew that's what field trips were really about—even Mrs. Carpenter. I could tell she did, because she was smiling and whistling as we drove toward the town square where we would turn east on Main Street and head out toward the state park.

But we didn't turn east; nope, instead, Mr. Trotman stood up and whispered in the driver's ear. She stopped smiling and looked up into the principal's face like she might just slam on the brakes and cause him to crash through the windshield.

She shook her head like she couldn't hardly believe what Mr. Trotman had told her, but she drove right through the square and straight down one block to stop in front of my crappy, old apartment. Mr. Trotman walked back to me and said, "You have five minutes to go inside and change into trousers without holes. If you don't, I'm going to turn this bus around and this field trip is over. All because of you. Now, get to it!"

I didn't want to be the blame for keeping my classmates from their fun. So, I put my stubbornness on hold and gave in. Walking down the aisle toward the door, I heard everybody whispering questions about what was going on. I couldn't blush any deeper than I was, and as I passed the driver, I heard her whisper, "Sorry, kid."

My mother was still in her bed because she had the depression. So, I changed into my good pair of jeans, the ones she told me never to wear unless I was dressing up. I snuck back out to the bus, never saying a word to her because I didn't want her to feel worse than she already was. I knew she was in no shape to have it out with Trotman, and I was worried I was keeping my class from their fieldtrip.

Coming out my front door, the other kids started clapping and yelling like I had won a race or something. I knew right then they didn't understand what was going on. I didn't blame them, but I wasn't going to cry or complain to them about it. I didn't want the reputation of being a whiner.

Trotman was standing in the bus door looking at his watch and grinning like I have seen some evil men do in the past. He said, "Step it up! We have a schedule to keep."

Not feeling so great, now, I took the empty bench seat at the back and slid down so no one could see me. The bus took off and we were finally on our way. After a while I peeked over the top of the seat in front of me and glared at Mr. Trotman. He was smiling away and talking to the bus driver like everything was alright.

But he was wrong, it wasn't.

I knew his wife, Julie. I knew his kids. I spent a lot of time with them when he wasn't home in the evenings—with nobody being able to say where he had gone. Supposedly, he just jumped in the car and took off. Mandy Vale told me once she had gone up to Coogan to see her cousin and saw Trotman hanging around out front of a tavern called The Hitchin' Post, with his arm around some blond woman.

I was still feeling bad about fieldtrip day and Mrs. Trotman could tell I was. So, she started prodding me into telling her what was wrong. I finally gave in and did just that because some grownups just have this way of getting by your defenses. I told her all about the day her husband made me go home and change into the only other pair of jeans that I owned, and he did it right in front of a bus load of kids. She knew how poor we were, and no doubt, (because she had three kids of her own) she knew that pants cost a ton of money. Only kind people like Julie Trotman would understand how I felt.

I came to their house every day after that, just to hang out, drink hot chocolate, and talk about all kinds of things. Then came the one afternoon where I was walking up their driveway in my holey jeans, and I saw my now ex-principal coming out the front door. He was also on his way to becoming the ex-husband, of a wonderful wife, and mother, who I was soon calling mom.

He saw me standing there and quickly looked away as he carried his two suitcases out and stuck them in the trunk of his car. After he finished, he turned and stared at me, but he wasn't grinning like he had been doing on fieldtrip day. I could see the meanness in his eyes as I passed him to go inside the house that was no longer his. I figured he had learned by now that, like holes in the knees of jeans, cheating on your wife also didn't look good in high school. Looking back over my shoulder as I went in the front door, I wondered if I should wave goodbye.

#15

Lori

Having a tough time of it on a Saturday just didn't seem fair. The weekend always meant freedom to me, and that included time to write poetry. School ended yesterday, and they had set me free from the 8th grade. I planned on writing poetry all summer long, and today, being the first day, I should have fell right into it. But the words weren't coming. I was in the park with my Rod McKuen book, *Come To Me In Silence* (not really one of my favorites). I hoped it would prime the pump and get me started.

Now, don't get me wrong; it's not my first time. I've been writing poetry all my life. Besides that, my name is, Poet. Poet Rowett, to be exact. My ma's sense of humor. It didn't end there. When my little brother was born five years ago (back in 1968), she went and named him Stowit.

When her and my dad brought him home, I asked what his name was, and when they told me, I said, "Why such a dumb name?" and ma said, "Just so I can say to him, 'Stow it, Rowett!' whenever he gets on my nerves." Ha-ha, very funny, ma.

What I should tell you is, my folks are hippies. They're tall and lanky (my grandpa's word) with long curly hair. My ma's, blonde. My dad's brown. This of course made mine, brownish-blonde, and it was just as long. Stowit's turned out pretty much the same as mine. I figure by the time he's my age, his hair will be down to his butt.

My folks are always getting high. No drinking, no hard drugs, just smoking Mary Jane. They have a special closet in our apartment which is upstairs in the old post office. It's a pretty large closet where they threw big pillows all over the floor and hung some fancy tapestries along with a few posters, and of course, there were lots of ashtrays. It's got a black light and a little window at the back for the smoke to get out. They also had some serious rules for smoking in there. Number 1-Smoke only after work.

Number 2-No toking until Stowit had gone to bed. And Number 3-Always wear your personal smoking robe so you didn't smell like a stoner every time you went outside.

Sometimes they would invite other couples over and would be in there until way after I fell asleep. I could hear them in there talking about what it was like to have kids, their jobs, and all the different things that happened here in Clarksburg. They'd be laughing and smoking up a storm. I didn't mind because that's better than fighting and arguing like my pal Louie's parents were always doing.

My folks didn't allow me to be in there. That was their free space. Some night I'm just going to go and throw the door wide open and yell, "What's going on in here?" Kind of like I think the town marshal might do. I'd get in trouble, for sure, but it might be worth the laugh.

Now, don't misunderstand, they're good parents—or at least, I thought so. My dad worked at the school as a janitor. Everybody liked him and sometimes he ate lunch with me. Ma worked at the old folk's home as a kind of nurse, and it seemed everybody over there loved her. I never heard anyone ever say anything bad about either of them. Well, except for Earl over at the little Standard gas station on the square.

I heard him going at it one day while I was standing there drinking a soda. He got to complaining about all the hippies moving into town. Then he brought up my folks, but ol' Ray Beasley who stopped in for a handful of sausage sticks, told him. "You just leave Rams and Flower out of this. They're wonderful folk… been nothing but good for Clarksburg."

He winked at me before walking out. I downed my orange soda so I could get the hell out of there before ol' Earl started in on me.

Anyway, laying there on the grass in the park, I couldn't get any words to come. All I got after about two hours, was:

The night brings a treacherous descent
Birthing a fear of the bent and broken
Earthbound until the dawn
The sun shall see me fly

That was only the first verse. I wanted more, but I was tired of it. So, I decided to finish it later and went home. Coming in the back way, I cut through people's yards. When I passed my dad's 1965 VW camper van parked out back by the alley, I tapped a stick on each one of the huge flowers painted on the side, along with the words: 'FLOWER POWER!' He drove it for a long time when he and ma were just hanging around together before they got married. The engine blew a year or so ago, and there it sat. He kept the curtains closed so the upholstery wouldn't fade. I figured it would probably rot before it faded. There was a small mattress just inside, and I slept in there sometimes. I think other people did too—drunk people.

Calico, my little collie dog, came out of her house and barked at me. When she saw who it was, she rolled over on her back so I could rub her belly. I felt bad for her being tied out there all the time (ma didn't want her inside because of fleas). So, I let her loose, and she ran around the yard real crazy like about a hundred times. We played for a while, you know, chasing each other and me throwing sticks so she could bring them back and stuff like that.

I needed a break after chasing calico around so I hooked her back up. The shed door was open a crack, which was kind of unusual. There was an old red motorcycle in there without an engine. I think it was the Irish kid's who lived in the apartment below mine. I didn't want him to think I was messing with it, so I shut it and sat on the concrete step outside the door. Calico lay next to me panting like ol' man Soor at the Jack & Jill grocery whenever we watched him unload vegetables from the delivery truck.

I read poetry to her from my book, but she didn't seem to like McKuen any better than I did. She went into her house and fell asleep, snoring loud enough to wake the dead. I figured I'd done all I could for her and went inside the apartment for some lunch.

Later in the afternoon, I took Stowit down to the river. He liked hanging out under the bridge, skipping rocks, and asking a ton of questions. Ma took a shift for a friend of hers, so she was over at the old folks' home. Dad was inside the apartment working on a big balsawood model of a biplane and watching *Wide World of Sports*. I thought that was kind of weird because he never was an athlete. But he sure got excited about: 'The Thrill of Victory and the Agony of Defeat'. He'd be laughing and carrying on, talking to himself every time somebody crashed or fell down. I couldn't stand sports; way too rough for me.

"Are there any fish in there, Poet?" Stowit asked, failing miserably at skipping his last rock.

"Sure, why do you think all those guys are sitting around over there with their fishing poles? You think those are knitting needles and the Knitting Club came down to the river for a day out?"

"No… so… what kind of fish?"

"Well, there's carp, redhorse, and catfish, maybe a bass or two."

"What's a carp look like?" he asked in his search for more flat rocks to skip.

"Like any ol' fish does! It's got a head, a tail and lots of fins. Damn, Stowit, how am I supposed to tell you what a carp looks like?"

"Well… what color are they?"

"Damn, Stowit! They're kind of gold-like… and real slimy!"

"How come you're always saying, damn, Poet? Like, damn this, and damn that. Huh, Poet?"

"Because you drive me crazy, that's why," I said, and messed up his hair.

He laughed because he liked it. I was the only one who could do that, though. He'd punch anyone else. I suspect because I was his big brother. I found us some more flat rocks, and we spent the rest of the day there at the river.

When we were about ready to head home, Dickie Butz showed up, walking the bank with his pole and a stringer full of redhorse. We were in the same class at school. Dickie was a daredevil. He had a scar on his face just by his left eye to prove it. His dark blonde hair wasn't quite as long as mine, so you could still see the mark whenever he turned his head.

"What you doing, Poet? You know… throwing them rocks in the river only scare the fish."

"Ah, damn, Dickie, there ain't no one fishing around us. You didn't think I'd thought of that?"

"Well, I suppose… hey, we're going down to the Pits tonight, want to come?"

"What's the pits, Poet?" Stowit asked.

"Not your business, little brother. It's for the big boys. Someday you'll know, but for now, forget it."

I threw Dickie a look, and he made his 'Oops' face.

"What's the pits, Dickie?" Stowit asked. Dickie turned away and pretended like something had caught his attention upriver. I grabbed my little brothers' hand and towed him toward home. "See you later, Dickie," I said, and when he looked at me, I winked to let him know I'd be there.

"I seen that, Poet. You're going, aren't you? To those… pits."

"So, what?"

"So… I'm going to tell ma."

"Well, she doesn't care, cause… she trusts me."

"Does she trust me, Poet? Does she, huh?"

"Well, she might. But if you squeal on me, to make me feel bad, she won't. So, what do you want? You want to be trusted… or not."

"To… uh… BE TRUSTED! I guess."

"Then, shut up and let's go home."

He did, and we goofed off all the way there. After we ran up the long stairs outside the building to the balcony porch, we panted our way through the screen door and into the hallway. Ma was home and sitting on dad's lap. They were kissing. Stowit said, "Oh, yuk, ma! I don't need to see that," and he ran into our bedroom. Ma got up and chased him, saying, "Oh yes you do, little man." I heard them in there roughhousing. She must have been tickling him because he was laughing like crazy, and the bed springs were squeaking like a mouse convention.

"What's happening, Poet?" my dad said.

That's the hippie way of asking, 'How's it going?' I tried not to use it. But honestly, that was hard because even my friends were using it nowadays. It wasn't proper English, and I was into using proper English. I would be a freshman next year—so time to start talking right. My dad said it enough times to make up for me. So, nothing lost, you see?

"I'm doing fine, dad. Just down skipping rocks with Stowit at the river."

"Good. Learning to skip rocks is important. Want a Bratwurst? Going to cook some up."

"Sure," I said.

Stowit was on the couch watching TV. Ma was sewing on a shirt she had made for herself and I was helping dad paint his model. Soon we were eating bratwurst with our hands (after they cooled, of course, and after ma had wiped off all the grease). I must admit, I had one eye on the sun as it sank down behind the trees out across the alley. There were ants in my pants, so to speak, making it hard to sit still.

"Dad, I'm going to Louie's, okay? We're going to have a campout."

"Sure thing, kiddo," he said. "When you going?"

"Now."

He put down his little paint brush and spread his arms. I let him hug me, but when he tried to kiss me, I turned my head, and all he got was cheek.

"Too old to be kissing your ol' man, huh?"

"Yep, sorry," I said and pulled away, giving him my biggest smile.

"Not too old for your mom, though," and she grabbed me and planted one on my lips.

I sputtered and wiped them off. They both laughed. Running for the door, I yelled, "See you, Stowit."

"Go away," he yelled back from the living room, probably mad because I distracted him from watching *Science Fiction Theater* and eating his bratwurst.

The long stairs were kind of dangerous, so you had to be careful going down—no running. When I got to the bottom, I ducked right, down the shorter set that led into the back yard. The mother of the Irish kid who lived downstairs, was sitting in her wooden chair on the stoop, out front. I didn't want to talk to her. She scared me. The rumors going around said she'd been to the mental institution and just might be a little crazy.

The Pits sat just south of Clarksburg. They used to be a quarry, but someone turned them into a county park. Trees had grown up around all these big ponds and it was now a good place to camp. When I got to the spot where we usually hung out (next to the biggest of the ponds), I found the guys sitting around a fire with their shirts off. The sun went down, and it got dark, fast.

Dickie, Louie, Bailey, and Little Charley were trying to convince each other that they, at one time in their lives, had actually held a Playboy magazine in their hands. Little Charley tried to make us all believe he'd stolen one from the back rack at Nordon's Drug store. Taking off my shirt and dropping it with the others, I said, "Oh Charley, everybody knows ol' man Nordon keeps those behind the counter. They're even covered in brown paper so you can't tell, right off, what they are."

"No, no, I…"

"Ah, bullshit, Charley," Dickie said. "We all know better, so just quit trying, huh?"

"Fine then, don't believe me, but…"

Louie and Bailey were laughing so hard at the faces Little Charley was making that it got me and Dickie laughing too. Little Charley just dug at the sand with a stick and shook his head like he was fed up with us.

"So, what's happening, poet-but-don't-know-it?" Louie said, wiping water off his face. I figured he must have just climbed out of the pond.

"Not much," I said. "Except, I do know it! You… barbarian!"

Barbarian was my new favorite word. I used it mostly with my friends. They didn't mind. They knew me and expected me to be weird, mostly because I loved words and wrote poetry.

Little Charley said, "You're going to have to come up with a new word, Poet. That one's getting old."

"Okay… how about, redundant? Like, 'Little Charley, you're a redundant fool' What do you think? Good word?"

"What the hell does that even mean," he asked.

"Ah, go look it up, Charley," Bailey said. "Hey, you guys want to go swimming?"

"I see Louie's already been in. Is that what we're doing tonight?" I asked.

"Naw, he hasn't been in yet. He was just sticking his face under and opening his eyes to see if he could see any fish in there. But we're not going fishing, we're going swimming. But not until we've finished this," he said and standing up, he pulled a bottle of MD 20/20 from his back pocket.

Now, I knew that Mad Dog (as we called it) was the hard stuff. You didn't make any plans for later if you were going to drink that. Because, well, you wouldn't be able to do anything that required thinking, only stuff like, standing up, falling down, yelling, swearing, and talking about stuff that didn't make sense. Maybe a little running and some horseplay at first, but that wouldn't last.

Baily said, "Stole it from my dad. He won't miss it."

He twisted off the cap, took a long swig and passed it to Louie, and then on around. When it got to me, I sipped once and passed it on because I'd never drank before. Nobody seemed to notice that I didn't swig it like they did. Even the tiny bit I did get, burned all the way down. But like I said, Mad Dog was powerful stuff, and things got a little crazy.

We were down to our underwear and bare feet right away, running around, yelling, chasing each other, jumping in the pond, and all kinds of crap like that. When the headlights from a car cut through the trees, we ran to hide. Laying down behind a big log, we peeked over the top, trying hard to keep from laughing. Little Charley couldn't stop, and then he went to tickling us. Dickie just sat on him and I covered his mouth. He still tried to tickle us, anyway.

A path, just wide enough for a car, wound through the trees from the main road, and ended right at the clearing. The car stopped just inside that, and somebody got out to walk around in front of the headlights.

"Hey guys, where are you? I know you're here, so… give it up!"

It was Hank. He was a sophomore and only hung around with us sometimes. He could drive now, and drove a light blue, 1962 Oldsmobile (his brother Frank's car, actually). We all stood up and hollered, "Hank!"

"Hey guys, what's happening?"

He went back to the driver's side to turn off the headlights and kill the engine. I heard him talking to somebody, and the passenger door opened. I think we all wished we had stayed down behind the log when that girl walked out to lean on the hood of the Old's. Five sets of hands went straight down to protect private parts, bringing a wicked giggle from her mouth.

"Hey guys, this is Lori. Picked her up hitchhiking down in Cedar Rapids. She told me she's looking to make some new friends. Say hi to the guys, Lori."

"Hi guys," she said in a sexy voice. "Looks like I'm going to get to know you pretty quick like. Already got you down to your underwear, and I haven't even been here but a minute."

Me and the guys laughed nervously. Hank laughed like a crazy man. Lori chuckled in a way that kind of scared me. She just stood there, smirking at us, the firelight making her kind of shimmer like a little fairy. A wicked one.

She seemed barely five feet tall. Her almost perfect teeth shone in the firelight, and her eyes gleamed, or so I imagined. She wore her hair in a bob that made her round face even rounder. A face that I really couldn't make out all that well in the shadow.

Little Charley ran for his pants and we followed. Pulling mine on, I watched Hank set a brown grocery sack on the hood of the Olds and start pulling out bottles of liquor and beer.

"Ah, come on guys, you don't have to put those on," Lori teased.

Little Charley said, "Yeah, that's what you think."

"Maybe we'll take them off later after you take off yours," Louie added.

"I'm going to need a few more beers in me, before that happens," Bailey lied.

"That makes two of us," Dickie said, wanting to get in on Bailey's lie.

I stood there, quiet, keeping my face angled down so she couldn't see any more of it than I could see of hers. I stuffed my hands in the pockets of my Levi's and watched her through the hair that had fallen in my face.

"So, what about you, the quiet one? What? Nothing to say to your new friend?" Lori asked.

"That's Poet. He talks more than you think," Hank said. "Come on over here guys and have a drink, it's on me. Raided my big brother's cooler in the garage. He'll never know it's gone until it's too late."

The guys ran over and grabbed bottles of beer. I followed and tried to keep them between me and Lori. It didn't help. She grabbed a bottle of Peppermint Schnapps, twisted off the cap and I thought she would stand there and drink it; but no. She worked her way through the guys and walked right up to me, shoving the bottle in my face.

"Want a drink? Go on, take it, quiet boy."

I wanted to swipe it away, but I thought it better to be polite. Also, I was afraid of what Hank might think of me. So, I grabbed it and took a single sip as I stared into her eyes. At that distance, I could see they were green, her skin was pale, and she had freckles. She wore a red and white striped tube top. It made her boobs look like she had stuffed a couple of oranges in there. The carrot-colored short shorts she had on were almost too small for her. The blue sandals on her feet were like the cheap ones that you could get at the Royal Blue grocery for a dollar ninety-five.

She smelled like Patchouli (my ma's favorite) and Juicy Fruit gum. I could still smell her sweat through it all, and there was also that girl smell. The one I always noticed whenever I walked by their locker room at school. I got the feeling she just might be a barbarian.

I walked around her and went to lean against the front of the car. She didn't turn her whole body when her eyes followed me, just her head. Then she stood there, kind of staring at me like she was trying to figure me out. I looked her over from behind. She had a bubble-butt which hung out of her shorts a bit. Her waist was thin, but I think that was because of her butt, or… maybe it was her hips.

Hank reached over, patted me on the shoulder and said, "Cute, huh?"

His face looked weird in the firelight. He wore a thin beard and a mustache, the Fu-Manchu kind; the only guy in high school who did, or maybe—could.

I didn't answer his question because I got distracted by the guys. They weren't carrying on like they usually do. Everybody just stood around, staring at Lori. The way she was acting, made me think she really liked it.

I set the bottle on the hood of the Olds and took out my comb to run it through my hair just for something else to do besides drinking and staring at Lori. The next thing I knew, she was standing right in front of me, this time, even closer. What I saw in her eyes reminded me of a time when Calico had caught a rabbit, and I tried to take it away. This girl wasn't going to let me escape. Never, ever. She wanted something, and I was either too stupid, or to confused, to figure out what it was.

"What you got there… Poet," she said in that sexy voice.

"Well, ummm, it's a comb. What does it…" She didn't let me finish. Snatching it from my hand, she stuck it down her tube top between her boobs.

"Hey, what the…"

"You want it? Come and get it."

That shocked me. I felt like a little kid again. I was shaking and didn't know what to do next. This was something new. I looked past her to the guys for help, but they just stood shoulder to shoulder, grinning, waiting to see what I was going to do. Well, all except Little Charley, who, even in the dim light of the campfire, looked a little green around the gills. I turned to Hank, hoping he would jump in and save me. He grinned like a wolf and nodded toward her like he wanted me to do what she was telling me to do.

"Just give it back, okay?" I said, trying to sound tough. I heard Hank sigh, and everybody, including Little Charley, groaned, just not for the same reason. Two seconds later, he was running for the bushes. I hoped Lori would turn around to look so I could snatch the comb and make my getaway.

The problem was, something had gotten out of sync and my hand was already on its way toward her tube top before she turned to look at Little Charley. She took that as a sign and jumped on me, her arms going over my shoulders and those short legs clamping my hips. Then her lips went to working on mine. I thought to push her away, but a voice inside my head said, "Don't you dare."

I never kissed anyone before. Well, except for my ma (and dad, in my younger days) and this—wasn't that. I didn't know a person could do so much with their tongue. My hands went to her waist, and I felt her hot skin and the curve of her hip. I felt a kind of warmness form at my crotch, and I thought I might start sweating. One of her hands slipped behind my back and down inside the waist band of my Levi's. My own butt now felt what it was like to be bread dough. Then she let go, dropped down, and stepped back. I could see her eyes in the dark and they seemed to be glowing. "Like that, did you?" she said. I was going to say no, but the bulge at my crotch said the opposite. My hands automatically went down to cover it.

Everybody howled, and Louie said, "Alright! I'm next," and she was on him in an instant, doing the same. Picking up the comb that had fallen out of her tube top, I walked away to the edge of the pond, embarrassed.

"Where you going, Poet?" Hank called out.

I didn't look back but raised my hand as if to say, 'Go away! Leave me alone.' I decided to take a walk around the shore of the pond. I left the tiny beach and followed a strip of sand that went all the way around. I felt more confusion than I'd ever felt before. I figured this must be what my dad meant when he said, "I feel a little conflicted about that." I mean, the guys and I had talked about this kind of thing. It was more like a group fantasy of how there would be this girl who liked us all—and at the same time. There had been many talks (just to pass the time) and they had been about what that girl would look like. We finally came to an agreement on what that would be. But it wasn't Lori.

I figured out about halfway around the pond that the reason I felt like I did was because Lori had jumped right on Louie after me and—I didn't want to share. It didn't seem right for her to do what she did before I got to know her better, or maybe, it was because she didn't ask first.

When I got all the way around and back to the campfire, I saw Lori walking away from Dickie, wiping her mouth and grinning. Little Charley lay curled up on his side next to the campfire, passed out cold. She walked over and looked down at him. Then shaking her head, she went back to the car. I suspected Little Charley might regret having drank too much and would complain later that it wasn't fair that he didn't get his turn.

"Well, look who's back. Hey, quiet boy, you want another? I got plenty."

"Naw! Lori, let's take off. I want to show you something I got plenty of," Hank said, and grinning, he slapped a hand over his crotch and pulled it upward.

"Oh, Hank, you brute!" she said, and moving over to him, she took his hand away and her's took its place. She stood there beside him with one hand on his crotch, looking at us out of the tops of her eyes, grinning like—a barbarian.

Hank set the liquor and beer in the bushes beside the little road and said, "You guys can keep this," and then they climbed into the Olds. When the car was pointing in the right direction to get out of there, Lori hollered out of the window, "Bye boys, see you around town," and waved like crazy.

Then they were gone. All I heard was crickets, frogs, and Little Charley's snores. Things changed so drastically that it left me feeling weird. Dickie staggered by me and picked up another beer.

"Get me one," Louie said, even though he could barely stand. Bailey still had the bottle of Mad Dog, but instead of drinking, he just held it, his eyes half closed. By the time Dickie got back with the beers, Bailey had fallen straight down onto his butt, and crossing his legs, he sat staring at the fire, hugging the Mad Dog. Louie and Dickie sat down close by, kind of hunched over like they were falling asleep. I grabbed the abandon bottle of Schnapps and after taking a tiny sip, I sat down and hugged the bottle like Bailey.

Louie said, "Can you believe that shit? Man! That was just like we imagined. Remember, Poet?"

"Yeah, I remember."

Dickie slurred, "Charley is going to be so jealous. Too bad he missed out."

"Well, we don't need to tell him. Then he won't feel bad," I said.

"Don't tell him! Hell, Poet, I'm going to tell everybody! People got to know."

"Yeah," said Bailey, his dark hair looking even wilder than before.

"You know that girl's only seventeen? Oh man! She sure knew a lot stuff for only being that old," Dickie added.

"We got bragging rights, now," Louie said and collapsed backwards on the ground, spilling his beer. He lay there for a minute and said to the sky, "Man, I'm really drunk." The rest of us just squinted at him until his snores matched Little Charley's. "Think I'm going to sleep, too," Bailey said, and propping the Mad Dog against the log we used for sitting, he lay down and put his head on his arm. Dickie sat leaning forward, his beer bottle trapped inside his crossed legs. He'd passed out sitting up.

I thought of just walking home, but I didn't want to go down that scary road through the woods in the dark. Since no one was looking, I tossed the bottle of Schnapps into the weeds, put on my shirt, and added more wood to the fire.

Going back to my spot, I lay down in the grass. I thought about what had happened and wondered why it bothered me so much. If Lori was only seventeen, how come she acted like a woman of twenty. Maybe there was something wrong with her? I mean, mentally. The guys at school joked about how they'd like to meet a Nymphomaniac. But I think that just might be an actual disease. So, maybe Lori was one of those. I supposed I could look it up, or if I got the guts, ask dad. That would be embarrassing, though. He wouldn't judge me or anything. He'd probably just figure it was time for the 'Birds & Bees' talk. You know the one.

I fell asleep but not for long because a group of hippies showed up to go skinny dipping. I barely remembered a naked woman, probably older than my ma, just standing there, looking at us, talking to some naked guy, who said, "Oh, just leave 'em alone, Sal, they'll be okay. You don't have to be everybody's mom, you know? Hell, they was drinking anyway, see all them bottles?"

I laid there, not moving, peeking through half-closed eyes. That's when a girl I knew from the high school walked up and stood beside them without a stitch of clothes on. Molly Blake. She was tall and slender, with perfect boobs, long blond hair, and the friendliest of smiles. I could hardly believe what I was seeing.

Molly said, "Oh, I know that kid! They call him Poet. He's a cute one."

She turned and walked away. I watched the cheeks of her beautiful behind, rise and fall until she disappeared into the dark. The other two turned and followed her, but I closed my eyes completely, so I wouldn't have to look at theirs. There were a few more people down by the water, and I thought about joining them, but I fell back to sleep listening to them splash, laugh, and carry-on.

I woke up to a Blue Jay making a hell of a racket in the tree above my head. The other guys moved a bit, but no one woke up. Little Charley was snoring the loudest, and I felt kind of sorry for him. I didn't know him all that well, but I knew he got picked on a lot by bigger kids. I came to his rescue a couple times and got knocked around for it. I wasn't afraid. I just didn't see the sense in it all.

The sun sat just below the horizon and the sky behind the trees showed a beautiful shade of blue. Because the dark had left the woods, I figured I could head home. I got up and walked down to the pond. The skinny-dipping party had left behind some beer bottles, the tail end of a few marijuana cigarettes (my folks call them roaches), a sock, a pair of Paisley bikini underwear, and a red bandana; Molly's red bandana. I could see she had folded and knotted it so she could wear it over her hair. That sparked an idea.

I could save it and give it to her when I saw her next. I could be her hero and we could become friends. Now, it's not a normal thing for a freshman to be friends with a senior, but there's always a first time. Snatching it out of the sand, I stuck it in my back pocket and took off for home.

I found myself with nothing to do on the next Monday, so I went up to the square. I just got home from letting Calico run in the woods south of town. She needed it pretty badly, and I knew she would love me forever for taking her there.

I ran into Willowbough Boyd while I was down there. She's this American Indian girl with a little Jack Russell that's smart as a whip. The dogs sniffed each other's butts and then ignored each other while they hunted. I yelled, "Hey, Willowbough," across the timber, but she just smiled, and then ignored me. She was shy and didn't say much in school. She hung out with Conor Sullivan, who we thought had drown, but then like a miracle, came back to life.

I think they're boyfriend and girlfriend now, but it's hard to tell because she wouldn't ever hold his hand or hug him in public.

Anyway, so I am standing on the corner and I see Hank's car coming up the street. He honked at me and guess who I see sitting on the passenger side; you guessed it, Lori. If she was still hanging around, where was she staying? Maybe Hank had her stashed away up in his attic. Who knows? She leaned out the window and hollered, "Hey! What's happening, quiet boy!"

My new nickname bugged the crap out of me, so I yelled, "Barbarian!" She laughed and looked over at Hank and got him laughing too. She still wore the same clothes she had on that night, leaving me to wonder if she had washed them yet. In the daylight, she didn't seem so scary. I think it was because she's what my ma called, direct, or maybe—aggressive. That made her frightening. She didn't wait for permission—she just helped herself. That bothered me, but I can't say why.

She hung around with Hank for about a week, then I ran into him, alone, at the Standard station, getting gas. Bill Johnson, the owner, had the coldest soda in Clarksburg, so I went in there to grab a bottle.

"Hey, Poet, what's happening," he said, climbing out of his Olds.

"Not a thing, just having a soda. Hey, where's Lori?"

"Why? You want a turn, too?"

"What? I, uhhh… No! Why?"

"Forget it," he said, like he was pissed off because I made him think about her.

Did I want a turn? What the hell? That pissed me off, so I kept at him. "So, ummm… you aren't together anymore?"

"Naw, she got tired of me. Started hanging around with Manny. You know that guy… drives that super loud Charger with the big wheels?"

"Yeah, I know it, the big yellow Dodge? That guy works over at the DX gas station. I think he's a mechanic. Kind of older, isn't he? Like—thirty something?"

"I suppose. Hey, Poet, I got to git, I'm going to Cedar Rapids. Hey! You want to come along?"

"Nope, got to get back home before Stowit wakes up from his nap. My dad's up at the school, waxing the gym floor. I got to get back home before he gets there."

"Alright, you don't know what you're missing. See you, buddy," he said, and paying Earl five bucks for the gas, he jumped in is his car and squealed away, leaving black marks on the concrete apron in front of the pumps.

"Damn kids," Earl yelled, and then looking at me, he said, "And… damn hippies!"

"Leave the kid alone, Earl," I heard Bill yell from the little office at the back. Earl grumbled something and went out into the mechanic's bay. I finished off my bottle, just as Bill stuck his head out of the door, "My ma's living over at the old folks home. She sure likes your ma. So, tell your folks I said hi, hey kiddo?"

"Sure thing," I said, and headed for home.

Lori had left Hank for Manny. Kind of weird since he was almost twice her age. I wanted to know more. I had about half an hour before dad would get home. So, I ran over to the sidewalk on the Blue Front side of the street and walked down to Hale's Hardware. The store sat on the corner right across from the DX.

I went inside to pretend I was looking for something. Old Howard Hale had a super cool bicycle in the big display window, so I pretended to be looking at it. But really, I was looking across the street, scoping out the gas station. The big yellow Charger sat parked at the side, between the station and the alley, away from all the other cars. Somebody's small, bare feet were sticking out of the passenger side window. Whoever it was, they must have been laying down on the seat. I could see that Manny guy working in one of the two bays. He was wearing green coveralls and was fixing something under a car up on the lift.

"You like that bike?" somebody said, and I about peed my pants.

I turned around real quick and saw Keli Hale standing there in a blue apron with Hale's Hardware in big white letters across the front. She was a grade above me, and I knew she had a crush on that Irish kid who lived downstairs. She seemed nice, but that was a wild group they belonged too. I didn't want any part of that.

"Um, yeah… it's super. How much does your dad want for it?"

"Eighty-five bucks. But he's out for lunch. If you buy it from me, I'll let you have it for seventy… as long as you buy it before he gets back."

I could tell she had just gotten a permanent because her blond hair was all curly now and pushed up on top of her head. My ma wouldn't like it if I said it out loud, but Keli had a face like a pig with small beady eyes and a big, flat nose that turned up. Other kids called her 'Pig Face' and sometimes loud enough for her to hear. I just kept my opinion to myself. It was what my ma called, 'The Thumper Method'. If I didn't have something nice to say, don't say anything at all. I didn't follow it all of the time, like when someone was trying to make me feel bad. Keli didn't do that, so she was safe.

She stuck her hands inside her apron and kind of swiveled back and forth at her ankles. Her eyes went up and down my body like she was sizing me up. I didn't want to be friends with her, so I figured I'd better get out of there.

"Okay… hey thanks. I'll go see what my folks say. Seventy, right?"

"Yeah," she said softly, and grinned.

I heard the back door open and shut. "Oops! Too late," she said. "Bye! See you later."

She turned away as her dad yelled, "Keli?" kind of like she was lost or something.

I escaped as quickly as I could. But instead of going home, I did the stupid thing and went across the street. I walked into the alley and snuck up to the Charger. All four windows were down, and Nazareth's *Broke Down Angel* was pouring out. I stopped just outside and peeked over the dirty feet.

Lori lay on her back, on the bench seat, her eyes closed, rocking out to the music. I thought about running, but my shadow fell over her face and those green eyes popped open.

She sat up in a flash as I backed away. Getting up on her knees in the passenger seat she grinned like a vampire and shouted, "Oh… quiet boy. What you doing?" Crossing her arms on the sill, she rested her chin on them and cocked her head.

I stopped and came back a couple steps. "I can't hear you, the music's too loud."

She turned it down and came back to the window. "You come for another kiss? You're so cute. You know, I could just eat you alive."

"I heard you broke up with Hank?"

"Broke up? So childish... Nope, no breakup. I mean, how fifties is that?"

"I don't know. So, you're with this Manny guy? I heard you're only seventeen?"

"Yeah, so? Lips are lips, and a dick's a dick. It's all the same."

"People are going to think you're trash. I mean, not me… but you know the gossip, right?"

"Yeah… but what I know is, it's okay for you… I mean, guys, to go around with a different girl every night, but one girl comes along who does the same thing, and… well, you know, quiet boy, I don't think that's fair. So, I'm going to change a few things."

"But Manny's old enough to be your dad."

"Not hardly, but you are so sweet. Are you worried about me, quiet boy? Little… shy boy."

"It's Poet."

"Don't I know it. You want to write me something? Something sweet?"

She got lower in the seat so that only her head showed and then she started rising up real slow as she pressed her chest against the door just below the sill. Our eyes met and I can't explain what I saw in them. She looked down at her chest and I realized she was scraping her tube top down and any second her boobs were going to pop out. She kept looking down at them and back at me, grinning.

"Uh oh! They are going to get loose. Oh my, what should I do?"

I noticed her extra-long dog teeth and the dark circles under her eyes. It magnified the vampire thing. I didn't want to see boobs, right then, and I wasn't going to wait for them. I turned and ran just as I heard a man shout, "Hey! What are you doing over there?" I looked back as I hightailed it up the street and saw Manny walk to the car, wiping his hands on a rag. Lori and he started yelling at each other, so I picked up my pace and got home before my dad did. Stowit was already up, eating a bowl of Captain Crunch, and watching *The Undersea World Of Jacques Cousteau.*

"Sorry, Stowit," I needed to get out for a minute."

"Don't worry about me, besides, you're not my boss."

"Okay, fine, I'm not your boss. Just don't tell ma or dad, huh?"

"Take me down to the river, later?"

"What? Why?"

Dad walked in about then, looking beat.

"Dad, guess what Poet did?"

I gave him my, 'You're such a traitor' look and said, "Hey, Stowit, want to go down to the river later?"

"You darn tootin', sounds like fun."

"So… what did Poet do, Stowit?" dad asked.

"He fixed me a bowl of Captain Crunch."

"Good man, Poet," my dad said and went into the kitchen.

I stayed off the street for a couple of days after that, taking the backyards to hang out at Louie's and Dickie's houses. We wandered The Pits, got rides on Conor's raft for a quarter apiece and hung around the Fairgrounds watching the harness races. We talked about Lori and what they would like to do to her. Which, I thought was funny because none of us had any experience with sex. They were just making stuff up. When they asked what I would do, because I was being so quiet, I just said, "The same." That way I could get them off my back. They both told me how Lori had ridden past their houses real slow in a clunky, old, green Pontiac and it kind of freaked me out. That girl had something up her sleeve, and I had a good idea what it was.

I had to go to the Jack & Jill for milk on Friday. I jay-walked across Main Street as a junky old, green Pontiac pulled up to the stop sign. Harry Fulton owned that car. Harry was another one of the Irish boy's friends. A quiet guy, but with a bad temper. Lori sat in the front seat, right up against him as he drove. Even though I hid my face, she recognized me and yelled, "Poet!" I pretended like I didn't see her and ducked inside the store.

Three days later, I had Stowit over to Nordon's for root beer floats. Nordon owned an old-fashion soda fountain, and he worked it himself. Sucking away on our straws, I saw Molly stop outside the window to talk with short, chubby, Mrs. Butters, my reading teacher. The red bandana was still folded neatly in my back pocket. Ma washed it for me, and I figured now was the time to give it back.

"Wait here, Stowit, got to talk to Molly."

"For another root beer float, I will."

"Geez, Stowit you're going to break me. Mr. Nordon, another float for this…"

"Coming right up," old man Nordon said before I finished.

Stowit giggled and went to spinning around on his stool. Running to the door, I flung it open. Mrs. Butters saw me first and said, "Poet, how are you? Are you still writing, young man? Don't ever stop writing, you hear me?"

"I won't, already have a few new ones."

"Great! So, good luck in high school. Come down and see me sometime and bring your poetry. I know that you know where my room is! Good… day, miss Molly" she said and chuckled. Shaking her head, and grinning, like something was funny, she walked away toward the beauty salon. Molly looked at me and shrugged. She didn't get why Mrs. Butters had chuckled. I felt kind of proud because I did.

"What was that all about, do you suppose?"

"CCR! You know? 'Good Golly, Miss Molly, and about her rocking at the house of blue lights?"

"Oh, yeah, okay. You are so clever. I'd a never guessed that in a million years."

She stood there, looking at me, smiling, and I think I saw her eyes twinkle. "So… Poet, you are an actual poet, right?"

"Um, yeah, kind of… well, I want to be, anyway."

"So cool. I saw you down at The Pits. You were out cold, or—were you?"

I blushed, and I could feel the red creeping up my neck to my face. I couldn't lie to her, so I said, "No, I knew you were there… barely awake, but I knew."

"Sooo… you saw me naked?"

"Ummm…"

"No big deal, we skinny dip all the time. You should come with us some night. That would be fun."

I didn't say anything and whipped the red bandana from my pocket. Holding it up for her to see, she gasped and giggled. "Oh my! You found it! I thought I'd lost it. You're so sweet." She leaned in and kissed my cheek when she took the bandanna from my hand. I think I blushed deeper than I ever had before. We stood there talking with her acting so natural, and me as nervous as hell. I kept my eyes on her face because she had on this thin, white peasant blouse and just happened to be braless.

We yakked away with me thinking how good she was at talking; so free and easy. We were nearly three years apart in age, but she made me feel like we were best friends. That's when Mike T came up 4th Street from the square behind me. He had those Cherry Bomb mufflers on his '57 Chevy and the windows of the stores rattled like there was an earthquake.

Molly and I turned together to watch, waiting for him to pass. Lori hung halfway out the passenger side window, just staring. She looked bored. Her lips formed the word, "Poet." But the car was too loud to hear anything. I glanced at Molly to see her reaction. She didn't have one. She simply watched like she was curious.

Lori had a black eye.

I shuddered at the thought, suspecting Manny. Molly said, "Hey, who was that? I've never seen her before. Did you see it? She had a black eye, like someone punched her."

"Yeah, I saw it."

"I know Mike from school, he's just a grade under me. But I thought he was dating Shelagh Bennett?"

I didn't want to talk about that, so I said, "Molly, I got to go, my little brothers inside."

"Is he a poet, too?"

"Naw, just a little kid who likes root beer floats."

She chuckled and said, "Okay, so Poet... skinny dipping some night, huh? And oh, let me read some of your poetry sometime? I love poetry. Mrs. Butters is a great teacher. So, I bet you're good at it."

She leaned in and kissed me on the forehead this time, and said, "See you later, and thanks for saving my favorite bandana."

"Okay, ummm... your welcome. Let me know about the skinny dipping, huh?"

She smiled this big, beautiful smile and walked away down the street, her tight, low riding, big belled jeans swishing, and her long, straight blond hair blowing in the breeze. I went back inside to find Stowit had just finished his float. "Who was that, Poet? Your girlfriend? Yeah, I'll bet your girlfriend. She was kissing you. Poets got a girlfriend! Poets got a girlfriend!"

"Oh, shut up. We got to get home, mom's making Shake N Bake tonight... and you're going to help."

"Am I really, wow! That ought to be fun."

I heard Mr. Nordon chuckle as we walked out. I suspected he knew all about the Shake N Bake commercial.

Stowit peed his bed that night. I had to promise to buy him red licorice the next time we went to the drugstore. It was the only way he wouldn't tell ma or dad that I let him have two root beer floats instead of one. My money came from my weekly allowance for doing chores. I never could save any of it with Stowit around.

Two weeks passed since that first night Lori kissed me. The last time I saw her, I was walking out of the library with a book of Robert Frost poems. She zoomed by with Crazy Vaughn in his lime colored, hunk of junk, pickup truck. They were laughing. Vaughn drove by too quick for her to yell anything.

Two more nights went by before the morning I got up early to do some fishing. I felt kind of tired because Calico's barking kept waking me up. I packed my note book and pencils along with my tackle box and pole. I actually spent more time writing, then fishing. The mist floated in the air as I walked out across the yard to the alley. The sun was just peeking over the dentist's office behind me across the street, and I loved how mysterious it all felt.

A noise came from inside the VW as I went by, and one of the side doors burst open. Dickie crawled out and fell on the ground at my feet. Rolling over on his back, he zipped up his shorts, shouting, "Hey, Poet, what's happening!"

"Dickie! What are you doing in my dad's bus?"

"Needed a place to sleep last night, hope it's alright?"

Somebody else pushed open the other side door. Lori lay there, wearing only a pair of pink, bikini underwear. Pulling her foot back from the door, she said, "Hey, Poet! Want to come in here with us?"

"Come on, Lori! Dickie said. "I got to get home. So… it's only the two of you!" Looking back and forth between her and me, he said, "She's all yours, Poet. See you later." He ran off, adjusting his shorts, leaving me alone with a nearly naked Lori.

I couldn't take my eyes off her. I was always kind of afraid that if I ever saw her that way, I'd be hooked. My thoughts went back to Molly that night at the pits. I couldn't figure out why seeing my goddess in her birthday suit made me feel differently than standing there looking at a topless Lori. A little voice whispered in my head, saying, "Do it. Climb in there with her. What are you afraid of?" But then there was a louder, stronger voice that said, "Don't you dare, Poet Rowett!"

Dickie was fifteen, but just a month older than me, and I knew he was a virgin before Lori showed up. We all were. She had taken his cherry, and now, she wanted mine.

"Hey Poet, you coming in, or not?"

I just wasn't ready. The louder voice won out and summoning all my strength, I said, "Nope!" and slammed both doors shut at the same time. She hollered, "Poet!" in kind of a sad way, and I took off at a run chasing Dickie.

I caught him at the bridge and grabbed the back of his shirt to stop him.

"What's going on, Dickie? You got to tell me and be honest. What's going on?"

"What do you mean? What? Are you stupid or something, Poet? Sex is going on, that's what. It's the thing we all wished for, remember? This girl shows up, and she wants to do it with everybody. We all dreamed of this happening, and now… it really is! Plain and simple, pal. I think you're the only one who hasn't done it with her."

"What do you mean by that? So, like Louie and Bailey? I mean, I know Hank has, but… Little Charley, even?"

"Naw, not Charley. She's not interested in him, she told me. But she also said, let's see, how'd she put it… oh yeah, 'You can bet I'm going to get into Poets pants—even if it kills me' So, it's your turn at home base, buddy."

"Louie and Bailey?"

"What did I just say? They went before me, and you should go back to that van right now and jump on that… unless you're queer or something."

"Well, I'm not, but… hey, what's wrong with being queer?"

"Everything… in this town. See you later, got to get home and have me a shower. Take my advice, Poet. Go back there, screw her brains out, and then forget about her. It's the best thing."

Dickie walked away from me as I stood on the end of that bridge, my mouth hanging open. I couldn't think straight, there were so many things that didn't add up. But the one thing I did know; it was not the best thing, no matter what Dickie said.

My folks had already talked to me about this. They had been talking about how people treat other people like objects instead of the warm blooded, feeling people that they were. I remember asking, "What do you mean by objects?" and they started in on me (lesson time!). That led into how I should treat girls. So, based on what my folks said, I knew Lori had become an object—not a subject. She stopped being a person. But she seemed to want it that way. That's what I couldn't figure out. It all became a jumbled-up mess in my head.

I spent the morning on the river, but I didn't write a single word. I just sat there on a big rock, my line in the water, mulling the situation over and over. I wanted Lori to leave. To go back to wherever she'd came from. That would solve everything. Then Clarksburg could get back to normal, and I could put all my energy into Molly.

After hours of running it through my mind, I realized what really troubled me most. Mrs. Butters had the class read Dr. Jekyll and Mr. Hyde, back in April. After we finished, she held an open discussion in the class room about Robert Louis Stevenson and his novel. Dr. Jekyll had taken a potion, but Mrs. Butters said it was really about the duality of man and that all humans have a darker side. After she talked about it, I started looking for it in grown-ups, and sure enough, I found it in a few. And now—it was in me. That whispering in my head was its voice, and it wanted to be the boss. Maybe Lori had found her dark side a long time ago and she had come to bring ours out. It all made me wonder if Lori was evil.

I didn't sleep well that night. Stowit squirmed and talked in his sleep and that didn't help matters. Ma and dad didn't smoke in their room either. Instead, they sat up watching old movies, ate popcorn, and talked about living in Clarksburg. They brought up the strange little red-haired girl they saw hanging out around the Blue Front tavern. I wanted to get up, stomp right into the living room and tell them all about her. But I couldn't bring myself to do it.

I woke up about eleven o'clock the next morning feeling super tired. I took a shower and washed myself, scrubbing like I hoped it would get rid of my problem. I stayed away from the square and kept my attention on Stowit and Calico. I didn't want to see the guys—or Lori.

Two days went by before I laid eyes on her again. I'd been sitting on the window seat at the front of our apartment, reading a Carl Sandburg book I got from the library and watching the street. An old, green '65 Chevy came around the corner up by the tavern. I knew that car– Red Dog Finney. He had a wife and kids, but there sat Lori, right in the front seat.

She leaned out of the window on the passenger side, staring up at my apartment. I pulled back from the screen a bit, and watched the car turn out of sight down by Ernie B's lawnmower shop.

Red Dog worked over at Slade's auto body because he got fired from his job at the turkey farm. Kind of a nice guy, but a real smart ass. He stood as tall as me and wore his red hair like Elvis Presley. I could never tell if he liked me or not. I decided not to care, and then it didn't matter. Sometimes my dad went to the Blue Front tavern and would come home to tell us all about the stories that he had heard from Red Dog.

Another day passed before I realized I couldn't stand it anymore and I went up to the corner. Clarksburg was dead, like every Sunday. On the way up, I saw Hank standing there, smoking, and leaning against the lamp pole. For just being a teenager, he sure fooled a lot of people. The mustache and the beard said he was much older. I wondered how soon I'd get hair on my face.

"Hank! How's it going? Where's your car?"

"What's happening, Poet! Hey, haven't seen you around for a while. Where you been hiding?"

"Oh… had to take care of my little brother, you know."

"No, I wouldn't know. But anyway, cars in the shop, getting some new mufflers and tires. So, got to hoof-it for the weekend. My brother Frank let me have it for free because he got a GTO. So, I had to fork out a few bucks because my dad wouldn't let me drive it again until it was safer. Frank just beat the shit out of that Olds when he drove it."

"Sounds expensive."

"You're telling me, had to save like crazy. Been working out on old man Holub's farm. Man! What a penny pincher. Never seem to make enough cash. Anyway, you seen the guys around? Seems everybody's staying home these days."

"Haven't seen them, either."

I decided not to tell him that had been my goal. About that time, the reason for not wanting too, stepped out of the Blue Front tavern across the street. It opened at noon and stayed that way until ten on Sundays. Some people just needed their beer, and Arnie, the owner, took advantage of that.

Lori looked different. She looked clean with her hair brushed and was wearing what looked like a brand-new hot pants sailor suit with the big collar and the little black and white stripes at her throat. The sandals were gone, and now she wore white, slip on sneakers.

I could tell she wanted to talk to us, but some guy who I knew only as Buzz, leaned out the door with a pool cue in his hand and said something to her. She turned to talk to him, and I saw, as usual, her buns were hanging out of her shorts. There was also a short plaster cast on her left arm that didn't quite reach her elbow.

"Pumpkin butt," Hank mumbled. "Man, you remember Poet… that first night. She had on those orange short-shorts, remember? The tight, knit ones. Want to talk about looking like a pumpkin… wow!"

"I didn't want to."

"What?"

"Talk about it," I said, a little worried where things were going.

"What the hell, Poet?"

"Nothing, Hank. Just forget it."

Lori went back inside the tavern and I breathed a sigh of relief. I figured I'd better leave before she came back out. But Hank got to talking and kept me there.

"So, did you hear Lori was hanging around with Red Dog Finney?"

I lied, shaking my head no. "Well, I guess his ol' lady came home with the kids and found them in bed together. That's why she's wearing that cast. Ol' lady Finney broke her arm in a fight. Well… maybe just a slight fracture. I heard Lori yanked out some of her hair. My ma… you know her? She's a nurse over at Doc Brandhal's office." He pointed toward it over by the Royal Blue grocer, as if I didn't know. "She told me this little midget of a redhaired girl came in, and they had to cast her up even though she didn't have any money. So, you can just guess who that was, right?"

"Right," was all I said, part of me wanting to run home, and part of me wanting to stay and hear the rest. "Rumor has it, ol' Red Dog bought her new clothes from Lottie's shop. Heard they had to settle for 'Big Girls' stuff because extra small in women's, were still too big."

Hank's ma was a gossip, one of the worst kinds. She and Lottie were good friends. So, I knew where the information was coming from. Then Hank had to go and ask, "So, Poet… you get any of that, yet? I see she's still in town. So… I guess not. She told me a week ago that she wasn't leaving Clarksburg until she had a piece of you."

"You know, Hank, I wish she'd go. Just leave us all alone and go away."

"What are you talking about? I told you; she's not going anywhere until she makes it with you. Just give in, let her have it, and walk away. What… are you queer or something?"

There it was again. I felt the anger coming up, and I didn't usually get mad about stuff that easily. But I think being angry was part of the dark side and the bigger it grew, the easier it was to get mad at things.

"No, I'm not queer. And if I hear that one more time, I'm going to explode."

"Why? Did someone else call you a queer? I mean, asking is one thing… but accusing you is another, get my drift? Who was it, Poet, I'll kick their ass, just say the word."

"Naw, it's okay. I'm out of here. See you around."

"Hey, wait! He grabbed my shoulder and spun me around. It kind of shocked me, but then I could see he just wanted to give me advice. His left hand was on my shoulder and he looked right into my eyes, like my dad always did.

"I just wanted to say, let her have it, Poet. No sense in fighting the urge. You know you want to."

His brotherly advice sounded almost like begging. It made me think maybe he wanted her to go away, too, and only I could save the day. It made me wonder how many others were hoping for her to go. He took his hand away, lit another cigarette and said, "Hear me?"

I didn't say anything and just walked toward home. Before I went up the long stairs, I looked back and saw him wave like he wasn't sure if he should or not.

I went in my bedroom and sat on the edge of my bed to think. So, I knew I wasn't queer because every time I thought of Molly, I got excited. I mean, I think I was in love with her. The picture of her that night at the pond was still strong in my head, and I hoped it would stay forever. On the other hand, when Lori kissed me, I'd turned to stone, like Louie was always saying. But I wasn't one of those people who cared if other people were queer or not. Like I said, my folks talked to me about it and then I met my ma's brother, Allan, who just happened to be queer. She introduced me on-purpose last year at Thanksgiving, and he was the nicest guy I'd ever met. I couldn't see why anyone would want to be mean to him; but I guess they were.

All this thinking brought me around to Lori and why she was different. I'd met tons of girls in my life, but not one of them was like her. I still felt something was wrong with her. Where were her folks? Where did she live? Was she a runaway? Was somebody out looking for her?

I sat for the longest time, running it through my head. Then the thought that if I just let her have her way, what could it hurt? The word 'dignity' popped into my head. Was that it? Would I lose my dignity? Maybe I needed to sacrifice that to solve the problem. Then she would go away, and that's what I wanted. She'd already gotten to the other guys. Hank seemed no different for it, and neither did the others. But maybe they didn't care about their dignity, and from the way Lori acted, I don't think she did either. So, why did I?

There were too many questions. I needed to stop thinking about it or I was going to drive myself crazy. I would just let her have her way and I would figure the rest out later. Being with her would be awkward and scary, but I think that's supposed to be part of life. Moments would come, just like this

155

one, and I would have to deal with them. I told a lot of people that I couldn't wait to grow up, but I guess it wasn't as easy as I thought it was.

The door opened and Stowit walked in. He stopped, gave me a weird look, and said, "I didn't know you were home. Does ma and dad know you're here?"

"Probably not."

"You know, Poet, you look kind of scared of something. Is somebody chasing you? A monster? Is it a monster? Because if it is, I need to go lock the front door."

"No, silly, it's not a monster."

He came over and sat next to me on the bed. I didn't know what to say to him because he was too young to understand. So, I said, "What are you up to?" He surprised me by saying, "Don't change the subject, what are you scared of?"

"Nothing… it's nothing, Stowit. So, don't worry about me."

"Well, okay, I'll try, but I doubt it will work. Because you know, we're brothers, and dad says brothers got to stick together." Then he threw an arm around me and squeezed, adding, "Don't worry Poet, I love you, no matter how scared you are."

That knocked me for a loop. I mean, it wasn't the first time he ever said that. It was just he seemed so in tune with how I was feeling and knew just what to say to make me feel better. Jumping up, he headed toward the door. He stopped just before he got there and grabbed a Yo-Yo off the top of my dresser.

"Hey, can I play with this?"

"Sure… yeah, go for it."

"Thanks," he said and left the room wrapping the string around a finger as he went.

A sudden wave of emotion came over me and I felt happy to have my family, but I also felt like I was going to cry. I fought back against the tears and they never came, but I'd come awfully damn close. I realized that I had my family, and Lori wasn't going to change that. In fact, very little would change. I just had to admit to myself that, like Stowit said, I was scared. But now, I felt afraid and confident, all at the same time.

I figured the next time I saw Lori, I would force myself to act like we were the best of pals. I had friends in school that were girls, and I could always hang around with them without a problem. So, I could act with Lori, the same that I did with them. Now, I just had to wait until I saw her again.

I didn't have to wait long because she came to me. Late the next morning, I was sitting on the sofa with Stowit, showing him how to do Dot to Dot. I was trying to explain how he had to follow the numbers. In the middle of doing a duck picture by myself to show him how to count, ma walked in and asked if we wanted an early lunch. She said she had to get over to the home, so she wanted to make it now. Dad had taken his vacation and was sitting in the kitchen at the table, reading the plans for the new flyable Spitfire model he'd gotten at Nordon's. I saw it was almost eleven o'clock and said, 'Yeah, we can do that. Lunch is good.'

"Yeah, lunch is always good," Stowit said. "Can we have spaghetti?"

That's about the time someone knocked on the door. Ma went and answered. I couldn't see who it was from where I was sitting, but I thought it was weird that I didn't hear them come up the long stairs. They usually thumped like crazy.

I heard someone imitate a little child and ask, "Can Poet come out and play?" It was Lori.

My ma said, "Just a second, I'll go get him." I dreaded every single one of her footsteps as they came down the hallway. Then she stopped just outside the living room door and said, "What's your name, by the way?"

"Lori. Tell him, Lori's here."

Ma stepped into the room and kind of whispered, "It's a girl. That little redheaded one... said her name is Lori. She's got a broken arm."

"Yeah, I know," I said, rolling my eyes. But the nervousness was coming, and I tried to hide it the best I could. I came out of the living room into the hall. Stowit followed to stand in the door, looking bashful.

Lori stood just inside the screen door. She saw him and said, "Hey, little boy. You're so cute. Are you Poet's little brother?"

Stowit didn't say anything. Ma grabbed his hand and led him into the kitchen. "Come on, little man, let's eat something."

"Ah ma, I wanted to look at that girl. She's got really, really, red hair."

"Yeah, she sure does," ma said.

"Whose got red hair?" my dad asked.

"Poets new girlfriend," Stowit said.

"She's here—now? Why don't you invite her in?"

"Because I think it might be best to leave Poet and her alone. That's why. Hey, honey, you want spaghetti?"

I didn't hear his answer because I was busy looking at Lori. She had those carrot colored short-shorts back on, but it looked like they had been washed. She wore a pink summer top, covered with little yellow and blue flowers. It had string for straps, leaving her shoulders bare and showing more freckles. Elastic ran around it just up under her boobs, and the blouse hung loose from there down to her waist. The cheap sandals were back, showing clean feet with pink painted toenails. Her black eye had faded to light green and only a few spots of purple showed. There were names scribbled all over her cast.

"What are you doing here?" I whispered, trying hard to sound mean.

"I think we have a date, don't we?" she said, making big eyes at me and showing those vampire teeth.

I didn't say anything and went passed her to stand on the porch. I held the door for her and when she was out of my apartment, I let it slam shut. At the bottom of the stairs, I went south, and she followed. We walked toward the railroad tracks and the woods on the other side. I was trying hard to stay calm. At first, she walked behind me. I could hear the flip-flop of her sandals. She finally hurried to catch up, and walked beside me, not saying a word.

Me and the guys had a fort made of logs and stuff down by the river in those woods. That's where we were going. I didn't say a single word and every time I looked at her, she'd grin up at me. She had this look in her eye like the one I had seen in Stowit's when we are in the toy isle at the store. I could smell her too, but it was just soap and perfume. I wondered if she had cleaned up just for me.

Climbing the levee around the sewer plant, I took her hand and helped her up. I dropped it as soon as it felt proper. Walking along the river side of the levee, I could see Conor Sullivan's raft tied to the sandbar. It looked kind of lonely floating out there all by itself. Soon Lori and I walked down the other side and into the trees. There was a sandy path under the fluttering leaves and it was shady in there. I found myself hoping Willowbough wasn't hanging around because that was her territory. I didn't want her dog announcing to the world that I was down there.

Leading Lori to the fort, we stopped about twenty feet away. I looked down into her face and then back at the fort. She seemed to be studying it. We still hadn't spoken a word. Turning back to me, our eyes met. The nervousness filled me from head to toe and I wondered if she could see how scared I was. I smiled as a sign of surrender. She returned it, but surprisingly, in a gentle way. Not the smart ass, smirking Lori—but a kind, almost, motherly Lori. Taking my hand again, she walked me inside.

#16

Kissing Lewis

My name is Bailey, my family are the Barnes. I became a freshman in high school just last year in 1973. I couldn't be happier about it. I like to drink, and I don't mean iced tea or pop. I mean beer, and anything else like it. Some of my friends call me 'Alky' because they think I'm an alcoholic. But I know damn well that I'm not old enough to be one of those. I've seen those guys coming out of the Blue Front tavern up on the square and they are definitely alcoholics. They can barely walk. I figure by the time I get old enough to go in that tavern, I'll be gone out of Clarksburg, anyway. Then, I can start a whole new life and start liking something else. But right now, I like it. I think that's because it makes the other guys puke, and me, I never do. So, all my friends kind of look up to me because of that.

So, becoming a freshman at Clarksburg high was how I started finding out about parties. They were always some kind of a secret and were usually at some kids house when their parents had gone away for the weekend. Notes would get passed in school and if you were lucky enough to intercept one, you could just show up. It was a thing the upperclassman did. If you showed up as a freshman, there was a good chance you could get your ass beat, or maybe, stripped naked and left out on some country road to walk home in the dark. That kind of scared me; drunk and naked in the middle of nowhere. I wasn't going to let that stop me, though. I had to be tough. Being tough was important in Clarksburg. That's my opinion. Of course, opinions are like a... oh, forget it, it don't matter.

There were two things on everybody's mind at my school: getting drunk and getting laid. It's all we talked about. After that, it was, cars, boats, motorcycles, movies, baseball, football, basketball, and some kids even talked about being afraid that they wouldn't graduate. Not me!

So, nothing, and I mean, nothing, topped the first two. That's what parties were for. They really served no other purpose. When my friend, Dickie, told me about a note he had snatched up when a girl was passing it to another girl. It was about a party on a farm out east of town. I decided I was going to go with him and crash it.

"Bailey, be ready by 7:30. We'll hitchhike. Maybe we can catch a ride before it gets too late."

"How in the hell will we get home?"

"We can catch a ride with someone from school, but we probably won't be leaving until after the sun comes up. So, tell your folks you and I are going to the Pits to camp out, just like we used to. I'll take my tent, but I'll dump it in your backyard behind some bushes, okay?"

"Okay, but what if we can't get a ride?"

"Then we'll just have to walk home."

"Sounds like a stupid plan, Dickster."

"Oh, don't be such a wuss. Walking through the country on a Sunday morning is kind of nice. Besides, it's not going to be that far away. So, you going or not?"

"I'm going. Meet you tomorrow."

"See ya!" Dicky said and left me sitting in the lunch room to think about it.

I honestly didn't want to walk home after a night of drinking, but it was my first, real party. I didn't want to miss it. I called other guys to see if they were going. Louie said no, he was grounded for letting a squirrel loose in the house. He said it didn't go as planned and the little critter wrecked the place before they could herd it out the door. Louie's the kind of guy who never thinks ahead.

I talked to Poet's ma up at the Royal Blue, but she said Poet was going to a writing camp this weekend. Little Charley was still mad at me for pushing him into Marie Niemeyer when we were walking down the hall at school. He had a crush on her but was too chicken to let her know. I was just helping move things along. He's still not talking to me.

The good news is, I heard Marie tell Copper Birdsong that she thought Little Charley was cute for running into her on purpose. She was going to see if he wanted to go to the Prairieville Ballroom some Saturday night. I figured he'd thank me later. So, that was it, just me and the Dickster.

I had ants in my pants all day Saturday and when Dickie showed up, I was chomping the bit. "Okay, Bailey, the party's at Carrot Smith's place. It's only a couple miles outside of town."

"Yeah, I know where Carrot lives. Just remember, don't call him Carrot to his face or he'll floor you."

"Yeah, but it just makes sense to call him Carrot; he's got red hair. So… what the hell is his real name anyway?'

"Uh… I think it's Marion."

"Well, hell, that's worse than Carrot."

"Yeah, but he hates Carrot. Some of the upper classmen call him Smitty. Just call him Smitty."

"But I'm not an upper classmen, yet. What if he kicks my ass for that?"

"I think you'll get it worse if you call him Carrot. So, just call him Smitty and if he doesn't like it because you're not an upper classman, then… run like hell."

"Yeah, but…"

"Dickie! Drop it. Let's go."

"Okay, but if I get my ass kicked…"

I glared at him and he quit talking, but then started mumbling to himself, instead. We headed east on Main Street. It was early May, so the weather was good. I wasn't sure what we'd do if it were winter. Surely wouldn't be walking, that's for sure. Every time a car was coming by, we'd run up under a streetlight and stick out our thumbs. The second car to come along was a truck. It was Red Dog Finney's truck, but Red Dog wasn't driving; it was his buddy, Buzz. First, I have to say, I was glad it was Buzz and not Red Dog. Buzz was this quiet guy who wasn't married even though he must have been at least forty. But Red Dog was married, had like… three kids, was older than Buzz, and he was still too wild for me.

"Where you going?" Buzz asked after rolling down his window.

"Carrot Smith's place," Dickie said.

"Oh yeah, big party, I 'spect? Jump in back, I'll drop you off at the crossroads, it's only about half a mile down Club Road from there. Down in that hollow."

"You can't take us all the way?" Dickie whined.

"Listen kid, I'm headed over to Prairieville and I'm already late, so…take it or leave it."

"But…"

"Shut up, Dickie," I said and dragged him back to the tailgate. I heard Buzz say, "Yeah, Dickie, listen to the smart kid."

"Smartass is more like it," Dickie said.

"You can just kiss my smart ass, Dickie," I said as we climbed over the tailgate. We didn't even get to sit down before Buzz gunned the engine and took off, knocking us down. Then I heard him laugh.

We moved up to sit with our backs against the cab. When the truck started to slow down, Dickie stood up and rode looking over the top. Buzz stopped at a gravel road that crossed the highway and yelled out, "Here you go."

Dickie and I dropped over the side and Buzz called out, "Come here a minute."

We walked over and he told us, "Just a word for the wise… maybe that's you, smart kid. Don't call him Carrot, or he'll definitely kick your ass. So…"

"WE KNOW," Dickie and I said together. Buzz started laughing and burned rubber on down the highway toward Prairieville, leaving us coughing in the smoke.

"Geez, what a prick," Dickie said.

"Yeah, but he was nice enough to give us a lift. What more do you want? Dinner and a movie?"

Dickie muttered something and I didn't make him tell me what it was. I just laughed and took off walking down the gravel.

Buzz was wrong about how far it was. It was more like a mile down Jordan's Road and then another mile at the crossroads where we had to take a left and go down into Wapsi Hollow. We had to rest a bunch of times with Dickie complaining every step of the way. Now, what I didn't understand was, why in the hell Carrot's folks lived down there. They were farmers, but they lived in a hollow. There was a river (The Wapsi) and they lived just on the other side of the bridge in this big house, in the trees, up on a hill. There wasn't a farm field around for at least a mile. It was kind of wild down there, I mean like… Sleepy Hollow wild. You know that book, right? Dark and scary.

Dickie and I were walking along in the dark, and the gravel was crunching under our feet. I kept looking back because I kept getting a feeling that someone was following us. But there was no one. Dickie kept looking at me, and I could see how big his eyes were. So, I knew he was scared too. Then, when we were passing the game club, we saw somebody coming down the road toward us in the dark. The moon was rising, and I could just make out the white tee shirt they were wearing. It was Timmy Brecht. He was this tough kid we knew who was supposed to be a junior but got held back a year.

"Hey, Timmy," I said.

"Whoa! Shit! You guys about scared the crap outta me. I ought to kick your asses for that."

"Ah come on, Timmy, we didn't do it on purpose, geez," Dickie said.

"Okay… so you guys headed for the party? Let me tell you… worst party ever. If I were you, I'd turn around right now and go back home. Hey! You could walk with me back to Clarksburg."

Naw," said Dickie. "We came all this ways, so… we're going."

"Have it your way."

"So… Timmy, why are you leaving so early?" I asked.

"That rat, Carrot head, kicked me out."

"What the hell for?" Dickie said. "You trying to have sex with his girl?"

"I ought to kick your ass," Timmy said and went after Dickie, but he ran off down the road and left me standing there. Timmy didn't go after him, he just turned around and looked at me.

I was afraid it was my turn. So, I tried to distract him by saying, "So, where is this place?"

It worked and he got all friendly again and pointed up the road. "The Smiths live up on that hill across the bridge. See it over there? You can just see the lights through the trees. Well… don't go up there. Carrots got his own trailer on this side of the river up on the little hill, down, over there. See them shiny grain bins up on that flat area? There's a lane leads up to 'em. Party's up there."

"Thanks a bunch, Timmy. See you next week in school, huh."

"Not if I see you first," he said, and laughing, he took off at a jog in the direction we had come from.

I could see Dickie had stopped up the road a piece. He was bent over like he had a stitch in his side. When I got to him, he stood up and said, "So, that creep leave?"

"Yeah, but I'd be careful when you go back to school on Monday."

"Ah, he don't scare me."

"Well, I'm just saying..."

"Yeah, I hear you. So… where's the party?"

I pointed it out to Dickie, and we took off in that direction. Pretty soon there were people walking by or just standing in groups on the road. Some were sitting on cars parked along the edge, smoking, drinking, and making out. Looking up, we saw this huge, white mobile home sitting on the edge of this short limestone cliff. If anyone fell off, they'd smack right into the middle of the road where we were standing. So, we went up the lane that started about a hundred yards farther on and kind of curved around to what looked like a big, flat gravel parking lot. I figured that's where grain trucks came to sit and unload corn into those bins. There were woods all around it, well, except for the cliff side.

Because Carrot had his own mobile home, it made me wonder if maybe Carrot's folks didn't like him all that much. They must have gotten him this long, ol' trailer to live in so they wouldn't have to be around him.

There were kids hanging out in the open door and just before we went in, I heard someone yelling and swearing. Dickie and I looked over the edge of the cliff. There were two guys fighting right in the middle of the bridge. I knew one of them was Carrot because of his voice, and sometimes his hair flashed red in the moonlight.

"That's Carrot's voice, I'd know it anywhere," Dickie said. "He's down there kicking someone's ass."

"Do you suppose they were stupid enough to go and call him Carrot?"

"No doubt."

"So… remember, Dickie, call him Smitty, or it's you whose going to be getting your butt kicked over there on that bridge."

"Yeah, I heard you the first time."

"Yep," I said and pushed my way inside the mobile home. Dickie followed me and I sat down on the end of the couch by the door. It was the only open seat because the place was packed. The cushion was still warm, so I figured somebody must have just got up and left it. If there was a fire, kids were going to die. I didn't want to think about that, so I said something to Dickie about getting a beer but when I looked where I thought he was, he wasn't... People were looking at me weird because I was talking to myself. He had just disappeared. Then some upperclassman, who I didn't know, walked over and handed me an Old Milwaukee.

"Want a beer?"

"Uh, sure, thanks."

"Going to get drunk?"

"If I can."

"Going to get laid?"

"Ummm… sure, if I can."

"Good luck with that. I've been here nearly two hours and still nothing."

He just walked away. I watched him step up into the kitchen and grab a PBR from an open cooler and then disappear into a room at the back. The beer he gave me was already open and I was hoping he had given it to me because it wasn't his favorite brand and not because he had spit in it. I looked inside and didn't see anything floating around, so I took a sip. It was still cold and tasted okay, so I took a long swig and started my search.

I sat there, drank my beer, and checked out all the girls that were in sight. After I decided none of them were for me, I just watched all the drunk kids and listened to some pretty stupid talk. The more beer I drank, the less stupid it seemed. Now, like I said, I've been out drinking before. Me and my friends always went down to the Pits. That's where I took my first swig of Mad Dog 2020 and met the first girl I ever had sex with. Her name was Lori, but I'm really trying to forget that.

So, partying with a ton of other kids that I didn't know was a whole new thing. There were more girls than boys in there, so I thought the odds of meeting somebody was in my favor. Some guy in a Clarksburg football jersey came out of the back and met a girl whose name was Keli Hale. Her dad owned Hale's Hardware. They had stopped right in front of me and he handed her a drink that looked like whiskey. He started drinking his as they talked, but she didn't. Instead, she got mad at him, set her drink on the arm of the couch, and stomped out. She was pushing people out of her way, saying, "I hate you, Chuck. I hate you." Then she disappeared outside. Chuck followed her, kind of begging her to stay, and saying "Ah come on, Keli. You'll like it, I promise." Then they were gone. I figured she wasn't coming back for her drink, so I took it.

Finishing my beer, I started in on the whiskey. I had a pretty good buzz going. I was looking for Dickie and starting to feel like maybe I should get up and go find him. I wasn't caring so much about having a place to sit anymore, besides, all the kids sitting on the couch were starting to bug me. Then the guy next to me started making out with the girl next to him. They were making some pretty slobbery noises with the kissing, and then she started in with this moaning noise. They must have been seniors. So, they probably didn't care who was watching.

That's when things changed. I mean, the party had been going like I figured it would and nothing was really new or different. I was still thinking about getting up when I saw her come out of the back room. She just stood there, looking like she was checking to see if anyone new had showed up. They called her Lewis.

I didn't know if that was her first name or last. Somebody once told me never too ask her that question. The problem with that, nobody else would ever share it with me. It was like some big mystery. I'd seen her around school a lot and I guess I should tell you that's because she was the tallest kid in the place. She wasn't skinny by no means, just a student with a grown woman's body. I think outside of school, people could easily mistake her for an adult. She had this long hair like dark chocolate with eyes to match. Her face was square-like, and she had what my ma always called 'a heavy jaw' The thing is, she had the lips and eyebrows of a woman. Her nose was a normal woman's nose. Honestly, I always thought she was kind of pretty because all the parts fit together nicely.

Tonight, she was wearing jeans and a white and blue plaid flannel shirt with the sleeves rolled up and tied at the front showing her belly button. I'd never seen her with make-up on, but I don't think she needed it. She was definitely a farmer's daughter. Her hands were big, and her arms were pretty muscley. I imagined her tossing hay bales or wrestling the bull out of the barn for the spring breeding. I figured that was the reason why she got so big. It didn't seem fair because she'd never get to be a miss America or something like that. But she did play basketball, and I have to admit, she was pretty damn good at it.

I didn't mess with her at school, not like a lot of the other guys who picked on her. Some of the seniors made fun of her, saying that she was really a man in drag. I didn't know what that meant, but I heard a couple of those guys got pounded by her later. Once, I just happened to be in the right place at the right time. Shelly Anderson was standing in the hall between classes, talking with some other students. I was at my locker, getting a different book for my next class. Louie was standing with me talking about some girl he'd met. He was wondering aloud if she might go out with him if he asked her nicely. I really wasn't listening all that close. Louie was a yakker, he was always spouting some crap about stuff that wasn't important.

So, I was trying to work this big, ol' history book out of my locker without knocking other stuff on the floor and kind of listening to Louie, when Lewis walked by. I heard Shelly laugh and say loud enough for everyone to hear, "Oh, look, here comes King Kong, everybody run." Then she laughed with Peggy Bowman and Denise Donnelly about it. Lewis walked right up to her, and after pushing Peggy out of the way, she just stood there, staring down at Shelly. Lewis didn't look mad or nothing. So, I didn't know what to expect. Shelly said, "Oops," and I watched her turn around like she was going to walk away into the principal's office. The others kids had all moved back so there was a pretty big open space around the two. I thought Lewis might smack her or pull her hair. Nope, Lewis just reached out and depantsed her. She grabbed Shelly's pink slacks at the sides and yanked them right down to her knees. Shelly let out a scream and then the other kids started laughing and some were even whistling. Peggy and Denise left in a hurry. Shelly had her arms full of books and she could either drop them and pull up her slacks or try to run into the girls restroom. She dropped the books.

They hit the floor with a loud smack and that brought Mr. Hansen, the Principal, out of his office. He saw Shelly standing there in her sky blue, bikini underwear, trying to pull up her pants. Lewis pointed at her and said, "Mr. Hansen, this has got to stop. This is the second time Shelly assumed we wanted to see her new underwear." Then Lewis walked away shaking her head like she was pretending to be disgusted.

I was a little shocked, and not so much because a girl was standing in the hallway in her underwear, but mostly because I'd never heard Lewis talk before. I figured she'd have this deep voice, but it was just a normal girls voice and honestly, she sounded smart. You know what I mean? It's just the way some people talk that tells you that you may not have been giving them credit where credit was do.

So now, Lewis was looking around the trailer at all the other kids and then she walked into the room we were in and kind of stood there, looking at all of us. I wasn't sure what she was doing, but she seemed to be searching for something—or someone. Then Carrot came running in, all out of breath. He sat down on the arm of the couch that was across the room and then looked right at me.

"Who in the hell are you?" he asked.

"Oh, hey Smitty. Um… Bailey Barnes. Seen you down there on the bridge beating the crap out of that guy. Looked like he deserved it."

He stared at me for a minute, then he smiled, nodded, and started talking to the senior sitting beside him. I felt relieved. I was really buzzing from the whiskey, but I had come up with the right thing to say because he just started ignoring me after that. That was until he noticed Lewis standing there. I saw it happen. That look just came over his face and I wondered if she could kick his butt. I was sure he was going to start in on her and the fight would be on.

"What are you looking for, Lewis? You lose something?" he asked.

"Thinking I might want a place to sit," she said still looking around. The room had gotten kind of quiet now. I figured everybody was getting ready for the crap to hit the fan.

"I thought you might be looking for someone to kiss? You want a kiss, Lewis," Carrot said.

She looked right at him and said, "Not from you."

"Well... then who?"

That's when the upperclassman at the end of my couch hollered out, "That guy," and when I looked at him, I saw he was pointing at me. Everybody else laughed and Carrot said, "Yeah, that guy. That… what's your name again?"

"Bailey."

"Yeah, Bailey-schmayley. Give him a smooch, Lewis. A big one."

Everybody on my couch got up and were just standing around looking at Carrot, who was looking at Lewis, who was looking at me. Then someone started chanting, "Kiss em, kiss em."

I was just drunk enough that I sat there, grinning at everyone like it was all a joke, and I was some kind of a ditz. I realized Lewis hadn't said anything. She was looking at me like she was thinking she just might do it. Then she handed Carrot her beer. Everybody in the room was on their feet now and I was thinking it might be time to run. It was getting loud in there with, "Kiss Bailey Schmayley! Kiss Bailey Schmayley!" Other kids were attracted to the racket and were filling up the room. They joined in and it got louder. Before I could stand up, Lewis walked over to the couch, lay down on her back, and put her head in my lap. She grinned up at me and I couldn't help but think how nice her teeth were. Then she clamped my head in her hands, pulled my face down, and laid one on me.

It seemed to go on forever. I started kissing her back and things got kind of slobbery. Then it was over, and she let go of my head. Everybody cheered like it had been a touchdown. Lewis stayed where she was, just staring up at me. I thought she would leave, but nope, she made herself comfortable.

Now, it wasn't as bad as I thought it was going to be. I mean, I remember kissing that Lori, and kissing Lewis wasn't no different. Except maybe kissing Lewis was a little better. Her lips were bigger, or maybe the right words is, fuller. She lay there looking up at me and not saying a word. I didn't know what to say, either. We just kind of studied each other. I have to say the look on her face told me she might be coming back for another. I will admit right now, I wouldn't have minded.

All the kids who had been sitting on the couch went outside and everybody else went back to their business now that the show was over. After a minute, Lewis finally spoke.

"That was kind of nice. What's your name, again?"

"Um, Bailey, Bailey Barnes," I said and grinned bigger.

"So, it's like you have two last names."

"Yeah, kinda," I said, and then thought maybe I could solve that mystery and ask her whether her name was her first, or last.

"So, what about…"

"You can call me Lewis, that's all you need to know."

So much for that idea.

"I like you, your kind of nice… and cute too," she said.

"Uh… thanks?"

She pushed the hair out of my face with a finger and then cupped my cheek with her big hand. "You don't mind if I stay here for a while? I need to sober up a bit before I drive home. Your legs are pretty comfortable."

"Yeah, that's okay, I don't mind."

She rolled onto her side and keeping her head in my lap, she just went and passed out. I mean, she just dropped off. Some people were looking at us and I was just grinning at them like it happened all the time. Other people were looking and whispering. The buzz was wearing off and I realized then that some of those people weren't drinking. The ones whispering.

Carrot looked over at us and said, "Ahhh, someone's going to get laid tonight!" I gave him a grin that was more like a sneer; like it just might be true. I wasn't counting on it. I just never thought I'd be with Lewis. But for some reason, it didn't bother me. I was starting to like her, and I really thought we could get together. I have to admit, the feeling was a new one. I had favorites in school, or should I say, girls I thought I wanted to date. Most of them never gave me a second look. Others just said hi, but that was all. When I tried to talk to them, maybe to see if they might want to go out with me, they would make excuses. Then they'd get up and walk away. It made me think I wasn't looking at things the right way and maybe I wasn't the stud I thought I was. Something was changing, and not around me, but inside me.

I had my eye on the clock hanging on the wall, watching the big hand move around. I really couldn't get up because Lewis had me pinned. So, I wasn't going anywhere until Lewis did. People were leaving and by about twelve thirty, the crowd inside the mobile home started to thin out. Some kids were passed out on the floor and other kids had to walk around them. That was about the time Dickie showed up. He had a beer in his hand and when he saw me, he said, "Hey, Bailey." Then he saw Lewis in my lap and his eyes went right to mine. I kind of shrugged and he grinned. Then he looked at Carrot, who was sitting there, staring right at him.

Now, I'm going to tell this because you need to know. Dickie is dense. That's also what my folks say (that's where I first heard the word). A lot of kids at school say the same, and my friend, Poet, who is usually too nice to say anything bad about anybody, even said, "You know, Bailey, I don't think Dickie could keep his mouth shut if his life depended on it. I think he just might be dense." There's no getting around it, Dickie was most certainly going to get himself killed.

So, he was looking at Carrot, and Carrot was looking right back and said, "So, who the hell are you?"

"Oh, come on. Everybody knows me. I'm Dickie. Dickie Butz. And your Carrot, right?"

There it was. He was doing just what I told him not to do. The same for Buzz, who was a grown man who knew what he was talking about. Then there were a dozen others who said, "Don't do it."

Carrot didn't say anything, but I watched his face grow mean. His eyes turned into slits and he was showing his teeth, but he wasn't smiling. Dickie was just standing there. He should have been running. Quicker than a flash, Carrot was off that couch, heading right for Dickie. I think the one thing Dickie had in his favor was that he could run. He ran track and was big on the 100-yard dash.

"You little twerp," Carrot hollered as he came across the floor.

"Oh, crap!" Dickie yelled.

He dropped that beer bottle, splashing the carpet and about half a dozen other kids at the same time. The door was still propped open and he was outside before Carrot even got to where Dickie had been standing. Then he was gone, and I heard a lot of yelling, mostly, something like, "You get back here, you…" That's all there was.

All the yelling and laughing and cussing (because of the splashing beer) woke Lewis up and she jumped to her feet. She stood there, rubbing her eyes, saying, "What the hell?" Everybody quieted down again. I thought she just might start pounding people, but all she did was look at her watch, mumble something about getting the hell out of there and started for the door. I just watched her go. I thought I would be relieved when she got up off me, but honestly, I felt kind of rejected. I didn't want her to go. That feeling didn't last long, though. She stopped halfway to the door, looked back at me, and said, "Are you coming, or what?"

I have to admit, I was off that couch and over there in one second. She took my hand and people made that noise. You know the one? Kind of a, 'Ahhh' noise, like it was the sweetest thing they ever saw.

Lewis never said anymore, she just towed me to an old, white Chevy Corvair parked by the big silver bins. I thought it was weird that she would drive a car like that, but that's because I was expecting a pickup truck. We got in, she found her keys, and we drove away, trying not to run over any drunks. I figured we would see Dickie on the road, but we saw Carrot, instead. He flagged us down and when he saw it was Lewis and me, he started being nice. I think it was because of the way Lewis was looking at him. He kind of ducked down and looked in the car at me and said, "Hey, Bailey, you see that kid? The one you came here with?"

"Uh, naw, I thought maybe you killed him and threw him in the river."

"No, but if I find him, I just might."

Lewis wasn't saying anything, she was just watching Carrot like any minute things might go to hell. She looked like she was ready to mix it up with Carrot if she had too.

"Alright… hey, see you at school, huh?" he said.

Lewis just drove away, saying, "Not if I see you first." Then she looked over at me, smiled, and patted my leg. I grinned back, still a little taken by her smile, and I thought I'd like to see it more often. I was glad I was getting a ride home and wasn't going to have to walk. But that's not what happened.

She took me to the Pits. Then she drove around down there on those little roads until she found a small open space that looked like a tiny clover field. It was right next to a pond and probably a good place to camp. She stopped the car, got out, and opened the trunk (which was in the front), and pulled out an old quilt. Then she went out into the center of that space and spread it on the ground. After that, she looked at me, smiled again, and said, "You coming, Bailey?"

"Sure thing," I hollered, got out, and went over there. We lay down on it together, with arms behind our heads, just looking up at the moon and the stars. It was quiet down there and you could hear the owls hooting and the fox barking. One time a coyote started howling somewhere out in somebody's pasture. Lewis wasn't doing much talking. Then she rolled onto her side and whispered like she was afraid other people might hear us and said, "Kiss me, again, will you Bailey." So, I did.

We spent the whole night there. Now, I know what you're thinking, and no, it was nothing like that. She wasn't Lori. We talked a lot, and sometimes we kissed. We held hands and before we nodded off, she asked me if she could lay with her head on my chest. So, I let her, and that's the way we woke up. She had nodded off before me and I lay there for a while listening to the night sounds. I was thinking that I was never going to be the same again after this night. There's this thing called 'growing up' and I suspect that's just what was happening. I couldn't stop it. And maybe, in less than one night, I might have fallen in love. That didn't make sense, but I wasn't going to try and stop that either. I learned a lot about Lewis before I dozed off. She actually was, a farmer's daughter, her parents were also very large people, especially her dad, and she had two older brothers. She was good in school and she never had a boyfriend before. She asked if I would be hers because, if I would, I could change her whole life.

Oh! And she finally confessed her name wasn't just Lewis, but she was too embarrassed to let people know her whole name, saying she had to hurt a few kids who found out and called her that in public. She said she was named after her grandmother, and of course, her folks had no clue that their choice wasn't going to be such a good idea until Lewis started growing. I promised her I wouldn't tell anyone. So… sorry everybody.

What's that? If I don't tell you, it just might drive you crazy? Well, okay, because you don't know her… and besides that, I wouldn't want anyone going nuts because of me… here it is, (and don't you dare tell a soul!) it's… Minnie.